Everyman, I will go with thee,
and be thy guide

Dylan Thomas

THE COLLECTED STORIES

Edited by
WALFORD DAVIES
University of Wales, Aberystwyth

Introduced by
LESLIE NORRIS
Brigham Young University, Provo, Utah

EVERYMAN
J. M. DENT · LONDON

First published in Great Britain by J.M.Dent 1983
This paperback edition first published by J.M.Dent 1984
Reprinted 1985, 1986
Reissued in Everyman in 1993

Printed in Great Britain by
The Guernsey Press Co. Ltd, Guernsey, C.I.

for
J.M.Dent
Orion Publishing Group
Orion House
5 Upper St Martin's Lane, London WC2H 9EA

British Library in Publication Data is available
ISBN 0 460 87330 X

CONTENTS

NOTE ON THE AUTHOR AND EDITORS

Dylan Marlais Thomas was born in Swansea in 1914. After leaving school he worked briefly as a junior reporter on the *South Wales Evening Post* before embarking on a literary career in London. Here he rapidly established himself as one of the finest poets of his generation. *18 Poems* appeared in 1934, *Twenty-five Poems* in 1936, and *Deaths and Entrances* in 1946; his *Collected Poems* was published in 1952. Throughout his life Thomas wrote short stories, his most famous collection being *Portrait of the Artist as a Young Dog*. He also wrote filmscripts, broadcast stories and talks, lectured in America, and wrote the radio play *Under Milk Wood*. In 1953, shortly after his thirty-ninth birthday, he collapsed and died in New York. His body is buried in Laugharne, Wales, his home for many years.

Leslie Norris is a Welsh poet and story-writer. *Sliding*, a collection of his stories, won the David Higham Prize for Fiction in 1978. He is currently on the staff of the Department of English at Brigham Young University, Provo, Utah.

Professor Walford Davies is Director of Extra-Mural Studies at the University of Wales, Aberystwyth. His other work on Dylan Thomas includes the following editions: *Dylan Thomas: Early Prose Writings* (1971); *Dylan Thomas: New Critical Essays* (1972); *Dylan Thomas: Collected Poems 1934–1953* (with Ralph Maud, 1988); *Dylan Thomas: Selected Poems (1974 and 1993).*

INTRODUCTION

When I told some friends I was about to write this introduction to Dylan Thomas's stories, their eyes lit up, they smiled, they began at once to tell their own stories. About Dylan Thomas. He was a man around whom anecdotes crowded, like pigeons in Trafalgar Square, and many of them are good stories, highly coloured and amusing, and not all of them are apocryphal. That Dylan Thomas still exists for many people, the type of the bohemian poet, a man whose extraordinary and inexplicable gift for poetry was all the more amazing when one considers what seemed the chaos of his life.

He was, of course, far more disciplined an artist than legend allows. Among other things, he knew himself very well. It would have been impossible for him to have written the many graceful, acute, brilliantly funny letters of apology without being completely aware of his own faults. Those letters are documents of self-knowledge, as well as evidence that he knew other people very well too; and they are written, nearly always, in marvellous prose. In short, Dylan Thomas possessed all the deliberate qualities of a writer of stories. He knew this. From the very beginning of his career he knew he was not simply a poet. He wrote to Glyn Jones, in a letter written when he was nineteen: 'You ask me to tell you about myself, but my life is so uneventful it is not worth recording. I am a writer of poems and stories.' And he was always a writer of poems and stories, although his life was to be neither uneventful nor unrecorded. He had already contributed stories as well as poems to the *Swansea Grammar School Magazine*, of which he was editor, and four of these early narratives are included here in an appendix. There is plenty of evidence that he considered poems and stories equal products of his gift, drawing no clear distinction between them, knowing they came from the same source. Even his projected magazine, which never appeared, was to be called *Prose and Verse*. When friends visited him at his parents' house in Cwmdonkin Drive he read his stories to them as well as his poems.

The early stories, like 'The Tree' which he published in the *Adelphi*, or any of the pieces which were to appear in *The Map of Love*, are indeed very like the poems. They possess the same obsessive imagery, are written in heightened rhythms, deal with the same interior world. They are very clearly the work of the young man who wrote the poems. And when Dylan Thomas left home late in 1934 to become a freelance writer in London, he found his poems and stories equally admired.

'Young Mr Thomas was at the moment without employment, but it was understood that he would soon be leaving for London to make a career in Chelsea as a free-lance journalist; he was penniless, and hoped, in a vague way, to live on women.' So wrote Dylan of a young man exactly like himself in 'Where Tawe Flows', one of the stories in the autobiographical *Portrait of the Artist as a Young Dog*. Certainly he had no job to go to when he arrived in London on Sunday, 11 November 1934, carrying his meagre luggage, his poems and stories. He had been encouraged in his move by winning the *Sunday Referee* poetry prize, part of which was the publication of his first book, *18 Poems*. This appeared a few weeks after Dylan's arrival in London, and with it he was launched into the small world of contemporary poets. It may be that this first public recognition of his ability as a poet also marked the beginning of a comparative neglect of his stories. If this were so, Dylan was unaware of it. From the chaotic room off the Fulham Road which he shared with his Swansea friend Fred Janes, and where he could see 'for yards around nothing but poems, poems, poems, butter, eggs, mashed potatoes, mashed among my stories and Janes' canvases', he wrote with pride of the stories which had been 'accepted by various periodicals'. He was still a writer of stories.

They were not, however, collected into a volume, as the poems were. *18 Poems* had created a small sensation and Thomas was already a famous young poet. His reputation was further enhanced when *Twenty-Five Poems* appeared in September 1936 and went rapidly into four impressions. It was widely and passionately reviewed. At twenty-two Thomas was firmly established as a leading poet.

But not a rich one. He was always careless about money and, despite its phenomenal sales for a book of verse, it is doubtful that he made much from *Twenty-Five Poems*. The book sold at a mere half-crown. Contemplating marriage, Dylan needed money more than ever, and took his stories to Richard Church, his editor at Dent's. He had already, early in 1936, tried to interest Church in a book of stories, but Church refused them, thinking them obscene. He saw no reason to change his opinion, a point of view shared by the printers who refused a little later to set them for another publisher. In the event, Dylan married Caitlin Macnamara on 11 July 1937, the stories uncollected, the financial future uncertain.

Dylan remained convinced that the stories deserved to appear in book form, and David Higham, who had become his agent, was able to arrange that six of them were included with sixteen new poems in one volume. This was *The Map of Love*, which came out in August 1939. It carried the sub-title, 'Verse and Prose', as if Dylan were keeping faith with his old Swansea dream of editing a magazine of an almost identical name. Certainly he was once more making it clear that he was 'a writer of poems and stories'. This was the book which introduced me, a young man beginning to read contemporary work, to Dylan's prose, and a heady experience it was. The book was handsome, beautifully produced, with a reproduction of the famous romantic portrait by Augustus John as frontispiece. In December of the same year *The World I Breathe*, a collection of all the poems in the first three books and three stories in addition to those in *The Map of Love*, was published in America. The early stories, it seemed, had found a home.

Much the same had happened to Dylan. He and Caitlin had moved into a small house in Laugharne, the little Carmarthenshire town which was to be his home for much of the rest of his life. Here Dylan was happily engaged in writing stories which were quite unlike those he had already published. Glyn Jones, whose commentaries are among the most sensitive on Dylan's work, tells us:

Dylan very early urged me to write short stories, and in 1937 my first collection, *The Blue Bed*, appeared. In Llanstephan in, I think it was, the summer of 1938, I mentioned to Caitlin Thomas that I had started a second volume, a series of short stories about childhood . . . She seemed very surprised and told me that Dylan had already started doing the same thing. His were the autobiographical stories

which in 1940 appeared as *Portrait of the Artist as a Young Dog*.
(Glyn Jones, *The Dragon has Two Tongues*, Dent 1968.)

The new stories were direct, vivid and uncomplicated evocations
of the Swansea in which Dylan had grown up; gone was the
charged prose of the early work. Thomas had already thought
of 'a book about Wales . . . an intimate chronicle of my personal
Journey among people and places', and Richard Church had
also suggested to him that he write of his early years. It is
obvious that the old manner would not suit either of these
projects, but the sources of the new, more conventional style are
a matter of conjecture. Dylan was certainly a reader of short
stories and knew the work of Lawrence, H. E. Bates and Liam
O'Flaherty among others. He was also particularly interested in
the work of Caradoc Evans, whose stories had already used a
Welsh background with success. With Glyn Jones he had visited
the older writer in Aberystwyth in 1936. The two young men
had driven north, wearing each other's hats, to talk with 'the
great Caradoc Evans', as Dylan calls him through a character in
Portrait of the Artist as a Young Dog. Dylan may well have
admired Evans enough to wish to write more directly, to attempt
for urban Swansea what Evans had done for rural Cardiganshire. Again, he had been living unprotected in the world for
years, his eye sharpened, his naturally observant senses at work.
He was probably ready to abandon the interior universe of his
adolescent work and to create a world more like the one about
him. Above all, he had become a great story-teller, famous
among the bars. He realized there were great areas of his ability
and personality that he would never be able to use in lyric
poetry, but that he could use them in his stories. Most of us
believe that poetry is a solemn art, its themes restricted to the
few great subjects, its puns and word-play grave and serious.
Dylan certainly felt like this about his poetry and served his
serious muse with dedication; but he was also a brilliantly funny
man. In the ten stories which make up *Portrait of the Artist as a
Young Dog* a comic Dylan makes his appearance, and he is a
virtuoso of comedy. He is master of the whole range, from slap-
stick to that pathetic laughter which moves us to tears. He is the
sharp citizen of Swansea, a comedian of suburban manners, his
ear a meticulous recorder of the speech of that city, his eye
noting everything. He is a young dog moving from the innocence

of the first three stories, 'The Peaches', 'A Visit to Grandpa's' and 'Patricia, Edith and Arnold' to the knowing young man of 'Old Garbo', his 'new hat on one side', his cigarette worn in admiring imitation of the old reporter he accompanies. It is probably the introduction of humour that was the most important element in the making of the new style and marks the clear division between the poetry and prose from now on.

The stories are full of wonderful talk. We hear and recognize the voices of the characters as they describe how Swansea Male Voice 'did the *Messiah*', tell the stories of their small lives as, huddled out of the rain, they stare at the sea, cheek school teachers, joke and wise-crack and argue their way to the coast. Always an actor, Thomas was able to use his gift for mimicry in his stories. We begin to hear the voice in which he would read them aloud. It is in them that Thomas is best able to use his exceptional narrative skills; his humour, his sense of place, his fine ear for speech, his eye, appreciative and unjudging, for the people he creates. These are the qualities which made him a famous writer, as distinct from a famous poet. Had he not written the stories his death would have been, comparatively speaking, a still drop.

Portrait of the Artist as a Young Dog is a title said to have been suggested by Richard Hughes, author of *A High Wind in Jamaica* and other distinguished work and a neighbour of Dylan's in Laugharne. Hughes had befriended the young Thomases, but I'm not sure he should be given the entire credit for the title. It does, of course, pay tribute to James Joyce's *Portrait of the Artist as a Young Man*, but Thomas's stories are closer to those in Joyce's *Dubliners*. And Dylan had almost used his title years before, when he wrote in 1933 to his friend Trevor Hughes, long before he had gone to Laugharne. In his letter Dylan had advised his friend to dive 'Into the sea of yourself like a young dog'. Dylan, in his own stories, had certainly dived into the sea of his childhood and youth.

Portrait was published in 1940, the last of Dylan's books to appear in England until after the war. After a short period of uncertainty, Dylan began to work in films and to make increasingly frequent broadcasts. He wrote fewer and fewer stories and poems.

He was, however, engaged on a novel. I heard of this when, a newly published poet, I travelled to London to meet my publisher. His name was Peter Baker and he had already printed a small pamphlet of my poems, all I had written at that time, and was prepared to take a larger collection. I had never met a publisher. It was disconcerting when Baker turned out to be younger than I was. The year was 1943 and I was twenty-two. Baker asked me what I was working on apart from poetry. Desperately, not wishing him to know I had never thought of working on anything else, I told him firmly that I was writing a novel. He was interested. A humorous novel, I said. He lost interest at once, telling me that it seemed to him that every poet in the country, intent on self-destruction, was writing a funny novel. Relieved, I threw away the new-born idea of a comic novel. Even Dylan Thomas, said Baker, had written one, or part of one. He had himself read it only a few weeks before and thrown it back as rubbish. I perked up considerably. If Dylan Thomas couldn't write one it was certain I couldn't. Dylan's novel, never completed and published posthumously in 1955, was called *Adventures in the Skin Trade*.

Despite its late appearance, most of it seems to have been written in the early summer of 1941, before Dylan was employed as a scriptwriter for Strand Films. I read the first section of it after I had spoken to Peter Baker, discovering that it had been published in 1941 in *Folios of New Writing*, but I didn't see the rest of the work until Putnam issued it, with an interesting Foreword by Thomas's friend, the poet Vernon Watkins. In a sense the novel is a continuation of the fictionalized autobiography Dylan had started in *Portrait*, his hero, Samuel Bennet, leaving Swansea early in the narrative by the train that Dylan had taken when he left home to live in London. Watkins felt that the novel had not been finished because of the impact of war, particularly the London air-raids, on what he called Thomas's 'essentially tragic vision', but he also suggests that Thomas mistrusted his own facility. Certainly he was able to write this kind of prose very quickly, in marked contrast to the painstaking, phrase-by-phrase way in which he wrote his poetry. Reading the book now, many years later, I still find it funny and inventive, and I can only think that Thomas did not continue with it because he had come to the end of what he had to say. He was not a novelist, he was a natural writer of short stories. The novel was too long for him. The short story, like the poem, is a selective form, but you can pack anything into the novel. And while Thomas recognized his kinship with Dickens when he called *Adventures in the Skin Trade* 'a mixture of Oliver Twist, Little Dorrit, Kafka, Beachcomber, and good old 3-adjectives-a-penny belly-churning Thomas, the Rimbaud of Cwmdonkin Drive', it was Dickens's energy, humour and poetry that he acknowledged, not the novel form. Still, this fragmentary novel, incomplete as it is, bears the mark of its author. Its characters are as logical as life, and as unexpected; it has bounce and colour. Dylan still hoped to complete it years after he set it aside, suggesting as late as 1953, the year of his death, that he would go on with it.

It was put away for all practical considerations when Dylan went to London to work as a scriptwriter. This work left him little time for his own writing, and in addition he was in increasing demand as a broadcaster and, later, as a reader of his own poems and those of other poets. There are left only seven short prose narratives from this late period, and six of these were written for broadcasting. It is ironic that his great popular reputation rests on one or two of these. But it is also understandable, for they are memorable pieces, bringing us the whole man, his warmth, his humour, his incredible memory for the days of childhood and youth, his moving sadness for what was irrecoverable, his poetry even. The first of these late stories, 'Quite Early One Morning', was written in 1944 and reads now like the first draft of *Under Milk Wood*, dealing as it does with the dreams of the sleeping town in the early morning, where Captain Tiny Evans, predecessor without doubt of Captain Cat, sleeps through his 'big seas of dreams' and watches 'a rainbow hail of flying fishes'.

But it is 'A Child's Christmas in Wales' that everyone knows. Compounded of two similar stories, 'Memories of Christmas' and 'Conversation about Christmas', this is the unforgettable narrative we hear broadcast every year. What is there to say about this rich confection, as full as a Christmas stocking with gifts: great, sheepish uncles and singing aunts, snow by the skyful, those Polar cats sleek and long as jaguars, wonderful Miss Prothero who 'said the right thing, always', the cosy, terrifying ghost story that sends the boys scuttling home? It's the best Christmas since Dickens.

'The Followers' is a ghost story. It is filled with hard evidence of the real world. I read it often, never failing to be convinced of the existence of the wet streets, listening to the voices of the 'youngish men from the offices, bundled home against the thistly wind' as they call to each other. It is in this palpable and recognizable world that the two young men begin to follow an unknown girl, an ordinary girl. In such a world ghosts should not exist, but there is one, entirely credible, in this story.

Of these late narratives 'The Followers' is the only one not written for broadcasting, and 'A Story' the only one written for television. I saw Thomas tell this story on the old black and white screen. He filled it with action and colour with his unaided words. His enormous uncle, 'the loud check meadow of his waistcoat littered, as though after a picnic, with cigarette ends, peelings, cabbage stalks, birds' bones, gravy', grew out of words bigger than John Wayne. The tale is the account of an outing to Porthcawl, in which the small Dylan is both participant and, as a child, observer. The ancient boys who go on the trip never reach Porthcawl, since they stop at every public house on the way. The child, left to 'keep an eye on the charra', stays outside, listening and watching. I recognize delightedly the confrontation between a stranger and Enoch Davies in the Hermit's Nest on the journey home, the men having stopped for 'a rum to keep out the cold'.

'I played for Aberavon in 1898,' said a stranger to Enoch Davies.
'Liar,' said Enoch Davies.
'I can show you photos,' said the stranger.
'Forged,' said Enoch Davies.
'And I'll show you my cap at home.'
'Stolen.'
'I got friends to prove it,' the stranger said in a fury.
'Bribed,' said Enoch Davies.

I have myself taken part in such a duel. Some years ago, John Ormond, distinguished film-maker, friend of Dylan Thomas and himself a poet, was shooting a film in west Wales. I was involved in this programme and was to go down to the Teifi river, very photogenic in spate, and cast a line into the water. This was strictly illegal, the fishing season having closed, but we cleared this by getting permission from the agent of the estate through which the stretch of water ran. It would be fine, he said, as long as I didn't put a lure on my line. Dressed in my fishing garb, I stood on the rocks above a foam of water and cast my harmless line. The cameras rolled. For about five minutes. Then the river bailiff appeared, large and implacable.

'What's this?' he said.

'I'm pretending to fish,' I said, 'so that these men can make a film.'

'Not allowed,' he said, 'the river's closed.'

'We've seen the agent,' I said.

'You may have,' he said, 'but I'm the river bailiff and I say you stop now.'

'For God's sake,' I said, 'I'm only pretending.'

'So you say,' he said.

'Look,' I said, reeling in my line, 'I don't have a hook on. What do you think I'm going to do, lasso the fish?'

'You might,' he said darkly.

The ghost of Dylan Thomas, I felt, was not far away.

The ghost of Dylan Thomas. He is certainly present in 'Return Journey', the long narrative in which Dylan goes back to Swansea to find his former selves, the first of whom he described unflinchingly as 'above medium height. Above medium height for Wales, I mean, he's five foot six and a half. Thick blubber lips; snub nose; curly mousebrown hair; one front tooth broken after playing a game called Cats and Dogs, in the Mermaid, Mumbles; speaks rather fancy; truculent; plausible; a bit of a shower-off; plus-fours and no breakfast, you know' – before passing down the years through 'the departed stages' of the boy he was pursuing. At the end of the journey, the park-keeper who 'knew him well', had 'known him by the thousands', says he is 'Dead . . . Dead . . . Dead . . . Dead . . . Dead . . . Dead.'

I still find that death unnecessary, all these years later, particularly after reading these stories, so full of the man, his warmth, his voices. Toward the end of his life he wrote to his friend Dr Daniel Jones (whom we met as a boy in *Portrait of the Artist as a Young Dog*): 'Isn't life awful? Last week I hit Caitlin with a plate of beetroot, and I'm still bleeding. I can't finish a poem or begin a story'.

He was to the end 'a writer of poems and stories'. One of my friends told me that his mother would not read Dylan Thomas 'because he was such a horrible man'. Persuaded to read these stories, she has changed her mind and is convinced he's a wonderful man. I agree with her.

Leslie Norris

BRIEF CHRONOLOGY

27 Oct 1914	Dylan Marlais Thomas born in Swansea
Sept 1925	Enters Swansea Grammar School, where his father was Senior English Master
27 Apr 1930	Starts the first of the 'Notebooks' into which he copied his early poems. (The Notebooks continued until Apr 1934)
Aug 1931	Leaves school. Employed as Reporter on the *South Wales Evening Post* (until Dec 1932)
Mar 1933	First poem published in London ('And death shall have no dominion' in the *New English Weekly*)
Aug 1933	First visit to London
Sept 1933	First poem published in 'Poet's Corner' of the *Sunday Referee* ('That Sanity be Kept'). Correspondence with Pamela Hansford Johnson begins
22 Apr 1934	Wins Book Prize of the 'Poet's Corner' – i.e., the *Sunday Referee*'s sponsorship of his first collection of poems
Feb–Nov. 1934	Several visits to London
10 Nov 1934	Moves to live in London
18 Dec 1934	*18 Poems* published
Apr 1936	Meets Caitlin Macnamara
10 Sept 1936	*Twenty-five Poems* published
21 Apr 1937	First radio broadcast ('Life and the Modern Poet')
11 July 1937	Marries Caitlin Macnamara
May 1938	First moved to live in Laugharne, Carmarthenshire

30 Jan 1939	First son (Llewelyn) born, in Hampshire
24 Aug 1939	*The Map of Love* (poems and stories) published
20 Dec 1939	*The World I Breathe* (a selection of his poetry and prose)—his first volume publication in America
4 Apr 1940	*Portrait of the Artist as a Young Dog* (short stories) published
July 1940	Leaves Laugharne for London
Sept 1940	Begins work as script-writer for films with the Strand Film Company
1940–2	Living partly in London, partly in Wales
Late 1942	Brings wife and son to live in Chelsea
Feb 1943	*New Poems* (USA)
3 Mar 1943	Daughter (Aeronwy) born
1943	Continuous work as broadcaster begins
Sept 1944– Summer 1945	Living at New Quay, Cardiganshire
Summer 1945– Spring 1946	Living in London
7 Feb 1946	*Deaths and Entrances* published
Mar 1946–May 1949	Living in or near Oxford
8 Nov 1946	*Selected Writings* (USA)
Apr–Aug 1947	Visits Italy
Sept 1947	Moves to live in South Leigh, Oxfordshire
1948	Writing feature films for Gainsborough
Mar 1949	Visits Prague as guest of Czechoslovak government
May 1949	Laugharne again becomes his main home (The Boat House)
24 July 1949	Second son (Colm) born
Feb–June 1950	First American tour
Jan 1951	In Iran, writing film script for the Anglo Iranian Oil Company
Jan–May 1952	Second American tour
Feb 1952	*In Country Sleep* (USA)

10 Nov 1952	*Collected Poems 1934–1952* published
16 Dec 1952	The poet's father dies
31 Mar 1953	*Collected Poems* (USA)
Apr–June 1953	Third American tour
14 May 1953	First performance of *Under Milk Wood* in New York
14 May 1953	*The Doctor and the Devils.* The first of the film scripts to be published
Oct 1953	Leaves on final American tour
9 Nov 1953	Dies in St Vincent's Hospital, New York City

THE COLLECTED STORIES

AFTER THE FAIR

The fair was over, the lights in the coconut stalls were put out, and the wooden horses stood still in the darkness, waiting for the music and the hum of the machines that would set them trotting forward. One by one, in every booth, the naphtha jets were turned down and the canvases pulled over the little gaming tables. The crowd went home, and there were lights in the windows of the caravans.

Nobody had noticed the girl. In her black clothes she stood against the side of the roundabouts, hearing the last feet tread upon the sawdust and the last voices die in the distance. Then, all alone on the deserted ground, surrounded by the shapes of wooden horses and cheap fairy boats, she looked for a place to sleep. Now here and now there, she raised the canvas that shrouded the coconut stalls and peered into the warm darkness. She was frightened to step inside, and as a mouse scampered across the littered shavings on the floor, or as the canvas creaked and a rush of wind set it dancing, she ran away and hid again near the roundabouts. Once she stepped on the boards; the bells round a horse's throat jingled and were still; she did not dare breathe again until all was quiet and the darkness had forgotten the noise of the bells. Then here and there she went peeping for a bed, into each gondola, under each tent. But there was nowhere, nowhere in all the fair for her to sleep. One place was too silent, and in another was the noise of mice. There was straw in the corner of the Astrologer's tent, but it moved as she touched it; she knelt by its side and put out her hand; she felt a baby's hand upon her own.

Now there was nowhere, so slowly she turned towards the caravans on the outskirts of the field, and found all but two to be unlit. She waited, clutching her empty bag, and wondering which caravan she should disturb. At last she decided to knock upon the window of the little, shabby one near her, and, standing on tiptoes, she looked in. The fattest man she had ever

seen was sitting in front of the stove, toasting a piece of bread.
She tapped three times on the glass, then hid in the shadows.
She heard him come to the top of the steps and call out 'Who?
Who?' but she dare not answer. 'Who? Who?' he called
again.

She laughed at his voice which was as thin as he was fat.

He heard her laughter and turned to where the darkness
concealed her. 'First you tap,' he said, 'then you hide, then you
laugh.'

She stepped into the circle of light, knowing she need no
longer hide herself.

'A girl,' he said. 'Come in, and wipe your feet.' He did not
wait but retreated into his caravan, and she could do nothing
but follow him up the steps and into the crowded room. He was
seated again, and toasting the same piece of bread. 'Have you
come in?' he said, for his back was towards her.

'Shall I close the door?' she asked, and closed it before he
replied.

She sat on the bed and watched him toast the bread until it
burnt.

'I can toast better than you,' she said.

'I don't doubt it,' said the Fat man.

She watched him put the charred toast upon a plate by his
side, take another round of bread and hold that, too, in front of
the stove. It burnt very quickly.

'Let me toast it for you,' she said. Ungraciously he handed her
the fork and the loaf.

'Cut it,' he said, 'toast it, and eat it.'

She sat on the chair.

'See the dent you've made on my bed,' said the Fat Man.
'Who are you to come in and dent my bed?'

'My name is Annie,' she told him.

Soon all the bread was toasted and buttered, so she put it in
the centre of the table and arranged two chairs.

'I'll have mine on the bed,' said the Fat Man. 'You'll have it
here.'

When they had finished their supper, he pushed back his chair
and stared at her across the table.

'I am the Fat Man,' he said. 'My home is Treorchy; the
Fortune-Teller next door is Aberdare.'

'I am nothing to do with the fair,' she said, 'I am Cardiff.'

'There's a town,' agreed the Fat Man. He asked her why she had come away.

'Money,' said Annie.

Then he told her about the fair and the places he had been to and the people he had met. He told her his age and his weight and the names of his brothers and what he would call his son. He showed her a picture of Boston Harbour and the photograph of his mother who lifted weights. He told her how summer looked in Ireland.

'I've always been a fat man,' he said, 'and now I'm the Fat Man; there's nobody to touch me for fatness.' He told her of a heat-wave in Sicily and of the Mediterranean Sea. She told him of the baby in the Astrologer's tent.

'That's the stars again,' he said.

'The baby'll die,' said Annie.

He opened the door and walked out into the darkness. She looked about her but did not move, wondering if he had gone to fetch a policeman. It would never do to be caught by the policeman again. She stared through the open door into the inhospitable night and drew her chair closer to the stove.

'Better to be caught in the warmth,' she said. But she trembled at the sound of the Fat Man approaching, and pressed her hands upon her thin breast as he climbed up the steps like a walking mountain. She could see him smile through the darkness.

'See what the stars have done,' he said, and brought in the Astrologer's baby in his arms.

After she had nursed it against her and it had cried on the bosom of her dress, she told him how she had feared his going.

'What should I be doing with a policeman.'

She told him that the policeman wanted her. 'What have you done for a policeman to be wanting you?'

She did not answer but took the child nearer to her wasted breast. He saw her thinness.

'You must eat, Cardiff,' he said.

Then the child began to cry. From a little wail its voice rose into a tempest of despair. The girl rocked it to and fro on her lap, but nothing soothed it.

'Stop it! Stop it!' said the Fat Man, and the tears increased. Annie smothered it in kisses, but it howled again.

'We must do something,' she said.

'Sing it a lullaby.'

She sang, but the child did not like her singing.

'There's only one thing,' said Annie, 'we must take it on the roundabouts.' With the child's arm around her neck she stumbled down the steps and ran towards the deserted fair, the Fat Man panting behind her.

She found her way through the tents and stalls into the centre of the ground where the wooden horses stood waiting, and clambered up on a saddle. 'Start the engine,' she called out. In the distance the Fat Man could be heard cranking up the antique machine that drove the horses all the day into a wooden gallop. She heard the spasmodic humming of the engines; the boards rattled under the horse's feet. She saw the Fat Man get up by her side, pull the central lever, and climb on to the saddle of the smallest horse of all. As the roundabout started, slowly at first and slowly gaining speed, the child at the girl's breast stopped crying and clapped its hands. The night wind tore through its hair, the music jangled in its ears. Round and round the wooden horses sped, drowning the cries of the wind with the beating of their hooves.

And so the men from the caravans found them, the Fat Man and the girl in black with a baby in her arms, racing round and round on their mechanical steeds to the ever-increasing music of the organ.

THE TREE

Rising from the house that faced the Jarvis hills in the long distance, there was a tower for the day-birds to build in and for the owls to fly around at night. From the village the light in the tower window shone like a glow-worm through the panes; but the room under the sparrows' nests was rarely lit; webs were spun over its unwashed ceilings; it stared over twenty miles of the up-and-down county, and the corners kept their secrets where there were claw marks in the dust.

The child knew the house from roof to cellar; he knew the irregular lawns and the gardener's shed where flowers burst out of their jars; but he could not find the key that opened the door of the tower.

The house changed to his moods, and a lawn was the sea or the shore or the sky or whatever he wished it. When a lawn was a sad mile of water, and he was sailing on a broken flower down the waves, the gardener would come out of his shed near the island of bushes. He too would take a stalk, and sail. Straddling a garden broom, he would fly wherever the child wished. He knew every story from the beginning of the world.

'In the beginning,' he would say, 'there was a tree.'

'What kind of a tree?'

'The tree where that blackbird's whistling.'

'A hawk, a hawk,' cried the child.

The gardener would look up at the tree, seeing a monstrous hawk perched on a bough or an eagle swinging in the wind.

The gardener loved the Bible. When the sun sank and the garden was full of people, he would sit with a candle in his shed, reading of the first love and the legend of apples and serpents. But the death of Christ on a tree he loved most. Trees made a fence around him, and he knew of the changing of the seasons by the hues on the bark and the rushing of sap through the covered roots. His world moved and changed as spring moved along the branches, changing their nakedness; his God grew up like a tree from the apple-shaped earth, giving bud to His children and letting His children be blown from their places by the breezes of winter; winter and death moved in one wind. He would sit in his shed and read of the crucifixion, looking over the jars on his window-shelf into the winter nights. He would think that love fails on such nights, and that many of its children ·ʹ are cut down.

The child transfigured the blowsy lawns with his playing. The gardener called him by his mother's name, and seated him on his knee, and talked to him of the wonders of Jerusalem and the birth in the manger.

'In the beginning was the village of Bethlehem,' he whispered to the child before the bell rang for tea out of the growing darkness.

'Where is Bethlehem?'

'Far away,' said the gardener, 'in the East.'

To the east stood the Jarvis hills, hiding the sun, their trees drawing up the moon out of the grass.

The child lay in bed. He watched the rocking-horse and wished that it would grow wings so that he could mount it and ride into the Arabian sky. But the winds of Wales blew at the curtains, and crickets made a noise in the untidy plot under the window. His toys were dead. He started to cry and then stopped, knowing no reason for tears. The night was windy and cold, he was warm under the sheets; the night was as big as a hill, he was a boy in bed.

Closing his eyes, he stared into a spinning cavern deeper than the darkness of the garden where the first tree on which the unreal birds had fastened stood alone and bright as fire. The tears ran back under his lids as he thought of the first tree that was planted so near him, like a friend in the garden. He crept out of bed and tiptoed to the door. The rocking-horse bounded forward on its springs, startling the child into a noiseless scamper back to bed. The child looked at the horse and the horse was quiet; he tiptoed again along the carpet, and reached the door, and turned the knob around, and ran on to the landing. Feeling blindly in front of him, he made his way to the top of the stairs; he looked down the dark stairs into the hall, seeing a host of shadows curve in and out of the corners, hearing their sinuous voices, imagining the pits of their eyes and their lean arms. But they would be little and secret and bloodless, not cased in invisible armour but wound around with cloths as thin as a web; they would whisper as he walked, touch him on the shoulder, and say S in his ear. He went down the stairs; not a shadow moved in the hall, the corners were empty. He put out his hand and patted the darkness, thinking to feel some dry and velvet head creep under the fingers and edge, like a mist, into the nails. But there was nothing. He opened the front door, and the shadows swept into the garden.

Once on the path, his fears left him. The moon had lain down on the unweeded beds, and her frosts were spread on the grass. At last he came to the illuminated tree at the long gravel end, older even than the marvel of light, with the woodlice asleep under the bark, with the boughs standing out from the body like the frozen arms of a woman. The child touched the tree; it bent as to his touch. He saw a star, brighter than any in the sky, burn steadily above the first birds' tower, and shine on nowhere but on the leafless boughs and the trunk and the travelling roots.

The child had not doubted the tree. He said his prayers to it, with knees bent on the blackened twigs the night wind fetched to the ground. Then, trembling with love and cold, he ran back over the lawns towards the house.

There was an idiot to the east of the county who walked the land like a beggar. Now at a farmhouse and now at a widow's cottage he begged for his bread. A parson gave him a suit, and it lopped round his hungry ribs and shoulders and waved in the wind as he shambled over the fields. But his eyes were so wide and his neck so clear of the country dirt that no one refused him what he asked. And asking for water, he was given milk.

'Where do you come from?'

'From the east,' he said.

So they knew he was an idiot, and gave him a meal to clean the yards.

As he bent with a rake over the dung and the trodden grain, he heard a voice rise in his heart. He put his hand into the cattle's hay, caught a mouse, rubbed his hand over its muzzle, and let it go away.

All day the thought of the tree was with the child; all night it stood up in his dreams as the star stood above its plot. One morning towards the middle of December, when the wind from the farthest hills was rushing around the house, and the snow of the dark hours had not dissolved from lawns and roofs, he ran to the gardener's shed. The gardener was repairing a rake he had found broken. Without a word, the child sat on a seedbox at his feet, and watched him tie the teeth, and knew that the wire would not keep them together. He looked at the gardener's boots, wet with snow, at the patched knees of his trousers, at the undone buttons of his coat, and the folds of his belly under the patched flannel shirt. He looked at his hands as they busied themselves over the golden knots of wire; they were hard, brown hands, with the stains of the soil under the broken nails and the stains of tobacco on the tips of the fingers. Now the lines of the gardener's face were set in determination as time upon time he knotted the iron teeth only to feel them shake insecurely from the handle. The child was frightened of the strength and the uncleanliness of the old man; but, looking at the long, thick beard, unstained and white as fleece, he soon became reassured. The beard was the beard of an apostle.

'I prayed to the tree,' said the child.

'Always pray to a tree,' said the gardener, thinking of Calvary and Eden.

'I pray to the tree every night.'

'Pray to a tree.'

The wire slid over the teeth.

'I pray to that tree.'

The wire snapped.

The child was pointing over the glasshouse flowers to the tree that, alone of all the trees in the garden, had no sign of snow.

'An elder,' said the gardener, but the child stood up from his box and shouted so loud that the unmended rake fell with a clatter on the floor.

'The first tree. The first tree you told me of. In the beginning was the tree, you said. I heard you,' the child shouted.

'The elder is as good as another,' said the gardener, lowering his voice to humour the child.

'The first tree of all,' said the child in a whisper.

Reassured again by the gardener's voice, he smiled through the window at the tree, and again the wire crept over the broken rake.

'God grows in strange trees,' said the old man. 'His trees come to rest in strange places.'

As he unfolded the story of the twelve stages of the cross, the tree waved its boughs to the chid. An apostle's voice rose out of the tarred lungs.

So they hoisted him up on a tree, and drove nails through his belly and his feet.

There was the blood of the noon sun on the trunk of the elder, staining the bark.

*   *   *

The idiot stood on the Jarvis hills, looking down into the immaculate valley from whose waters and grasses the mists of morning rose and were lost. He saw the dew dissolving, the cattle staring into the stream, and the dark clouds flying away at the rumour of the sun. The sun turned at the edges of the thin and watery sky like a sweet in a glass of water. He was hungry for light as the first and almost invisible rain fell on his lips; he plucked at the grass, and, tasting it, felt it lie green on his tongue. So there was light in his mouth, and light was a sound at his ears, and the whole dominion of light in the valley that had such a curious name. He had known of the Jarvis Hills; their shapes rose over the slopes of the county to be seen for miles around, but no one had told him of the valley lying under the hills. Bethlehem, said the idiot to the valley, turning over the sounds of the word and giving it all the glory of the Welsh morning. He brothered the world around him, sipped at the air, as a child newly born sips and brothers the light. The life of the Jarvis valley, steaming up from the body of the grass and the trees and the long hand of the stream, lent him a new blood. Night had emptied the idiot's veins, and dawn in the valley filled them again.

'Bethlehem,' said the idiot to the valley.

The gardener had no present to give the child, so he took out a key from his pocket and said: 'This is the key to the tower. On Christmas Eve I will unlock the door for you.'

Before it was dark, he and the child climbed the stairs to the tower, the key turned in the lock, and the door, like the lid of a secret box, opened and let them in. The room was empty. 'Where are the secrets?' asked the child, staring up at the matted rafters and into the spider's corners and along the leaden panes of the window.

'It is enough that I have given you the key,' said the gardener, who believed the key of the universe to be hidden in his pocket along with the feathers of birds and the seeds of flowers.

The child began to cry because there were no secrets. Over and over again he explored the empty room, kicking up the dust to look for a colourless trap-door, tapping the unpanelled walls for the hollow voice of a room beyond the tower. He brushed the webs from the window, and looked out through the dust into the snowing Christmas Eve. A world of hills stretched far away into the measured sky, and the tops of hills he had never seen climbed up to meet the falling flakes. Woods and rocks, wide seas of barren land, and a new tide of mountain sky sweeping through the black beeches, lay before him. To the east were the outlines of nameless hill creatures and a den of trees.

'Who are they? Who are they?'

'They are the Jarvis hills,' said the gardener, 'which have been from the beginning.'

He took the child by the hand and led him away from the window. The key turned in the lock.

That night the child slept well; there was power in snow and darkness; there was unalterable music in the silence of the stars; there was a silence in the hurrying wind. And Bethlehem had been nearer than he expected.

*   *   *

On Christmas morning the idiot walked into the garden. His hair was wet and his flaked and ragged shoes were thick with the dirt of the fields. Tired with the long journey from the Jarvis hills, and weak for the want of food, he sat down under the elder-tree where the gardener had rolled a log. Clasping his hands in front of him, he saw the desolation of the flower-beds and the weeds that grew in profusion on the edges of the paths. The tower stood up like a tree of stone and glass over the red eaves. He pulled his coat-collar round his neck as a fresh wind sprang up and struck the tree; he looked down at his hands and saw that they were praying. Then a fear of the garden came over him, the shrubs were his enemies, and the trees that made an avenue down to the gate lifted their arms in horror. The place was too high, peering down on to the tall hills; the place was too low, shivering up at the plumed shoulders of a new mountain. Here the wind was too wild, fuming about the silence, raising a Jewish voice out of the elder boughs; here the silence beat like a human heart. And as he sat under the cruel hills, he heard a voice that was in him cry out: 'Why did you bring me here?'

He could not tell why he had come; they had told him to come and had guided him, but he did not know who they were. The voice of a people rose out of the garden beds, and rain swooped down from heaven.

'Let me be,' said the idiot, and made a little gesture against the sky. There is rain on my face, there is wind on my cheeks. He brothered the rain.

So the child found him under the shelter of the tree, bearing the torture of the weather with a divine patience, letting his long hair blow where it would, with his mouth set in a sad smile.

Who was this stranger? He had fires in his eyes, the flesh of his neck under the gathered coat was bare. Yet he smiled as he sat in his rags under a tree on Christmas Day.

'Where do you come from?' asked the child.

'From the east,' answered the idiot.

The gardener had not lied, and the secret of the tower was true; this dark and shabby tree, that glistened only in the night, was the first tree of all.

But he asked again:

'Where do you come from?'

'From the Jarvis hills.'

'Stand up against the tree.'

The idiot, still smiling, stood up with his back to the elder.

'Put out your arms like this.'

The idiot put out his arms.

The child ran as fast as he could to the gardener's shed, and, returning over the sodden lawns, saw that the idiot had not moved but stood, straight and smiling, with his back to the tree and his arms stretched out.

'Let me tie your hands.'

The idiot felt the wire that had not mended the rake close round his wrists. It cut into the flesh, and the blood from the cuts fell shining on to the tree.

'Brother,' he said. He saw that the child held silver nails in the palm of his hand.

THE TRUE STORY

The old woman upstairs had been dying since Helen could remember. She had lain like a wax woman in her sheets since Helen was a child coming with her mother to bring fresh fruit and vegetables to the dying. And now Helen was a woman under her apron and print frock and her pale hair was bound in a bunch behind her head. Each morning she got up with the sun, lit the fire, let in the red-eyed cat. She made a pot of tea and, going up to the bedroom at the back of the cottage, bent over the old woman whose unseeing eyes were never closed. Each morning she looked into the hollows of the eyes and passed her hands over them. But the lids did not move, and she could not tell if the old woman breathed. 'Eight o'clock, eight o'clock now,' she said. And at once the eyes smiled. A ragged hand came out from the sheets and stayed there until Helen took it in her padded hand and closed it round the cup. When the cup was empty Helen filled it, and when the pot was dry she pulled back the white sheets from the bed. There the old woman was, stretched out in her nightdress, and the colour of her flesh was grey as her hair. Helen tidied the sheets and attended to the old woman's wants. Then she took the pot away.

Each morning she made breakfast for the boy who worked in the garden. She went to the back door, opened it, and saw him in the distance with his spade. 'Half past eight now,' she said. He was an ugly boy and his eyes were redder than the cat's, two crafty cuts in his head forever spying on the first shadows of her breast. She put his food in front of him. When he stood up he always said, 'Is there anything you want me to do?' She had never said, 'Yes.' The boy went back to dig potatoes out of the patch or to count the hens' eggs, and if there were berries to be picked off the garden bushes he joined her before noon. Seeing the red currants pile up in the palm of her hand, she would think of the stain of the money under the old woman's mattress. If there were hens to be killed she could cut their throats far more cleanly than the boy who let his knife stay in the wound and wiped the blood on the knife along his sleeve. She caught a hen and killed it, felt its warm blood, and saw it run headless up the path. Then she went in to wash her hands.

It was in the first weeks of spring that she made up her mind to kill the old woman upstairs. She was twenty years old. There was so much that she wanted. She wanted a man of her own and a black dress for Sundays and a hat with a flower. She had no money at all. On the days that the boy took the eggs and the vegetables to market she gave him sixpence that the old woman gave her, and the money the boy brought back in his handkerchief she put into the old woman's hand. She worked for her food and shelter as the boy worked for his, though she slept in a room upstairs and he slept in a straw bed over the empty sheds.

On a market morning she walked into the garden so that the plan might be cooled in her head. It was a fine May day with no more than two clouds in the sky, two unshapely hands closing round the head of the sun. 'If I could fly,' she thought, 'I could fly in at the open window and fix my teeth in her throat.' But the cool wind blew the thought away. She knew that she was no common girl, for she had read books in the winter evenings when the boy was dreaming in the straw and the old woman was alone in the dark. She had read of a god who came down like money, of snakes with the voices of men, and of a man who stood on the top of a hill talking with a piece of fire.

At the end of the garden where the fence kept out the wild, green fields she came to a mound of earth. There she had buried the dog she had killed for catching and killing the hens. On a rough cross the date of the death was written backwards so that the dog had not died yet. 'I could bury her here,' said Helen to herself, 'By the side of the grave, so that nobody could find her.' And she patted her hands and reached the back door of the cottage before the two clouds got round the sun.

Inside there was a meal to be prepared for the old woman, potatoes to be mashed up in the tea. With the knife in her hand and the skins in her lap, she thought of the murder she was about to do. The knife made the only sound, the wind had dropped down, her heart was as quiet as though she had wrapped it up. Nothing moved in the cottage; her hand was dead on her lap; she could not think that smoke went up the chimney and out into the still sky. Her mind, alone in the world, was ticking away. Then, when all things were dead, a cock crew, and she remembered the boy who would soon be back from market. She had made up her mind to kill before he returned, but the grave must be dug and the hole filled up. Helen felt her hand die again in her lap. And in the middle of death she heard the boy's hand lift the latch. He came into the kitchen, saw that she was cleaning the potatoes, and dropped his handkerchief on the table. Hearing the rattle of money, she looked up at him and smiled. He had never seen her smile before.

Soon she put his meal in front of him, and sat sideways by the fire. As he raised the knife to his mouth, he felt the full glance of her eyes on the sides of his eyes. 'Have you taken up her dinner?' he asked. She did not answer. When he had finished he stood up from the table and asked, 'Is there anything you want me to do?' as he had asked a thousand times. 'Yes,' said Helen.

She had never said 'Yes' to him before. He had never heard a woman speak as she did then. The first shadow of her breast had never been so dark. He stumbled across the kitchen to her and she lifted her hands to his shoulders. 'What will you do for me?' she said, and loosened the straps of her frock so that it fell about her and left her breast bare. She took his hand and placed it on her flesh. He stared at her nakedness, then said her name and caught hold of her. She held him close. 'What will you do for me?' She let her frock fall on the floor and tore the rest of her clothes away. 'You will do what I want,' she said as his hands dropped on her.

After a minute she struggled out of his arms and ran softly across the room. With her naked back to the door that led upstairs, she beckoned him and told him what he was to do. 'You help me, we shall be rich,' she said. He smiled and nodded. He tried to finger her again but she caught his fingers and opened the door and led him upstairs. 'You stay here quiet,' she said. In the old woman's room she looked around her as if for the last time, at the cracked jug, the half-open window, the bed and the text on the wall. 'One o'clock now,' she said into the old woman's ear, and the blind eyes smiled. Helen put her fingers round the old woman's throat. 'One o'clock now,' she said, and with a sudden movement knocked the old woman's head against the wall. It needed but three little knocks, and the head burst like an egg.

'What have you done?' cried the boy. Helen called for him to come in. He stared at the naked woman who cleaned her hands on the bed and at the blood that made a round, red stain on the wall, and screamed out in horror. 'Be quiet,' said Helen, but he screamed again at her quiet voice and scurried downstairs.

'So Helen must fly,' she said to herself. 'Fly out of the old woman's room.' She opened the window wider and stepped out. 'I am flying,' she said.

But she was not flying.

THE ENEMIES

It was morning in the green acres of the Jarvis valley, and Mr Owen was picking the weeds from the edges of his garden path. A great wind pulled at his beard, the vegetable world roared under his feet. A rook had lost itself in the sky, and was making a noise to its mate; but the mate never came, and the rook flew into the west with a woe in its beak. Mr Owen, who had stood up to ease his shoulders and look at the sky, observed how dark the wings beat against the red sun. In her draughty kitchen Mrs Owen grieved over the soup. Once, in past days, the valley had housed the cattle alone; the farm-boys came down from the hills to holla at the cattle and to drive them to be milked; but no stranger set foot in the valley. Mr Owen, walking lonely through the country, had come upon it at the end of a late summer evening when the cattle were lying down still, and the stream that divided it was speaking over the pebbles. Here, thought Mr Owen, I will build a small house with one storey, in the middle of the valley, set around by a garden. And, remembering clearly the way he had come along the winding hills, he returned to his village and the questions of Mrs Owen. So it came about that a house with one story was built in the green fields; a garden was dug and planted, and a low fence put up around the garden to keep the cows from the vegetables.

That was early in the year. Now summer and autumn had gone over; the garden had blossomed and died; there was frost at the weeds. Mr Owen bent down again, tidying the path, while the wind blew back the heads of the nearby grasses and made an oracle of each green mouth. Patiently he strangled the weeds; up came the roots, making war in the soil around them; insects were busy in the holes where the weeds had sprouted, but, dying between his fingers, they left no stain. He grew tired of their death, and tireder of the fall of the weeds. Up came the roots, down went the cheap, green heads.

Mrs Owen, peering into the depths of her crystal, had left the soup to bubble on unaided. The ball grew dark, then lightened as a rainbow moved within it. Growing hot like a sun, and cooling again like an arctic star, it shone in the folds of her dress where she held it lovingly. The tea-leaves in her cup at breakfast had told of a dark stranger. What would the crystal tell her? Mrs Owen wondered.

Up came the roots, and a crooked worm, disturbed by the probing of the fingers, wriggled blind in the sun. Of a sudden the valley filled all its hollows with the wind, with the voice of the roots, with the breathing of the nether sky. Not only a mandrake screams; torn roots have their cries; each weed Mr Owen pulled out of the ground screamed like a baby. In the village behind the hill the wind would be raging, the clothes on the garden lines would be set to strange dances. And women with shapes in their wombs would feel a new knocking as they bent over the steamy tubs. Life would go on in the veins, in the bones, the binding flesh, that had their seasons and their weathers even as the valley binding the house about with the flesh of the green grass.

The ball, like an open grave, gave up its dead to Mrs Owen. She stared on the lips of women and the hairs of men that wound into a pattern on the face of the crystal world. But suddenly the patterns were swept away, and she could see nothing but the shapes of the Jarvis hills. A man with a black hat was walking down the paths into the invisible valley beneath. If he walked any nearer he would fall into her lap. 'There's a man with a black hat walking on the hills,' she called through the window. Mr Owen smiled and went on weeding.

It was at this time that the Reverend Mr Davies lost his way; he had been losing it most of the morning, but now he had lost it altogether, and stood perturbed under a tree on the rim of the Jarvis hills. A great wind blew through the branches, and a great grey-green earth moved unsteadily beneath him. Wherever he looked the hills stormed up to the sky, and wherever he sought to hide from the wind he was frightened by the darkness. The farther he walked, the stranger was the scenery around him; it rose to undreamed-of-heights, and then fell down again into a valley no bigger than the palm of his hand. And the trees walked like men. By a divine coincidence he reached the rim of the hills just as the sun reached the centre of the sky. With the wide world rocking from horizon to horizon, he stood under a tree and looked down into the valley. In the fields was a little house with a garden. The valley roared around it, the wind leapt at it like a boxer, but the house stood still. To Mr Davies it seemed as though the house had been carried out of a village by a large bird and placed in the very middle of the tumultuous universe.

But as he climbed over the craggy edges and down the side of the hill, he lost his place in Mrs Owen's crystal. A cloud displaced his black hat, and under the cloud walked a very old phantom, a shape of air with stars all frozen in its beard, and a half-moon for a smile. Mr Davies knew nothing of this as the stones scratched his hands. He was old, he was drunk with the wine of the morning, but the stuff that came out of his cuts was a human blood.

Nor did Mr Owen, with his face near the soil and his hands on the necks of the screaming weeds, know of the transformation in the crystal. He had heard Mrs Owen prophesy the coming of the black hat, and had smiled as he always smiled at her faith in the powers of darkness. He had looked up when she called, and, smiling, had returned to the clearer call of the ground. 'Multiply, multiply,' he had said to the worms disturbed in their channelling, and had cut the brown worms in half so that the halves might breed and spread their life over the garden and go out, contaminating, into the fields and the bellies of the cattle.

Of this Mr Davies knew nothing. He saw a young man with a beard bent industriously over the garden soil; he saw that the house was a pretty picture, with the face of a pale young woman pressed up against the window. And, removing his black hat, he introduced himself as the rector of a village some ten miles away.

'You are bleeding,' said Mr Owen.

Mr Davies's hands, indeed, were covered in blood.

When Mrs Owen had seen to the rector's cuts, she sat him down in the arm-chair near the window, and made him a strong cup of tea.

'I saw you on the hill,' she said, and he asked her how she had seen him, for the hills are high and a long way off.

'I have good eyes,' she answered.

He did not doubt her. Her eyes were the strangest he had seen.

'It is quiet here,' said Mr Davies.

'We have no clock,' she said, and laid the table for three.

'You are very kind.'

'We are kind to those that come to us.'

He wondered how many came to the lonely house in the valley, but did not question her for fear of what she would reply. He guessed she was an uncanny woman loving the dark because it was dark. He was too old to question the secrets of darkness, and now, with the black suit torn and wet and his thin hands bound with the bandages of the stranger woman, he felt older than ever. The winds of the morning might blow him down, and the sudden dropping of the dark be blind in his eyes. Rain might pass through him as it passes through the body of a ghost. A tired, white-haired old man, he sat under the window, almost invisible against the panes and the white cloth of the chair.

Soon the meal was ready, and Mr Owen came in unwashed from the garden.

'Shall I say grace?' said Mr Davies when all three were seated around the table.

Mrs Owen nodded.

'O Lord God Almighty, bless this our meal,' said Mr Davies. Looking up as he continued his prayer, he saw that Mr and Mrs Owen had closed their eyes. 'We thank Thee for the bounties that Thou hast given us.' And he saw that the lips of Mr and Mrs Owen were moving softly. He could not hear what they said, but he knew that the prayers they spoke were not his prayers.

'Amen,' said all three together.

Mr Owen, proud in his eating, bent over the plate as he had bent over the complaining weeds. Outside the window was the brown body of the earth, the green skin of the grass, and the breasts of the Jarvis hills; there was a wind that chilled the animal earth, and a sun that had drunk up the dews on the fields; there was creation sweating out of the pores of the trees; and the grains of sand on far-away seashores would be multiplying as the sea rolled over them. He felt the coarse foods on his tongue; there was a meaning in the rind of the meat, and a purpose in the lifting of food to mouth. He saw, with a sudden satisfaction, that Mrs Owen's throat was bare.

She, too, was bent over her plate, but was letting the teeth of her fork nibble at the corners of it. She did not eat, for the old powers were upon her, and she dared not lift up her head for the greenness of her eyes. She knew by the sound which way the wind blew in the valley; she knew the stage of the sun by the curve of the shadows on the cloth. Oh, that she could take her crystal, and see within it the stretches of darkness covering up this winter light. But there was a darkness gathering in her mind, drawing in the light around her. There was a ghost on her left; with all her strength she drew in the intangible light that moved around him, and mixed it in her dark brains.

Mr Davies, like a man sucked by a bird, felt desolation in his veins, and, in a sweet delirium, told of his adventures on the hills, of how it had been cold and blowing, and how the hills went up and down. He had been lost, he said, and had found a dark retreat to shelter from the bullies in the wind; but the darkness had frightened him, and he had walked again on the hills where the morning tossed him about like a ship on the sea. Wherever he went he was blown in the open or frightened in the narrow shades. There was nowhere, he said pityingly, for an old man to go. Loving his parish, he had loved the surrounding lands, but the hills had given under his feet or plunged him into the air. And, loving his God, he had loved the darkness where men of old had worshipped the dark invisible. But now the hill caves were full of shapes and voices that mocked him because he was old.

'He is frightened of the dark,' thought Mrs Owen, 'the lovely dark.' With a smile, Mr Owen thought: 'He is frightened of the worm in the earth, of the copulation in the tree, of the living grease in the soil.' They looked at the old man, and saw that he was more ghostly than ever. The window behind him cast a ragged circle of light round his head.

Suddenly Mr Davies knelt down to pray. He did not understand the cold in his heart nor the fear that bewildered him as he knelt, but, speaking his prayers for deliverance, he stared up at the shadowed eyes of Mrs Owen and at the smiling eyes of her husband. Kneeling on the carpet at the head of the table, he stared in bewilderment at the dark mind and the gross dark body. He stared and he prayed, like an old god beset by his enemies.

THE DRESS

They had followed him for two days over the length of the county, but he had lost them at the foot of the hills, and hidden in a golden bush, had heard them shouting as they stumbled down the valley. Behind a tree on the ridge of the hills he had peeped down on to the fields where they hurried about like dogs, where they poked the hedges with their sticks and set up a faint howling as a mist came suddenly from the spring sky and hid them from his eyes. But the mist was a mother to him, putting a coat around his shoulders where the shirt was torn and the blood dry on his blades. The mist made him warm; he had the food and the drink of the mist on his lips; and he smiled through her mantle like a cat. He worked away from the valleywards side of the hill into the denser trees that might lead him to light and fire and a basin of soup. He thought of the coals that might be hissing in the grate, and of the young mother standing alone. He thought of her hair. Such a nest it would make for his hands. He ran through the trees, and found himself on a narrow road. Which way should he walk : towards or away from the moon ? The mist had made a secret of the position of the moon, but, in a corner of the sky, where the mist had fallen apart, he could see the angles of the stars. He walked towards the north where the stars were, mumbling a song with no tune, hearing his feet suck in and out of the spongy earth.

Now there was time to collect his thoughts, but no sooner had he started to set them in order than an owl made a cry in the trees that hung over the road, and he stopped and winked up at her, finding a mutual melancholy in her sounds. Soon she would swoop and fasten on a mouse. He saw her for a moment as she sat screeching on her bough. Then, frightened of her, he hurried on, and had not gone more than a few yards into the darkness when, with a fresh cry, she flew away. Pity the hare, he thought, for the weasel will drink her. The road sloped to the stars, and the trees and the valley and the memory of the guns faded behind.

He heard footsteps. An old man, radiant with rain, stepped out of the mist.

'Good night, sir,' said the old man.

'No night for the son of woman,' said the madman.

The old man whistled, and hurried, half running, in the direction of the roadside trees.

Let the hounds know, the madman chuckled as he climbed up the hill, let the hounds know. And, crafty as a fox, he doubled back to where the misty road branched off three ways. Hell on the stars, he said, and walked towards the dark.

The world was a ball under his feet; it kicked as he ran; it dropped; up came the trees. In the distance a poacher's dog yelled at the trap on its foot, and he heard it and ran the faster, thinking the enemy was on his heels. 'Duck, boys, duck,' he called out, but with the voice of one who might have pointed to a falling star.

Remembering of a sudden that he had not slept since the escape, he left off running. Now the waters of the rain, too tired to strike the earth, broke up as they fell and blew about in the wind like the sandman's grains. If he met sleep, sleep would be a girl. For the last two nights, while walking or running over the empty county, he had dreamed of their meeting. 'Lie down,' she would say, and would give him her dress to lie on, stretching herself out by his side. Even as he had dreamed, and the twigs under his running feet had made a noise like the rustle of her dress, the enemy had shouted in the fields. He had run on and on, leaving sleep farther behind him. Sometimes there was a sun, a moon, and sometimes under a black sky he had tossed and thrown the wind before he could be off.

'Where is Jack?' they asked in the gardens of the place he had left. 'Up on the hills with a butcher's knife,' they said, smiling. But the knife was gone, thrown at a tree and quivering there still. There was no heat in his head. He ran on and on, howling for sleep.

And she, alone in the house, was sewing her new dress. It was a bright country dress with flowers on the bodice. Only a few more stitches were needed before it would be ready to wear. It would lie neat on her shoulders, and two of the flowers would be growing out of her breasts.

When she walked with her husband on Sunday mornings over the fields and down into the village, the boys would smile at her behind their hands, and the shaping of the dress round her belly would set all the widow women talking. She slipped into her new dress, and, looking into the mirror over the fire-place, saw that it was prettier than she had imagined. It made her face paler and her long hair darker. She had cut it low.

A dog out in the night lifted its head up and howled. She turned away hurriedly from her reflection, and pulled the curtains closer.

Out in the night they were searching for a madman. He had green eyes, they said, and had married a lady. They said he had cut off her lips because she smiled at men. They took him away, but he stole a knife from the kitchen and slashed his keeper and broke out into the wild valleys.

From afar he saw the light in the house, and stumbled up to the edge of the garden. He felt, he did not see, the little fence around it. The rusting wire scraped on his hands, and the wet, abominable grass crept over his knees. And once he was through the fence, the hosts of the garden came rushing to meet him, the flower-headed, and the bodying frosts. He had torn his fingers while the old wounds were still wet. Like a man of blood he came out of the enemy's darkness on to the steps. He said in a whisper : 'Let them not shoot me.' And he opened the door.

She was in the middle of the room. Her hair had fallen untidily, and three of the buttons at the neck of her dress were undone. What made the dog howl as it did ? Frightened of the howling, and thinking of the tales she had heard, she rocked in her chair. What became of the woman ? she wondered as she rocked. She could not think of a woman without any lips. What became of women without any lips ? she wondered.

The door made no noise. He stepped into the room, trying to smile, and holding out his hands.

'Oh, you've come back,' she said.

Then she turned in her chair and saw him. There was blood even by his green eyes. She put her fingers to her mouth. 'Not shoot,' he said.

But the moving of her arm drew the neck of her dress apart, and he stared in wonder at her wide, white forehead, her frightened eyes and mouth, and down on to the flowers on her dress. With the moving of her arm, her dress danced in the light. She sat before him, covered in flowers. 'Sleep,' said the madman. And, kneeling down, he put his bewildered head upon her lap.

THE VISITOR

His hands were weary, though all night they had lain over the sheets of his bed and he had moved them only to his mouth and his wild heart. The veins ran, unhealthily blue streams, into the white sea. Milk at his side steamed out of a chipped cup. He smelt the morning, and knew that cocks in the yard were putting back their heads and crowing at the sun. What were the sheets around him if not the covering sheets of the dead? What was the busy-voiced clock, sounding between photographs of mother and dead wife, if not the voice of an old enemy? Time was merciful enough to let the sun shine on his bed, and merciless to chime the sun away when night came over and even more he needed the red light and the clear heat.

Rhianon was attendant on a dead man, and put the chipped edge of the cup to a dead lip. It could not be heart that beat under the ribs. Hearts do not beat in the dead. While he had lain ready for the inch-tape and the acid, Rhianon had cut open his chest with a book-knife, torn out the heart, put in the clock. He heard her say, for the third time, Drink the lovely milk. And, feeling it run sour over his tongue, and her hand caress his forehead, he knew he was not dead. He was a living man. For many miles the months flowed into the years, rounding the dry days.

Callaghan to-day would sit and talk with him. He heard in his brain the voices of Callaghan and Rhianon battle until he slept, and tasted the blood of words. His hands were weary. He brooded over his long, white body, marking the ribs stick through the sides. The hands had held other hands and thrown a ball high into the air. Now they were dead hands. He could wind them about his hair and let them rest untingling on his belly or lose them in the valley between Rhianon's breasts. It did not matter what he did with them. They were as dead as the hands of the clock, and moved to clockwork.

Shall I close the windows until the sun's warmer? said Rhianon.

I'm not cold.

He would tell her that the dead feel neither cold nor warmth, sun and wind could never penetrate his cloths. But she would laugh in her kind way and kiss him on the forehead and say to him, Peter, what's getting you down? You'll be out and about one day. One day he would walk on the Jarvis hills like a boy's ghost, and hear the people say, There walks the ghost of Peter, a poet, who was dead for years before they buried him.

Rhianon tucked the sheets around his shoulders, gave him a morning kiss, and carried the chipped cup away.

A man with a brush had drawn a rib of colour under the sun and painted many circles around the circle of the sun. Death was a man with a scythe; but that summer day no living stalk was to be cut down.

The invalid waited for his visitor. Peter waited for Callaghan. His room was a world within a world. A world in him went round and round, and a sun rose in him and a moon fell. Callaghan was the west wind, and Rhianon blew away the chills of the west wind like a wind from Tahiti.

He let his hand rest on his head, stone on stone. Never had the voice of Rhianon been so remote as when it told him that the sour milk was lovely. What was she but a sweetheart talking madly to her sweetheart under a coffin of garments? Somebody in the night had turned him up and emptied him of all but a false heart. That under the ribs' armour was not his, not his the beating of a vein in the foot. His arms could no longer make their movements nor a circle around a girl to shield her from winds and robbers. There was nothing more remote under the sun than his own name, and poetry was a string of words stringed on a beanstick. With his lips he rounded a little ball of sound into some shape, and spoke a word.

There was no to-morrow for dead men. He could not think that after the next night and its sleeping, life would sprout up again like a flower through a coffin's cracks.

His room around him was a vast place. From their frames the lying likenesses of women looked down on him. That was the face of his mother, that nearly yellow oval in its frame of old gold and thinning hair. And, next to her, dead Mary. Though Callaghan blew hard, the walls around Mary would never fall down. He thought of her as she had been, remembered her Peter, darling, Peter, and her smiling eyes.

He remembered he had not smiled since that night, seven years ago, when his heart had trembled so violently within him that he had fallen to the ground. There had been strengthening in the unbelievable setting of the sun. Over the hills and the roof went the broad moons, and summer came after spring. How had he lived at all when Callaghan had not blown away the webs of the world with a great shout, and Rhianon spread her loveliness about him ? But the dead need no friends. He peered over the turned coffin-lid. Stiff and straight, a man of wax stared back. Taking away the pennies from those dead eyes, he looked on his own face.

Breed, cardboard on cardboard, he had cried, before I blow down your paste huts with one bellow out of my lungs. When Mary came, there was nothing between the changing of the days but the divinity he had built around her. His child killed Mary in her womb. He felt his body turn to vapour, and men who had been light as air walked, metal-hooved, through and beyond him.

He started to cry, Rhianon, Rhianon, someone has upped and kicked me in the side. Drip, drip, goes my blood in me. Rhianon, he cried.

She hurried upstairs, and time and time over again wiped away the tears from his cheeks with the sleeve of her dress.

He lay still as the morning matured and grew up into a noble noon. Rhianon passed in and out, her dress, he smelt as she bent over him, smelling of clover and milk. With a new surprise he followed her cool movements around the room, the sweep of her hands as she brushed the dead Mary in her frame. With such surprise, he thought, do the dead follow the movements of the quick, seeing the bloom under the living skin. She should be singing as she moved from mantelpiece to window, putting things right, or should be humming like a bee about her work. But if she had spoken, or laughed, or struck her nails against the thin metal of the candlesticks, drawing forth a bellnote, or if the room had been suddenly crowded with the noises of birds, he would have wept again. It pleased him to look upon the unmoving waves of the bedclothes, and think himself an island set somewhere in the south sea. Upon this island of rich and miraculous plants, the seeds grown fruits hung from the trees and, smaller than apples, dropped with the pacific winds on to the ground to lie there and be the harbourers of the summer slugs.

And thinking of the island set somewhere in the south caverns, he thought of water and longed for water. Rhianon's dress, rustling about her, made the soft noise of water. He called her over to him and touched the bosom of her dress, feeling the water on his hands. Water, he told her, and told her how, as a boy, he had lain on the rocks, his fingers tracing cool shapes on the surfaces of the pools. She brought him water in a glass, and held the glass up level with his eyes so that he could see the room through a wall of water. He did not drink, and she set the glass aside. He imagined the coolness under the sea. Now on a summer day soon after noon, he wished again for water to close utterly around him, to be no island set above the water but a green place under, staring around a dizzy cavern. He thought of some cool words, and made a line about an olive-tree that grew under a lake. But the tree was a tree of words, and the lake rhymed with another word.

Sit and read to me, Rhianon.

After you have eaten, she said, and brought him food.

He could not think that she had gone down into the kitchen and, with her own hands, prepared his meal. She had gone and had returned with food, as simply as a maiden out of the Old Testament. Her name meant nothing. It was a cool sound. She had a strange name out of the Bible. Such a woman had washed the body after it had been taken off the tree, with cool and competent fingers that touched on the holes like ten blessings. He could cry out to her, Put a sweet herb under my arm. With your spittle make me fragrant.

What shall I read you? she asked when at last she sat by his side.

He shook his head, not caring what she read so long as he could hear her speak and think of nothing but the inflections of her voice.

Ah! gentle may I lay me down, and gentle rest my head,
And gentle sleep the sleep of death, and gentle hear the voice
Of Him that walketh in the garden in the evening time.

She read on until the Worm sat on the Lily's leaf.

Death lay over his limbs again, and he closed his eyes.

There was no ease from pain nor from the figures of death that went about their familiar business even in the darkness of the heavy lids.

Shall I kiss you awake? said Callaghan. His hand was cold on Peter's hand.

And all the lepers kissed, said Peter, and fell to wondering what he had meant.

Rhianon saw that he was no longer listening to her, and went on tiptoes away.

Callaghan, left alone, leant over the bed and spread the soft ends of his fingers on Peter's eyes. Now it is night, he said. Where shall we go to-night?

Peter opened his eyes again, saw the spreading fingers and the candles glowing like the heads of poppies. A fear and a blessing were on the room.

The candles must not be blown out, he thought. There must be light, light, light. Wick and wax must never be low. All day and all night the three candles, like three girls, must blush over my bed. These three girls must shelter me.

The first flame danced and then went out. Over the second and the third flame Callaghan pursed his grey mouth. The room was dark. Where shall we go to-night? he said, but waited for no answer, pulling the sheets back from the bed and lifting Peter in his arms. His coat was damp and sweet on Peter's face.

Oh, Callaghan, Callaghan, said Peter with his mouth pressed on the black cloth. He felt the movements of Callaghan's body, the tense, the relaxing, muscles, the curving of the shoulders, the impact of the feet on the racing earth. A wind from under the clay and the limes of the earth swept up to his hidden face. Only when the boughs of trees scraped on his back did he know that he was naked. So that he might not cry aloud, he shut his lips firmly together over a damp fold of flesh. Callaghan, too, was naked as a baby.

Are we naked? We have our bones and our organs, our skin and our flesh. There is a ribbon of blood tied in your hair. Do not be frightened. You have a cloth of veins around your thighs. The world charged past them, the wind dropped to nothing, blowing the fruits of battle under the moon. Peter heard the songs of birds, but no such songs as he had heard the birds, on his bedroom sill, fetch out of their throats. The birds were blind.

Are they blind? said Callaghan. They have worlds in their

eyes. There is white and black in their whistling. Do not be frightened. There are bright eyes under the shells of their eggs.

He came suddenly to a stop, Peter light as a feather in his arms, and set him gently down on a green globe of soil. Below there was a valley journeying far away with its burden of lame trees and grass into the distance where the moon hung on a navelstring from the dark. From the woods on either side came the sharp cracks of guns and the pheasants falling like a rain. But soon the night was silent, softening the triggers of the fallen twigs that had snapped out under Callaghan's feet.

Peter, conscious of his sick heart, put a hand to his side but felt none of the protecting flesh. The tips of his fingers tingled around the driving blood, but the veins were invisible. He was dead. Now he knew he was dead. The ghost of Peter, wound invisible about the ghost of the blood, stood on his globe and wondered at the corrupting night.

What is this valley ? said Peter's voice.

The Jarvis valley, said Callaghan. Callaghan, too, was dead. Not a bone or a hair stood up under the steadily falling frost.

This is no Jarvis valley.

This is the naked valley.

The moon, doubling and redoubling the strength of her beams, lit up the barks and the roots and the branches of the Jarvis trees, the busy lice in the wood, the shapes of the stones and the black ants travelling under them, the pebbles in the streams, the secret grass, the untiring death-worms under the blades. From their holes in the flanks of the hills came the rats and weasels, hairs white in the moon, breeding and struggling as they rushed downward to set their teeth in the cattle's throats. No sooner did the cattle fall sucked on to the earth and the weasels race away, then all the flies, rising from the dung of the fields, came up like a fog and settled on the sides. There from the stripped valley rose the smell of death, widening the mountainous nostrils on the face of the moon. Now the sheep fell and the flies were at them. The rats and the weasels, fighting over the flesh, dropped one by one with a wound for the sheep's fleas staring out of their hair. It was to Peter but a little time before the dead, picked to the symmetrical bone, were huddled in under the soil by the wind that blew louder and harder as the fat flies dropped on to the grass. Now the worm and the death-beetle undid the fibres of the animal bones, worked at them brightly and minutely, and the weeds through the sockets and the flowers on the vanished breasts sprouted up with the colours of the dead life fresh on their leaves. And the blood that had flowed flowed over the ground, strengthening the blades of the grass, fulfilling the wind-planted seeds in its course, into the mouth of the spring. Suddenly all the streams were red with blood, a score of winding veins all over the twenty fields, thick with their clotted pebbles.

Peter, in his ghost, cried out with joy. There was life in the naked valley, life in his nakedness. He saw the streams and the beating water, how the flowers shot out of the dead, and the blades and roots were doubled in their power under the stride of the spilt blood.

And the streams stopped. Dust of the dead blew over the spring, and the mouth was choked. Dust lay over the waters like a dark ice. Light, that had been all-eyed and moving, froze in the beams of the moon.

Life in this nakedness, mocked Callaghan at his side, and Peter knew that he was pointing, with the ghost of a finger, down on to the dead streams. But as he spoke, and the shape that Peter's heart had taken in the time of the tangible flesh was aware of the knocks of terror, a life burst out of the pebbles like the thousand lives, wrapped in a boy's body, out of the womb. The streams again went on their way, and the light of the moon, in a new splendour, shone on the valley and magnified the shadows of the valley and pulled the moles and the badgers out of their winter into the deathless midnight season of the world.

Light breaks over the hill, said Callaghan, and lifted the invisible Peter in his arms. Dawn, indeed, was breaking far over the Jarvis wilderness still naked under the descending moon.

As Callaghan raced along the rim of the hills and into the woods and over an exultant country where the trees raced with him, Peter cried out joyfully.

He heard Callaghan's laughter like a rattle of thunder that the wind took and doubled. There was a shouting in the wind, a commotion under the surface of the earth. Now under the roots and now on the tops of the wild trees, he and his stranger were racing against the cock. Over and under the falling fences of the light they climbed and shouted.

Listen to the cock, cried Peter, and the sheets of the bed rolled up to his chin.

A man with a brush had drawn a red rib down the east. The ghost of a circle around the circle of the moon spun through a cloud. He passed his tongue over his lips that had miraculously clothed themselves with skin and flesh. In his mouth was a strange taste, as if last night, three hundred nights ago, he had squeezed the head of a poppy and drunk and slept. There was the old rumour of Callaghan down his brain. From dawn to dark he had talked of death, had seen a moth caught in the candle, had heard the laughter that could not have been his ring in his ears. The cock cried again, and a bird whistled like a scythe through wheat.

Rhianon, with a sweet, naked throat, stepped into the room.

Rhianon, he said, hold my hand, Rhianon.

She did not hear him, but stood over his bed and fixed him with an unbreakable sorrow.

Hold my hand, he said. And then : Why are you putting the sheet over my face ?

THE VEST

He rang the bell. There was no answer. She was out. He turned the key.

The hall in the late afternoon light was full of shadows. They made one almost solid shape. He took of his hat and coat, looking sideways, so that he might not see the shape, at the light through the sitting-room door.

'Is anybody in?'

The shadows bewildered him. She would have swept them up as she swept the invading dust.

In the drawing-room the fire was low. He crossed over to it and sat down. His hands were cold. He needed the flames of the fire to light up the corners of the room. On the way home he had seen a dog run over by a motorcar. The sight of the blood had confused him. He had wanted to go down on his knees and finger the blood that made a round pool in the middle of the road. Someone had plucked at his sleeve, asking him if he was ill. He remembered that the sound and strength of his voice had drowned the first desire. He had walked away from the blood, with the stained wheels of the car and the soaking blackness under the bonnet going round and round before his eyes. He needed the warmth. The wind outside had cut between his fingers and thumbs.

She had left her sewing on the carpet near the coal-scuttle. She had been making a petticoat. He picked it up and touched it, feeling where her breasts would sit under the yellow cotton. That morning he had seen her head enveloped in a frock. He saw her, thin in her nakedness, as a bag of skin and henna drifting out of the light. He let the petticoat drop on to the floor again.

Why, he wondered, was there this image of the red and broken dog? It was the first time he had seen the brains of a living creature burst out of the skull. He had been sick at the last yelp and the sudden caving of the dog's chest. He could have killed and shouted, like a child cracking a blackbeetle between its fingers.

A thousand nights ago, she had lain by his side. In her arms, he thought of the bones of her arms. He lay quietly by her skeleton. But she rose next morning in the corrupted flesh.

When he hurt her, it was to hide his pain. When he struck her cheek until the skin blushed, it was to break the agony of his own head. She told him of her mother's death. Her mother had worn a mask to hide the illness at her face. He felt the locust of that illness on his own face, in the mouth and the fluttering eyelid.

The room was darkening. He was too tired to shovel the fire into life, and saw the last flame die. A new coldness blew in with the early night. He tasted the sickness of the death of the flame as it rose to the tip of his tongue, and swallowed it down. It ran around the pulse of the heart, and beat until it was the only sound. And all the pain of the damned. The pain of a man with a bottle breaking across his face, the pain of a cow with a calf dancing out of her, the pain of the dog, moved through him from his aching hair to the flogged soles of his feet.

His strength returned. He and the dripping calf, the man with the torn face, and the dog on giddy legs, rose up as one, in one red brain and body, challenging the beast in the air. He heard the challenge in his snapping thumb and finger, as she came in.

He saw that she was wearing her yellow hat and frock.

'Why are you sitting in the dark?' she said.

She went into the kitchen to light the stove. He stood up from his chair. Holding his hands out in front of him as though they were blind, he followed her. She had a box of matches in her hand. As she took out a dead match and rubbed it on the box, he closed the door behind him. 'Take off your frock,' he said.

She did not hear him, and smiled.

'Take off your frock,' he said.

She stopped smiling, took out a live match and lit it.

'Take off your frock,' he said.

He stepped towards her, his hands still blind. She bent over the stove. He blew the match out.

'What is it?' she said.

His lips moved, but he did not speak.

'Why?' she said.

He slapped her cheek quite lightly with his open hand.

'Take off your frock,' he said.

He heard her frock rustle over her head, and her frightened sob as he touched her. Methodically his blind hands made her naked.

He walked out of the kitchen, and closed the door.

In the hall, the one married shadow had broken up. He could not see his own face in the mirror as he tied his scarf and stroked the brim of his hat. There were too many faces. Each had a section of his features, and each a stiffened lock of his hair. He pulled up the collar of his coat. It was a wet winter night. As he walked, he counted the lamps. He pushed a door open and stepped into the warmth. The room was empty. The woman behind the bar smiled as she rubbed two coins together. 'It's a cold night,' she said.

He drank up the whisky and went out.

He walked on through the increasing rain. He counted the lamps again, but they reached no number.

The corner bar was empty. He took his drink into the saloon, but the saloon was empty.

The Rising Sun was empty.

Outside, he heard no traffic. He remembered that he had seen nobody in the streets. He cried aloud in a panic of loneliness :

'Where are you, where are you ?'

Then there was traffic, and the windows were blazing. He heard singing from the house on the corner.

The bar was crowded. Women were laughing and shouting. They spilt their drinks over their dresses and lifted their dresses up. Girl were dancing on the sawdust. A woman caught him by the arm, and rubbed his face on her sleeve, and took his hand in hers and put it on her throat. He could hear nothing but the voices of the laughing women and the shouting of the girls as they danced. Then the ungainly women from the seats and the corners rocked towards him. He saw that the room was full of women. Slowly, still laughing, they gathered close to him.

He whispered a word under his breath, and felt the old sickness turn sour in his belly. There was blood before his eyes.

Then he, too, burst into laughter. He stuck his hands deep in the pockets of his coat, and laughed into their faces.

His hand clutched around a softness in his pocket. He drew out his hand, the softness in it.

The laughter died. The room was still. Quiet and still, the women stood watching him.

He raised his hand up level with his eyes. It held a piece of soft cloth.

Who'll buy a lady's vest,' he said, 'Going, going, ladies, who'll buy a lady's vest.'

The meek and ordinary women in the bar stood still, their glasses in their hands, as he leant with his back to the counter and shouted with laughter and waved the bloody cloth in front of them.

THE BURNING BABY

They said that Rhys was burning his baby when a gorse bush broke into fire on the summit of the hill. The bush, burning merrily, assumed to them the sad white features and the rickety limbs of the vicar's burning baby. What the wind had not blown away of the baby's ashes, Rhys Rhys had sealed in a stone jar. With his own dust lay the baby's dust, and near him the dust of his daughter in a coffin of white wood.

They heard his son howl in the wind. They saw him walking over the hill, holding a dead animal up to the light of the stars. They saw him in the valley shadows as he moved, with the motion of a man cutting wheat, over the brows of the fields. In a sanatorium he coughed his lung into a basin, stirring his fingers delightedly in the blood. What moved with invisible scythe through the valley was a shadow and a handful of shadows cast by the grave sun.

The bush burned out, and the face of the baby fell away with the smoking leaves.

It was, they said, on a fine sabbath morning in the middle of the summer that Rhys Rhys fell in love with his daughter. The gorse that morning had burst into flames, Rhys Rhys, in clerical black, had seen the flames shoot up to the sky, and the bush on the edge of the hill burn red as God among the paler burning of the grass. He took his daughter's hand as she lay in the garden hammock, and told her that he loved her. He told her that she was more beautiful than her dead mother. Her hair smelt of mice, her teeth came over her lip, and the lids of her eyes were red and wet. He saw her beauty come out of her like a stream of sap. The folds of her dress could not hide from him the shabby nakedness of her body. It was not her bone, nor her flesh, nor her hair that he found suddenly beautiful. The poor soil shudders under the sun, he said. He moved his hand up and down her arm. Only the awkward and ugly, only the barren bring forth fruit. The flesh of her arm was red with the smoothing of his hand. He touched her breast. From the touch of her breast he knew each inch of flesh upon her. Why do you touch me there ? she said.

In the church that morning he spoke of the beauty of the harvest, of the promise of the standing corn and the promise in the sharp edge of the scythe as it brings the corn low and whistles through the air before it cuts into the ripeness. Through the open windows at the end of the aisles, he saw the yellow fields upon the hillside and the smudge of heather on the meadow borders. The world was ripe.

The world is ripe for the second coming of the son of man, he said aloud.

But it was not the ripeness of God that glistened from the hill. It was the promise and the ripeness of the flesh, the good flesh, the mean flesh, flesh of his daughter, flesh, flesh, the flesh of the voice of thunder howling before the death of man.

That night he preached of the sins of the flesh. O God in the image of our flesh, he prayed.

His daughter sat in the front pew, and stroked her arm. She would have touched her breast where he had touched it, but the eyes of the congregation were upon her.

Flesh, flesh, flesh, said the vicar.

His son, scouting the fields for a mole's hill or the signs of a red fox, whistling to the birds and patting the calves as they stood untimid at their mother's sides, came upon a dead rabbit sprawling on a stone. The rabbit's head was riddled with pellets, the dogs had torn open its belly, and the marks of a ferret's teeth were upon its throat. He lifted it gently up, tickling it behind the ears. The blood from its head dropped on his hand. Through the rip in the belly, its intestines had dropped out and coiled on the stone. He held the little body close to his jacket, and ran home through the fields, the rabbit dancing against his waistcoat. As he reached the gate of the vicarage, the worshippers dribbled out of church. They shook hands and raised their hats, smiling at the poor boy with his long green hair, his ass's ears, and death buttoned under his jacket. He was always the poor boy to them.

Rhys Rhys sat in his study, the stem of his pipe stuck between his flybuttons, the bible unopened upon his knees. The day of God was over, and the sun, like another sabbath, went down behind the hills. He lit the lamp, but his own oil burned brighter.

He drew the curtains, shutting out the unwelcome night. But he opened his own heart up, and the bald pulse that beat there was a welcome stranger. He had not felt love like this since the woman who scratched him, seeing the woman witch in his male eyes, had fallen into his arms and kissed him, and whispered Welsh words as he took her. She had been the mother of his daughter and had died in her pains, stealing, when she was dead, the son of his second love, and leaving the greenhaired changeling in its place. Merry with desire, Rhys Rhys cast the bible on the floor. He reached for another book, and read, in the lamplit darkness, of the old woman who had deceived the devil. The devil is poor flesh, said Rhys Rhys.

His son came in, bearing the rabbit in his arms. The lank, redcoated boy was a flesh out of the past. The skin of the unburied dead patched to his bones, the smile of the changeling to his mouth, and the hair of the sea rising from his scalp, he stood before Rhys Rhys. A ghost of his mother, he held the rabbit gently to his breast, rocking it to and fro. Cunningly, from under halfclosed lids, he saw his father shrink away from the vision of death. Be off with you, said Rhys Rhys. Who was this green stranger to carry in death and rock it, like a baby under a warm shawl of fur, before him? For a minute the flesh of the world lay still; the old terror set in; the waters of the breast dried up; the nipples grew through the sand. Then he drew his hand over his eyes, and only the rabbit remained, a little sack of flesh, half empty, swaying in the arms of his son. Be off, he said. The boy held the rabbit close, and rocked it, and tickled it again.

Changeling, said Rhys Rhys. He is mine, said the boy, I'll peel him and keep the skull. His room in the attic was crowded with skulls and dried pelts, and little bones in bottles.

Give it to me.

He is mine.

Rhys Rhys tore the rabbit away, and stuffed it deep in the pocket of his smoking coat. When his daughter came in, dressed and ready for bed, with a candle in her hand, Rhys Rhys had death in his pocket.

She was timid, for his touch still ached on her arm and breast but she bent unblushing over him. Saying good-night, she kissed him, and he blew her candle out. She was smiling as he lowered the wick of the lamp.

Step out of your shift, said he. Shiftless, she stepped towards his arms.

I want the little skull, said a voice in the dark.

From his room at the top of the house, through the webs on the windows, and over the furs and the bottles, the boy saw a mile of green hill running away into the darkness of the first dawn. Summer storm in the heat of the rain, flooring the grassy mile, had left some new morning brightness, out of the dead night, in each reaching root.

Death took hold of his sister's legs as she walked through the calf-deep heather up the hill. He saw the high grass at her thighs. And the blades of the upgrowing wind, out of the four windsmells of the manuring dead, might drive through the soles of her feet, up the veins of the legs and stomach, into her womb and her pulsing heart. He watched her climb. She stood, gasping for breath, on a hill of the wider hill, tapping the wall of her bladder, fondling her matted chest (for the hair grew on her as on a grown man), feeling the heart in her wrist, loving her coveted thinness. She was to him as ugly as the sowfaced woman Llareggub who had taught him the terrors of the flesh. He remembered the advances of that unlovely woman. She blew out his candle as he stepped towards her on the night the great hail had fallen and he had hidden in her rotting house from the cruelty of the weather. Now half a mile off his sister stood in the morning, and the vermin of the hill might spring upon her as she stood, uncaring, rounding the angles of her ugliness. He smiled at the thought of the devouring rats, and looked around the room for a bottle to hold her heart. Her skull, fixed by a socket to the nail above his bed, would be a smiling welcome to the first pains of waking.

But he saw Rhys Rhys stride up the hill, and the bowl of his sister's head, fixed invisibly above his sheets, crumbled away. Standing straight by the side of a dewy tree, his sister beckoned. Up went Rhys Rhys through the calfdeep heather, the death in the grass, over the boulders and up through the reaching ferns, to where she stood. He took her hand. The two shadows linked hands, and climbed together to the top of the hill. The boy saw them go, and turned his face to the wall as they vanished, in one dull shadow, over the edge, and down to the dingle at the west foot of the lovers' alley.

Later, he remembered the rabbit. He ran downstairs and

crumbles. There lay the poor star of flesh that had dropped, like the bead of a woman's milk through the nipples of a wormy tree.

He stacked the torn heathers in the midst of the circle where the stones still howled on the sabbaths. On the head of the purple stack, he piled the dead grass. A stack of death, the heather grew as tall as he, and loomed at last over his windy hair.

Behind a boulder moved the accompanying shadow, and the shadow of the boy was printed under the fiery flank of a tree. The shadow marked the boy, and the boy marked the bones of the naked baby under their chilly cover, and how the grass scraped on the bald skull, and where his father picked out a path in the cancerous growths of the silent circle. He saw Rhys Rhys pick up the baby and place it on the top of the stack, saw the head of a burning match, and heard the crackle of the bush, breaking like a baby's arms.

The stack burst into flame. Rhys Rhys, before the red eye of the creeping fire, stretched out his arms and beckoned the shadow from the stones. Surrounded by shadows, he prayed before the flaming stack, and the sparks of the heather blew past his smile. Burn, child, poor flesh, mean flesh, flesh, flesh, sick sorry flesh, flesh of the foul womb, burn back to dust, he prayed.

And the baby caught fire. The flames curled round its mouth and blew upon the shrinking gums. Flame round its red cord lapped its little belly till the raw flesh fell upon the heather.

A flame touched its tongue. Eeeeeh, cried the burning baby, and the illuminated hill replied.

THE ORCHARDS

He had dreamed that a hundred orchards on the road to the sea village had broken into flame; and all the windless afternoon tongues of fire shot through the blossom. The birds had flown up as a small red cloud grew suddenly from each branch; but as night came down with the rising of the moon and the swinging-in of the mile-away sea, a wind blew out the fires and the birds returned. He was an apple-farmer in a dream that ended as it began: with the flesh-and-ghost hand of a woman pointing to the trees. She twined the fair and dark tails of her hair together, smiled over the apple-fields to a sister figure who stood in a circular shadow by the walls of the vegetable garden; but the birds flew down on to her sister's shoulders, unafraid of the scarecrow face and the cross-wood nakedness under the rags. He gave the woman a kiss, and she kissed him back. Then the crows came down to her arms as she held him close; the beautiful scarecrow kissed him, pointing to the trees as the fires died.

Marlais awoke that summer morning with his lips still wet from her kiss. This was a story more terrible than the stories of the reverend madmen in the Black Book of Llareggub, for the woman near the orchards, and her sister-stick by the wall, were his scarecrow lovers for ever and ever. What were the sea-village burning orchards and the clouds at the ends of the branches to his love for these bird-provoking women? All the trees of the world might blaze suddenly from the roots to the highest leaves, but he would not sprinkle water on the shortest fiery field. She was his lover, and her sister with birds on her shoulders held him closer than the women of LlanAsia.

Through the top-storey window he saw the pale blue, cloud-less sky over the tangle of roofs and chimneys, and the promise of a lovely day in the rivers of the sun. There, in a chimney's shape, stood his bare, stone boy and the three blind gossips, blowing fire through their skulls, who huddled for warmth in all weathers. What man on a roof had turned his weathercock's head to stare at the red-and-black girls over the town and, by his turning, made them stone pillars? A wind from the world's end had frozen the roof-walkers when the town was a handful of houses; now a circle of coal table-hills, where the children played Indians, cast its shadow on the black lots and the hundred streets; and the stone-blind gossips cramped together by his bare boy and the brick virgins under the towering crane-hills.

The sea ran to the left, a dozen valleys away, past the range of volcanoes and the great stack forests and ten towns in a hole. It met the Glamorgan shores where a half-mountain fell westward out of the clump of villages in a wild wood, and shook the base of Wales. But now, thought Marlais, the sea is slow and cool, full of dolphins; it flows in all directions from a green centre, lapping the land stones; it makes the shells speak on the blazing half-mountain sand, and the lines of time even shall not join the blue sea surface and the bottomless bed.

He thought of the sea running; when the sun sank, a fire went in under the liquid caverns. He remembered, while he dressed. the hundred fires around the blossoms of the apple-trees, and the uneasy salt rising of the wind that died with the last pointing of the beautiful scarecrow's hand. Water and fire, sea and apple-tree, two sisters and a crowd of birds, blossomed, pointed, and flew down all that mid-summer morning in a top-storey room in the house on a slope over the black-housed town.

He sharpened his pencil and shut the sky out, shook back his untidy hair, arranged the papers of a devilish story on his desk, and broke the pencil-point with a too-hard scribble of 'sea' and 'fire' on a clean page. Fire would not set the ruled lines alight, adventure, burning, through the heartless characters, nor water close over the bogy heads and the unwritten words. The story was dead from the devil up; there was a white-hot tree with apples where a frozen tower with owls should have rocked in a wind from Antarctica; there were naked girls, with nipples like berries, on the sand in the sun, where a cold and unholy woman should be wailing by the Kara Sea or the Sea of Azov. The morning was against him. He struggled with his words like a man with the sun, and the sun stood victoriously at high noon over the dead story.

Put a two-coloured ring of two women's hair round the blue

world, white and coal-black against the summer-coloured
boundaries of sky and grass, four-breasted stems at the poles of
the summer sea-ends, eyes in the sea-shells, two fruit-trees out
of a coal-hill : poor Marlais's morning, turning to evening, spins
before you. Under the eyelids, where the inward night drove
backwards through the skull's base, into the wide, first world
on the far-away eye, two love-trees smouldered like sisters. Have
an orchard sprout in the night, an enchanted woman with a
spine like a railing burn her hand in the leaves, man-on-fire a
mile from a sea have a wind put out your heart : Marlais's death
in life in the circular going down of the day that had taken no
time blows again in the wind for you.

The world was the saddest in the turning world, and the stars
in the north, where the shadow of a mock moon spun until a
wind put out the shadow, were the ravaged south faces. Only
the fork-tree breast of the woman's scarecrow could bear his
head like an apple on the white wood where no worm would
enter, and her barbed breast alone pierce the worm in the dream
under her sweetheart's eyelid. The real round moon shone on
the women of LlanAsia and the love-torn virgins of This street.

The word is too much with us. He raised his pencil so that its
shadow fell, a tower of wood and lead, on the clean paper ; he
fingered the pencil tower, the half-moon of his thumb-nail rising
and setting behind the leaden spire. The tower fell, down fell the
city of words, the walls of a poem, the symmetrical letters. He
marked the disintegration of the ciphers as the light failed, the
sun drove down into a foreign morning, and the word of the sea
rolled over the sun. 'Image, all image,' he cried to the fallen
tower as the night came on. 'Whose harp is the sea ? Whose
burning candle is the sun ?' An image of man, he rose to his feet
and drew the curtains open. Peace, like a simile, lay over the
roofs of the town. 'Image, all image,' cried Marlais, stepping
through the window on to the level roofs.

The slates shone around him, in the smoke of the magnified
stacks and through the vapours of the hill. Below him, in a
world of words, men on their errands moved to no purpose but
the escape of time. Brave in his desolation, he scrambled to the
edge of the slates, there to stand perilously above the tiny traffic
and the lights of the street signals. The toy of the town was at
his feet. On went the marzipan cars, changing gear, applying
brake, over the nursery carpets into a child's hands. But soon

height had him and he swayed, feeling his legs grow weak beneath him and his skull swell like a bladder in the wind. It was the image of an infant city that threw his pulses into confusion. There was dust in his eyes; there were eyes in the grains of dust ascending from the street. Once on the leveller roofs, he touched his left breast. Death was the bright magnets of the streets; the wind pulled off the drag of death and the falling visions. Now he was stripped of fear, strong, night-muscled. Over the housetops he ran towards the moon. There the moon came, in a colder glory than before, attended by stars, drawing the tides of the sea. By a parapet he watched her, finding a word for each stage of her journey in the directed sky, calling her same-faced, wondering at her many masks. Death mask and dance mask over her mountainous features trans-formed the sky; she struggled behind a cloud, and came with a new smile over the wall of wind. Image, and all was image, from Marlais, ragged in the wind, to the appalling town, he on the roofs invisible to the street, the street beneath him blind to his walking word. His hand before him was five-fingered life.

A baby cried, but the cry grew fainter. It is all one, the loud voice and the still voice striking a common silence, the dowdy lady flattening her nose against the panes, and the well-mourned lady. The word is too much with us, and the dead word. Cloud, the last muslin's rhyme, shapes above tenements and bursts in cold rain on the suburban drives. Hail falls on cinder track and the angelled stone. It is all one, the rain and the macadam; it is all one, the hail and cinder, the flesh and the rough dust. High above the hum of the houses, far from the skyland and the frozen fence, he questioned each shadow; man among ghosts, and ghost in clover, he moved for the last answer.

The bare boy's voice through a stone mouth, no longer smoking at this hour, rose up unanswerably: 'Who walks, mad among us, on the roofs, by my cold, brick-red side and the weathercock-frozen women, walks over This street, under the image of the Welsh summer heavens walks all night loverless, has two sister lovers ten towns away. Past the great stack forests to the left and the sea his lovers burn for him endlessly by a hundred orchards.' The gossips' voices rose up unanswerably: 'Who walks by the stone virgins is our virgin Marlais, wind and fire, and the coward on the burning roofs.'

He stepped through the open window.

Red sap in the trees bubbled from the cauldron roots to the last spray of blossom, and the boughs, that night after the hollow walk, fell like candles from the trunks but could not die for the heat of the sulphurous head of the grass burned yellow by the dead sun. And flying there, he rounded, half mist, half man, all apple circles on the sea-village road in the high heat of noon as the dawn broke; and as the sun rose like a river over the hills so the sun sank behind a tree. The woman pointed to the hundred orchards and the black birds who flocked around her sister, but a wind put the trees out and he woke again. This was the intolerable, second waking out of a life too beautiful to break, but the dream was broken. Who had walked by the virgins near the orchards was a virgin, wind and fire, and a coward in the destroying coming of the morning. But after he had dressed and taken breakfast, he walked up This street to the hilltop and turned his face towards the invisible sea.

'Good morning, Marlais,' said an old man sitting with six greyhounds in the blackened grass.

'Good morning, Mr David Davies.'

'You are up very early,' said David Two Times.

'I am walking towards the sea.'

'The wine-coloured sea,' said Dai Twice.

Marlais strode over the hill to the greener left, and down behind the circle of the town to the rim of Whippet valley where the trees, for ever twisted between smoke and slag, tore at the sky and the black ground. The dead boughs prayed that the roots might shoulder up the soil, leaving a dozen channels empty for the leaves and the spirit of the cracking wood, a hole in the valley for the mole-handed sap, a long grave for the last spring's skeleton that once had leapt, when the blunt and forked hills were sharp and straight, through the once-green land. But Whippet's trees were the long dead of the stacked south of the country; who had vanished under the hacked land pointed, thumb-to-hill, these black leaf-nailed and warning fingers. Death in Wales had twisted the Welsh dead into those valley cripples.

The day was a passing of days. High noon, the story-killer and the fire bug (the legends of the Russian seas died as the trees awoke to their burning), passed in all the high noons since the fall of man from the sun and the first sun's pinnacling of the half-made heavens. And all the valley summers, the once monu-mental red and the now headstone-featured, all that midsummer afternoon were glistening in the seaward walk. Through the ancestral valley where his fathers, out of their wooden dust and full of sparrows, wagged at a hill, he walked steadily; on the brink of the hole that held LlanAsia as a grave holds a town, he was caught in the smoke of the forests and, like a ghost from the clear-cut quarters under the stack roots, climbed down on to the climbing streets.

'Where are you walking, Marlais?' said a one-legged man by a black flower-bed.

'Towards the sea, Mr William Williams.'

'The mermaid-crowded sea,' said Will Peg.

Marlais passed out of the tubercular valley on to a waste mountain, through a seedy wood to a shagged field; a crow, on a molehill, in Prince Price's skull cawed of the breadth of hell in the packed globe; the afternoon broke down, the stumped land heaving, and, like a tree or lightning, a wind, roots up, forked between smoke and slag as the dusk dropped; surrounded by echoes, the red-hot travellers of voices, and the devils from the horned acres, he shuddered on his enemies' territory as a new night came on in the nightmare of an evening. 'Let the trees collapse,' the dusty journeymen said, 'the boulders flake away and the gorse rot and vanish, earth and grass be swallowed down on to a hill's v balancing on the grave that proceeds to Eden. Winds on fire, through vault and coffin and fossil we'll blow a manfull of dust into the garden. Where the serpent sets the tree alight, and the apple falls like a spark out of its skin, a tree leaps up; a scarecrow shines on the cross-boughs, and, by one in the sun, the new trees arise, making an orchard round the crucifix.' By midnight two more valleys lay beneath him, dark with their two towns in the palms of the mined mountains; a valley, by one in the morning, held Aberbabel in its fist beneath him. He was a young man no longer but a legendary walker, a folk-man walking, with a cricket for a heart; he walked by Aberbabel's chapel, cut through the graveyard over the unstill headstones, spied a red-cheeked man in a nightshirt two foot above ground.

The valleys passed; out of the water-dipping hills, the moments of mountains, the eleventh valley came up like an hour. And coming out timelessly through the dwarf's eye of the telescope, through the ring of light like a circle's wedding on the last hill before the sea, the shape of the hundred orchards

magnified with the immaculate diminishing of the moon. This
was the spectacle that met the telescope, and the world Marlais
saw in the morning following upon the first of the eleven untold
adventures : to his both sides the unbroken walls, taller than the
beanstalks that married a story on the roof of the world, of
stone and earth and beetle and tree ; a graveyard before him the
ground came to a stop, shot down and down, was lost with the
devil in bed, rose shakily to the sea-village road where the
blossoms of the orchards hung over the wooden walls and sister-
roads ran off into the four white country points ; a rock line
thus, straight to the hill-top, and the turning graph scored with
trees ; dip down the county, deep as the history of the final fire
burning through the chamber one story over Eden, the first
green structure after the red downfall ; down, down, like a stone
stuck with towns, like the river out of a glass of places, fell his
foot-holding hill. He was a folk-man no longer but Marlais the
poet walking, over the brink into ruin, up the side of doom,
over hell in bed to the red left, till he reached the first of the
fields where the unhatched apples were soon to cry fire in a
wind from a half-mountain falling westward to the sea. A man-
in-a-picture Marlais, by noon's blow to the centre, stood by a
circle of apple-trees and counted the circles that travelled over
the shady miles into a clump of villages. He laid himself down
in the grass, and noon fell back bruised to the sun ; and he slept
till a handbell rang over the fields. It was a windless afternoon
in the sisters' orchards, and the fair-headed sister was ringing
the bell for tea.

He had come very near to the end of the indescribable journey.
The fair girl, in a field sloping seaward three fields and a stile
from Marlais, laid out a white cloth on a flat stone. Into one of
a number of cups she poured milk and tea, and cut the bread so
thin she could see London through the white pieces. She stared
hard at the stile and the pruned, transparent hedge, and as
Marlais climbed over, ragged and unshaven, his stripped breast
burned by the sun, she rose from the grass and smiled and
poured tea for him. This was the end to the untold adventures.
They sat in the grass by the stone table like lovers at a picnic,
too loved to speak, desireless familiars in the shade of the hedge
corner. She had taken a handbell for her sister, and called a
lover over eleven valleys to her side. Her many lovers' cups were
empty on the flat stone.

And he who had dreamed that a hundred orchards had broken into flame saw suddenly then in the windless afternoon tongues of fire shoot through the blossom. The trees all around them kindled and crackled in the sun, the birds blew up as a small red cloud grew from each branch, the bark caught like gorse, the unborn, blazing apples whirled down devoured in a flash. The trees were fireworks and torches, smouldered out of the furnace of the fields into a burning arc, cast down their branded fruit like cinders on the charred roads and fields.

Who had dreamed a boy's dream of her flesh-and-ghost hand in the windless afternoon saw then, at the red height, when the wooden step-roots splintered at the orchard entrance and the armed towers came to grief, that she raised her hand heavily and pointed to the trees and birds. There was a flurry in the sky, of wing and fire and near-to-evening wind in the going below of the burned day. As the new night was built, she smiled as she had done in the short dream eleven valleys old; lame like Pisa, the night leaned on the west walls; no trumpet shall knock the Welsh walls down before the last crack of music; she pointed to her sister in a shadow by the disappearing garden, and the dark-headed figure with crows on her shoulders appeared at Marlais's side.

This was the end of a story more terrible than the stories of the quick and the undead in mountainous houses on Jarvis hills, and the unnatural valley that Idris waters is a children's territory to this eleventh valley in the seaward travel. A dream that was no dream skulked there; the real world's wind came up to kill the fires; a scarecrow pointed to the extinguished trees.

This he had dreamed before the blossom's burning and the putting-out, before the rising and the salt swinging-in, was a dream no longer near these orchards. He kissed the two secret sisters, and a scarecrow kissed him back. He heard the birds fly down on to his lovers' shoulders. He saw the fork-tree breast, the barbed eye, and the dry, twig hand.

THE END OF THE RIVER

Twelve generations of the Quincey family, that dogfaced line, had left their mark upon the manor. The walls remained steadfast, but covered with a green fungus that sprouted upon the Quincey habitations, regardless of pruning. The gardener had not neglected the lawns, and the flower-beds, though pale and blowsy, were tended with all his senile care, for Chubb could never die, bound, as he was, so inextricably to the Quincey bosom. But weeds grew thick where weeds were little expected to grow. Ivy climbed up the walls of the coach house, and, in spite of the daily attentions of the youngest housemaid but one, moss invaded the front steps and rust lay thick upon the knocker. Hens upon the bird-limed patch beyond the kitchen died at a premature age, while the eggs they contrived to lay were rarely oval and often of a withered shape and a rather unpleasant mottled colour. The pigs were fed as heartily as pigs could wish, but they grew thin and died. The cows' milk tasted like vinegar.

The Quincey manor, with its portrait gallery of canine gentlemen, its dining-hall furnished in three periods, and its perilous verandahs from which the bloodless Quinceys, on midsummer nights, would pass their gravish comments on the moon, had resolved to crumble, spurning renovations and improvements, sitting on the camel hill over the disagreeable river, waiting for its end.

And Sir Peregrine, twelfth baron, had nothing but sympathy for it. It had sheltered twelve generations of doggy aristocrats and their litters, had seen small boys grow to be small men, had seen them meet, mate, and lie, at last, in the depths of the family vault, their dead paws on their chests. It had entertained near-royalty, and consequently had allotted a royal bedroom to its left wing. Over all the passions of a most impure world it had spread its painted roofs, and, on one notable occasion, had hidden, in a cellar full of stale wine and rats, the murdered body of poor Sir Thomas.

The manor, thought Sir Peregrine, was old enough to die, had pondered enough upon the human follies and felt no fear of death.

Stroking a three-days' beard, he placed a deck-chair on the safest part of the verandah, looked up into the sun and turned to the year 1889 in the Quincey Chronicles.

Somewhere a romantic daughter spelt out her Sunday music. His lady, in the quiet of her room, was writing to an Australian cousin. In his apartment the butler was reading from the literary pages of the *Observer*. Chubb, in the not very far distance, leaned on a garden gate and smoked.

Peregrine, read the twelfth baron from the Chronicles, took up the title on the death of his father, Belphigor, in 1889. In 1902 he married the Honourable Katerina Hautley, second daughter of Lord and Lady Winch of Alltheway Park, Gloucestershire. From this union were born three daughters: Katerina, who died of influenza in her second year, Astasia, and Phoebe Mary. Sir Peregrine was a colonel in the Territorial Army up to the Great War (1914–1918), and an official in the Ministry of War during those troubled years. He was elected Master of the Tidhampton Hunt in 1920, following upon the death of Alderman Alcock, and in 1922 broke his arm while riding with the hounds. In the following year Phoebe Mary married the Honourable Douglas Dougal, son of Sir Douglas and Lady Dougal of Halfandhalf Castle, Perth. In 1924 Phoebe Mary died in childbirth.

That was all. The Chronicles of the previous Quincey generations were written in detail and with an ornamentation of style that did credit to the literary accomplishments of the family. But Sir Peregrine dealt in facts, and facts alone. His life until that moment, but shorn of its hopes and foolishness, its strength and weaknesses, delights and dolours, spread over half a page of the ponderous book. This little life set between the eccentricities of the longwinded Belphigor and ...

Sir Peregrine put the book down.

Chubb was still leaning and smoking. The smoke rose up vertically into the windless air. Chubb had not moved. His eyes rested on the river which went Sir Peregrine knew not where, meandering, he supposed, through a world of fields and rushes, making noise over pebbles, till it came to a sudden stop. He had always called it the one river that did not wind safely to the sea.

Astasia had stopped her playing.

Life was good, he found, on most Sunday afternoons. But to-day he was restless, and could not sit, as he had for so many years, dreamily upon the verandah, feeling the world grow and hum around him, hearing the music of a sweetly untuned piano or the songs of birds.

The day was beautiful. Clouds sailed on the sky. There was a warm sun. He looked down to where the Chronicles lay at his feet, and knew, quite suddenly and almost happily, all that was the matter. The time had come for the dissolution of the Quinceys, for the fall of their manor and the end of their dynasty.

Sir Peregrine, lifting the book, took out a pencil used to a stump through the solving of innumerable crossword puzzles.

In 1924 he read again, Phoebe Mary died in childbirth.

Phoebe Mary had been his favourite daughter. He had cried for six nights after she was buried. Then he, too, had buried her, under the clouds and mists of his mind. Once he had forgotten her name. Phoebe Mary? he said, and had fallen to wondering who that could be with such a name.

Phoebe Mary died in childbirth.

The end of the Quinceys, he wrote with the pencil.

Then he added the date.

In the garden he looked around him, at the flowers whose colours were as even as those in a toy paint box. The little wind there was moved the petals so that they seemed, to him, to breathe for the last time the sweet air of the surrounding beds. He knew they were aware of climax, and loved them for their serenity. Chubb had nurtured them, and the end of the world would see the gardener like a god, waiting in a woman's blue smock, for his reward.

The end of the world was the end of the manor. And Chubb, though he would say nothing of it, neither affirm nor contradict, had tended the first bed for the first young baron.

Sir Peregrine found him at the end of the path. The gardener did not move. His arms were resting on the gate that led to the seven fields going down to the river.

Sir Peregrine, wiping a remnant of dinner from his ancient waistcoat, looked down to where the water rolled over the dirty stones. At the end of the water was the end of everything. Today he was to walk over the fields and follow the river where it went, through towns or countries, over hills or under, until the sudden stop.

The garden was humming behind them.

The clouds moved on softly to some stop.

How old are you, Chubb? asked Sir Peregrine. You were the gardener here when Lady Astasia rode to her Queen, Elizabeth, over the rocky roads on a piebald horse. You tended the flowers when Quentin, third of the Quinceys, wrote to his lady in an ivory tower, wrapping the verses round a pigeon's throat. At Christmas you made snowmen for me. How many years have you brooded over the dirty river? You always knew the end of all things lay where it stopped. I only knew to-day. It came to me suddenly and I knew.

The immortal Chubb made no answer. He tilted his felt hat further back on his head, and sent up a ring of smoke from a white pipe. His face, fringed with a yellowing beard, was as round and expressionless as a saucer. At any time a breath of wind might send another crack along its surface, and make a thousand smiles or frowns. Through a space in his teeth he breathed and whistled, and made a succession of mysterious tunes as he drew at his pipe.

The exterior Chubb belied what was divine beneath. He looked like nothing more than an ancient gardener, with his woman's smock pinned untidily around him.

Chubb, I am going.

Sir Peregrine waited for the words to pierce the gardener's smoky armour.

I am going to follow the river to its end. Tell me one word of cheer before I go. Say good-bye, undying Chubb.

The birds, said the gardener, 'ave 'ad the seeds.

It was enough. Sir Peregrine climbed quickly over the gate and ran down the field. At the end was a stile. He climbed it, and ran again over the uneven grass, his hair leaping about his head and his brass-buttoned waistcoat flapping against his sides. Three fields. Four fields. Sweat ran down his forehead on to his neck and collar. He could hear his heart thundering in his ears. But he kept at the same crazy jog, over another stile, along another field, stopping to climb through a small hole in the hedge, then on again, snorting and blowing.

A crow, perched on a scarecrow's shoulder, suddenly started cawing as the twelfth baron galloped past, then flew above him, spurring him on with harsh cries.

Now he could hear the noise of the river. On the low bank above it, he stared down on to the little fishes and the shining pebbles. The crow, seeing him stop, gave a final sardonic caw, and flew back to its lone companion, who was swinging a ragged arm in the wind.

Sir Peregrine felt a great elation surging through him. He turned around, and saw the Quincey manor, on its imperial hill, squinting down upon him. He followed the river bank through the dirty fields and through a wood brown with owls' wings. He saw the sun lowering in the sky. Now he no longer ran, but stumbled over the fields, his eyes dim, covered in tears, half unseeing. His clothes were damp about him. His hair that had, in the mad run down the seven fields, leapt so proudly on his head, straggled on to his wet brow. He was thirsty and tired. But he stumbled on.

Where does the river end? he called out to an old woman driving cows over a green field.

Where does it end? he asked. But the hedges and the ferns and the talking pebbles never replied.

He came at last to a well by the side of a meadow, and there a girl-child was washing clothes. He saw her through his tears and heard her voice singing.

Is this the end?

Yes, said the girl-child.

The end, said Sir Peregrine in a whisper. The end of the manor, the Quinceys, and me.

The words made such a nice little rhythm that he started to sing them in his old voice.

The end of the manor, the Quinceys and me.

The child was frightened.

For twelve generations, he said, the Quinceys have lived their little lives up there. And he pointed with a bewildered hand towards the sky. This is the end, he said.

Yes, said the child.

What is the end? he said. What have you to give? What at the end?

He held his arms out.

With a frightened cry, the girl-child thrust an un-washed

napkin into his hand. He clasped it, and she ran away. Not looking, but holding it to his breast and making soft, delighted noises in his throat, Sir Peregrine lay down upon the grass. The moon came up. Chubb had not failed.

And that immortal gardener, as the twelfth baron lay down on a bed of grass and soft manure, was smoking a white pipe in the quiet of the Quincey gardens. Sunday was almost passed, and then there would be another day. Contentedly the ancient gardener, in his woman's smock, leaned on the garden gate and smoked.

THE LEMON

Early one morning, under the arc of a lamp, carefully, silently, in smock and rubber gloves, the doctor grafted a cat's head on to a chicken's trunk. The cat-headed creature, in a house of glass, swayed on its legs; though it stared through the slits of its eyes, it saw nothing; there was the flutter of a strange pulse under its fur and feathers; and, lifting its foot to the right of the glass wall, it rocked again to the left. Change the sex of a dog: it cries like a bitch in a high heat, and sniffs, bewildered, over the blind litter. Such a strange dog, with a grafted ovary, howled in its cage. The doctor put his ear to the glass, hoping for a new sound. The sun blew in through the laboratory windows, and the light of the wind was the colour of the sun. With music in his ears, he moved among the phials and the bottles of life; the mutilated were silent; the new born in the rabbits' cages drew down the hygienic air delightedly into their lungs. To-morrow there were to be mastoids for the ferret by the window, but to-day it leapt in the sun.

The hill was as big as a mountain, and the house swelled like a hill on the topmost peak. Holding too many rooms, the house had a room for the wild owls, and a cellar for the vermin that multiplied on clean straw and grew fat as rabbits. The people in the house moved like too many ghosts among the white-sheeted tables, met face to face in the corridors and covered their eyes for fear of a new stranger, or suddenly crowded together in the central hall, questioning one another as to the names of the new born. One by one the faces vanished, but there was always one to take its place, a woman with a child at her breast, or a blind man from the world. All had possession of the keys of the house.

There was one boy among them who had the name of the house, and, son of the house that was called a hill, he played with the shadows in the corridors and slept at night in a high room shuttered from the stars. But the people of the house slept in sight of the moon; they heard the gulls from the sea, the noise of the waves, when the wind blew from the south, breaking on sand, and slept with their eyes open.

The doctor woke up with the birds, seeing the sun rise each morning in a coloured water, and the day, like the growths in his jars, grow brighter and stronger as the growing hours let the rain or the shine and the particles of winter light fall from them. As was his custom, he turned, this one morning, from the window where the weazel leapt, to the life behind glass. He marked with an unmortal calm, with the never-ended beginning of a smile no mother bared with the mouth of her milk, how the young lapped at their mothers and his creatures, and the newly hatched fluttered, and the papped birds opened their beaks. He was power and the clay knife, he was the sound and the substance, for he made a hand of glass, a hand with a vein, and sewed it upon the flesh, and it strengthened with the heat of the false light, and the glass nails grew long. Life ran from his fingers, in the heat of his acids, on the surface of the boiling herbs; he had death in a thousand powders; he had frozen a crucifix of steam; all the great chemistries of the earth, the mystery of matter – 'See,' he said aloud, 'a brand on a frog's forehead where there was neither' – in his room at the top of the house had no mystery.

The house was one mystery. Everything happens in a blaze of light; the groping of the boy's blind hands along the walls of the corridors was a movement of light, though the last candle dimmed by the head of the stairs and the lines of light at the feet of the locked doors were suddenly taken away. Nant, the boy, was not alone; he heard a frock rustle, a hand beneath his own scrape on the distemper. 'Whose hand?' he said softly. Then, flying in a panic down the dark carpets, he cried more loudly: 'Never answer me.' 'Your hand,' said the dark, and Nant stopped still.

Death was too long for the doctor, and eternity took too much time.

I was that boy in a dream, and I stood stock still, knowing myself to be alone, knowing that the voice was mine and the dark not the death of the sun but the dark light thrown back by the walls of the windowless corridors. I put out my arm, and it turned into a tree.

Early that morning, under the arch of a lamp, the doctor made a new acid, turning it round and round with a spoon, seeing it have colour in its beaker and then, by the change of heat, be the colour of water. It was the strongest acid, burning the air, but it struggled through his fingers sweet as a syrup and did not burn at all. Carefully, silently, he raised the beaker and opened the door of a cage. This was a new milk for the cat. He poured the acid into a saucer, and the cat-headed creature slipped down to drink. I was that cat-head in a dream; I drank the acid, and I slept; I woke up in death, but there I forgot the dream and moved on a different being in the image of the boy who was terrified of the dark. And, my arm no longer the branch of a tree, like a mole I hurried from light and to the light; for one blind moment I was a mole with a child's hands digging, up or down, I knew not which, in the Welsh earth. I knew that I was dreaming, but suddenly I awoke to the hard, real lack of light in the corridors of the house. There was nobody to guide me; the doctor, the foreigner in a white coat making a new logic in his tower of birds, was my only friend. Nant raced for the doctor's tower. Up spiral stairs and a broken ladder, reading, by candle, a sign that said To London and the Sun, he climbed in my image, I in his, and we were two brothers climbing.

The key was on a chain ringed from my waist. Opening the door, I found the doctor as I always found him, staring through the walls of a glass cage. He smiled but paid no heed to me who had lusted a hundred seconds for his smile and his white coat. 'I gave it my acid and it died,' the doctor said. 'And, after ten minutes, the dead hen rose to its feet; it rubbed against glass like a cat, and I saw its cat's head. This was ten minutes' death.'

A storm came up, black bodied, from the sea, bringing rain and twelve winds to drive the hillbirds off the face of the sky; the storm, the black man, the whistler from the sea bottom and the fringe of the fish stones, the thunder, the lightning, the mighty pebbles, these came up; as a sickness, an afterbirth, coming up from the belly of weathers; mad as a mist coming up, the antichrist from a seaflame or a steam crucifix, coming up the putting on of rain; as the acid was stronger, the multiplying storm, the colour of temper, the whole, the unholy, rock-handed, came up coming up.

This was the exterior world.

And the shadows, that were web and cloven footed in the house, with the beaks of birds, the shifted shadows that bore a woman in each hand, had no casting substances; and the foam horses of the exterior sea climbed like foxes on the hills. This that held Nant and the doctor, the bone of a horse head, the ox and black man arising from the clay picture, was the interior world. This was the interior world where the acid grew stronger, and the death in the acid added ten days to the dead time.

Still the doctor did not see me. I who was the doctor in a dream, the foreign logician, the maker of birds, engrossed in the acid strengthening and the search for oblivion, soon raised the beaker to my mouth as the storm came up. There was thunder as I drank; and, as he fell, the lightning crossed on the wind.

'There is a dead man in the tower,' a woman said to her companion as they stood by the door of the central hall.

'There is a dead man in the tower,' said the corner echoes, and their voices rose through the house. Suddenly the hall was crowded, and the people of the house moved among one another, questioning as to the name of the new dead.

Nant stood over the doctor. Now the doctor was dead. There was a corridor leading to the tower of ten days' death, and there a woman danced alone, with the hands of a man upon her shoulders. And soon the virgins joined her, bared to the waist, and made the movements of dancing; they danced towards the open doors of the corridors, stood lightly in the doorways; they danced four steps towards the doors, and then danced four steps away. In the long hall they danced in celebration of the dead. This was the dance of the halt, the blind, and the half dead, this the dance of the abnegation of the dead, this the dance of the children, the grave girls bared to the waist, this the dance of the dreamers, the open-eyed and the naked hopheads, sleeping as they moved. The doctor was dead at my feet. I knelt down to count his ribs, to raise his jaw, to take the beaker of acid from his hand. But the dead hand stiffened.

Said a voice at my elbow: 'Unlock the hand.' I moved to obey the voice, but a softer voice said at my ear: 'Let the hand stiffen.' 'Strike the second voice.' 'Strike the first voice.' 'Unlock the hand.' 'Let the hand stiffen.' I struck at the two voices with my fist, and Nant's hand turned into a tree.

At noon the storm was stronger; all afternoon it shook the tower, pulling the slates from the roof; it came from the sea and the earth from the sea beds and the roots of the forests. I could hear nothing but the voice of the thunder that drowned the two stricken voices; I saw the lightning stride up the hill, a bright, forked man blinding me through the tower windows. And still they danced, into the early evening, the storm increasing, and still the half-naked virgins danced to the doors. This was the dance of the celebration of death in the interior world.

I heard a voice say over the thunder: 'The dead shall be buried. This was not everlasting death, but a death of days; this was a sleep with no heart. We bury the dead,' said the voice that heard my heart, the brief and the everlasting. The storm up the wind measured off the distances of the voice, but a lull in the rain let the two struggling voices at my side recall me to the hand and the acid. I dragged up the stiffening hand, unlocked the fingers, and raised the beaker to my mouth. As the glass burned me, there came a knocking at the door and a cry from the people of the house. They who were seeking the body of the new dead worried the door. My boy's heart was breaking. Swiftly I glanced towards the table where a lemon lay on a plate. I punctured the skin of the lemon, and poured in the acid. Then down came the storm of the dark voices and the knocks, and the tower door broke on its hinges. The dead was found. I fought between the shoulders of the entering strangers and, leaving them to their picking, spiralled down, sped through the corridors, the lemon at my breast.

Nant and I were brothers in this wild world far from the border villages, from the sea that has England in its hand, from the lofty spires and the uneaten graves beneath them. As one, one-headed, two-footed, we ran through the passages and the halls, seeing no shadows, hearing none of the wicked intimacies of the house. The rooms were empty of wickedness. We looked for a devil in the corners, but their secrets were ours. So we ran on, afraid of our footfalls, exulting in the beating of the blood, for death was at our breast, a sharp fruit, a full and yellow tumour shaped to the skin. Nant was a lonely runner in the house; I parted from him, leaving a half ache and a half terror, going my own way, the way of the light breaking over Cathmarw hill and the Black Valley. And, going his own way, he climbed alone up a stone stairs to the last tower. He put his mouth to her cheek and touched her nipple. The storm died as she touched him.

He cut the lemon in half with the scissors dangling from the rope of her skirt.

And the storm came up as they drank.

This was the coming of death in the interior world.

THE HORSE'S HA

He saw the plague enter the village on a white horse. It was a cancerous horseman, with a furuncle for a hat, that galloped the beast over grass and cobble and the coloured hill. Plague, plague, cried Tom Twp as the horse on the horizon, scenting the stars, lifted a white head. Out came the grocer with an egg in his hand, and the butcher in a bloody coat. They followed the line of the lifted finger, but the horse had gone, the trees were no speakers, and the birds who flew criss-cross on the sky said no word of warning to the parson's rookery or the chained starlings in the parlour of ApLlewelyn. As white, said Tom Twp, as the egg in your hand. He remembered the raw head of the horseman, and whispered shyly ; As red as mother's rump in your window. The clouds darkened, the sun went in, the suddenly ferocious wind broke down three fences, and the cows, blue-eyed with plague, nibbled at the centres of the marrow beds. The egg fell, and the red yolk struggled between the spaces of the cobbles, the white mixed with the rain that dripped from the scarlet coat. In went the grocer with a stained hand, and the butcher among the hands of veal. Tom Twp, following his finger towards the horizon where the horse of plague had stamped and vanished, reached the dark church as the rain grew sick of the soil and drew back to heaven. He ran between the graves where the worm rubbed in the tradesman's hands. Mrs ApLlewelyn raised a stone breast above the grass. Softly opening the door, he came upon the parson praying for disarmament in the central aisle. Disarm the forces of the army and the navy, he heard the parson murmur to the Christ of stained glass who smiled like a nannygoat above him, hearing the cries from Cardiff and the smoking West. Disarm the territorial forces, the parson prayed. In anger, God smote him. There is plague, said Tom Twp. ApLlewelyn in the organ loft reached for the bass stops. The white plague drifted through the church to the music of the savage voluntary. Parson and sinner stood beneath the reflections of the Holy Family, marking in each ginger halo the hair of blood. There was to one the voice of an arming God in the echo of each chord, and, to the other, the horse's ha.

One by one the starlings died; the last remaining bird, with a pain in its crop, whistled at the late afternoon. Ap Llewelyn, returning from music and marvelling at the sky, heard the last starling's voice as he walked up the drive. Why is there no welcome, wondered the keeper, from my starling charges. Every day of the year they had lost their tempers, tore at the sashes of the window watching on the flying world; they had scraped on the glass, and fetched up their wings from the limed bar, signalling before him. On the rug at his feet lay six starlings, cold and stiff, the seventh mourning. Death in his absence had laid six singers low. He who marks the sparrows fall has no time for my birds, said ApLlewelyn. He smote big, bloody death, and death, relenting, pulled a last fart from the bodies of the dead birds.

Plague, plague, cried Tom Twp, standing in a new rain. Where the undertaker's house had died in the trees, he holla'd, like ApLlewelyn, of big, bloody death; he heard the rooks cawing in the trees, and saw a galloping shadow. The trees smelt of opium and mice, to Tom two sorts of the hell-headed animal who ran in the skirtings of the grave. There were, on the branches of the trees and hanging upright from the earth, the owls that ate the mice and the mouths of the rosy flowers that fed on opium. To the chimneys of Last House and the one illuminated window he called the plague. Out came the under-taker in a frock coat; distrusting the light of the moon, he carried a candle in his gloved hand, the candle casting three shadows. To the middle shadow Tom Twp addressed his words of the white coming. Shall I measure, said the shadow on the left, the undead of Wales? Plague on a horse, said Tom Twp to the left shadow, and heard the darker shadow on the right reply.

No drug of man works on the dead. The parson, at his pipe, sucked down a dead smoke from the nostrils of the travelling horse who now, on a far-off mountain, neighed down at Africa. Smitten by God, the parson, as the dark rose deepest where the moon rose in a blaze of light, counted his blessings, the blazing fire, the light in the tobacco, and the shape of the deep bowl. Hell was this fire, the dark denial burning like a weed, and the poppy out of the smoking earth. The lines of the bowl, that patterned his grave, were the lines of the weedy world; the light in the tobacco faded; the weed was at the parson's legs, worrying him into a longer fall than the fall from heaven, and, heavier than the poppy, into a long sleep.

Butcher and baker fell asleep that night, their women sleeping at their sides. Butcher and baker took their women in no image; their women broke again for them the accustomed maidenheads, their erected saviours crossing, in my language, the hill of hairs. Over the shops, the cold eggs that had life, the box where the rats worked all night on the high meat, the shopkeepers gave no thought to death. They felt, in the crowded space between hip and belly, the action of a third lover. Death, in the last gristle, broke on the minutes, and, by twelve beneath Cathmarw steeple, the towers fell.

Shall I measure the undead? This, said the undertaker in his parlour, pointing through the uncurtained window to the shape of the night, is the grave for the walking and the breathing. Here lay the sleepy body, the smoking body, the flesh that burned a candle, and the lessening manwax. Go home and die, he had told Tom Twp, and, telling it again to the mad moon, he remembered the story of the resurrection-men who had snatched a talking body out of the Cathmarw yards. He heard the dead die round him, and a live man, in his grafted suit, break up the gravel on the drive of Last House. Cathmarw, in a bath of blood, slept still for the light day, Tom twisted in the hedge, butcher and baker stiff by their loves, and parson with a burnt-out pipe loose in his jaws. ApLlewelyn skinned the six starlings; he dropped to the ground at last, holding two handfuls of red and broken feathers; the seventh bird, naked as its dead mates, still shivering, sang on the limed bar. Plague is upon us, said Mr Montgomery, the undertaker, for the wind was resounding with the noise of departure, and the smell of the departing flesh crept up the wind. In the skin of this Western Wales, through the veins of the county, the rub of the plague transformed into a circle of sick and invisible promise the globe of seeds; swollen in the tubers of the trees, death poisoned the green buds and coloured the birthmarks of the forest with a fresh stain. Mr Montgomery threw his glass of vinegar in the plague's face; the glass broke on the window, and the vinegar ran down the broken panes. He cardboarded each slit and crack, smelling the running acid as he nailed up a cloth to shield night from him;

he bolted and barred the doors of his wooden house and stuffed
the holes in the parlour corners, until, buried at last in a coffin
with chimneys, he took down his mother's book. Cures for the
sickness of the body and the sickness of the mind, ingredients
for a saucer for resurrection, calls to the dead, said Bronwen
Montgomery. The hand that wrote squarely to the crowded
planet held a worm, and rain beat down the letters of her living
name, and of Cathmarw's plague she said, in a translated
tongue, that the horse was a white beast ridden over the hill by
a raw-headed horseman. Take, said Bronwen, the blood of a
bird, and mix it with the stuff of man. Take, of a dead man and
bird, a bowl of death, and pour the bird's blood and the mortal
sap through the sockets of the bowl. Stir with a finger, and, if a
dead finger, drink my brew by me. He cast her aside. There was
a bird and man in the unbolted darkness, plague in the loin and
feather tickling the flesh and bone, uplifted fingers in the trees,
and an eye in the air. These were his common visions; plague
could not cloud the eye, nor the wind in the trees split the finger-
nail. Unbolting, unbarring the coffin with chimney, he walked
into the single vision of the night; the night was one bird's
blood, one pocket of man, one finger lifted in the many and the
upward world. He walked through the woods and onto the
dusty road that led to Wales all ways, to the left, to the right, to
the north, to the south, down through the vegetations, and up
through the eye of the air. Looking at the still trees in the
darkness, he came at last to the house of ApLlewelyn. He
opened the gate and walked up the drive. There, in the parlour,
lay ApLlewelyn, six featherless starlings at his side, the seventh
mourning. Take, take, said Bronwen out of the Cathmarw
yards, the blood of a bird. He gathered a dead bird up, tore at
its throat, and caught the cold blood in his hands. Drink my
brew by me, said Bronwen at his ear. He found a cup on the
dresser, and half filled it with the blood of the shrunken starling.
Though he rot he must wait, said Mr Montgomery to the
organist, till I drink her brew by her. Take, take, said his mother,
the stuff of man. He hurried out and on, hearing the last starling
mourn for the new departure.

Tom Twp was twisted in the hedge. He did not feel the jackknife at his finger, and the going of the grassy wedding ring
around it did not trouble him at all.

Parson, dead in his chair, did not cry aloud as his trousers slid down to his boots, and promise filled the bladder of a fountain-pen.

The cup was full. Mr Montgomery stirred it with a wedding finger, and drank from it in the Cathmarw yards by the grave of his mother. Down went the red brew. The graves spun around him, the angels shifted on their stones, and the lids, invisible to the silent drinker, creaked on their hinges. Poison stirred him and he spun, one foot in his mother's grave. Dead Cathmarw made a movement out of the wooden hamlet towards the hill of hairs. The hair rose on his scalp. Blood in his blood, and the cold ounce of the parson's seed edging to creation, he counted the diminishings of the moon; the stationary sun slipped down, and the system he could not take to the ground broke in half and in a hundred stars. Three days went by in a wind, the fourth rising cloudless and sinking again to too many strokes from the out-counted steeple. The fourth night got up like a man; the vision altering, a woman in the moon lit up the yards. He counted the diminishings of the sun. Too many days, he said, sick of his mother's brew and of the poisoned hours that passed and repassed him, leaving on the gravel path a rag and a bone in a faded frock coat. But as the days passed, so the dead grew tired of waiting. Tom, uneasy in the hedge, raised a four-fingered hand to stifle the yawn that broke up the last remaining skins upon his face. Butcher and baker ached in too long a love, and cursed the beds that bore them. The six naked starlings rose on their wings, the seventh singing, and ApLlewelyn, out of a deep sleep, drifted into a reawakened world where the birds danced about him. So, tired of waiting, the dead rose and sought the undertaker, for the rot had set in, and their flesh fell as they walked, in a strange procession, along the dusty road that led all ways to the graves of Cathmarw.

Mr Montgomery saw them come, and, as a new sunshine descended on the yards, offered them his cup of brew. But the dead refused his hand. Tom Twp hunched, the sterile parson, butcher and baker ungainly in their loves, and ApLlewelyn with his hands around the feathers, clawed at the earth, making a common grave. Far, far above them, the seven naked starlings scratched on the sky. A darkness descended on the yards, but lifted again as Mr Montgomery questioned the parson as to the God of death. What is God's death? Lifting his head from the soil, the parson said, God took my promise. And he smote the earth. I am your tombmaker, said Mr Montgomery as the unshrouded parson climbed into the grave. I, I took your promise, he said as the soil closed over. What is death's music? one note or many? the chord of contagion? Thus questioned the undertaker, the cup three quarters empty in his gloved hand. He who marks the sparrows fall has no time for my birds, said ApLlewelyn. What music is death? What should I know of the music of death who am no longer the keeper of birds? ApLlewelyn vanished into the second quarter of the grave. I, I slew your birds, said the undertaker to the vanishing man. The butcher was dead meat. Let me answer your platitudes, said the butcher's wife, scrubbing the surface of the double hole in the earth. I was love, I am̄ dead, and my man still walks in me. What is death's love? said the undertaker to the woman. Let me answer your platitudes, said the grocer's wife. I was dead, I am love, and my man still treads in me. They who filled and were filled, in a two-backed death, filled the third quarter. And Tom Twp, counting his fingers at the edge of their acre, found a tenth miraculous finger, with a nail red as blood and a clear half-moon, Death is my last finger, said Tom Twp, and dived into the closing grave. So Mr Montgomery was left alone, by the desolate church, under a disappearing moon. One by one the stars went out, leaving a hole in heaven. He looked upon the grave, and slowly removed his coat.

THE SCHOOL FOR WITCHES

On Cader Peak there was a school for witches where the doctor's daughter, teaching the unholy cradle and the devil's pin, had seven country girls. On Cader Peak, half ruined in an enemy weather, the house with a story held the seven girls, the cellar echoing, and a cross reversed above the entrance to the inner rooms. Here the doctor, dreaming of illness, in the centre of the tubercular hill, heard his daughter cry to the power swarming under the West roots. She invoked a particular devil, but the gehenna did not yawn under the hill, and the day and the night continued with their two departures; the cocks crew and the corn fell in the villages and yellow fields as she taught the seven girls how the lust of man, like a dead horse, stood up to his injected mixtures. She was short and fat-thighed; her cheeks were red; she had red lips and innocent eyes. But her body grew hard as she called to the black flowers under the tide of roots; when she fetched the curdlers out of the trees to bore through the cows' udders, the seven staring stared at the veins hardening in her breast; she stood uncovered, calling the devil, and the seven uncovered closed round her in a ring.

Teaching them the intricate devil, she raised her arms to let him enter. Three years and a day had vanished since she first bowed to the moon, and, maddened by the mid light, dipped her hair seven times in the salt sea, and a mouse in honey. She stood, still untaken, loving the lost man; her fingers hardened on light as on the breastbone of the unentering devil.

Mrs Price climbed up the hill, and the seven saw her. It was the first evening of the new year, the wind was motionless on Cader Peak, and a half red, promising dusk floated over the rocks. Behind the midwife the sun sank as a stone sinks in a marsh, the dark bubbled over it, and the mud sucked it down into the bubble of the bottomless fields.

In Bethlehem there is a prison for mad women, and in Cathmarw by the parsonage trees a black girl screamed as she laboured. She was afraid to die like a cow on the straw, and to the noises of the rooks. She screamed for the doctor on Cader Peak as the tumultuous West moved in its grave. The midwife heard her. A black girl rocked in her bed. Her eyes were stones. Mrs Price climbed up the hill, and the seven saw her.

Midwife, midwife, called the seven girls. Mrs Price crossed herself. A chain of garlic hung at her throat. Carefully, she touched it. The seven cried aloud, and ran from the window to the inner rooms where the doctor's daughter, bent on uncovered knees, counselled the black toad, her familiar, and the divining cat slept by the wall. The familiar moved its head. The seven danced, rubbing the white wall with their thighs until the blood striped the thin symbols of fertility upon them. Hand in hand they danced among dark symbols, under the charts that marked the rise and fall of the satanic seasons, and their white dresses swung around them. The owls commenced to sing, striking against the music of the suddenly awaking winter. Hand in hand the dancers spun around the black toad and the doctor's daughter, seven stags dancing, their antlers shaking, in the confusion of the unholy room.

She is a very black woman, said Mrs Price, and curtsied to the doctor.

He woke to the midwife's story out of a dream of illness, remembering the broken quicked, the black patch and echo, the mutilated shadows of the seventh sense.

She lay with a black scissor-man.

He wounded her deep, said the doctor, and wiped a lancet on his sleeve.

Together they stumbled down the rocky hill.

A terror met them at the foot, the terror of the blind tapping their white sticks and the stumps of the arms on the solid darkness ; two worms in the foil of a tree, bellies on the rubber sap and the glues of a wrong-grained forest, they, holding tight to hats and bags, crawled now up the path that led to the black birth. From right, from left, the cries of labour came in under the branches, piercing the dead wood, from the earth where a mole sneezed, and from the sky, out of the worms' sight.

They were not the only ones caught that night in the torrential blindness ; to them, as they stumbled, the land was empty of men, and the prophets of bad weather alone walked in their neighbourhoods. Three tinkers appeared out of silence by the chapel wall. Capel Cader, said the panman. Parson is down on tinkers, said John Bucket. Cader Peak, said the scissor-man, and up they went. They passed the midwife close; she heard the scissors clacking, and the branch of a tree drum on the buckets. One, two, three, they were gone, invisibly shuffling as she hugged her skirts. Mrs Price crossed herself for the second time that day, and touched the garlic at her throat. A vampire with a scissors was a Pembroke devil. And the black girl screamed like a pig.

Sister, raise your right hand. The seventh girl raised her right hand. Now say, said the doctor's daughter, Rise up out of the bearded barley. Rise out of the green grass asleep in Mr Griffith's dingle. Big man, black man, all eye, one tooth, rise up out of Cader marshes. Say the devil kisses me. The devil kisses me, said the girl cold in the centre of the kitchen. Kiss me out of the bearded barley. Kiss me out of the bearded barley. The girls giggled in a circle. Swive me out of the green grass. Swive me out of the green grass. Can I put on my clothes now? said the young witch, after encountering the invisible evil.

Throughout the hours of the early night, in the smoke of the seven candles, the doctor's daughter spoke of the sacrament of darkness. In her familiar's eyes she read the news of a great and an unholy coming; divining the future in the green and sleepy eyes, she saw, as clearly as the tinkers saw the spire, the towering coming of a beast in stag's skin, the antlered animal whose name read backwards, and the black, black, black wanderer climbing a hill for the seven wise girls of Cader. She woke the cat. Poor Bell, she said, smoothing his fur the wrong way. And, Ding dong, Bell, she said, and swung the spitting cat.

Sister, raise your left hand. The first girl raised her left hand. Now with your right hand put a needle in your left hand. Where is a needle? Here, said the doctor's daughter, Is a needle, here in your hair. She made a gesture over the black hair, and drew a needle out from the coil at her ear. Say I cross you. I cross you, said the girl, and, with the needle in her hand, struck at the black cat racked on the daughter's lap.

For love takes many shapes, cat, dog, pig or goat; there was a lover, spellbound in the time of mass, now formed and featured in the image of the darting cat; his belly bleeding, he sped past the seven girls, past parlour and dispensary, into the

night, on to the hill ; the wind got at his wound, and swiftly he
darted down the rocks, in the direction of the cooling streams.

He passed the three tinkers like lightning. Black cat is luck,
said the panman. Bloody cat is bad luck, said John Bucket. The
scissorman said nothing. They appeared out of silence by the
wall of the Peak house, and heard a hellish music through the
open door. They peered through the stained-glass window, and
the seven girls danced before them. They have beaks, said the
panman. Web feet, said John Bucket. The tinkers walked in.

At midnight the black girl bore her baby, a black beast with
the eyes of a kitten and a stain at the corner of its mouth. The
midwife remembering birthmarks, whispered to the doctor of
the gooseberry on his daughter's arm. Is it ripe yet? said Mrs
Price. The doctor's hand trembled, and his lancet cut the baby
under the chin. Scream you, said Mrs Price, who loved all
babies.

The wind howled over Cader, waking the sleepy rooks who
cawed from the trees and, louder than owls, disturbed the
midwife's meditations. It was wrong for the rooks, those sleepy
birds over the zinc roofs, to caw at night. Who put a spell on
the rooks ? The sun might rise at ten past one in the morning.

Scream you, said Mrs Price, the baby in her arms, This is a
wicked world. The wicked world, with a voice out of the wind,
spoke to the baby half smothering under the folds of the
midwife's overcoat. Mrs Price wore a man's cap, and her great
breasts heaved under the black blouse. Scream you, said the
wicked world, I am an old man blinding you, a wicked little
woman tickling you, a dry death parching you. The baby
screamed, as though a flea were on its tongue.

The tinkers were lost in the house, and could not find the
inner room where the girls still danced with the beaks of birds
upon them and their web feet bare on the cobblestones. The
panman opened the dispensary door, but the bottles and the
tray of knives alarmed him. The passages were too dark for
John Bucket, and the scissorman surprised him at a corner.
Christ defend me, he cried. The girls stopped dancing, for the
name of Christ rang in the outer halls. Enter, and, Enter, cried
the doctor's daughter to the welcome devil. It was the scissorman who found the door and turned the handle, walking into
candlelight. He stood before Gladwys on the threshold, a giant

black as ink with a three days' beard. She lifted her face to his, and her sackcloth fell away.

Up the hill, the midwife, cooing as she came, held the newborn baby in her arms, and the doctor toiled behind her with his black bag rattling. The birds of the night flew by them, but the night was empty, and these restless wings and voices, hindering emptiness forever, were the feathers of shadows and the accents of an invisible flying. What purpose there was in the shape of Cader Peak, in the bouldered breast of the hill and the craters poxing the green-black flesh, was no more than the wind's purpose that willy nilly blew from all corners the odd turfs and stones of an unmoulded world. The grassy rags and bones of the steep hill were, so the doctor pondered as he climbed behind the baby rocking into memory on a strange breast, whirled together out of the bins of chaos by a winter wind. But the doctor's conceits came to nothing, for the black child let out a scream so high and loud that Mr Griffiths heard it in his temple in the dingle. The worshipper of vegetables, standing beneath his holy marrow nailed in four places to the wall, heard the cry come down from the heights. A mandrake cried on Cader. Mr Griffiths hastened in the direction of the stars.

John Bucket and the panman stepped into candlelight, seeing a strange company. Now in the centre circle of the room, surrounded by the unsteady lights, stood the scissorman and a naked girl; she smiled at him, he smiled at her, his hands groped for her body, she stiffened and slackened, he drew her close, smiling she stiffened again, and he licked his lips.

John Bucket had not seen him as a power for evil baring the breasts and the immaculate thighs of the gentlewomen, a magnetic blackman with the doom of women in his smile, forcing open the gates of love. He remembered a black companion on the roads, sharpening the village scissors, and, in the shadows, when the tinkers took the night, a coal-black shadow, silent as the travelling hedges.

Was this tall man, the panman murmured, who takes the doctor's daughter with no how-d'you-do, was he Tom the scissorman? I remember him on the highways in the heat of the sun, a black, three-coated tinker.

And, like a god, the scissorman bent over Gladwys, he healed her wound, she stood his ointment and his fire, she burned at the tower altar, and the black sacrifice was done. Stepping out of his arms, her offering cut and broken, the gut of a lamb, she smiled and cried manfully: Dance, dance, my seven. And the seven danced, their antlers shaking, in the confusion of the unholy room. A coven, a coven, cried the seven as they danced. They beckoned the panman from the door. He edged towards them, and they caught his hands. Dance, dance, my strange man, the seven cried. John Bucket joined them, his buckets drumming, and swiftly they dragged him into the rising fury of the dance. The scissorman in the circle danced like a tower. They sped round and round, none crying louder than the two tinkers in the heart of the swirling company, and lightly the doctor's daughter was among them. She drove them to a faster turn of foot; giddy as weathercocks in a hundred changing winds, they were revolving figures in the winds of their dresses and to the music of the scissors and the metal pans; giddily she spun between the dancing hoops, the wheels of cloth and hair, and the bloody ninepins spinning; the candles grew pale and lean in the wind of the dance; she whirled by the tinker's side, by the scissorman's side, by his dark, damp side, smelling his skin, smelling the seven furies.

It was then that the doctor, the midwife, and the baby entered through the door as quietly as could be. Sleep well, Pembroke, for your devils have left you. And woe on Cader Peak that the black man dances in my house. There had been nothing for that savage evening but an end of evil. The grave had yawned, and the black breath risen up.

Here danced the metamorphoses of the dusts of Cathmarw. Lie level, the ashes of man, for the phoenix flies from you, woe unto Cader, into my nice, square house. Mrs Price fingered her garlic, and the doctor stood grieving.

The seven saw them. A coven, a coven, they cried. One, dancing past them, snatched at the doctor's hand; another dancing caught him around the waist, and, all bewildered by the white flesh of their arms, the doctor danced. Woe, woe on Cader he cried as he swirled among maidens, and his steps gathered speed. He heard his voice rising; his feet skimmed over the silver cobbles. A coven, a coven, cried the dancing doctor, and bowed in his measures.

Suddenly Mrs price, hugging the black baby, was surrounded at the entrance of the room. Twelve dancers hemmed her in, and the hands of strangers pulled at the baby on her breast. See,

But Mr Owen burst out laughing; he threw back his head, and laughed at the matting shadows, at the oil in the clear, glass bag of the lamp. That there could be seed, shuffling to the spring of heat, in the old man's glands. That there could be life in the ancient loins. Father of the jawbones of asses and the hair-thighed camel's fleas, Mr Davies swayed before him in a mist of laughter. He could blow the old man up the sky with a puff of his lungs.

He is your child, said Mrs Owen.

She smiled at the shadow between them, the eunuch shadow of a man that fitted between the curving of their shoulders.

So Mr Davies smiled again, knowing the shadow to be his. And Mr Owen, caring for no shadow but that cast on his veins by the rising and the setting of the blood, smiled at them both.

The holy gentlemen would honour them that night.

And the Six circled the three.

PROLOGUE TO AN ADVENTURE

As I walked through the wilderness of this world, as I walked through the wilderness, as I walked through the city with the loud electric faces and the crowded petrols of the wind dazzling and drowning me that winter night before the West died, I remembered the winds of the high, white world that bore me and the faces of a noiseless million in the busyhood of heaven staring on the afterbirth. They who nudged through the literate light of the city, shouldered and elbowed me, catching my trilby with the spokes of their umbrellas, who offered me matches and music, made me out of their men's eyes into a manshape walking. But take away, I told them silently, the flannel and cotton, the cheap felt and leather, I am the nakedest and baldest nothing between the pinnacle and the base, an alderman of ghosts holding to watch-chain and wallet on the wet pavement, the narrator of echoes moving in man's time. I have Old Moore by the beard, and the news of the world is no world's news, the gossips of heaven and the fallen rumours are enough and too much for a shadow that casts no shadow, I said to the blind beggars and the paperboys who shouted into the rain. They who were hurrying by me on the narrow errands of the world, time bound to their wrists or blinded in their pockets, who consulted the time strapped to a holy tower, and dodged between bonnets and wheels, heard in my fellow's footsteps the timeless accents of another walking. On the brilliant pavements under a smoky moon, their man's world turning to the bass roll of the traffic, they saw in the shape of my fellow another staring under the pale lids, and heard the spheres turn as he spoke. This is a strange city, gentlemen on your own, gentlemen arm-in-arm making a rehearsed salute, gentlemen with ladies, ladies this is a strange city. For them in the friendless houses in the streets of pennies and pleasures a million ladies and gentlemen moved up in bed, time moved with the practised moon over a million roofs that night, and grim policemen stood at each corner in the black wind. O mister lonely, said the ladies on their own, we shall be naked as new-born mice, loving you long in the short sparks of the night. We are not the ladies with feathers between their breasts, who lay eggs on the quilt. As I walked through the skyscraping centre, where the lamps walked at my side like volted men or the trees of a new scripture, I jostled the devil at my elbow, but lust in his city shadows dogged me under the arches, down the black blind streets. Now in the shape of a bald girl smiling, a wailing wanton with handcuffs for earings, or the lean girls that lived on pickings, now in ragged woman with a muckrake curtseying in the slime, the tempter of angels whispered over my shoulder, We shall be naked but for garters and black stockings, loving you long on a bed of strawberries and cream, and the nakeder for a ribbon that hides the nipples. We are not the ladies that eat into the brain behind the ear, or feed on the fat of the heart. I remembered the sexless shining women in the first hours of the world that bore me, and the golden sexless men that cried All Praise in the sounds of shape. Taking strength from a sudden shining, I have Old Scratch by the beard, I cried aloud. But the short-time shapes still followed, and the counsellor of an unholy nakedness nagged at my heels. No, not for nothing did the packed thoroughfares confront me at each cross and pavement's turning with these figures in the shapes of sounds, the lamp-chalked silhouettes and the walking frames of dreams, out of a darker allegory than the fictions of the earth could turn in twelve suns' time. There was more than man's meaning to the man-skulled bogies thumbing the skeletons of their noses, to the marrow-merry andrews scratching their armpits in a tavern light, and to the dead man, smiling through his bandages, who laid hand on my sleeve, saying in no man's voice, There is more than man's meaning in a stuffed man talking, split from navel to arsehole, and more in the horned ladies at your heels than a pinch of the cloven delights and the tang of sulphur. Heaven and hell shift up and down the city. I have the God of Israel in the image of a painted boy, and Lucifer, in a woman's shirt, pisses from a window in Damaroid Alley. See now, you shining ones, how the tuner of harps has fallen, and the painter of winds like a bag of henna into the gutter. The high hopes lie broken with broken bottles and suspender-belts, the white mud falls like feathers, there out of Pessary Court comes the Bishop of Bumdom, dressed like a ratcatcher, a holy sister in Gamarouche Mews sharpens her index tooth on a bloodstone, two weazels couple on All Paul's altar. It was an ungodly meaning, or the purpose of the fallen gods whose haloes magnified the wrong-cross-steepled horns on the pointed heads, that windily informed me of man's lower walking, and, as I thrust the dead-and-bandaged and a split-like-cabbage enemy to my right side, up sidled my no-bigger-than-a-thimble friends to the naked left. He who played the sorcerer, appearing all at one time in a dozen sulphurous beckonings, saying, out of a dozen mouths, We shall be naked as the slant-thighed queens of Asia in your dreams, was a symbol in the story of man's journey through the symboled city. And that which shifted with the greased lightning of a serpent from the nest holes in the bases of the cathedral pillars, tracking round the margins of the four cindery winds, was, too, a symbol in that city journey. In a mousetailed woman and a holy snake, the symbols of the city writhed before me. But by one red horn I had that double image, tore off the furry stays and leather jacket. We shall be naked, said Old Scratch variously emerging, as a Jewgirl crucified to the bedposts. We are all metaphors of the sound of shape of the shape of sound, break us we take another shape. Sideways the snake and the woman stroked a cross in the air. I saw the starfall that broke a cloud up, and dodged between bonnets and wheels to the iller-lit streets where I saw Daniel Dom lurching after a painted shadow.

We walked into the Seven Sins. Two little girls danced barefoot in the sawdust, and a bottle splintered on their legs. A negress loosened the straps of her yellow frock and bared a breast, holding a plate under the black flesh. Buy a pound, she said, and thrust her breast in Daniel's face. He faced the women as they moved, a yellow, noisy sea towards us, and caught the half-naked negress by the wrist. Like a woman confronted by a tower, You are so strong, my love, she said, and kissed him full on the mouth. But before the sea could circle us, we were out through the swing-doors into the street and the mid-winter night where the moonlight, salt white no longer, hung windlessly over the city. They were night's enemies who made a lamp out of the devil's eye, but we followed a midnight radiance around the corners, like two weird brothers trod in the glittering webprints. In their damp hats and raincoats, in the blaze of shopwindows, the people jostled against us on the pavements, and a gutterboy caught me by the sleeve. Buy an almanac, he said. It was the bitter end of the year. Now the starfall had ended, the sky was a hole in space. How long, how long, lord of the hail, shall my city rock on, and the seven deadly seas wait tidelessly for the moon, the bitter end the last tide-spinning of the full circle. Daniel lamented, trailing the midnight radiance to the door of the Deadly Virtue where the light went out and the seven webprints faded. We were forever climbing the steps of a sea-tower, crying aloud from the turret that we might warn us, as we clambered, of the rusty rack and the spiked maiden in the turret corners. Make way for Mister Dom and friend. Walking into the Deadly Virtue, we heard our names announced through the loudspeaker trumpet of the wooden image over the central mirror, and, staring in the glass as the oracle continued, we saw two distorted faces grinning through the smoke. Make way, said the loudspeaker, for Daniel, ace of Destruction, old Dom the toper of Doom's kitchen, and for the alderman of ghosts. Is the translator of man's manuscript, his walking chapters, said the trumpet-faced, a member of my Deadly Virtue? What is the colour of the narrator's blood? Put a leech on his forearm. Make way, the image cried, for bald and naked Mister Dreamer of the bluest veins this side of the blood-coloured sea. As the sea of faces parted, the bare-backed ladies scraped back from the counter, and the matchstick-waisted men, the trussed and cor-setted stilt-walkers with the tits of ladies, sought out the darker recesses of the saloon, we stumbled forward to the fiery bottles. Brandy for the dreamer and the pilgrim, said the wooden voice. Gentlemen, it is my call, said the live loudspeaker, death on my house. It was then, in the tangled hours of a new morning, surrounded by the dead faces of the drinkers, the wail of lost voices, and the words of the one electric image, that Daniel, hair-on-end, lamented first to me of the death on the city and the lost hero of the heart. There can be no armistice for the sexless, golden singers and the sulphurous hermaphrodites, the flying beast and the walking bird that war about us, for the horn and the wing. I could light the voices of the fiery virgins winking in my glass, catch the brandy-brown beast and bird as they fumed before my eyes, and kiss the two-antlered angel. No, not for nothing were these two intangible brandymaids neighbour-ing Daniel who cried, syringe in hand, Open your coke-white legs, you ladies of needles, Dom thunder Daniel is the lightning drug and the doctor.

Now a wind sprang through the room from the dead street; from the racked tower where two men lay in chains and a hole broke in the wall, we heard our own cries travel through the fumes of brandy and the loudspeaker's music; we pawed, in our tower agony, at the club shapes dancing, at the black girls tattooed from shoulder to nipple with a white dancing shape, frocked with snail-headed rushes and capped like antlers. But they slipped from us into the rubber corners where their black lovers waited invisibly; and the music grew louder until the tower cry was lost among it; and again Daniel lurched after a painted shadow that led him, threading through smoke and dancers, to the stained window.

Beneath him lay the city sleeping, curled in its streets and houses, lamped by its own red-waxed and iron stars, with a built moon above it, and the spires crossed over the bed. I stared down, rocking at his side, on to the unsmoking roofs and the burned-out candles. Destruction slept. Slowly the room behind us flowed, like four waters, down the seven gutters of the city into a black sea. A wave, catching the live loudspeaker in its mouth, sucking up the wood and music; for the last time a mountainous wave circled the drinkers and dragged them down, out of the world of light, to a crawling sea-bed; we saw a wave jumping and the last bright eyes go under, the last raw head, cut like a straw, fall crying through the destroying water. Daniel and I stood alone in the city. The sea of destruction lapped around our feet. We saw the starfall that broke the night up. The glass lights on iron went out, and the waves grew down into the pavements.

THE MAP OF LOVE

Here dwell, said Sam Rib, the two-backed beasts. He pointed to his map of Love, a square of seas and islands and strange continents with a forest of darkness at each extremity. The two-backed island, on the line of the equator, went in like the skin of lupus to his touch, and the blood sea surrounding found a new motion in its waters. Here seed, up the tide, broke on the boiling coasts; the sand grains multiplied; the seasons passed; summer, in a father's heat, went down to the autumn and the first pricks of winter, leaving the island shaping the four contrary winds out of its hollows.

Here, said Sam Rib, digging his fingers in the hills of a little island, dwell the first beasts of love. And here the get of the first loves mixed, as he knew, with the grasses that oiled their green upgoings, with their own wind and sap nurtured the first rasp of love that never, until spring came, found the nerves' answer in the fellowing blades.

Beth Rib and Reuben marked the green sea around the island. It ran through the landcracks like a boy through his first caves. Under the sea they marked the channels, painted in skeleton, that linked the first beasts' island with the boggy lands. For shame of the half-liquid plants sprouting from the bog, the pen-drawn poisons seething in the grass, and the copulation in the second mud, the children blushed.

Here, said Sam Rib, two weathers move. He traced with his finger the lightly drawn triangles of two winds, and the mouths of two cornered cherubs. The weathers moved in one direction. Singly they crawled over the abominations of the swamp, content in the shadow of their own rains and snowings, in the noise of their own sighs, and the pleasures of their own green achings. The weathers, like a girl and a boy, moved through the tossing world, the sea storm dragging under them, the clouds divided in many rages of movement as they stared on the raw wall of wind.

Return, synthetic prodigals, to thy father's laboratory, declaimed Sam Rib, and the fatted calf in a test-tube. He indicated the shift of locations, the pen lines of the separate weathers travelling over the deep sea and the second split between the lovers' worlds. The cherubs blew harder; wind of the two tossing weathers and the sprays of the cohering sea drove on and on; on the single strand of two coupled countries, the weathers stood. Two naked towers on the two-loves-in-a-grain of the million sands, they mixed, so the map arrows said, into a single strength. But the arrows of ink shot them back; two weakened towers, wet with love, they trembled at the terror of their first mixing, and two pale shadows blew over the land.

Beth Rib and Reuben scaled the hill that cast an eye of stone on the striped valley; hand-in-hand they ran down the hill, singing as they went, and took off their gaiters at the wet grass of the first of the twenty fields. There was a spirit in the valley that would roll on when all the hills and trees, all the rocks and streams, had been buried under the West death. Here was the first field wherein mad Jarvis, a hundred years before, had sown his seed in the belly of a bald-headed girl who had wandered out of a distant county and lain with him in the pains of love.

Here was the fourth field, a place of wonder, where the dead might spin all drunken-legged out of the dry graves, or the fallen angels battle upon the waters of the streams. Planted deeper in the soil of the valley than the blind roots could burrow after their mates, the spirit of the fourth field rose out of darkness, drawing the deep and the dark from the hearts of all who trod the valley a score or more miles from the borders of the mountainous county.

In the tenth and the central field Beth Rib and Reuben knocked at the doors of the bungalows, asking the location of the first island surrounded by loving hills. They knocked at the back door and received a ghostly admonishment.

Barefooted and hand-in-hand, they ran through the ten remaining fields to the edge of the Idris water where the wind smelt of seaweed and the valley spirit was wet with sea rain. But night came down, hand on thigh, and shapes in the further stretches of the now misty river drew a new shape close to them. An island shape walled round with darkness a half-mile up river. Stealthily Beth Rib and Reuben tiptoed to the lapping water.

They saw the shape grow, unlocked their fingers, took off their summer clothes, and, naked, raced into the river.

Up river, up river, she whispered.

Up river, he said.

They floated down river as a current tugged at their legs, but they fought off the current and swam towards the still growing island. Then mud rose from the bed of the river and sucked at Beth's feet.

Down river, down river, she called, and struggled from the mud.

Reuben, weed-bound, fought with the grey heads that fought his hands, and followed her back to the brink of the sea-going valley.

But, as Beth swam, the water tickled her; the water pressed on her side.

My love, cried Reuben, excited by the tickling water and the hands of the weeds.

And, as they stood naked on the twentieth field, My love, she whispered.

First fear shot them back. Wet as they were, they pulled their clothes on them.

Over the fields, she said.

Over the fields, in the direction of the hills and the hill-home of Sam Rib, like weakened towers the children ran, no longer linked, bewildered by the mud and blushing at the first tickle of the misty island water.

Here dwell, said Sam Rib, the first beasts of love. In the cool of a new morning the children listened, too frightened to touch hands. He touched again the sagging hill above the island, and pointed the progression of the skeleton channels linking mud with mud, green sea with darker, and all love-hills and islands into one territory. Here the grass mates, the green mates, the grains, said Sam Rib, and the dividing waters mate and are mated. The sun with the grass and the green, sand with water, and water with the green grass, these mate and are mated for the bearing and fostering of the globe. Sam Rib had mated with a green woman, as Great-Uncle Jarvis with his bald girl; he had mated with a womanly water for the bearing and the fostering of the child who blushed by him. He marked how the boggy lands lay so near the first beast doubling a back, the round of doubled beasts under as high a hill as Great-Uncle's hill that had frowned last night and wrapped itself in stones. Great-Uncle's hill had cut the children's feet, for the daps and the gaiters were lost for ever in the grass of the first field.

Thinking of the hill, Beth Rib and Reuben sat quiet. They heard Sam say that the hill of the first island grew soft as wool for the descent, or smooth as ice for tobogganing. They remembered the tame descent last night.

Tame hill, said Sam Rib, grows wild for the ascending. Lining the adolescents' hill was a white route of stone and ice marked with the sliding foot or sledge of the children going down; another route, at the foot, climbed upwards in a line of red stone and blood marked with the cracking prints of the ascending children. The descent was soft as wool. Fail on the first island, and the ascending hill wraps itself in a sharp thing of stones.

Beth Rib and Reuben, never forgetful of the humpbacked boulders and the flints in the grass, turned to each other for the first time that day. Sam Rib had made her and would mould him, would make and mould the boy and girl together into a double climber that sought the island and melted there into a single strength. He told them again of the mud, but did not frighten them. And the grey heads of the weeds were broken, never to swell again in the hands of the swimmer. The day of ascending was over; the first descent remained, a hill on the map of love, two branches of stone and olive in the children's hands.

Synthetic prodigals returned that night to the room of the hill, through caves and chambers running to the roof, discerning the roof of stars, and happy in their locked hands. There lay the striped valley before them, and the grass of the twenty fields fed the cattle; the night cattle moved by the hedges or lapped at warm Idris water. Beth Rib and Reuben ran down the hill, and the tender stones lay still under their feet; faster, they ran down the Jarvis flank, the wind at their hair, smells of the sea blown to their quivering nostrils from the north and the south where there was no sea; and, slowing their speed, they reached the first field and the rim of the valley to find their gaiters placed neatly in a cow-cloven spot in the grass.

They buttoned on their gaiters, and ran through the falling blades.

Here is the first field, said Beth Rib to Reuben.

The children stopped, the moonlight night went on, a voice spoke from the hedge darkness.

Said the voice, You are the children of love.

Where are you?

I am Jarvis.

Who are you?

Here, my dears, here in the hedge with a wise woman.

But the children ran away from the voice in the hedge.

Here in the second field.

They stopped for breath, and a weasel, making his noise, ran over their feet.

Hold harder.

I'll hold you harder.

Said a voice, Hold hard, the children of love.

Where are you?

I am Jarvis.

Who are you?

Here, here, lying with a virgin from Dolgelley.

In the third field the man of Jarvis lay loving a green girl, and, as he called them the children of love, lay loving her ghost and the smell of buttermilk on her breath. He loved a cripple in the fourth field, for the twist in her limbs made loving longer, and he cursed the straight children who found him with a straight-limbed lover in the fifth field marking the quarter.

A girl from Tiger Bay held Jarvis close, and her lips marked a red, cracked heart upon his throat; this was the sixth and the weather-tracked field where, turning from the maul of her hands, he saw their innocence, two flowers wagging in a sow's ear. My rose, said Jarvis, but the seventh love smelt in his hands, his fingering hands that held Glamorgan's canker under the eighth hedge. From the Convent of Bethel's Heart, a holy woman served him the ninth time.

And the children in the central field cried as ten voices came up, came up, came down from the ten spaces of the half-night and the hedging world.

It was full night when they answered, when the voices of one voice compassionately answered the two-voiced question ringing on the strokes of the upward, upward, and the downward air.

We, said they, are Jarvis, Jarvis under the hedge, in the arms of a woman, a green woman, a woman bald as a badger, on a nun's thigh.

They counted the numbers of their loves before the children's ears. Beth Rib and Reuben heard the ten oracles, and shyly they surrendered. Over the remaining fields, to the whispers of the last ten lovers, to the voice of ageing Jarvis, grey-haired in the final shadows, they sped to Idris. The island shone, the water babbled, there was a gesture of the limbs in each wind's stroke denting the flat river. He took off her summer clothes, and she shaped her arms like a swan. The bare boy stood at her shoulder; and she turned and saw him dive into the ripples in her wake. Behind them her fathers' voices slipped out of sound.

Up river, called Beth, up river.

Up river, he answered.

Only the warm, mapped waters ran that night over the edges of the first beasts' island white in a new moon.

IN THE DIRECTION OF THE BEGINNING

In the light tent in the swinging field in the great spring evening, near the sea and the shingled boat with a mast of cedar-wood, the hinderwood decked with beaks and shells, a folded, salmon sail, and two finned oars; with gulls in one flight high over, stork, pelican, and sparrow, flying to the ocean's end and the first grain of a timeless land that spins on the head of a sand glass, a hoop of feathers down the dark of the spring in a topsyturvy year; as the rocks in history, by every feature and scrawled limb, eye of a needle, shadow of a nerve, cut in the heart, by rifted fibre and clay thread, recorded for the rant of odyssey the dropping of the bay-leaf toppling of the oak-tree splintering of the moonstone against assassin avatar undead and numbered waves, a man was born in the direction of the beginning. And out of sleep, where the moon had raised him through the mountains in her eyes and by the strong, eyed arms that fall behind her, full of tides and fingers, to the blown sea, he wrestled over the edge of the evening, took to the beginning as a goose to the sky, and called his furies by their names from the wind-drawn index of the grave and waters. Who was this stranger who came like a hailstone, cut in ice, a snow-leafed seabush for her hair, and taller than a cedarmast, the north white rain descending and the whale-driven sea cast up to the caves of the eye, from a fishermen's city on the floating island? She was salt and white and travelling as the field, on one blade, swung with its birds around her, evening centred in the neverstill heart, he heard her hands among the treetops – a feather dived, her fingers flowed over the voices – and the world went drowning down through a siren stranger's vision of grass and waterbeasts and snow. The world was sucked to the last lake's drop; the cataract of the last particle worried in a lather to the ground, as if the rain from heaven had let its clouds fall turtle-turning like a manna made of the soft-bellied seasons, and the hard hail, falling, spread and flustered in a cloud half flower half ash or the comb-footed scavenger's wind through a pyramid raised high with mud or the soft slow drift of mingling steam and leaves. In the exact centre of enchantment he was a shoreman in deep sea, lashed by his hair to the eye in the cyclop breast, with his swept thighs strung among her voice; white bears swam and sailors drowned to the music she scaled and drew with hands and fables from his upright hair; she plucked his terror by the ears, and bore him singing into light through the forest of the serpent-haired and the stone-turning voice. Revelation stared back over its transfixed shoulder. Which was her genesis, the last spark of judgment or the first whale's spout from the waterland? The conflagration at the end, a burial fire jumping, a spent rocket hot on its tail, or, where the first spring and its folly climbed the sea barriers and the garden locks were bruised, capped and douting water over the mountain candle-head? Whose was the image in the wind, the print on the cliff, the echo knocking to be answered? She was orioled and serpent-haired. She moved in the swallowing, salty field, the chronicle and the rocks, the dark anatomies, the anchored sea itself. She raged in the mule's womb. She faltered in the galloping dynasty. She was loud in the old grave, kept a still, quick tongue in the sun. He marked her outcast image, mapped with a nightmare's foot in poison and framed against the wind, print of her thumb that buckled on its hand with a webbed shadow, interrogation of the familiar echo: which is my genesis, the granite fountain extinguishing where the first flame is cast in the sculptured world, or the bonfire maned like a lion in the threshold of the last vault? One voice then in that evening travelled the light and water waves, one lineament took on the sliding moods, from where the gold green sea cantharis dyes the trail of the octopus one venom crawled through foam, and from the four map corners one cherub in an island shape puffed the clouds to sea.

AN ADVENTURE FROM A WORK
IN PROGRESS

The boat tugged its anchor, and the anchor flew up from the seabed like an iron arrow and hung poised in a new wind and pointed over the corkscrew channels of the sea to the dark holes and caves in the horizon. He saw birds searing out of the pitted distance blind by his anchor as he swam with a seal at his side to the boat that stamped the water. He gripped on the bows like a mane, the arrowing anchor shot north, and the boat sped beneath it with winds and invisible fire puffing and licking. His animal boat split the water into a thousand boatsized seas, bit deep into the flying shoals, halved and multiplied the flying fishes, it dived under waves like a wooden dolphin and wagged the fingering wrack off its stern, it swerved past a black and gold buoy with cathedral chimes and kept cold north. Spray turned to ice as it whipped through his hair, and pierced his cheeks and eyelids, and the running blood froze hard. He saw through a coat of red ice that the sea was transparent; under his boat the drowned dead burned in a pale green, grass-high fire; the sea rained on the flames. But on through the north, between glass hills on which shebears climbed and saw themselves reflected, eating the sea between the paddling floes, a shell of lightning fibres skimming and darting under an anchor-bolt, tossed and magnified among the frozen window weeds, through a slow snow-storm whose flakes fell like hills one at a time down the white air, lost in a round sudden house of the six year night and slipping through an arch of sleeping birds each roosted on an icicle, the boat came into blue water. Birds with blue feathers set alight by the sun, with live flames for their crests, flew by the hovering anchor to the trees and bushes on the rims of soft sand round the sea that brushed his boat slowly and whispered it like a name in letters of parting water towards a harbour grove and a slowly spinning island with lizards in its lap. The salmon of the still sail turned to the blue of the birds' eggs in the tips of the fringing forest of each wave. The feathers crackled from the birds and drifted down and fell upon bare rods and stalks that fenced the island entrance, the rods and stalks grew into trees with musical leaves still burning. The history of the boat was spelt in knocking water on the hanging harbour bank; each syllable of his adventure struck on grass and stone and rang out in the passages of the disturbed rock-plants and was chattered from flame to tree. The anchor dived to rest. He strode through the blazing fence. The print of the ice was melting. The island spun. He saw between trees a tall woman standing on the opposite bank. He ran directly towards her but the green thighs closed. He ran on the rim towards her but she was still the same distance from him on the roundabout island. Time was about to fall; it had slept without sound under and over the blaze and spinning; now it was raised ready. Flowers in the centre of the island caught its tears in a cup. It hardened and shouted and shone in dead echoes and pearls. It fell as he ran on the outer rim, and oaks were felled in the acorn and lizards laid in the shell. He held the woman drowning in his arms, her driftwood limbs, her winking ballast head of glass; he fought with her blood like a man with a waterfall turning to fishdust and ash, and her salvaged seaweed hair twisted blindly about his eyes. The boat with anchor hovering and finned oars trembling for water after land, the beaks at the stern gabbling and the shells alive, was blown alongside him, by a wind that took a corner on one breath, from the harbour bank where roots of trees drove up the sky and foliage in cinders smouldered down, the lopped leg of a bird scratched against rock, a thundering cave sat upright and bolted mouthdown into the sea; he dipped the gills of the oars, the cedarmast shook like a cloth, warm north the boat sped off again from an island no longer spinning but split into vanishing caves and contrary trees. Time that had fallen rested in the edges of its knives and the hammock of its fires, the memory of the woman was strong on his hands, her claws and anemones, weedwrack and urchin hair, the sea was deserted and colourless, direction was dead as the island and north was a circle, a bird above the anchor spurted through a stationary cloud to catch its cry, the boat with gilled oars swimming ploughed through the foam in the wake, her pale brow glistened in the new moon of his nails and the drenched thread of her nerves sprang up and down behind them, the stern beaks quacked and yawned, crabs clacked from the shells, a mist rose up that dressed and unshaped the sky and the sea flowed in secret. Through the mist, dragging a black weather with it, a spade-shaped shoal of clouds tacked to its peak, a broken moon, a wind with trumpets, came a mountain in a moment. The boat struck rock. The beaks were still. The shells snapped shut. He leaped into mud as the wind cried his name to the flapping shoals; his name rolled down the mountain, echoed through caves and crevices, ducked in venomous pools, slap on black walls, translated into the voice of dying stone, growling through slime into silence. He gazed at the mountain peak; a cloud obscured it, cords of light from the moon were looped around the tentacles of the crags. Lightning with a horn and bone on, with gristle white as a spine hardening and halving the forked sides, struck through the tacked cloud cap, lit the stone head, scorched the mist-curled fringe, cut through the cords until the moon sailed upwards like a kite. With the turning out of the lightning, the jackknife doubling up of the limp spine, the weather in tow rocked to work and flight in a sealed air, the mountain vanished leaving a hole in space to keep the shape of his horror as he sank, as the monuments of the dark mud toppled and his raised arms were cemented against rock with the wet maggot sacks and the mixed, crawling beasts of statues and creatures who once stood on the ledges of the mountain foot or blocked the crying mouths of caves. The wind, blowing matter with a noise, stuck to his cheek. The sea climbed his limbs like a sailor. Bound and drowning in that dismembered masonry, his eyes on a level with the shuffled circle of headpieces floating, he saw the lightning dart to strike again, and the horned bone stiffen among the forks; hope, like another muscle, broke the embraces of the nuzzling bodies, thrust off the face that death-masked his, for the mountain appeared on the strike of light and the hollow shape of his horror was filled with crags and turrets, rock webs and dens, spinning black balconies, the loud packed smashing of separate seas, and the abominable substances of a new colour. The world happened at once. There was the furnished mountain built in a flash and thunderclap colliding. The shapes of rain falling made a new noise and number. And the lightning stayed striking; its charted shaft of sawteeth struck and bit in continual light; one blind flash was a year of mornings. The mummyfolds, the mudpots, the wet masks, the quick casts, the closing sheathes, melted under the frostbite heat of that unwinking lightning. He boxed free from the statues and the caved and toppling watchers. From a man-sized dent in a melting thigh he came up strung with shells and mussed with weed like a child from the roots of the original sea into a dazzling bed. Once on hard land, with shells that swung from his hair ringing from the tail of a weed, and shells repeating the sea, he shook away calamity, bounced the weeds off his bare breast, threw back his head until the pealing shells took in their echo the voices of all miscellaneous water, and grappled with the mountainside. His shadow led and beckoned; he turned curves of the eel-backed paths, his shadow pointed to the footprints that appeared before his feet; he followed where his footprints led, saw the smudged outline of his hand on a wet stone as he quarrelled with stones and trees towards it up an attacking valley; animals closed their lips round the shout of a wind walking by and scooped his name to welcome it up hollow trunks and walls. He followed the flight of his name: it slipped to a stop at the peak: there a tall woman caught the flying name to her lips. He flourished in the middle of the pain of the mountain and joy sped with his shadow, the strong memory of the driftwrack woman was dead on his hands digging deep in the soil towards this stranger tall as a pulled tree and whiter at that great shortening distance than the lightning-coloured sea a hundred dangers below. The thighs smooth as groundstone and sensual cleft, limpet eye and musselmouth, the white boulders bent, blue shadows and pricked berries, the torrential flowers and blacks of the bush on the skull and the muffed pits, the draped cellars, the lashed stones, the creased face on the knees, all for a moment while he stood in love were still and near. Then slowly her peak in a cloud's alcove – carved animals on an abbey, wind in an amice, arching accusing her – rose with his lovely dashing from stillness. Slowly her peak got up the cloudy arches, the stones he stumbled on followed her at the same speed. Though he hugged like a bear and climbed fast, she kept her distance from him. The mountain in the intervals of his breathing grew many times its size until time fell and cut and burned it down. The peak collapsed, the mountain folded, he clasped the woman diminishing in his arms; the downpours of her hair were short falls, her limbs stunted, her hands blunt, her teeth were small and square as dice and the rot marked them. A halo cracked like china, wings were spoked. Blood flapped behind all the windows of the world. And with the wasting of her limbs suddenly she grew young. Holding her small body, he cried in the nightmare of a naked child kissing and blaspheming close, breasts small as pears with milk foaming from them, the innocent holes of the open eyes, the thin, rouged musselmouth, when the head falls, the eyes loll, the small throat snaps, and the headless child lies loving in the dark. The mad bug trotted in at the ear with the whole earth on a feeler. With his cries she caved in younger. He held her hard. The marrow in her bones was soft as syrup. From a scar in the peak came a shadow with black gamp and scarlet basin. She dangled there with bald and monstrous skull, bunched monkey face and soaked abdominal tail. Out of the webbed sea-pig and water-nudging fish a white pool spat in his palm. Reeling to run seaward and away, he trod the flats of waves. The splintered claw of a crab struck from the killed hindershells. And, after the anchor burrowing through blind cloud, he rowed and sailed, that the world might happen to him once, past the events of revolving islands and elastic hills, on the common sea.

PORTRAIT OF THE ARTIST
AS A YOUNG DOG*

* The title under which the following ten stories were first printed together.

THE PEACHES

The grass-green cart, with 'J. Jones, Gorsehill' painted shakily on it, stopped in the cobblestone passage between 'The Hare's Foot' and 'The Pure Drop.' It was late on an April evening. Uncle Jim, in his black market suit with a stiff white shirt and no collar, loud new boots, and a plaid cap, creaked and climbed down. He dragged out a thick wicker basket from a heap of straw in the corner of the cart and swung it over his shoulder. I heard a squeal from the basket and saw the tip of a pink tail curling out as Uncle Jim opened the public door of 'The Pure Drop.'

'I won't be two minutes,' he said to me. The bar was full; two fat women in bright dresses sat near the door, one with a small dark child on her knee; they saw Uncle Jim and nudged up on the bench.

'I'll be out straight away,' he said fiercely, as though I had contradicted him, 'you stay there quiet.'

The woman without the child raised up her hands. 'Oh, Mr Jones,' she said in a high laughing voice. She shook like a jelly.

Then the door closed and the voices were muffled.

I sat alone on the shaft of the cart in the narrow passage, staring through a side window of 'The Hare's Foot.' A stained blind was drawn half over it. I could see into half of a smoky, secret room, where four men were playing cards. One man was huge and swarthy, with a handlebar moustache and a love-curl on his forehead; seated by his side was a thin, bald, pale old man, with his cheeks in his mouth; the faces of the other two were in shadow. They all drank out of brown pint tankards and never spoke, laying the cards down with a smack, scraping at their match-boxes, puffing at their pipes, swallowing unhappily, ringing the brass bell, ordering more, by a sign of the fingers, from a sour woman with a flowered blouse and a man's cap.

The passage grew dark too suddenly, the walls crowded in, and the roofs crouched down. To me, staring timidly there in the dark passage in a strange town, the swarthy man appeared like a giant in a cage surrounded by clouds, and the bald old man withered into a black hump with a white top; two white hands darted out of the corner with invisible cards. A man with spring-heeled boots and a two-edged knife might be bouncing towards me from Union Street.

I called, 'Uncle Jim, Uncle Jim,' softly so that he should not hear.

I began to whistle between my teeth, but when I stopped I thought the sound went hissing on behind me. I climbed down from the shaft and stepped close to the half-blind window; a hand clawed up the pane to the tassel of the blind; in the little, packed space between me on the cobbles and the card-players at the table, I could not tell which side of the glass was the hand that dragged the blind down slowly. I was cut from the night by a stained square. A story I had made in the warm, safe island of my bed, with sleepy midnight Swansea flowing and rolling round outside the house, came blowing down to me then with a noise on the cobbles. I remembered the demon in the story, with his wings and hooks, who clung like a bat to my hair as I battled up and down Wales after a tall, wise, golden, royal girl from Swansea convent. I tried to remember her true name, her proper, long, black-stockinged legs, her giggle and paper curls, but the hooked wings tore at me and the colour of her hair and eyes faded and vanished like the grass-green of the cart that was a dark, grey mountain now standing between the passage walls.

And all this time the old, broad, patient, nameless mare stood without stirring, not stamping once on the cobbles or shaking her reins. I called her a good girl and stood on tiptoe to try to stroke her ears as the door of 'The Pure Drop' swung open and the warm lamplight from the bar dazzled me and burned my story up. I felt frightened no longer, only angry and hungry. The two fat women near the door giggled 'Good night, Mr Jones' out of the rich noise and the comfortable smells. The child lay curled asleep under the bench. Uncle Jim kissed the two women on the lips.

'Good night.'
'Good night.'
'Good night.'
Then the passage was dark again.
He backed the mare into Union Street, lurching against her

side, cursing her patience and patting her nose, and we both climbed into the cart.

'There are too many drunken gipsies,' he said as we rolled and rattled through the flickering lamp-lit town.

He sang hymns all the way to Gorsehill in an affectionate bass voice, and conducted the wind with his whip. He did not need to touch the reins. Once on the rough road, between hedges twisting out to twig the mare by the bridle and poke our caps, we stopped at a whispered 'Whoa,' for uncle to light his pipe and set the darkness on fire and show his long, red, drunken fox's face to me, with its bristling side-bushes and wet, sensitive nose. A white house with a light in one bedroom window shone in a field on a short hill beyond the road.

Uncle whispered, 'Easy, easy, girl,' to the mare, though she was standing calmly, and said to me over his shoulder in a suddenly loud voice : 'A hangman lived there.'

He stamped on the shaft, and we rattled on through a cutting wind. Uncle shivered, pulling down his cap to hide his ears ; but the mare was like a clumsy statue trotting, and all the demons of my stories, if they trotted by her side or crowded together and grinned into her eyes, would not make her shake her head or hurry.

'I wish he'd have hung Mrs Jesus,' uncle said.

Between hymns he cursed the mare in Welsh. The white house was left behind, the light and the hill were swallowed up.

'Nobody lives there now,' he said.

We drove into the farm-yard of Gorsehill, where the cobbles rang and the black, empty stables took up the ringing and hollowed it so that we drew up in a hollow circle of darkness and the mare was a hollow animal and nothing lived in the hollow house at the end of the yard but two sticks with faces scooped out of turnips.

'You run and see Annie,' said uncle. 'There'll be hot broth and potatoes.'

He led the hollow, shappy statue towards the stable ; clop, clop to the mice-house. I heard locks rattle as I ran to the farm-house door.

The front of the house was the single side of a black shell, and the arched door was the listening ear. I pushed the door open and walked into the passage out of the wind. I might have been walking into the hollow night and the wind, passing through a tall vertical shell on an island sea-shore. Then a door at the end of the passage opened; I saw the plates on the shelves, the lighted lamp on the long, oil-clothed table, 'Prepare to Meet Thy God' knitted over the fire-place, the smiling china dogs, the brown-stained settle, the grandmother clock, and I ran into the kitchen and into Annie's arms.

There was a welcome, then. The clock struck twelve as she kissed me, and I stood among the shining and striking like a prince taking off his disguise. One minute I was small and cold, skulking dead-scared down a black passage in my stiff, best suit, with my hollow belly thumping and my heart like a time bomb, clutching my grammar school cap, unfamiliar to myself, a snub-nosed story-teller lost in his own adventures and longing to be home; the next I was a royal nephew in smart town clothes, embraced and welcomed, standing in the snug centre of my stories and listening to the clock announcing me. She hurried me to the seat in the side of the cavernous fireplace and took off my shoes. The bright lamps and the ceremonial gongs blazed and rang for me.

She made a mustard bath and strong tea, told me to put on a pair of my cousin Gwilym's socks and an old coat of uncle's that smelt of rabbit and tobacco. She fussed and clucked and nodded and told me, as she cut bread and butter, how Gwilym was still studying to be a minister, and how Aunt Rach Morgan, who was ninety years old, had fallen on her belly on a scythe.

Then Uncle Jim came in like the devil with a red face and a wet nose and trembling, hairy hands. His walk was thick. He stumbled against the dresser and shook the coronation plates, and a lean cat shot booted out from the settle corner. Uncle looked nearly twice as tall as Annie. He could have carried her about under his coat and brought her out suddenly, a little, brown-skinned, toothless, hunchbacked woman with a cracked sing-song voice.

'You shouldn't have kept him out so long,' she said, angry and timid.

He sat down in his special chair, which was the broken throne of a bankrupt bard, and lit his pipe and stretched his legs and puffed clouds at the ceiling.

'He might catch his death of cold,' she said.

She talked at the back of his head while he wrapped himself in clouds. The cat slunk back. I sat at the table with my supper finished, and found a little empty bottle and a white balloon in the pockets of my coat.

'Run off to bed, there's a dear,' Annie whispered.

'Can I go and look at the pigs?'

'In the morning, dear,' she said.

So I said good night to Uncle Jim, who turned and smiled at me and winked through the smoke, and I kissed Annie and lit my candle.

'Good night.'

'Good night.'

'Good night.'

I climbed the stairs; each had a different voice. The house smelt of rotten wood and damp and animals. I thought that I had been walking long, damp passages all my life, and climbing stairs in the dark, alone. I stopped outside Gwilym's door on the draughty landing.

'Good night.'

The candle flame jumped in my bedroom where a lamp was burning very low, and the curtains waved; the water in a glass on a round table by the bed stirred, I thought, as the door closed, and lapped against the sides. There was a stream below the window; I thought it lapped against the house all night until I slept.

'Can I go and see the pigs?' I asked Gwilym next morning. The hollow fear of the house was gone, and, running downstairs to my breakfast, I smelt the sweetness of wood and the fresh spring grass and the quiet untidy farm-yard, with its tumble-down dirty-white cow-house and empty stables open.

Gwilym was a tall young man aged nearly twenty, with a thin stick of a body and spade-shaped face. You could dig the garden with him. He had a deep voice that cracked in half when he was excited, and he sang songs to himself, treble and bass, with the same sad hymn tune, and wrote hymns in the barn. He told me stories about girls who died for love. 'And she put a rope round the tree but it was too short,' he said; 'she stuck a pen-knife in her bosoms but it was too blunt.' We were sitting together on the straw heaps that day in the half-dark of the shuttered stable. He twisted and leaned near to me, raising his big finger, and the straw creaked.

'She jumped in the cold river, she jumped,' he said, his mouth against my ear, 'arse over tip and Diu, she was dead.' He squeaked like a bat.

The pigsties were at the far end of the yard. We walked towards them, Gwilym dressed in minister's black, though it was a weekday morning, and me in a serge suit with a darned bottom, past three hens scrabbling the muddy cobbles and a collie with one eye, sleeping with it open. The ramshackle outhouses had tumbling, rotten roofs, jagged holes in their sides, broken shutters, and peeling whitewash; rusty screws ripped out from the dangling, crooked boards; the lean cat of the night before sat snugly between the splintered jaws of bottles cleaning its face, on the tip of the rubbish pile that rose triangular and smelling sweet and strong to the level of the riddled cart-house roof. There was nowhere like that farm-yard in all the slapdash county, nowhere so poor and grand and dirty as that square of mud and rubbish and bad wood and falling stone, where a bucketful of old and bedraggled hens scratched and laid small eggs. A duck quacked out of the trough in one deserted sty. Now a young man and a curly boy stood staring and sniffing over a wall at a sow, with its tits on the mud, giving suck.

'How many pigs are there?'

'Five. The bitch ate one,' said Gwilym.

We counted them as they squirmed and wriggled, rolled on their backs and bellies, edged and pinched and pushed and squealed about their mother. There were four. We counted again. Four pigs, four naked pink tails curling up as their mouths guzzled down and the sow grunted with pain and joy.

She must have ate another,' I said, and picked up a scratching stick and prodded the grunting sow and rubbed her crusted bristles backwards. 'Or a fox jumped over the wall,' I said.

'It wasn't the sow or the fox,' said Gwilym. 'It was father.'

I could see uncle, tall and sly and red, holding the writhing pig in his two hairy hands, sinking his teeth in its thigh, crunching its trotters up: I could see him leaning over the wall of the sty with the pig's legs sticking out of his mouth. 'Did Uncle Jim eat the pig?'

Now, at this minute, behind the rotting sheds, he was standing, knee-deep in feathers, chewing off the live heads of the poultry.

'He sold it to go on the drink,' said Gwilym in his deepest

rebuking whisper, his eyes fixed on the sty. 'Last Christmas he took a sheep over his shoulder, and he was pissed for ten days.'

The sow rolled nearer the scratching stick, and the small pigs sucking at her, lost and squealing in the sudden darkness, struggled under her folds and pouches.

'Come and see my chapel,' said Gwilym. He forgot the lost pig at once and began to talk about the towns he had visited on a religious tour, Neath and Bridgend and Bristol and Newport, with their lakes and luxury gardens, their bright, coloured streets roaring with temptation. We walked away from the sty and the disappointed sow.

'I met actress after actress,' he said.

Gwilym's chapel was the last old barn before the field that led down to the river; it stood well above the farm-yard, on a mucky hill. There was one whole door with a heavy padlock, but you could get in easily through the holes on either side of it. He took out a ring of keys and shook them gently and tried each one in the lock. 'Very posh,' he said; 'I bought them from the junk-shop in Carmarthen.' We climbed into the chapel through a hole.

A dusty wagon with the name painted out and a white-wash cross on its side stood in the middle. 'My pulpit cart,' he said, and walked solemnly into it up the broken shaft. 'You sit on the hay; mind the mice,' he said. Then he brought out his deepest voice again, and cried to the heavens and the bat-lined rafters and the hanging webs: 'Bless us this holy day, O Lord, bless me and Dylan and this Thy little chapel for ever and ever, Amen. I've done a lot of improvements to this place.'

I sat on the hay and stared at Gwilym preaching, and heard his voice rise and crack and sink to a whisper and break into singing and Welsh and ring triumphantly and be wild and meek. The sun through a hole, shone on his praying shoulders, and he said: 'O God, Thou art everywhere all the time, in the dew of the morning, in the frost of the evening, in the field and the town, in the preacher and the sinner, in the sparrow and the big buzzard. Thou canst see everything, right down deep in our hearts; Thou canst see us when the sun is gone; Thou canst see us when there aren't any stars, in the gravy blackness, in the deep, deep, deep, deep pit; Thou canst see and spy and watch us all the time, in the little black corners, in the big cowboys' prairies, under the blankets when we're snoring fast, in the terrible shadows; pitch black, pitch black; Thou canst see everything we do, in the night and day, in the day and the night, everything, everything; Thou canst see all the time. O God, mun, you're like a bloody cat.'

He let his clasped hands fall. The chapel in the barn was still, and shafted with sunlight. There was nobody to cry Hallelujah or God-bless; I was too small and enamoured in the silence. The one duck quacked outside.

'Now I take a collection,' Gwilym said.

He stepped down from the cart and groped about in the hay beneath it and held out a battered tin to me.

'I haven't got a proper box,' he said.

I put two pennies in the tin.

'It's time for dinner,' he said, and we went back to the house without a word.

Annie said, when we had finished dinner: 'Put on your nice suit for this afternoon. The one with stripes.'

It was to be a special afternoon, for my best friend, Jack Williams, from Swansea, was coming down with his rich mother in a motor car, and Jack was to spend a fortnight's holiday with me.

'Where's Uncle Jim?'

'He's gone to market,' said Annie.

Gwilym made a small pig's noise. We knew where uncle was; he was sitting in a public house with a heifer over his shoulder and two pigs nosing out of his pockets, and his lips wet with bull's blood.

'Is Mrs Williams very rich?' asked Gwilym.

I told him she had three motors cars and two houses, which was a lie. 'She's the richest woman in Wales, and once she was a mayoress,' I said. 'Are we going to have tea in the best room?'

Annie nodded. 'And a large tin of peaches,' she said.

'That old tin's been in the cupboard since Christmas,' said Gwilym, 'mother's been keeping it for a day like this.'

'They're lovely peaches,' Annie said. She went upstairs to dress like Sunday.

The best room smelt of moth balls and fur and damp and dead plants and stale, sour air. Two glass cases on wooden coffin-boxes lined the window wall. You looked at the weed-grown vegetable garden through a stuffed fox's legs, over a partridge's head, along the red-paint-stained breast of a stiff wild duck. A case of china and pewter, trinkets, teeth, family brooches, stood beyond the bandy table; there was a large oil lamp on the patchwork table-cloth, a Bible with a clasp, a tall vase with a draped woman about to bathe on it, and a framed photograph of Annie, Uncle Jim, and Gwilym smiling in front of a fern-pot. On the mantelpiece were two clocks, some dogs, brass candlesticks, a shepherdess, a man in a kilt, and a tinted photograph of Annie, with high hair and her breasts coming out. There were chairs around the table and in each corner, straight, curved, stained, padded, all with lace cloths hanging over their backs. A patched white sheet shrouded the harmonium. The fireplace was full of brass tongs, shovels, and pokers. The best room was rarely used. Annie dusted and brushed and polished there once a week, but the carpet still sent up a grey cloud when you trod on it, and dust lay evenly on the seats of the chairs, and balls of cotton and dirt and black stuffing and long black horse hairs were wedged in the cracks of the sofa. I blew on the glass to see the pictures. Gwilym and castles and cattle.

'Change your suit now,' said Gwilym.

I wanted to wear my old suit, to look like a proper farm boy and have manure in my shoes and hear it squelch as I walked, to see a cow have calves and a bull on top of a cow, to run down in the dingle and wet my stockings, to go out and shout, 'Come on, you b—,' and pelt the hens and talk in a proper voice. But I went upstairs to put my striped suit on.

From my bedroom I heard the noise of a motor car drawing up the yard. It was Jack Williams and his mother.

Gwilym shouted, 'They're here, in a Daimler!' from the foot of the stairs, and I ran down to meet them with my tie undone and my hair uncombed.

Annie was saying at the door: 'Good afternoon, Mrs Williams, good afternoon. Come right in, it's a lovely day, Mrs Williams. Did you have a nice journey then? This way, Mrs Williams, mind the step.'

Annie wore a black, shining dress that smelt of moth balls, like the chair covers in the best room; she had forgotten to change her gym-shoes, which were caked with mud and all holes. She fussed on before Mrs Williams down the stone passage, darting her head round, clucking, fidgeting, excusing the small house, anxiously tidying her hair with one rough, stubby hand.

Mrs Williams was tall and stout, with a jutting bosom and thick legs, her ankles swollen over her pointed shoes; she was fitted out like a mayoress or a ship, and she swayed after Annie into the best room.

She said: 'Please don't put yourself out for me, Mrs Jones, there's a dear.' She dusted the seat of a chair with a lace handkerchief from her bag before sitting down.

'I can't stop, you know,' she said.

'Oh, you must stay for a cup of tea,' said Annie, shifting and scraping the chairs away from the table so that nobody could move and Mrs Williams was hemmed in fast with her bosom and her rings and her bag, opening the china cupboard, upsetting the Bible on the floor, picking it up, dusting it hurriedly with her sleeve.

'And peaches,' Gwilym said. He was standing in the passage with his hat on.

Annie said, 'Take your hat off, Gwilym, make Mrs Williams comfortable,' and she put the lamp on the shrouded harmonium and spread out a white table-cloth that had a tea stain in the centre, and brought out the china and laid knives and cups for five.

'Don't bother about me, there's a dear,' said Mrs Williams. 'There's a lovely fox!' She flashed a finger of rings at the glass case.

'It's real blood,' I told Jack, and we climbed over the sofa to the table.

'No, it isn't,' he said, 'it's red ink.'

'Oh, your shoes!' said Annie.

'Don't tread on the sofa, Jack, there's a dear.'

'If it isn't ink it's paint then.'

Gwilym said, 'Shall I get you a bit of cake, Mrs Williams?'

Annie rattled the tea-cups. 'There isn't a single bit of cake in the house,' said she; 'we forgot to order it from the shop; not a single bit. Oh, Mrs Williams!'

Mrs Williams said: 'Just a cup of tea thanks.' She was still sweating because she had walked all the way from the car. It spoiled her powder. She sparkled her rings and dabbed at her face.

'Three lumps,' she said. 'And I'm sure Jack will be very happy here.'

'Happy as sandboys,' Gwilym sat down.

'Now you must have some peaches, Mrs Williams, they're lovely.'

'They should be, they've been here long enough,' said Gwilym. Annie rattled the tea-cups at him again.

'No peaches, thanks,' Mrs Williams said.

'Oh, you must, Mrs Williams, just one. With cream.'

'No, no, Mrs Jones, thanks the same,' she said. 'I don't mind pears or chunks, but I can't bear peaches.'

Jack and I had stopped talking. Annie stared down at her gym-shoes. One of the clocks on the mantelpiece coughed, and struck. Mrs Williams struggled from her chair.

'There, time flies !' she said.

She pushed her way past the furniture, jostled against the sideboard, rattled the trinkets and brooches, and kissed Jack on the forehead.

'You've got scent on,' he said.

She patted my head.

'Now behave yourselves.'

To Annie, she said in a whisper : 'And remember, Mrs Jones, just good plain food. No spoiling his appetite.'

Annie followed her out of the room. She moved slowly now. 'I'll do my very best, Mrs Williams.'

We heard her say, 'Good-bye then, Mrs Williams,' and go down the steps of the kitchen and close the door. The motor car roared in the yard, then the noise grew softer and died.

Down the thick dingle Jack and I ran shouting, scalping the brambles with our thin stick-hatchets, dancing, hallooing. We skidded to a stop and prowled on the bushy banks of the stream. Up above, sat one-eyed, dead-eyed, sinister, slim, ten-notched Gwilym, loading his guns in Gallows Farm. We crawled and rat-tatted through the bushes, hid, at a whistled signal, in the deep grass, and crouched there, waiting for the crack of a twig or the secret breaking of boughs.

On my haunches, eager and alone, casting an ebony shadow, with the Gorsehill jungle swarming, the violent, impossible birds and fishes leaping, hidden under four-stemmed flowers the height of horses, in the early evening in a dingle near Carmar-then, my friend Jack Williams invisibly near me, I felt all my young body like an excited animal surrounding me, the torn knees bent, the bumping heart, the long heat and depth between the legs, the sweat prickling in the hands, the tunnels down to the eardrums, the little balls of dirt between the toes, the eyes in the sockets, the tucked-up voice, the blood racing, the memory around and within flying, jumping, swimming, and waiting to pounce. There, playing Indians in the evening, I was aware of me myself in the exact middle of a living story, and my body was my adventure and my name. I sprang with excitement and scrambled up through the scratching brambles again.

Jack cried: 'I see you! I see you!' He scampered after me. 'Bang! bang! you're dead!'

But I was young and loud and alive, though I lay down obediently.

'Now you try and kill me,' said Jack. 'Count a hundred.'

I closed one eye, saw him rush and stamp towards the upper field, then tiptoe back and begin to climb a tree, and I counted fifty and ran to the foot of the tree and killed him as he climbed. 'You fall down,' I said.

He refused to fall, so I climbed too, and we clung to the top branches and stared down at the lavatory in the corner of the field. Gwilym was sitting on the seat with his trousers down. He looked small and black. He was reading a book and moving his hands.

'We can see you!' we shouted.

He snatched his trousers up and put the book in his pocket.

'We can see you, Gwilym!'

He came out into the field. 'Where are you, then?'

We waved our caps at him.

'In the sky!' Jack shouted.

'Flying!' I shouted.

We stretched our arms out like wings.

'Fly down here.'

We swung and laughed on the branches.

'There's birds!' cried Gwilym.

Our jackets were torn and our stockings were wet and our shoes were sticky; we had green moss and brown bark on our hands and faces when we went in for supper and a scolding. Annie was quiet that night, though she called me a ragamuffin and said she didn't know what Mrs Williams would think and told Gwilym he should know better. We made faces at Gwilym and put salt in his tea, but after supper he said: 'You can come to the chapel if you like. Just before bed.'

He lit a candle on the top of the pulpit cart. It was a small light in the big barn. The bats were gone. Shadows still clung upside down along the roof. Gwilym was no longer my cousin in a Sunday suit, but a tall stranger shaped like a spade in a cloak, and his voice grew too deep. The straw heaps were lively. I thought of the sermon on the cart: we were watched, Jack's heart was watched, Gwilym's tongue was marked down, my whisper, 'Look at the little eyes,' was remembered always.

'Now I take confessions,' said Gwilym from the cart.

Jack and I stood bareheaded in the circle of the candle, and I could feel the trembling of Jack's body.

'You first.' Gwilym's finger, as bright as though he had held it in the candle flame until it burned, pointed me out, and I took a step towards the pulpit cart, raising my head.

'Now you confess,' said Gwilym.

'What have I got to confess?'

'The worst thing you've done.'

I let Edgar Reynolds be whipped because I had taken his homework; I stole from my mother's bag; I stole from Gwyneth's bag; I stole twelve books in three visits from the library, and threw them away in the park; I drank a cup of my water to see what it tasted like; I beat a dog with a stick so that it would roll over and lick my hand afterwards; I looked with Dan Jones through the keyhole while his maid had a bath; I cut my knee with a penknife, and put the blood on my handkerchief and said it had come out of my ears so that I could pretend I was ill and frighten my mother; I pulled my trousers down and showed Jack Williams; I saw Billy Jones beat a pigeon to death with a fire-shovel, and laughed and got sick; Cedric Williams and I broke into Mrs Samuels' house and poured ink over the bedclothes.

I said: 'I haven't done anything bad.'

'Go on, confess,' said Gwilym. He was frowning down at me.

'I can't! I can't!' I said. 'I haven't done anything bad.'

'Go on, confess!'

'I won't! I won't!'

Jack began to cry. 'I want to go home,' he said.

Gwilym opened the chapel door and we followed him into the yard, down past the black, humped sheds, towards the house, and Jack sobbed all the way.

In bed together, Jack and I confessed our sins.

'I steal from my mother's bag, too; there are pounds and pounds.'

'How much do you steal?'

'Threepence.'

'I killed a man once.'

'No you didn't then.'

'Honest to Christ, I shot him through the heart.'

'What was his name?'

'Williams.'

'Did he bleed?'

I thought the stream was lapping against the house.

'Like a bloody pig,' I said.

Jack's tears had dried. 'I don't like Gwilym, he's barmy.'

'No he isn't. I found a lot of poems in his bedroom once. They were all written to girls. And he showed them to me afterwards, and he'd changed all the girls' names to God.'

'He's religious.'

'No, he isn't, he goes with actresses. He knows Corinne Griffith.'

Our door was open. I liked the door locked at night, because I would rather have a ghost in the bedroom than think of one coming in; but Jack liked it open, and we tossed and he won. We heard the front door rattle and footsteps in the kitchen passage.

'That's Uncle Jim.'

'What's he like?'

'He's like a fox, he eats pigs and chickens.'

The ceiling was thin and we heard every sound, the creaking of the bard's chair, the clatter of plates, Annie's voice saying: 'Midnight!'

'He's drunk,' I said. We lay quite still, hoping to hear a quarrel.

'Perhaps he'll throw plates,' I said.

But Annie scolded him softly. 'There's a fine state, Jim.'

He murmured to her.

'There's one pig gone,' she said. 'Oh, why do you have to do it, Jim? There's nothing left now. We'll never be able to carry on.'

'Money! money! money!' he said. I knew he would be lighting his pipe.

Then Annie's voice grew so soft we could not hear the words, and uncle said: 'Did she pay you the thirty shillings?'

'They're talking about your mother,' I told Jack.

For a long time Annie spoke in a low voice, and we waited for words. 'Mrs Williams,' she said, and 'motor car,' and 'Jack,' and 'peaches.' I thought she was crying for her voice broke on the last word.

Uncle Jim's chair creaked again, he might have struck his fist on the table, and we heard him shout: 'I'll give her peaches! Peaches, peaches! Who does she think she is? Aren't peaches good enough for her? To hell with her bloody motor car and her bloody son! Making us small.'

'Don't, don't Jim!' Annie said, 'you'll wake the boys.'

'I'll wake them and whip the hell out of them, too!'

'Please, please, Jim!'

'You send the boy away,' he said, 'or I'll do it myself. Back to his three bloody houses.'

Jack pulled the bedclothes over his head and sobbed into the pillow: 'I don't want to hear, I don't want to hear, I'll write to my mother. She'll take me away.'

I climbed out to close the door. Jack would not talk to me again, and I fell asleep to the noise of the voices below, which soon grew gentle.

Uncle Jim was not at breakfast. When we came down, Jack's shoes were cleaned for him and his jacket was darned and pressed. Annie gave two boiled eggs to Jack and one to me. She forgave me when I drank tea from the saucer.

After breakfast, Jack walked to the post office. I took the one-eyed collie to chase rabbits in the upper fields, but it barked at ducks and brought me a tramp's shoe from a hedge, and lay down with its tail wagging in a rabbit hole. I threw stones at the deserted duck pond, and the collie ambled back with sticks.

Jack went skulking into the damp dingle, his hands in his pockets, his cap over one eye. I left the collie sniffing at a molehill, and climbed to the tree-top in the corner of the lavatory field. Below me, Jack was playing Indians all alone, scalping through the bushes, surprising himself round a tree, hiding from himself in the grass. I called to him once, but he pretended not to hear. He played alone, silently and savagely. I saw him standing with his hands in his pockets, swaying like a Kelly, on the mudbank by the stream at the foot of the dingle. My bough lurched, the heads of the dingle bushes spun up towards me like green tops, 'I'm falling!' I cried, my trousers saved me, I swung and grasped, this was one minute of wild adventure, but Jack did not look up and the minute was lost. I climbed, without dignity, to the ground.

Early in the afternoon, after a silent meal, when Gwilym was reading the scriptures or writing hymns to girls or sleeping in his chapel, Annie was baking bread, and I was cutting a wooden whistle in the loft over the stable, the motor car drove up in the yard again.

Out of the house Jack, in his best suit, ran to meet his mother, and I heard him say as she stepped, raising her short skirts, on to the cobbles: 'And he called you a bloody cow, and he said he'd whip the hell out of me, and Gwilym took me to the barn in the dark and let the mice run over me, and Dylan's a thief, and that old woman's spoilt my jacket.'

Mrs Williams sent the chauffeur for Jack's luggage. Annie came to the door, trying to smile and curtsy, tidying her hair, wiping her hands on her pinafore.

Mrs Williams said, 'Good afternoon,' and sat with Jack in the back of the car and stared at the ruin of Gorsehill.

The chauffeur came back. The car drove off, scattering the hens. I ran out of the stable to wave to Jack. He sat still and stiff by his mother's side. I waved my handkerchief.

A VISIT TO GRANDPA'S

In the middle of the night I woke from a dream full of whips and lariats as long as serpents, and runaway coaches on mountain passes, and wide, windy gallops over cactus fields, and I heard the man in the next room crying, 'Gee-up!' and 'Whoa!' and trotting his tongue on the roof of his mouth.

It was the first time I had stayed in grandpa's house. The floorboards had squeaked like mice as I climbed into bed, and the mice between the walls had creaked like wood as though another visitor was walking on them. It was a mild summer night, but curtains had flapped and branches beaten against the window. I had pulled the sheets over my head, and soon was roaring and riding in a book.

'Whoa there, my beauties!' cried grandpa. His voice sounded very young and loud, and his tongue had powerful hooves, and he made his bedroom into a great meadow. I thought I would see if he was ill, or had set his bedclothes on fire, for my mother had said that he lit his pipe under the blankets, and had warned me to run to his help if I smelt smoke in the night. I went on tiptoe through the darkness to his bedroom door, brushing against the furniture and upsetting a candlestick with a thump. When I saw there was a light in the room I felt frightened, and as I opened the door I heard grandpa shout, 'Gee-up!' as loudly as a bull with a megaphone.

He was sitting straight up in bed and rocking from side to side as though the bed were on a rough road; the knotted edges of the counterpane were his reins; his invisible horse stood in a shadow beyond the bedside candle. Over a white flannel nightshirt he was wearing a red waistcoat with walnut-sized brass buttons. The over-filled bowl of his pipe smouldered among his whiskers like a little, burning hayrick on a stick. At the sight of me, his hands dropped from the reins and lay blue and quiet, the bed stopped still on a level road, he muffled his tongue into silence, and the horses drew softly up.

'Is there anything the matter, grandpa?' I asked, though the clothes were not on fire. His face in the candlelight looked like a ragged quilt pinned upright on the black air and patched all over with goat-beards.

He stared at me mildly. Then he blew down his pipe, scattering the sparks and making a high, wet dog-whistle of the stem, and shouted: 'Ask no questions.'

After a pause, he said slyly: 'Do you ever have nightmares, boy?'

'I said: 'No.'

'Oh, yes, you do,' he said.

I said I was woken by a voice that was shouting to horses.

'What did I tell you?' he said. 'You eat too much. Who ever heard of horses in a bedroom?'

He fumbled under his pillow, brought out a small tinkling bag, and carefully untied its strings. He put a sovereign in my hand, and said: 'Buy a cake.' I thanked him and wished him good night.

As I closed my bedroom door, I heard his voice crying loudly and gaily, 'Gee-up! gee-up!' and the rocking of the travelling bed.

In the morning I woke from a dream of fiery horses on a plain that was littered with furniture, and of large, cloudy men who rode six horses at a time and whipped them with burning bedclothes. Grandpa was at breakfast, dressed in deep black. After breakfast he said, 'There was a terrible loud wind last night,' and sat in his arm-chair by the hearth to make clay balls for the fire. Later in the morning he took me for a walk, through Johnstown village and into the fields on the Llanstephan road.

A man with a whippet said, 'There's a nice morning, Mr Thomas,' and when he had gone, leanly as his dog, into the short-treed green wood he should not have entered because of the notices, grandpa said: 'There, do you hear what he called you? Mister!'

We passed by small cottages, and all the men who leant on the gates congratulated grandpa on the fine morning. We passed through the wood full of pigeons, and their wings broke the branches as they rushed to the tops of the trees. Among the soft, contented voices and the loud, timid flying, grandpa said, like a man calling across a field: 'If you heard those old birds in the night, you'd wake me up and say there were horses in the trees.'

We walked back slowly, for he was tired, and the lean man stalked out of the forbidden wood with a rabbit held as gently over his arm as a girl's arm in a warm sleeve.

On the last day but one of my visit I was taken to Llanstephan in a governess cart pulled by a short, weak pony. Grandpa might have been driving a bison, so tightly he held the reins, so ferociously cracked the long whip, so blasphemously shouted warning to boys who played in the road, so stoutly stood with his gaitered legs apart and cursed the demon strength and wilfulness of his tottering pony.

'Look out, boy!' he cried when we came to each corner, and pulled and tugged and jerked and sweated and waved his whip like a rubber sword. And when the pony had crept miserably round each corner, grandpa turned to me with a sighing smile: 'We weathered that one, boy.'

When we came to Llanstephan village at the top of the hill, he left the cart by the 'Edwinsford Arms' and patted the pony's muzzle and gave it sugar, saying: 'You're a weak little pony, Jim, to pull big men like us.'

He had strong beer and I had lemonade, and he paid Mrs Edwinsford with a sovereign out of the tinkling bag; she inquired after his health, and he said that Llangadock was better for the tubes. We went to look at the churchyard and the sea, and sat in the wood called the Sticks, and stood on the concert platform in the middle of the wood where visitors sang on midsummer nights and, year by year, the innocent of the village was elected mayor. Grandpa paused at the churchyard and pointed over the iron gate at the angelic headstones and the poor wooden crosses. 'There's no sense in lying there,' he said.

We journeyed back furiously: Jim was a bison again.

I woke late on my last morning, out of dreams where the Llanstephan sea carried bright sailing-boats as long as liners; and heavenly choirs in the Sticks, dressed in bards' robes and brass-buttoned waistcoats, sang in a strange Welsh to the departing sailors. Grandpa was not at breakfast; he rose early. I walked in the fields with a new sling, and shot at the Towy gulls and the rooks in the parsonage trees. A warm wind blew from the summer points of the weather; a morning mist climbed from the ground and floated among the trees and hid the noisy birds; in the mist and the wind my pebbles flew lightly up like hailstones in a world on its head. The morning passed without a bird falling.

I broke my sling and returned for the midday meal through the parson's orchard. Once, grandpa told me, the parson had bought three ducks at Carmarthen Fair and made a pond for them in the centre of the garden, but they waddled to the gutter under the crumbling doorsteps of the house, and swam and quacked there. When I reached the end of the orchard path, I looked through a hole in the hedge and saw that the parson had made a tunnel through the rockery that was between the gutter and the pond and had set up a notice in plain writing: 'This way to the pond.'

The ducks were still swimming under the steps.

Grandpa was not in the cottage. I went into the garden, but grandpa was not staring at the fruit-trees. I called across to a man who leant on a spade in the field beyond the garden hedge: 'Have you seen my grandpa this morning?'

He did not stop digging, and answered over his shoulder: 'I seen him in his fancy waistcoat.'

Griff, the barber, lived in the next cottage. I called to him through the open door: 'Mr Griff, have you seen my grandpa?'

The barber came out in his shirtsleeves.

I said: 'He's wearing his best waistcoat.' I did not know if it was important, but grandpa wore his waistcoat only in the night.

'Has grandpa been to Llanstephan?' asked Mr Griff anxiously.

'He went there yesterday in a little trap,' I said.

He hurried indoors and I heard him talking in Welsh, and he came out again with his white coat on, and he carried a striped and coloured walking-stick. He strode down the village street and I ran by his side.

When we stopped at the tailor's shop, he cried out, 'Dan!' and Dan Tailor stepped from his window where he sat like an Indian priest but wearing a derby hat. 'Dai Thomas has got his waistcoat on,' said Mr Griff, 'and he's been to Llanstephan.'

As Dan Tailor searched for his overcoat, Mr Griff was striding on. 'Will Evans,' he called outside the carpenter's shop, 'Dai Thomas has been to Llanstephan, and he's got his waistcoat on.'

'I'll tell Morgan now,' said the carpenter's wife out of the hammering, sawing darkness of the shop.

We called at the butcher's shop and Mr Price's house, and Mr Griff repeated his message like a town crier.

We gathered together in Johnstown square. Dan Tailor had his bicycle, Mr Price his pony trap. Mr Griff, the butcher, Morgan carpenter, and I climbed into the shaking trap, and we trotted off towards Carmarthen town. The tailor led the way, ringing his bell as though there were a fire or a robbery, and an old woman by the gate of a cottage at the end of the street ran inside like a pelted hen. Another woman waved a bright handkerchief.

'Where are we going?' I asked.

Grandpa's neighbours were as solemn as old men with black hats and jackets on the outskirts of a fair. Mr Griff shook his head and mourned: 'I didn't expect this again from Dai Thomas.'

'Not after last time,' said Mr Price sadly.

We trotted on, we crept up Constitution Hill, we rattled down into Lammas Street, and the tailor still rang his bell and a dog ran, squealing, in front of his wheels. As we clip-clopped over the cobbles that led down to the Towy bridge, I remembered grandpa's nightly noisy journeys that rocked the bed and shook the walls, and I saw his gay waistcoat in a vision and his patchwork head tufted and smiling in the candlelight. The tailor before us turned round on his saddle, his bicycle wobbled and skidded. 'I see Dai Thomas!' he cried.

The trap rattled on to the bridge, and I saw grandpa there: the buttons of his waistcoat shone in the sun, he wore his tight, black Sunday trousers and a tall, dusty hat I had seen in a cupboard in the attic, and he carried an ancient bag. He bowed to us. 'Good morning, Mr Price,' he said, 'and Mr Griff and Mr Morgan and Mr Evans.' To me he said: 'Good morning, boy.'

Mr Griff pointed his coloured stick at him.

'And what do you think you are doing on Carmarthen bridge in the middle of the afternoon,' he said sternly, 'with your best waistcoat and your old hat?'

Grandpa did not answer, but inclined his face to the river wind, so that his beard was set dancing and wagging as though he talked, and watched the coracle men move, like turtles, on the shore.

Mr Griff raised his stunted barber's pole. 'And where do you think you are going,' he said, 'with your old black bag?'

Grandpa said: 'I am going to Llangadock to be buried.' And he watched the coracle shells slip into the water lightly, and the gulls complain over the fish-filled water as bitterly as Mr Price complained:

'But you aren't dead yet, Dai Thomas.'

For a moment grandpa reflected, then: 'There's no sense in lying dead in Llanstephan,' he said. 'The ground is comfy in Llangadock; you can twitch your legs without putting them in the sea.'

His neighbours moved close to him. They said: 'You aren't dead, Mr Thomas.'

'How can you be buried, then?'

'Nobody's going to bury you in Llanstephan.'

'Come on home, Mr Thomas.'

'There's strong beer for tea.'

'And cake.'

But grandpa stood firmly on the bridge, and clutched his bag to his side, and stared at the flowing river and the sky, like a prophet who has no doubt.

PATRICIA, EDITH, AND ARNOLD

The small boy in his invisible engine, the Cwmdonkin Special,
its wheels, polished to dazzle, crunching on the small back
garden scattered with breadcrumbs for the birds and white with
yesterday's snow, its smoke rising thin and pale as breath in the
cold afternoon, hooted under the wash-line, kicked the dog's
plate at the washhouse stop, and puffed and pistoned slower
and slower while the servant girl lowered the pole, unpegged the
swinging vests, showed the brown stains under her arms, and
called over the wall; 'Edith, Edith, come here, I want you.'

Edith climbed on two tubs on the other side of the wall and
called back: 'I'm here, Patricia.' Her head bobbed up above the
broken glass.

He backed the Flying Welshman from the washhouse to the
open door of the coal-hole and pulled hard on the brake that
was a hammer in his pocket: assistants in uniform ran out with
fuel; he spoke to a saluting fireman, and the engine shuffled off,
round the barbed walls of China that kept the cats away, by the
frozen rivers in the sink, in and out of the coal-hole tunnel. But
he was listening carefully all the time, through the squeals and
whistles, to Patricia and the next-door servant, who belonged to
Mrs Lewis, talking when they should have been working, calling
his mother Mrs T., being rude about Mrs L.

He heard Patricia say: 'Mrs T. won't be back till six.'

And Edith next door replied: 'Old Mrs L. has gone to Neath
to look for Mr Robert.'

'He's on the randy again,' Patricia whispered.

'Randy, sandy, bandy,!' cried the boy out of the coal-hole.

'You get your face dirty, I'll kill you,' Patricia said absent-
mindedly.

She did not try to stop him when he climbed up the coal-heap.
He stood quietly on the top, King of the Coal Castle, his head
touching the roof, and listened to the worried voices of the girls.
Patricia was almost in tears, Edith was sobbing and rocking on

the unsteady tubs. 'I'm standing on top of the coal,' he said, and waited for Patricia's anger.

She said : 'I don't want to see him, you go alone.'

'We must, we must go together,' said Edith. 'I've got to know.'

'I don't want to know.'

'I can't stand it, Patricia, you must go with me.'

'You go alone, he's waiting for you.'

'Please, Patricia !'

'I'm lying on my face in the coal,' said the boy.

'No, it's your day with him. I don't want to know. I just want to think he loves me.'

'Oh, talk sense, Patricia, please ! Will you come or no ? I've got to hear what he says.'

'All right then, in half an hour. I'll shout over the wall.'

'You'd better come soon,' the boy said, 'I'm dirty as Christ knows what.'

Patricia ran to the coal-hole. 'The language ! Come out of there at once !' she said.

The tubs began to slide and Edith vanished.

'Don't you dare use language like that again. Oh ! your suit !' Patricia took him indoors.

She made him change his suit in front of her. 'Otherwise there's no telling.' He took off his trousers and danced around her, crying : 'Look at me, Patricia !'

'You be decent,' she said, 'or I won't take you to the park.'

'Am I going to the park, then ?'

'Yes, we're all going to the park ; you and me and Edith next door.'

He dressed himself neatly, not to annoy her, and spat on his hands before parting his hair. She appeared not to notice his silence and neatness. Her large hands were clasped together ; she stared down at the white brooch on her chest. She was a tall, thick girl with awkward hands, her fingers were like toes, her shoulders were wide as a man's.

'Am I satisfactory ?' he asked.

'There's a long word,' she said, and looked at him lovingly. She lifted him up and seated him on the top of the chest of drawers. 'Now you're as tall as I am.'

'But I'm not so old,' he said.

He knew that this was an afternoon on which anything might

happen; it might snow enough for sliding on a tray; uncles from America, where he had no uncles, might arrive with revolvers and St Bernards; Ferguson's shop might catch on fire and all the piece-packets fall on the pavements; and he was not surprised when she put her black, straight-haired heavy head on his shoulder and whispered into his collar: 'Arnold, Arnold Matthews.'

'There, there,' he said, and rubbed her parting with his finger and winked at himself in the mirror behind her and looked down her dress at the back.

'Are you crying?'

'No.'

'Yes, you are, I can feel the wet.'

She dried her eyes on her sleeve. 'Don't you let on that I was crying.'

'I'll tell everybody, I'll tell Mrs T. and Mrs L., I'll tell the policeman and Edith and my dad and Mr Chapman, Patricia was crying on my shoulder like a nanny goat, she cried for two hours, she cried enough to fill a kettle. I won't really,' he said.

As soon as he and Patricia and Edith set off for the park, it began to snow. Big flakes unexpectedly fell on the rocky hill, and the sky grew dark as dusk though it was only three in the afternoon. Another boy, somewhere in the allotments behind the houses, shouted as the first flakes fell. Mrs Ocky Evans opened the top bay-windows of Springmead and thrust her head and hands out, as though to catch the snow. He waited, without revolt, for Patricia to say, 'Quick! hurry back, it's snowing!' and to pack him in out of the day before his feet were wet. Patricia can't have seen the snow, he thought at the top of the hill, though it was falling heavily, sweeping against her face, covering her black hat. He dared not speak for fear of waking her, as they turned the corner into the road that led down to the park. He lagged behind to take his cap off and catch the snow in his mouth.

'Put on your cap,' said Patricia, turning, 'Do you want to catch your death of cold?'

She tucked his muffler inside his coat, and said to Edith: 'Will he be there in the snow, do you think? He's bound to be there, isn't he? He was always there on my Wednesdays, wet or fine.' The tip of her nose was red, her cheeks glowed like coals, she looked handsomer in the snow than in the summer, when her hair would lie limp on her wet forehead and a warm patch spread on her back.

'He'll be there,' Edith said. 'One Friday it was pelting down and he was there. He hasn't got anywhere else to go, he's always there. Poor Arnold!' She looked white and tidy in a coat with a fur piece, and twice as small as Patricia; she stepped through the thick snow as though she were going shopping.

'Wonders will never cease,' he said aloud to himself. This was Patricia letting him walk in the snow, this was striding along in a storm with two big girls. He sat down in the road. 'I'm on a sledge,' he said, 'pull me, Patricia, pull me like an Eskimo.'

'Up you get, you moochin, or I'll take you home.'

He saw that she did not mean it. 'Lovely Patricia, beautiful Patricia,' he said, 'pull me along on my bottom.'

'Any more dirty words, and you know who I'll tell.'

'Arnold Matthews,' he said.

Patricia and Edith drew closer together.

'He notices everything,' Patricia whispered.

Edith said: 'I'm glad I haven't got your job.'

'Oh,' said Patricia, catching him by the hand and pressing it on her arm, 'I wouldn't change him for the world!'

He ran down the gravel path on to the upper walk of the park. 'I'm spoilt!' he shouted, 'I'm spoilt! Patricia spoils me!'

Soon the park would be white all over; already the trees were blurred round the reservoir and fountain, and the training college on the gorse hill was hidden in a cloud. Patricia and Edith took the steep path down to the shelter. Following on the forbidden grass, he slid past them straight into a bare bush, but the bump and the pricks left him shouting and unhurt. The girls gossiped sadly now. They shook their coats in the deserted shelter, scattering snow on the seats, and sat down, close together still, outside the bowling-club window.

'We're only just on time,' said Edith. 'It's hard to be punctual in the snow.'

'Can I play by here?'

Patricia nodded. 'Play quietly then; don't be rough with the snow.'

'Snow! snow! snow!' he said, and scooped it out of the gutter and made a small ball.

'Perhaps he's found a job,' Patricia said.

'Not Arnold.'

'What if he doesn't come at all ?'

'He's bound to come, Patricia ; don't say things like that.'

'Have you brought your letters ?'

'They're in my bag. How many have you got ?'

'No, how many have you got, Edith ?'

'I haven't counted.'

'Show me one of yours,' Patricia said.

He was used to their talk by this time ; they were old and cuckoo, sitting in the empty shelter sobbing over nothing. Patricia was reading a letter and moving her lips.

'He told me that, too,' she said, 'that I was his star.'

'Did he begin : "Dear Heart ?" '

'Always : "Dear Heart." '

Edith broke into real loud tears. With a snowball in his hand, he watched her sway on the seat and hide her face in Patricia's snowy coat.

Patricia said, patting and calming Edith, rocking her head : 'I'll give him a piece of my mind when he comes !'

When who comes ? He threw the snowball high into the silently driving fall. Edith's crying in the deadened park was clear and thin as a whistle, and, disowning the soft girls and standing away from them in case a stranger passed, a man with boots to his thighs, or a sneering, bigger boy from the Uplands, he piled the snow against the wire of the tennis court and thrust his hands into the snow like a baker making bread. As he delved and moulded the snow into loaves, saying under his breath, 'This is the way it is done, ladies and gentlemen,' Edith raised her head and said : 'Patricia, promise me, don't be cross with him. Let's all be quiet and friendly.'

'Writing, "Dear Heart" to us both,' said Patricia angrily. 'Did he ever take off your shoes and pull your toes and – '

'No, no, you mustn't, don't go on, you mustn't speak like that !' Edith put her fingers to her cheeks. 'Yes, he did,' she said.

'Somebody has been pulling Edith's toes,' he said to himself, and ran round the other side of the shelter, chuckling. 'Edith went to market,' he laughed aloud, and stopped at the sight of a young man without an overcoat sitting in the corner seat and cupping his hands and blowing into them. The young man wore a white muffler and a check cap. When he saw the boy, he pulled his cap down over his eyes. His hands were pale blue and the ends of his fingers yellow.

The boy ran back to Patricia. 'Patricia, there's a man!' he cried.

'Where's a man?'

'On the other side of the shelter; he hasn't got an overcoat and he's blowing in his hands like this.'

Edith jumped up. 'It's Arnold!'

'Arnold Matthews, Arnold Matthews, we know you're there!' Patricia called round the shelter, and, after a long minute, the young man, raising his cap and smiling, appeared at the corner and leant against a wooden pillar.

The trousers of his sleek blue suit were wide at the bottoms; the shoulders were high and hard, and sharp at the ends; his pointed patent shoes were shining; a red handkerchief stuck from his breast pocket; he had not been out in the snow.

'Fancy you two knowing each other,' he said loudly, facing the red-eyed girls and the motionless, open-mouthed boy who stood at Patricia's side with his pockets full of snowballs.

Patricia tossed her head and her hat fell over one eye. As she straightened her hat, 'You come and sit down here, Arnold Matthews, you've got some questions to answer!' she said in her washing-day voice.

Edith clutched at her arm: 'Oh! Patricia you promised.' She picked at the edge of her handkerchief. A tear rolled down her cheek.

Arnold said softly then: 'Tell the little boy to run away and play.'

The boy ran round the shelter once and returned to hear Edith saying: 'There's a hole in your elbow, Arnold,' and to see the young man kicking the snow at his feet and staring at the names and hearts cut on the wall behind the girls' heads.

'Who did you walk out with on Wednesdays?' Patricia asked. Her clumsy hands held Edith's letter close to the sprinkled folds of her chest.

'You, Patricia.'

'Who did you walk out with on Fridays?'

'With Edith, Patricia.'

He said to the boy: 'Here, son, can you roll a snowball as big as a football?'

'Yes, as big as two footballs.'

Arnold turned back to Edith, and said: 'How did you come to know Patricia Davies? You work in Brynmill.'

'I just started work in Cwmdonkin,' she said. 'I haven't seen you since, to tell you. I was going to tell you to-day, but I found out. How could you Arnold? Me on my afternoon off, and Patricia on Wednesdays.'

The snowball had turned into a short snow man with a lop-sided, dirty head and a face full of twigs, wearing a boy's cap and smoking a pencil.

'I didn't mean any harm,' said Arnold. 'I love you both.'

Edith screamed. The boy jumped forward and the snow man with a broken back collapsed.

'Don't tell your lies, how can you love two of us?' Edith cried, shaking her handbag at Arnold. The bag snapped open, and a bundle of letters fell on the snow.

'Don't you dare pick up those letters,' Patricia said.

Arnold had not moved. The boy was searching for his pencil in the snow man's ruins.

'You make your choice, Arnold Matthews, here and now.'

'Her or me,' said Edith.

Patricia turned her back to him. Edith, with her bag in her hand hanging open, stood still. The sweeping snow turned up the top page of a letter.

'You two,' he said, 'you go off the handle. Sit down and talk. Don't cry like that, Edith. Hundreds of men love more than one woman, you're always reading about it. Give us a chance, Edith, there's a girl.'

Patricia looked at the hearts and arrows and old names. Edith saw the letters curl.

'It's you, Patricia,' said Arnold.

Still Patricia stood turned away from him. Edith opened her mouth to cry, and he put a finger to his lips. He made the shape of a whisper, too soft for Patricia to hear. The boy watched him soothing and promising Edith, but she screamed again and ran out of the shelter and down the path, her handbag beating against her side.

'Patricia,' he said, 'turn round to me. I had to say it. It's you, Patricia.'

The boy bent down over the snow man and found his pencil driven through its head. When he stood up he saw Patricia and Arnold arm in arm.

Snow dripped through his pockets, snow melted in his shoes, snow trickled down his collar into his vest. 'Look at you now,' said Patricia, rushing to him and holding him by the hands, 'you're wringing wet.'

'Only a bit of snow,' said Arnold, suddenly alone in the shelter.

'A bit of snow indeed, he's as cold as ice and his feet are like sponges. Come on home at once !'

The three of them climbed the path to the upper walk, and Patricia's footprints were large as a horse's in the thickening snow.

'Look, you can see our house, it's got a white roof !'

'We'll be there, ducky, soon.'

'I'd rather stay out and make a snow man like Arnold Matthews.'

'Hush ! hush ! your mother'll be waiting. You must come home.'

'No she won't. She gone on a randy with Mr Robert. Randy, sandy, bandy !'

'You know very well she's shopping with Mrs Partridge, you mustn't tell wicked lies.'

'Well Arnold Matthews told lies. He said he loved you better than Edith, and he whispered behind your back to her.'

'I swear I didn't, Patricia, I don't love Edith at all !'

Patricia stopped walking. 'You don't love Edith ?'

'No, I've told you, it's you. I don't love her at all,' he said. 'Oh ! my God, what a day ! Don't you believe me ? It's you Patricia. Edith isn't anything. I just used to meet her ; I'm always in the park.'

'But you told her you loved her.'

The boy stood bewildered between them. Why was Patricia so angry and serious ? Her face was flushed and her eyes shone. Her chest moved up and down. He saw the long black hairs on her leg through a tear in her stockings. Her leg is as big as my middle, he thought. I'm cold ; I want tea ; I've got snow in my fly.

Arnold backed slowly down the path. 'I had to tell her that or she wouldn't have gone away. I had to, Patricia. You saw what she was like. I hate her. Cross my heart !'

'Bang ! bang !' cried the boy.

Patricia was smacking Arnold, tugging at his muffler, knocking him with her elbows. She pummelled him down the path,

and shouted at the top of her voice, 'I'll teach you to lie to
Edith ! You pig ! you black ! I'll teach you to break her heart !'

He shielded his face from her blows as he staggered back.
'Patricia, Patricia, don't hit me ! There's people !'

As Arnold fell, two women with umbrellas up peered through
the whirling snow from behind a bush.

Patricia stood over him. 'You lied to her and you'd lie to me,'
she said. 'Get up, Arnold Matthews !'

He rose and set his muffler straight and wiped his eyes with
the red handkerchief, and raised his cap and walked toward the
shelter.

'And as for you,' Patricia said, turning to the watching
women, 'you should be ashamed of yourselves ! Two old women
playing about in the snow.'

They dodged behind the bush.

Patricia and the boy climbed, hand in hand, back to the upper
walk.

'I've left my cap by the snow man,' he remembered. 'It's my
cap with the Tottenham colours.'

'Run back quickly,' she said, 'you can't get any wetter than
you are.'

He found his cap half hidden under snow. In a corner of the
shelter, Arnold sat reading the letters that Edith had dropped,
turning the wet pages slowly. He did not see the boy, and the
boy, behind a pillar, did not interrupt him. Arnold read every
letter carefully.

'You've been a long time finding your cap,' Patricia said. 'Did
you see the young man ?'

'No,' he said, 'he was gone.'

At home, in the warm living-room, Patricia made him change
his clothes again. He held his hands in front of the fire, and soon
they began to hurt.

'My hands are on fire,' he told her, 'and my toes, and my
face.'

After she had comforted him, she said : 'There, that's better.
The hurting's gone. You won't call the king your uncle in a
minute.' She was bustling about the room. 'Now we've all had
a good cry to-day.'

THE FIGHT

I was standing at the end of the lower playground and annoying Mr Samuels, who lived in the house just below the high railings. Mr Samuels complained once a week that boys from the school threw apples and stones and balls through his bedroom window. He sat in a deck chair in a small square of trim garden and tried to read the newspaper. I was only a few yards from him. I was staring him out. He pretended not to notice me, but I knew he knew I was standing there rudely and quietly. Every now and then he peeped at me from behind his newspaper, saw me still and serious and alone, with my eyes on his. As soon as he lost his temper I was going to go home. Already I was late for dinner. I had almost beaten him, the newspaper was trembling, he was breathing heavily, when a strange boy, whom I had not heard approach, pushed me down the bank.

I threw a stone at his face. He took off his spectacles, put them in his coat pocket, took off his coat, hung it neatly on the railings, and attacked. Turning round as we wrestled on the top of the bank, I saw that Mr Samuels had folded his newspaper on the deck chair and was standing up to watch us. It was a mistake to turn round. The strange boy rabbit-punched me twice. Mr Samuels hopped with excitement as I fell against the railings. I was down in the dust, hot and scratched and biting, then up and dancing, and I butted the boy in the belly and we tumbled in a heap. I saw through a closing eye that his nose was bleeding. I hit his nose. He tore at my collar and spun me round by the hair.

'Come on! come on!' I heard Mr Samuels cry.

We both turned towards him. He was shaking his fists and dodging about in the garden. He stopped then, and coughed, and set his panama straight, and avoided our eyes, and turned his back and walked slowly to the deck chair.

We both threw gravel at him.

'I'll give him "Come on!",' the boy said, as we ran along the playground away from the shouts of Mr Samuels and down the steps on to the hill.

We walked home together. I admired his bloody nose. He said that my eye was like a poached egg, only black.

'I've never seen such a lot of blood,' I said.

He said I had the best black eye in Wales, perhaps it was the best black eye in Europe; he bet Tunney never had a black eye like that.

'And there's blood all over your shirt.'

'Sometimes I bleed in dollops,' he said.

On Walter's Road we passed a group of high school girls, and I cocked my cap and hoped my eye was as big as a bluebag, and he walked with his coat flung open to show the bloodstains.

I was a hooligan all during dinner, and a bully, and as bad as a boy from the Sandbanks, and I should have more respect, and I sat silently, like Tunney, over the sago pudding. That afternoon I went to school with an eye-shade on. If I had had a black silk sling I would have been as gay and desperate as the wounded captain in the book that my sister used to read, and that I read under the bedclothes at night, secretly with a flash-lamp.

On the road, a boy from an inferior school, where the parents did not have to pay anything, called me 'One eye!' in a harsh, adult voice. I took no notice, but walked along whistling, my good eye on the summer clouds sailing, beyond insult, above Terrace Road.

The mathematics master said: 'I see that Mr Thomas at the back of the class has been straining his eyesight. But it isn't over his homework, is it, gentlemen?'

Gilbert Rees, next to me, laughed loudest.

'I'll break your leg after school!' I said.

He'd hobble, howling, up to the head master's study. A deep hush in the school. A message on a plate brought by the porter. 'The head master's compliments, sir, and will you come at once?' 'How did you happen to break this boy's leg?' 'Oh! damn and bottom, the agony!' cried Gilbert Rees. 'Just a little twist,' I would say. 'I don't know my own strength. I apologize. But there's nothing to worry about. Let me set the leg, sir.' A rapid manipulation, the click of a bone. 'Doctor Thomas, sir, at your service.' Mrs Rees was on her knees. 'How can I thank you?' 'It's nothing at all, dear lady. Wash his ears every morning. Throw away his rulers. Pour his red and green inks down the sink.'

In Mr Trotter's drawing class we drew naked girls inaccurately on sheets of paper under our drawings of a vase and passed them along under the desks. Some of the drawings were detailed strangely, others were tailed off like mermaids. Gilbert Rees drew the vase only.

'Sleep with your wife, sir ?'

'What did you say ?'

'Lend me a knife, sir ?'

'What would you do if you had a million pounds ?'

'I'd buy a Bugatti and a Rolls and a Bentley and I'd go two hundred miles an hour on Pendine sands.'

'I'd buy a harem and keep the girls in the gym.'

'I'd buy a house like Mrs Cotmore-Richard's, twice as big as hers, and a cricket field and a football field and a proper garage with mechanics and a lift.'

'And a lavatory as big as, as big as the Melba pavilion, with plush seats and a golden chain and . . .'

'And I'd smoke cigarettes with real gold tips, better than Morris's Blue Book.'

'I'd buy all the railway trains, and only 4A could travel in them.'

'And not Gilbert Rees either.'

'What's the longest you've been ?'

'I went to Edinburgh.'

'My father went to Salonika in the War.'

'Where's that, Cyril ?'

'Cyril, tell us about Mrs Pussie Edwards in Hanover Street.'

'Well, my brother says he can do anything.'

I drew a wild guess below the waist, and wrote Pussie Edwards in small letters at the foot of the page.

'Cave !'

'Hide your drawings.'

'I bet you a greyhound can go faster than a horse.'

Everybody liked the drawing class, except Mr Trotter.

In the evening, before calling on my new friend, I sat in my bedroom by the boiler and read through my exercise-books full of poems. There were Danger Don'ts on the backs. On my bedroom walls were pictures of Shakespeare, Walter de la Mare torn from my father's Christmas *Bookman*, Robert Browning,

Stacy Aumonier, Rupert Brooke, a bearded man who I had discovered was Whittier, Watts's 'Hope,' and a Sunday school certificate I was ashamed to want to pull down. A poem I had had printed in the 'Wales Day by Day' column of the *Western Mail* was pasted on the mirror to make me blush, but the shame of the poem had died. Across the poem I had written, with a stolen quill and in flourishes: 'Homer Nods.' I was always waiting for the opportunity to bring someone into my bedroom – 'Come into my den; excuse the untidiness; take a chair. No! not that one, it's broken!' – and force him to see the poem accidentally. 'I put it there to make me blush.' But nobody ever came in except my mother.

Walking to his house in the early dusk through solid, deserted professional avenues lined with trees, I recited pieces of my poems and heard my voice, like a stranger's voice in Park Drive accompanied by the tap-tapping of nailed boots, rise very thinly up through the respectable autumn evening.

> 'My mind is fashioned
> In the ways of intertissue;
> Veiled and passioned
> Are the thoughts that issue
> From its well of furtive lust
> Raptured by the devil's dust.'

If I looked through a window on to the road, I would see a scarlet-capped boy with big boots striding down the middle, and would wonder who it could be. If I were a young girl watching, my face like Mona Lisa's, my coal-black hair coiled in earphones, I'd see beneath the 'Boys' Department' suit a manly body with hair and sun tan, and call him and ask, 'Will you have tea or cocktails?' and hear his voice reciting the *Grass Blade's Psalm* in the half-dark of the heavily curtained and coloured drawing-room hung about with famous reproductions and glowing with books and wine bottles:

> 'The frost has lain,
> Frost that is dark with flowered slain,
> Fragilely strewn
> With patches of illuminated moon,
> About my lonely head in flagged unlovely red,

'The frost has spake,
Frost secretive and thrilled in silent flake,
With unseen lips of blue
Glass in the glaze stars threw,
Only to my ears, has spake in visionary tears.

'The frost has known,
From scattered conclave by the few winds blown,
That the lone genius in my roots,
Bare down there in a jungle of fruits,
Has planted a green year, for praise in the heart of my
    upgrowing days.

'The frost has filled
My heart with longing that the night's sleeve spilled,
Frost of celestial vapour fraught,
Frost that the columns of unfallen snow have sought,
With desire for the fields of space hovering about my single
    place.'

'Look! there's a strange boy, walking alone like a prince.'
'No, no, like a wolf! Look at his long stride!' Sketty church
was shaking its bells for me.

'When I am strewn low
And all my ashes are
Dust in a dumb provoking show
Of minatory star . . .'

I recited. A young man and woman, arm in arm, suddenly
appeared from a black lane between houses. I changed my
recitation into a tune and hummed past them. They would be
tittering together now, with their horrid bodies close. Cissy,
moony, long hair. I whistled hard and loud, kicked a trades-
men's entrance, and glanced back over my shoulder. The couple
were gone. Here's a kick at 'The Elms'. 'Where are the bleedy
elms, mister?' Here's a handful of gravel, Mrs. 'The Croft', right
at your window. One night I would paint 'Bum' all over the
front gate of 'Kia-ora.'
    A woman stood on 'Lyndhurst' steps with a hissing pom, and,
stuffing my cap in my pocket, I was off down the road; and
there was Dan's house, 'Warmley,' with music coming loudly
out of it.

He was a composer and a poet too; he had written seven historical novels before he was twelve, and he played the piano and the violin; his mother made wool pictures, his brother was a clerk at the docks and syncopated, his aunt kept a preparatory school on the first floor, and his father wrote music for the organ. All this he had told me as we walked home bleeding, strutting by the gym-frocks waving to boys in the trams.

My new friend's mother answered the door with a ball of wool in her hand. Dan, in the upstairs drawing-room, heard my arrival and played the piano faster.

'I didn't hear you come in,' he said when I found him. He finished on a grand chord, stretching all his fingers.

The room was splendidly untidy, full of wool and paper and open cupboards stacked with things you could never find; all the expensive furniture had been kicked; a waistcoat hung on the chandelier. I thought I could live for ever in that room, writing and fighting and spilling ink, having my friends for picnics there after midnight with Walker's rum-and-butter and charlottes russes from Eynon's, and Cydrax and Vino.

He showed me his books and his seven novels. All the novels were about battles, sieges, and kings. 'Just early stuff,' he said.

He let me take out his violin and make a cat noise.

We sat on a sofa in the window and talked as though we had always known each other. Would the 'Swans' beat the 'Spurs'? When could girls have babies? Was Arnott's average last year better than Clay's?

'That's my father outside there on the road,' he said, 'the tall one waving his arms.'

Two men were talking on the tram lines. Mr Jenkyn looked at if he were trying to swim down Eversley Road, he breast-stroked the air and beat on the ground with his feet, and then he limped and raised one shoulder higher than the other.

'Perhaps he's describing a fight,' I said.

'Or telling Mr Morris a story about cripples,' said Dan. 'Can you play the piano?'

'I can do chords, but not tunes,' I said.

We played a duet with crossed hands.

'Now who's that sonata by?'

We made a Dr Percy, who was the greatest composer for four hands in the world, and I was Paul America, the pianist, and Dan was Winter Vaux.

I read him an exercise-book full of poems. He listened wisely, like a boy aged a hundred, his head on one side and his spectacles shaking on his swollen nose. 'This is called *Warp*, ' I said :

> 'Like suns red from running tears,
> Five suns in the glass,
> Together, separate yet, yet separately round,
> Red perhaps, but the glass is as pale as grass,
> Glide, without sound.
> In unity, five tears lid-awake, suns yet, but salt,
> Five inscrutable spears in the head,
> Each sun but an agony,
> Twist perhaps, pain bled of hate,
> Five into one, the one made of five into one, early
> Suns distorted to late.
> All of them now, madly and desolate,
> Spun with the cloth of the five, run
> Widely and foaming, wildly and desolate,
> Shoot through and dive. One of the five is the sun.'

The noise of the trams past the house clattered away as far as the sea or farther, into the dredgered bay. Nobody had ever listened like that before. The school had vanished, leaving on Mount Pleasant hill a deep hole that smelt of cloakrooms and locker mice, and 'Warmley' shone in the dark of a town I did not know. In the still room, that had never been strange to me, sitting in heaps of coloured wool, swollen-nosed and one-eyed, we acknowledged our gifts. The future spread out beyond the window, over Singleton Park crowded with lovers messing about, and into smoky London paved with poems.

Mrs Jenkyn peered round the door and switched the light on. 'There, that's more homely,' she said. 'You aren't cats.'

The future went out with the light, and we played a thumping piece by Dr Percy – 'Have you ever heard anything so beautiful ? Louder, louder, America !' said Dan. 'Leave a bit of bass for me,' I said – until the next-door wall was rapped.

'That's the Careys. Mr Carey's a Cape Horner,' Dan said.

We played him one harsh, whaling piece before Mrs Jenkyn, with wool and needles, ran upstairs.

When she had gone, Dan said : 'Why is a man always ashamed of his mother ?'

'Perhaps he isn't when he is older,' I said, but I doubted it. The week before I was walking down High Street with three boys after school, and I saw my mother with a Mrs Partridge outside the Kardomah. I knew she would stop me in front of the others and say, 'Now you be home early for tea,' and I wanted High Street to open and suck me down. I loved her and disowned her. 'Let's cross over,' I said, 'there's some sailor's boots in Griffith's window.' But there was only a dummy with a golf suit on, and a roll of tweed.

'Supper isn't for half an hour yet. What shall we do?'

'Let's see who can hold up that chair the longest,' I said.

'No, let's edit a paper : you do the literature, I'll do the music.'

'What shall we call it, then?'

He wrote, '*The*—, edited by D. Jenkyn and D. Thomas,' on the back of a hat-box from under the sofa. The rhythm was better with D. Thomas and D. Jenkyn, but it was his house.

'What about *The Maestersingers*?'

'No, that's too musical,' I said.

'*The Warmley Magazine*?'

'No,' I said, 'I live in "Glanrhyd."'

After the hat-box was covered, we wrote.

'*The Thunderer*, edited by D. $\frac{\text{Jenkyn,}}{\text{Thomas}}$ in chalk on a piece of cardboard and pinned it on the wall.

'Would you like to see our maid's bedroom?' asked Dan. We whispered up to the attic.

'What's her name?'

'Hilda.'

'Is she young?'

'No, she's twenty or thirty.'

Her bed was untidy. 'My mother says you can always smell a maid.' We smelled the sheets. 'I can't smell anything.'

In her brass-bound box was a framed photograph of a young man wearing plus-fours.

'That's her boy.'

'Let's give him a moustache.'

Somebody moved downstairs, a voice called, 'Supper now!' and we hurried out, leaving the box open. 'One night we'll hide under her bed,' Dan said as we opened the dining-room door.

Mr Jenkyn, Mrs Jenkyn, Dan's aunt, and a Reverend Bevan and Mrs Bevan were seated at the table.

Mr Bevan said grace. When he stood up, it was just as though he were still sitting down, he was so short. 'Bless our repast this evening,' he said, as though he didn't like the food at all. But once 'Amen' was over, he went at the cold meat like a dog.

Mrs Bevan didn't look all there. She stared at the table-cloth and made hesitant movements with her knife and fork. She appeared to be wondering which to cut up first, the meat or the cloth.

Dan and I stared at her with delight; he kicked me under the table and I spilt the salt. In the commotion I managed to put some vinegar on his bread.

Mrs Jenkyn said, while everyone except Mr Bevan was watching Mrs Bevan moving her knife slowly along the edge of her plate: 'I do hope you like cold lamb.'

Mrs Bevan smiled at her, assured, and began to eat. She was grey-haired and grey-faced. Perhaps she was grey all over. I tried to undress her, but my mind grew frightened when it came to her short flannel petticoat and navy bloomers to the knees. I couldn't even dare unbutton her tall boots to see how grey her legs were. She looked up from her plate and gave me a wicked smile.

Blushing, I turned to answer Mr Jenkyn, who was asking me how old I was. I told him, but added one year. Why did I lie then? I wondered. If I lost my cap and found it in my bedroom, and my mother asked me where I had found it, I would say, 'In the attic,' or 'Under the hall stand.' It was exciting to have to keep wary all the time in case I contradicted myself, to make up the story of a film I pretended to have seen and put Jack Holt in Richard Dix's place.

'Fifteen and three-quarters,' said Mr Jenkyn, 'that's a very exact age. I see we have a mathematician with us. Now see if he can do this little sum.'

He finished his supper and laid out matches on the plate.

'That's an old one, Dad,' Dan said.

'Oh, I'd like to see it very much,' I said in my best voice. I wanted to come to the house again. This was better than home, and there was a woman off her head, too.

When I failed to place the matches rightly, Mr Jenkyn showed me how it was done, and, still not understanding, I thanked him and asked him for another one. It was almost as good being a hypocrite as being a liar; it made you warm and shameful.

'What were you talking to Mr Morris about in the street, Dad?' asked Dan. 'We saw you from upstairs.'

'I was telling him how the Swansea and District Male Voice did the *Messiah*, that's all. Why do you ask?'

Mr Bevan couldn't eat any more, he was full. For the first time since supper began, he looked round the table. He didn't seem to like what he saw. 'How are studies progressing, Daniel?'

'Listen to Mr Bevan, Dan, he's asking you a question.'

'Oh, so so.'

'So so?'

'I mean they're going very well, thank you, Mr Bevan.'

'Young people should attempt to say what they mean.'

Mrs Bevan giggled, and asked for more meat. 'More meat,' she said.

'And you, young man, have you a mathematical bent?'

'No, sir,' I said, 'I like English.'

'He's a poet,' said Dan, and looked uncomfortable.

'A brother poet,' Mr Bevan corrected, showing his teeth.

'Mr Bevan has published books,' said Mr Jenkyn. '*Proserpine, Psyche*—'

'*Orpheus*,' said Mr Bevan sharply.

'And *Orpheus*. You must show Mr Bevan some of your verses.'

'I haven't got anything with me, Mr Jenkyn.'

'A poet,' said Mr Bevan, 'should carry his verses in his head.'

'I remember them all right,' I said.

'Recite me your latest one; I'm always very interested.'

'What a gathering,' Mrs Jenkyn said, 'poets, musicians, preachers. We only want a painter now, don't we?'

'I don't think you'll like the very latest one,' I said.

'Perhaps,' said Mr Bevan, smiling, 'I am the best judge of that.'

'Frivolous is my hate,' I said, wanting to die, watching Mr Bevan's teeth.

> 'Singed with bestial remorse
> Of unfulfilment of desired force,
> And lust of tearing late;
>
> 'Now could I raise
> Her dead, dark body to my own

And hear the joyous rustle of her bone
And in her eyes see deathly blaze;

'Now could I wake
To passion after death, and taste
The rapture of her hating, tear the waste
Of body. Break, her dead, dark body, break.'

Dan kicked my shins in the silence before Mr Bevan said 'The influence is obvious, of course. "Break, break, break, on thy cold, grey stones, O sea."'

'Hubert knows Tennyson backwards,' said Mrs Bevan, 'backwards.'

'Can we go upstairs now?' Dan asked.

'No annoying Mr Carey then.'

And we shut the door softly behind us and ran upstairs with our hands over our mouths.

'Damn! damn! damn!' said Dan. 'Did you see the reverend's face?'

We imitated him up and down the room, and had a short fight on the carpet. Dan's nose began to bleed again. 'That's nothing, it'll stop in a minute. I can bleed when I like.'

'Tell me about Mrs Bevan. Is she mad?'

'She's terribly mad, she doesn't know who she is. She tried to throw herself out of the window but he didn't take any notice, so she came up to our house and told mother all about it.'

Mrs Bevan knocked and walked in. 'I hope I'm not interrupting you.'

'No, of course not, Mrs Bevan.'

'I wanted a little change of air,' she said. She sat down in the wool on the sofa by the window.

'Isn't it a close night?' said Dan. 'Would you like the window open?'

She looked at the window.

'I can easily open it for you,' Dan said, and winked at me.

'Let me open it for you, Mrs Bevan,' I said.

'It's good to have the window open.'

'And this is a nice high window too.'

'Plenty of air from the sea.'

'Let it be, dear,' she said. 'I'll just sit here and wait for my husband.'

She played with the balls of wool, picked up a needle and tapped it gently on the palm of her hand.

'Is Mr Bevan going to be long ?'

'I'll just sit and wait for my husband,' she said.

We talked to her some more about windows, but she only smiled and undid the wool, and once she put the blunt end of the long needle in her ear. Soon we grew tired of watching her, and Dan played the piano – 'My twentieth sonata,' he said, 'this one is *Homage to Beethoven*' – and at half-past nine I had to go home.

I said good night to Mrs Bevan, who waved the needle and bowed sitting down, and Mr Bevan downstairs gave me his cold hand to shake, and Mr and Mrs Jenkyn told me to come again, and the quiet aunt gave me a Mars bar.

'I'll send you a bit of the way,' said Dan.

Outside, on the pavement, in the warm night, we looked up at the lighted drawing-room window. It was the only light in the road.

'Look ! there she is !'

Mrs Bevan's face was pressed against the glass, her hook nose flattened, her lips pressed tight, and we ran all the way down Eversley Road in case she jumped.

At the corner, Dan said: 'I must leave you now, I've got to finish a string trio to-night.'

'I'm working on a long poem,' I said, 'about the princes of Wales and the wizards and everybody.'

We both went home to bed.

EXTRAORDINARY LITTLE COUGH

One afternoon, in a particularly bright and glowing August, some years before I knew I was happy, George Hooping, whom we called Little Cough, Sidney Evans, Dan Davies, and I sat on the roof of a lorry travelling to the end of the Peninsula. It was a tall, six-wheeled lorry, from which we could spit on the roofs of the passing cars and throw our apple stumps at women on the pavement. One stump caught a man on a bicycle in the middle of the back, he swerved across the road, for a moment we sat quiet and George Hooping's face grew pale. And if the lorry runs him over, I thought calmly as the man on the bicycle swayed towards the hedge, he'll get killed and I'll be sick on my trousers and perhaps on Sidney's too, and we'll be arrested and hanged, except George Hooping who didn't have an apple.

But the lorry swept past; behind us, the bicycle drove into the hedge, the man stood up and waved his fist, and I waved my cap back at him.

'You shouldn't have waved your cap,' said Sidney Evans, 'he'll know what school we're in.' He was clever, dark, and careful, and had a purse and a wallet.

'We're not in school now.'

'Nobody can expel me,' said Dan Davies. He was leaving next term to serve in his father's fruit shop for a salary.

We all wore haversacks, except George Hooping whose mother had given him a brown-paper parcel that kept coming undone, and carried a suitcase each. I had placed a coat over my suitcase because the initials on it were 'N.T.' and everybody would know that it belonged to my sister. Inside the lorry were two tents, a box of food, a packing-case of kettles and saucepans and knives and forks, an oil lamp, a primus stove, ground sheets and blankets, a gramophone with three records, and a table-cloth from George Hooping's mother.

We were going to camp for a fortnight in Rhossilli, in a field above the sweeping five-mile beach. Sidney and Dan had stayed

there last year, coming back brown and swearing, full of stories
of campers' dances round the fires at midnight, and elderly girls
from the training college who sun-bathed naked on ledges of
rocks surrounded by laughing boys, and singing in bed that
lasted until dawn. But George had never left home for more
than a night; and then, he told me, one half-holiday when it
was raining and there was nothing to do but stay in the wash-
house racing his guineapigs giddily along the benches, it was
only to stay in St Thomas, three miles from his house, with an
aunt who could see through the walls and who knew what a
Mrs Hoskin was doing in the kitchen.

'How much further?' asked George Hooping, clinging to his
split parcel, trying in secret to push back socks and suspenders,
enviously watching the solid green fields skim by as though the
roof were a raft on an ocean with a motor in it. Anything upset
his stomach, even liquorice and sherbet, but I alone knew that
he wore long combinations in the summer with his name stitched
in red on them.

'Miles and miles,' Dan said.

'Thousands of miles,' I said. 'It's Rhossilli, USA. We're going
to camp on a bit of rock that wobbles in the wind.'

'And we have to tie the rock on to a tree.'

'Cough can use his suspenders,' Sidney said.

The lorry roared round a corner – 'Upsy-daisy! Did you feel
it then, Cough? It was on one wheel' – and below us, beyond
fields and farms, the sea, with a steamer puffing on its far edge,
shimmered.

'Do you see the sea down there, it's shimmering, Dan,' I said.

George Hooping pretended to forget the lurch of the slippery
roof and, from that height, the frightening smallness of the sea.
Gripping the rail of the roof, he said: 'My father saw a killer
whale.' The conviction in his voice died quickly as he began. He
beat against the wind with his cracked, treble voice, trying to
make us believe. I knew he wanted to find a boast so big it
would make our hair stand up and stop the wild lorry.

'Your father's a herbalist.' But the smoke on the horizon was
the white, curling fountain the whale blew through his nose,
and its black nose was the bow of the poking ship.

'Where did he keep it, Cough, in the wash-house?'

'He saw it in Madagascar. It had tusks as long as from here
to, from here to . . .'

'From here to Madagascar.'

All at once the threat of a steep hill disturbed him. No longer bothered about the adventures of his father, a small, dusty skullcapped and alpaca-coated man standing and mumbling all day in a shop full of herbs and curtained holes in the wall, where old men with backache and young girls in trouble waited for consultations in the half-dark, he stared at the hill swooping up and clung to Dan and me.

'She's doing fifty !'

'The brakes have gone, Cough !'

He twisted away from us, caught hard with both hands on the rail, pulled and trembled, pressed on a case behind him with his foot, and steered the lorry to safety round a stone-walled corner and up a gentler hill to a gate of a battered farm-house.

Leading down from the gate, there was a lane to the first beach. It was high tide, and we heard the sea dashing. Four boys on a roof – one tall, dark, regular-featured, precise of speech, in a good suit, a boy of the world ; one squat, ungainly, red-haired, his red wrists fighting out of short, frayed sleeves ; one heavily spectacled, small-paunched, with indoor shoulders and feet in always unlaced boots wanting to go different ways ; one small, thin, indecisively active, quick to get dirty, curly – saw their field in front of them, a fortnight's new home that had thick, pricking hedges for walls, the sea for a front garden, a green gutter for a lavatory, and a wind-struck tree in the very middle.

I helped Dan unload the lorry while Sidney tipped the driver and George struggled with the farm-yard gate and looked at the ducks inside. The lorry drove away.

'Let's build our tents by the tree in the middle,' said George.

'Pitch !' Sidney said, unlatching the gate for him.

We pitched our tents in a corner, out of the wind.

'One of us must light the primus,' Sidney said, and, after George had burned his hand, we sat in a circle outside the sleeping-tent talking about motor-cars, content to be in the country, lazily easy in each other's company, thinking to ourselves as we talked, knowing always that the sea dashed on the rocks not far below us and rolled out into the world, and that to-morrow we would bathe and throw a ball on the sands and stone a bottle on a rock and perhaps meet three girls. The oldest would be for Sidney, the plainest for Dan, and the youngest for me. George broke his spectacles when he spoke to girls ; he had

to walk off, blind as a bat, and the next morning he would say :
'I sorry I had to leave you, but I remembered a message.'

It was past five o'clock. My father and mother would have
finished tea ; the plates with famous castles on them were cleared
from the table ; father with a newspaper, mother with socks,
were far away in the blue haze to the left, up a hill, in a villa,
hearing from the park the faint cries of children drift over the
public tennis court, and wondering where I was and what I was
doing. I was alone with my friends in a field, with a blade of
grass in my mouth saying, 'Dempsey would hit him cold,' and
thinking of the great whale that George's father never saw
thrashing on the top of the sea, or plunging underneath, like a
mountain.

'Bet you I can beat you to the end of the field.'

Dan and I raced among the cowpads, George thumping at our
heels.

'Let's go down to the beach.'

Sidney led the way, running straight as a soldier in his khaki
shorts, over a stile, down fields to another, into a wooded valley,
up through heather on to a clearing near the edge of the cliff,
where two broad boys were wrestling outside a tent. I saw one
bite the other in the leg, they both struck expertly and savagely
at the face, one struggled clear, and, with a leap, the other had
him face to the ground. They were Brazell and Skully.

'Hallo, Brazell and Skully !' said Dan.

Skully had Brazell's arm in a policeman's grip ; he gave it two
quick twists and stood up, smiling.

'Hallo, boys ! Hallo, Little Cough ! How's your father ?'

'He's very well, thank you.'

Brazell, on the grass, felt for broken bones. 'Hallo, boys !
How are your fathers ?'

They were the worst and biggest boys in school. Every day
for a term they caught me before class began and wedged me in
the waste-paper basket and then put the basket on the master's
desk. Sometimes I could get out and sometimes not. Brazell was
lean, Skully was fat.

'We're camping in Button's field,' said Sidney.

'We're taking a rest cure here,' said Brazell. 'And how is Little
Cough these days ? Father given him a pill ?'

We wanted to run down to the beach, Dan and Sidney and
George and I, to be alone together, to walk and shout by the sea

in the country, throw stones at the waves, remember adventures and make more to remember.

'We'll come down to the beach with you,' said Skully.

He linked arms with Brazell, and they strolled behind us, imitating George's wayward walk and slashing the grass with switches.

Dan said hopefully: 'Are you camping here for long, Brazell and Skully?'

'For a whole nice fortnight, Davies and Thomas and Evans and Hooping.'

When we reached Mewslade beach and flung ourselves down, as I scooped up sand and it trickled, grain by grain through my fingers, as George peered at the sea through his double lenses and Sidney and Dan heaped sand over his legs, Brazell and Skully sat behind us like two warders.

'We thought of going to Nice for a fortnight,' said Brazell — he rhymed it with ice, dug Skully in the ribs, — 'but the air's nicer here for the complexion.'

'It's as good as a herb,' said Skully.

They shared an enormous joke, cuffing and biting and wrestling again, scattering sand in the eyes, until they fell back with laughter, and Brazell wiped the blood from his nose with a piece of picnic paper. George lay covered to the waist in sand. I watched the sea slipping out, with birds quarrelling over it, and the sun beginning to go down patiently.

'Look at Little Cough,' said Brazell. 'Isn't he extraordinary? He's growing out of the sand. Little Cough hasn't got any legs.'

'Poor Little Cough,' said Skully, 'he's the most extraordinary boy in the world.'

'Extraordinary Little Cough,' they said together, 'extraordinary, extraordinary, extraordinary.' They made a song out of it, and both conducted with their switches.

'He can't swim.'

'He can't run.'

'He can't learn.'

'He can't bowl.'

'He can't bat.'

'And I bet he can't make water.'

George kicked the sand from his legs. 'Yes, I can!'

'Can you swim?'

'Can you run?'

'Can you bowl?'

'Leave him alone,' Dan said.

They shuffled nearer to us. The sea was racing out now. Brazell said in a serious voice, wagging his finger: 'Now, quite truthfully, Cough, aren't you extraordinary? Very extraordinary? Say "Yes" or "No."'

'Categorically, "Yes" or "No."' said Skully.

'No,' George said. 'I can swim and I can run and I can play cricket. I'm not frightened of anybody.'

I said: 'He was second in the form last term.'

'Now isn't that extraordinary? If he can be second he can be first. But no, that's too extraordinary. Little Cough must be second.'

'The question is answered,' said Skully. 'Little Cough is extraordinary.' They began to sing again.

'He's a very good runner,' Dan said.

'Well, let him prove it. Skully and I ran the whole length of Rhossilli sands this morning, didn't we, Skull?'

'Every inch.'

'Can Little Cough do it?'

'Yes,' said George.

'Do it, then.'

'I don't want to.'

'Extraordinary Little Cough can't run,' they sang, 'can't run, can't run.'

Three girls, all fair, came down the cliff-side arm in arm, dressed in short, white trousers. Their arms and legs and throats were brown as berries; I could see when they laughed that their teeth were very white; they stepped on to the beach, and Brazell and Skully stopped singing. Sidney smoothed his hair back, rose casually, put his hands in his pockets, and walked towards the girls, who now stood close together, gold and brown, admiring the sunset with little attention, patting their scarves, turning smiles on each other. He stood in front of them, grinned, and saluted: 'Hallo, Gwyneth! do you remember me?'

'La-di-da!' whispered Dan at my side, and made a mock salute to George still peering at the retreating sea.

'Well, if this isn't a surprise!' said the tallest girl. With little studied movements of her hands, as though she were distributing flowers, she introduced Peggy and Jean.

Fat Peggy, I thought, too jolly for me, with hockey legs and tomboy crop, was the girl for Dan; Sidney's Gwyneth was a distinguished piece and quite sixteen, as immaculate and unapproachable as a girl in Ben Evans' stores; but Jean, shy and curly, with butter-coloured hair, was mine. Dan and I walked slowly to the girls.

I made up two remarks: 'Fair's fair, Sidney, no bigamy abroad,' and 'Sorry we couldn't arrange to have the sea in when you came.'

Jean smiled, wriggling her heel in the sand, and I raised my cap.

'Hallo!'

The cap dropped at her feet.

As I bent down, three lumps of sugar fell from my blazer pocket. 'I've been feeding a horse,' I said, and began to blush guiltily when all the girls laughed.

I could have swept the ground with my cap, kissed my hand gaily, called them señoritas, and made them smile without tolerance. Or I could have stayed at a distance, and this would have been better still, my hair blown in the wind, though there was no wind at all that evening, wrapped in mystery and staring at the sun, too aloof to speak to girls; but I knew that all the time my ears would have been burning, my stomach would have been as hollow and as full of voices as a shell. 'Speak to them quickly, before they go away!' a voice would have said insistently over the dramatic silence, as I stood like Valentino on the edge of the bright, invisible bull-ring of the sands. 'Isn't it lovely here!' I said.

I spoke to Jean alone; and this is love, I thought, as she nodded her head and swung her curls and said: 'It's nicer than Porthcawl.'

Brazell and Skully were two big bullies in a nightmare; I forgot them when Jean and I walked up the cliff, and, looking back to see if they were baiting George again or wrestling together, I saw that George had disappeared around the corner of the rocks and that they were talking at the foot of the cliff with Sidney and the two girls.

'What's your name?'

I told her.

'That's Welsh,' she said.

'You've got a beautiful name.'

'Oh, it's just ordinary.'

'Shall I see you again ?'

'If you want to.'

'I want to all right ! We can go and bathe in the morning. And we can try to get an eagle's egg. Did you know that there were eagles here ?'

'No,' she said. 'Who was that handsome boy on the beach, the tall one with dirty trousers ?'

'He's not handsome, that's Brazell. He never washes or combs his hair or anything. He's a bully and he cheats.'

'I think he's handsome.'

We walked into Button's field, and I showed her inside the tents and gave her one of George's apples. 'I'd like a cigarette,' she said.

It was nearly dark when the others came. Brazell and Skully were with Gwyneth, one each side of her holding her arms, Sidney was with Peggy, and Dan walked, whistling, behind with his hands in his pockets.

'There's a pair,' said Brazell, 'they've been here all alone and they aren't even holding hands. You want a pill,' he said to me.

'Build Britain's babies,' said Skully.

'Go on !' Gwyneth said. She pushed him away from her, but she was laughing, and she said nothing when he put his arm around her waist.

'What about a bit of fire ?' said Brazell.

Jean clapped her hands like an actress. Although I knew I loved her, I didn't like anything she said or did.

'Who's going to make it ?'

'He's the best, I'm sure,' she said, pointing at me.

Dan and I collected sticks, and by the time it was quite dark there was a fire crackling. Inside the sleeping-tent, Brazell and Jean sat close together; her golden head was on his shoulder; Skully, near them, whispered to Gwyneth; Sidney unhappily held Peggy's hand.

'Did you ever see such a sloppy lot ?' I said, watching Jean smile in the fiery dark.

'Kiss me, Charley !' said Dan.

We sat by the fire in the corner of the field. The sea, far out, was still making a noise. We heard a few nightbirds. ' "Tu-whit ! tu-whoo !" Listen ! I don't like owls,' Dan said, 'they scratch your eyes out !'—and tried not to listen to the soft voices in the tent. Gwyneth's laughter floated out over the suddenly moonlit field, but Jean, with the beast, was smiling and silent in the covered warmth ; I knew her little hand was in Brazell's hand.

'Women !' I said.

Dan spat in the fire.

We were old and alone, sitting beyond desire in the middle of the night, when George appeared, like a ghost, in the firelight and stood there trembling until I said : 'Where've you been ? You've been gone hours. Why are you trembling like that ?'

Brazell and Skully poked their heads out.

'Hallo, Cough my boy ! How's your father ? What have you been up to to-night ?'

George Hooping could hardly stand. I put my hand on his shoulder to steady him, but he pushed it away.

'I've been running on Rhossilli sands ! I ran every bit of it ! You said I couldn't, and I did ! I've been running and running !'

Someone inside the tent had put a record on the gramophone. It was a selection from *No, No, Nanette*.

'You've been running all the time in the dark, Little Cough ?'

'And I bet I ran it quicker than you did, too !' George said.

'I bet you did,' said Brazell.

'Do you think we'd run five miles ?' said Skully.

Now the tune was 'Tea for Two.'

'Did you ever hear anything so extraordinary ? I told you Cough was extraordinary. Little Cough's been running all night.'

'Extraordinary, extraordinary, extraordinary Little Cough,' they said.

Laughing from the shelter of the tent into the darkness, they looked like a boy with two heads. And when I stared round at George again he was lying on his back fast asleep in the deep grass and his hair was touching the flames.

JUST LIKE LITTLE DOGS

Standing alone under a railway arch out of the wind, I was looking at the miles of sands, long and dirty in the early dark, with only a few boys on the edge of the sea and one or two hurrying couples with their mackintoshes blown around them like balloons, when two young men joined me, it seemed out of nowhere, and struck matches for their cigarettes and illuminated their faces under bright-checked caps.

One had a pleasant face; his eyebrows slanted comically towards his temples, his eyes were warm, brown, deep, and guileless, and his mouth was full and weak. The other man had a boxer's nose and a weighted chin ginger with bristles.

We watched the boys returning from the oily sea; they shouted under the echoing arch, then their voices faded. Soon there was not a single couple in sight; the lovers had disappeared among the sandhills and were lying down there with broken tins and bottles of the summer passed, old paper blowing by them, and nobody with any sense was about. The strangers, huddled against the wall, their hands deep in their pockets, their cigarettes sparkling, stared, I thought, at the thickening of the dark over the empty sands, but their eyes may have been closed. A train raced over us, and the arch shook. Over the shore, behind the vanishing train, smoke clouds flew together, rags of wings and hollow bodies of great birds black as tunnels, and broke up lazily; cinders fell through a sieve in the air, and the sparks were put out by the wet dark before they reached the sand. The night before, little quick scarecrows had bent and picked at the track-line and a solitary dignified scavenger wandered three miles by the edge with a crumpled coal sack and a park-keeper's steel-tipped stick. Now they were tucked up in sacks, asleep in a siding, their heads in bins, their beards in straw, in coal-trucks thinking of fires, or lying beyond pickings on Jack Stiff's slab near the pub in the Fishguard Alley, where the methylated-spirit drinkers danced into the policemen's arms and women like lumps of clothes in a pool waited, in doorways and holes in the soaking wall, for vampires or firemen. Night was properly down on us now. The wind changed. Thin rain began. The sands themselves went out. We stood in the scooped, windy room of the arch, listening to the noises from the muffled town, a goods train shunting, a siren in the docks, the hoarse trams in the streets far behind, one bark of a dog, unplaceable sounds, iron being beaten, the distant creaking of wood, doors slamming where there were no houses, an engine coughing like a sheep on a hill.

The two young men were statues smoking, tough-capped and collarless watchers and witnesses carved out of the stone of the blowing room where they stood at my side with nowhere to go, nothing to do, and all the raining, almost winter, night before them. I cupped a match to let them see my face in a dramatic shadow, my eyes mysteriously sunk, perhaps, in a startling white face, my young looks savage in the sudden flicker of light, to make them wonder who I was as I puffed my last butt and puzzled about them. Why was the soft-faced young man, with his tame devil's eyebrows, standing like a stone figure with a glow-worm in it? He should have a nice girl to bully him gently and take him to cry in the pictures, or kids to bounce in a kitchen in Rodney Street. There was no sense in standing silent for hours under a railway arch on a hell of a night at the end of a bad summer when girls were waiting, ready to be hot and friendly, in chip shops and shop doorways and Rabbiotti's all-night café, when the public bar of the 'Bay View' at the corner had a fire and skittles and a swarthy, sensuous girl with different coloured eyes, when the billiard saloons were open, except the one in High Street you couldn't go into without a collar and tie, when the closed parks had empty, covered bandstands and the railings were easy to climb.

A church clock somewhere struck a lot, faintly from the night on the right, but I didn't count.

The other young man, less than two feet from me, should be shouting with the boys, boasting in lanes, propping counters, prancing and clouting in the Mannesmann Hall, or whispering around a bucket in a ring corner. Why was he humped here with a moody man and myself, listening to our breathing, to the sea, the wind scattering sand through the archway, a chained dog and a foghorn and the rumble of trams a dozen streets away, watching a match strike, a boy's fresh face spying in a shadow, the lighthouse beams, the movement of a hand to a fag, when the sprawling town in a drizzle, the pubs and the clubs and the coffee-shops, the prowlers' streets, the arches near the promenade, were full of friends and enemies? He could be playing nap by a candle in a shed in a wood-yard.

Families sat down to supper in rows of short houses, the wireless sets were on, the daughters' young men sat in the front rooms. In neighbouring houses they read the news off the table-cloth, and the potatoes from dinner were fried up. Cards were played in the front rooms of houses on the hills. In the houses on tops of the hills families were entertaining friends, and the blinds of the front rooms were not quite drawn. I heard the sea in a cold bit of the cheery night.

One of the strangers said suddenly, in a high, clear voice: 'What are we all doing then?'

'Standing under a bloody arch,' said the other one.

'And it's cold,' I said.

'It isn't very cosy,' said the high voice of the young man with the pleasant face, now invisible. 'I've been in better hotels than this.'

'What about that night in the Majestic?' said the other voice.

There was a long silence.

'Do you often stand here?' said the pleasant man. His voice might never have broken.

'No, this is the first time here,' I said. 'Sometimes I stand in the Brynmill arch.'

'Ever tried the old pier?'

'It's no good in the rain, is it?'

'Underneath the pier, I mean, in the girders.'

'No, I haven't been there.'

'Tom spends every Sunday under the pier,' the pug-faced young man said bitterly. 'I got to take him his dinner in a piece of paper.'

'There's another train coming,' I said. It tore over us, the arch bellowed, the wheels screamed through our heads, we were deafened and spark-blinded and crushed under the fiery weight and we rose again, like battered black men, in the grave of the arch. No noise at all from the swallowed town. The trams had rattled themselves dumb. A pressure of the hidden sea rubbed

away the smudge of the docks. Only three young men were
alive.

One said: 'It's a sad life, without a home.'

'Haven't you got a home then?' I said.

'Oh, yes, I've got a home all right.

'I got one, too.'

'And I live near Cwmdonkin Park,' I said.

'That's another place Tom sits in in the dark. He says he
listens to the owls.'

'I knew a chap once who lived in the country, near Bridgend,'
said Tom, 'and they had a munition works there in the War and
it spoiled all the birds. The chap I know says you can always tell
a cuckoo from Bridgend, it goes: "Cuckbloodyoo!
cuckbloodyoo!"'

'Cuckbloodyoo!' echoed the arch.

'Why are you standing under the arch, then?' asked Tom.
'It's warm at home. You can draw the curtains and sit by the
fire, snug as a bug. Gracie's on the wireless to-night. No
shananacking in the old moonlight.'

'I don't want to go home, I don't want to sit by the fire. I've
got nothing to do when I'm in and I don't want to go to bed. I
like standing about like this with nothing to do, in the dark all
by myself,' I said.

And I did, too. I was a lonely nightwalker and a steady
stander-at-corners. I liked to walk through the wet town after
midnight, when the streets were deserted and the window lights
out, alone and alive on the glistening tramlines in dead and
empty High Street under the moon, gigantically sad in the damp
streets by ghostly Ebenezer Chapel. And I never felt more a part
of the remote and overpressing world, or more full of love and
arrogance and pity and humility, not for myself alone, but for
the living earth I suffered on and for the unfeeling systems in the
upper air, Mars and Venus and Brazell and Skully, men in China
and St Thomas, scorning girls and ready girls, soldiers and
bullies and policemen and sharp, suspicious buyers of second-
hand books, bad, ragged women who'd pretend against the
museum wall for a cup of tea, and perfect, unapproachable
women out of the fashion magazines, seven feet high, sailing
slowly in their flat, glazed creations through steel and glass and
velvet. I leant against the wall of a derelict house in the
residential areas or wandered in the empty rooms, stood terrified

on the stairs or gazing through the smashed windows at the sea
or at nothing, and the lights going out one by one in the avenues.
Or I mooched in a half-built house, with the sky stuck in the
roof and cats on the ladders and a wind shaking through the
bare bones of the bedrooms.

'And you can talk,' I said. 'Why aren't you at home ?'

'I don't want to be home,' said Tom.

'I'm not particular,' said his friend.

When a match flared, their heads rocked and spread on the
wall, and shapes of winged bulls and buckets grew bigger and
smaller. Tom began to tell a story. I thought of a new stranger
walking on the sands past the arch and hearing all of a sudden
that high voice out of a hole.

I missed the beginning of the story as I thought of the man on
the sands listening in a panic or dodging, like a footballer, in
and out among the jumping dark towards the lights behind the
railway line, and remembered Tom's voice in the middle of a
sentence.

'. . . went up to them and said it was a lovely night. It wasn't
a lovely night at all. The sands were empty. We asked them
what their names were and they asked us what ours were. We
were walking along by this time. Walter here was telling them
about the glee party in the "Melba" and what went on in the
ladies' cloakroom. You had to drag the tenors away like ferrets.'

'What were their names ?' I asked.

'Doris and Norma,' Walter said.

'So we walked along the sands towards the dunes,' Tom said,
'and Walter was with Doris and I was with Norma. Norma
worked in the steam laundry. We hadn't been walking and
talking for more than a few minutes when, by God, I knew I
was head over heels in love with the girl, and she wasn't the
pretty one, either.'

He described her. I saw her clearly. Her plump, kind face,
jolly brown eyes, warm wide mouth, thick bobbed hair, rough
body, bottle legs, broad bum, grew from a few words right out
of Tom's story, and I saw her ambling solidly along the sands in
a spotted frock in a showering autumn evening with fancy
gloves on her hard hands, a gold bangle, with a voile handkerchief tucked in it, round her wrist, and a navy-blue handbag
with letters and outing snaps, a compact, a bus ticket, and a
shilling.

'Doris was the pretty one,' said Tom, 'smart and touched up and sharp as a knife. I was twenty-six years old and I'd never been in love, and there I was, gawking at Norma in the middle of Tawe sands, too frightened to put my finger on her gloves. Walter had his arm round Doris then.'

They sheltered behind a dune. The night dropped down on them quickly. Walter was a caution with Doris, hugging and larking, and Tom sat close to Norma, brave enough to hold her hand in its cold glove and tell her all his secrets. He told her his age and his job. He liked staying in in the evenings with a good book. Norma liked dances. He liked dances, too. Norma and Doris were sisters. 'I'd never have thought that,' Tom said, 'you're beautiful, I love you.'

Now the story-telling thing in the arch gave place to the loving night in the dunes. The arch was as high as the sky. The faint town noises died. I lay like a pimp in a bush by Tom's side and squinted through to see him round his hands on Norma's breast. 'Don't you dare!' Walter and Doris lay quietly near them. You could have heard a safety-pin fall.

'And the curious thing was,' said Tom, 'that after a time we all sat up on the sand and smiled at each other. And then we all moved softly about on the sand in the dark, without saying a word. And Doris was lying with me, and Norma was with Walter.'

'But why did you change over, if you loved her?' I asked.

'I never understood why,' said Tom. 'I think about it every night.'

'That was in October,' Walter said.

And Tom continued: 'We didn't see much of the girls until July. I couldn't face Norma. Then they brought two paternity orders against us, and Mr Lewis, the magistrate, was eighty years old, and stone deaf, too. He put a little trumpet by his ear and Norma and Doris gave evidence. Then we gave evidence, and he couldn't decide whose was which. And at the end he shook his head back and fore and pointed his trumpet and said: "Just like little dogs!"'

All at once I remembered how cold it was. I rubbed my numb hands together. Fancy standing all night in the cold. Fancy listening, I thought, to a long, unsatisfactory story in the frost-bite night in a polar arch. 'What happened then?' I asked.

Walter answered. 'I married Norma,' he said 'and Tom

married Doris. We had to do the right thing by them, didn't we? That's why Tom won't go home. He never goes home till the early morning. I've got to keep him company. He's my brother.'

It would take me ten minutes to run home. I put up my coat collar and pulled my cap down.

'And the curious thing is,' said Tom, 'that I love Norma and Walter doesn't love Norma or Doris. We've two nice little boys. I call mine Norman.'

We all shook hands.

'See you again,' said Walter.

'I'm always hanging about,' said Tom.

'Abyssinia!'

I walked out of the arch, crossed Trafalgar Square, and pelted up the steep streets.

WHERE TAWE FLOWS

Mr Humphries, Mr Roberts, and young Mr Thomas knocked on the front door of Mrs Emlyn Evans's small villa, 'Lavengro,' punctually at nine o'clock in the evening. They waited, hidden behind a veronica bush, while Mr Evans shuffled in carpet slippers up the passage from the back room and had trouble with the bolts.

Mr Humphries was a school teacher, a tall, fair man with a stammer, who had written an unsuccessful novel.

Mr Roberts, a cheerful, disreputable man of middle age, was a collector for an insurance company; they called him in the trade a body-snatcher, and he was known among his friends as Burke and Hare, the Welsh Nationalist. He had once held a high position in a brewery office.

Young Mr Thomas was at the moment without employment, but it was understood that he would soon be leaving for London to make a career in Chelsea as a free-lance journalist; he was penniless, and hoped, in a vague way, to live on women.

When Mr Evans opened the door and shone his torch down the narrow drive, lighting up the garage and hen-run but missing altogther the whispering bush, the three friends bounded out and cried in threatening voices: 'We're Ogpu men, let us in!'

'We're looking for seditious literature,' said Mr Humphries with difficulty, raising his hand in a salute.

'Heil, Saunders Lewis! and we know where to find it,' said Mr Roberts.

Mr Evans turned off his torch. 'Come in out of the night air, boys, and have a drop of something. It's only parsnip wine,' he added.

They removed their hats and coats, piled them on the end of the bannister, spoke softly for fear of waking up the twins, George and Celia, and followed Mr Evans into his den.

'Where's the trouble and strife, Mr Evans?' said Mr Roberts in a cockney accent. He warmed his hands in front of the fire and regarded with a smile of surprise, though he visited the house every Friday, the neat rows of books, the ornate roll-top desk that made the parlour into a study, the shining grandfather clock, the photographs of children staring stiffly at a dickybird, the still, delicious home-made wine, that had such an effect, in an old beer bottle, the sleeping tom on the frayed rug. 'At home with the *bourgeoisie*.'

He was himself a homeless bachelor with a past, much in debt, and nothing gave him more pleasure than to envy his friends their wives and comforts and to speak of them intimately and disparagingly.

'In the kitchen,' said Mr Evans, handing out glasses.

'A woman's only place,' said Mr Roberts heartily, 'with one exception.'

Mr Humphries and Mr Thomas arranged the chairs around the fire, and all four sat down, close and confidential and with full glasses in their hands. None of them spoke for a time. They gave one another sly looks, sipped and sighed, lit the cigarettes that Mr Evans produced from a draughts box, and once Mr Humphries glanced at the grandfather clock and winked and put his finger to his lips. Then, as the visitors grew warm and the wine worked and they forgot the bitter night outside, Mr Evans said with a little shudder of forbidden delight : 'The wife will be going to bed in half an hour. Then we can start the good work. Have you all got yours with you ?'

'And the tools,' said Mr Roberts, smacking his side pocket.

'What's the word until then ?' said young Mr Thomas.

Mr Humphries winked again. 'Mum !'

'I've been waiting for to-night to come round like I used to wait for Saturdays when I was a boy,' said Mr Evans, 'I got a penny then. And it all went on gob-stoppers and jelly-babies, too.'

He was a traveller in rubber, rubber toys and syringes and bath mats. Sometimes Mr Roberts called him the poor man's friend to make him blush. 'No ! no ! no !' he would say, 'you can look at my samples, there's nothing like that there.' He was a Socialist.

'I used to buy a packet of Cinderellas with my penny,' said Mr Roberts, 'and smoke them in the slaughter-house. The sweetest little smoke in the world. You don't see them now.'

'Do you remember old Jim, the caretaker, in the slaughter-house?' asked Mr Evans.

'He was after my time; I'm no chicken, like you boys.'

'You're not old, Mr Roberts, think of G.B.S.'

'No clean Shavianism for me, I'm an unrepentant eater of birds and beasts,' said Mr Roberts.

'Do you eat flowers, too?'

'Oh! oh! you literary men, don't you talk above my head now. I'm only a poor resurrectionist on the knocker.'

'He'd put his hand down in the guts-box and bring you out a rat with it's neck broken clean as a match for the price of a glass of beer.'

'And it was beer then.'

'Shop! shop!' Mr Humphries beat on the table with his glass, 'you mustn't waste stories, we'll need them all,' he said. 'Have you got the abattoir anecdote down in your memory book, Mr Thomas?'

'I'll remember it.'

'Don't forget, you can only talk at random now,' said Mr Humphries.

'Okay, Roderick!' Mr Thomas said quickly.

Mr Roberts put his hands over his ears. 'The conversation is getting esoteric,' he said. 'Excuse my French! Mr Evans, have you such a thing as a rook rifle? I want to scare the highbrows off. Did I ever tell you the time I lectured to the John O' London's Society on "The Utility of Uselessness"? That was a poser. I talked about Jack London all the time, and when they said at the end that it wasn't a lecture about what I said it was going to be, I said "Well, it was useless lecturing about that, wasn't it?" and they hadn't a word to say. Mrs Dr Davies was in the front row, you remember her? She gave that first lecture on W. J. Locke and got spoonered in the middle. Remember talking about the "Bevagged Loveabond," Mr Humphries?'

'Shop! Shop!' said Mr Humphries, groaning, 'keep it until after.'

'More parsnip?'

'It goes down the throat like silk, Mr Evans.'

'Like baby's milk.'

'Say when, Mr Roberts.'

'A word of four syllables denoting a period of time. Thank you! I read that on a matchbox.'

'Why don't they have serials on matchboxes? You'd buy the shop up to see what Daphne did next,' Mr Humphries said.

He stopped and looked round in embarrassment at the faces of his friends. Daphne was the name of the grass widow in Manselton for whom Mr Roberts had lost both his reputation and his position in the brewery. He had been in the habit of delivering bottles to her house, free of charge, and he had bought her a cocktail cabinet and given her a hundred pounds and his mother's rings. In return she held large parties and never invited him. Only Mr Thomas had noticed the name, and he was saying: 'No, Mr Humphries, on toilet rolls would be best.'

'When I was in London,' Mr Roberts said, 'I stayed with a couple called Armitage in Palmer's Green. He made curtains and blinds. They used to leave each other messages on the toilet paper every single day.'

'If you want to make a Venetain blind,' said Mr Evans, 'stick him in the eye with a hatpin.' He felt, always, a little left out of his evenings at home, and he was waiting for Mrs Evans to come in, disapprovingly, from the kitchen.

'I've often had to use, "Dear Tom, don't forget the Watkinses are coming to tea," or, "To Peggy, from Tom, in remembrance." Mr Armitage was a Mosleyite.'

'Thugs,' said Mr Humphries.

'Seriously, what are we going to do about this uniformication of the individual?' Mr Evans asked. Maud was in the kitchen still; he heard her beating the plates.

'Answering your question with another,' said Mr Roberts, putting one hand on Mr Evans's knee, 'what individuality is there left? The mass-age produces the mass-man. The machine produces the robot.'

'As its slave,' Mr Humphries articulated clearly, 'not, mark you, as its master.'

'There you have it. There it is. Tyrannic dominance by a sparking plug, Mr Humphries, and it's flesh and blood that always pays.'

'Any empty glasses?'

Mr Roberts turned his glass upside down. 'That used to mean, "I'll take on the best man in the room in a bout of fisticuffs," in Llanelly. But seriously, as Mr Evans says, the old-fashioned individualist is a square peg now in a round hole.'

'What a hole!' said Mr Thomas.

'Take our national – what did Onlooker say last week ? – our national misleaders.'

'You take them, Mr Roberts, we've got rats already,' Mr Evans said with a nervous laugh. The kitchen was silent. Maud was ready.

'Onlooker is a *nom de plume* for Basil Gorse Williams,' said Mr Humphries. 'Did any one know that ?'

'*Nom de guerre.* Did you see his article on Ramsay Mac ? "A sheep in wolf's clothing."'

'Know him !' Mr Roberts said scornfully, 'I've been sick on him.'

Mrs Evans heard the last remark as she came into the room. She was a thin woman with bitter lines, tired hands, the ruins of fine brown eyes, and a superior nose. An unshockable woman, she had once listened to Mr Roberts's description of his haemorrhoids for over an hour on a New year's Eve and had allowed him, without protest to call them the grapes of wrath. When sober, Mr Roberts addressed her as 'ma'am' and kept the talk to weather and colds. He sprang to his feet and offered her his chair.

'No, thank you, Mr Roberts,' she said in a clear, hard voice, 'I'm going to bed at once. The cold disagrees with me.'

Go to bed plain Maud, thought young Mr Thomas. 'Will you have a little warm, Mrs Evans, before you retire ?' he said.

She shook her head, gave the friends a thin smile, and said to Mr Evans : 'Put the world right before you come to bed.'

'Good night, Mrs Evans.'

'It won't be after midnight this time, Maud, I promise. I'll put Sambo out in the back.'

'Good night, ma'am.'

Sleep tight, hoity.

'I won't disturb you gentlemen any more,' she said. 'What's left of the parsnip wine for Christmas is in the boot cupboard, Emlyn. Don't let it waste. Good night.'

Mr Evans raised his eyebrows and whistled. 'Whew ! boys.' He pretended to fan his face with his tie. Then his hand stopped still in the air. 'She was used to a big house,' he said, 'with servants.'

Mr Roberts brought out pencils and fountain pens from his side pocket. 'Where's the priceless MS. ? Tempus is fugiting.'

Mr Humphries and Mr Thomas put notebooks on their knees,

took a pencil each, and watched Mr Evans open the door of the grandfather clock. Beneath the swinging weights was a heap of papers tied in a blue bow. These Mr Evans placed on the desk.

'I call order,' said Mr Roberts. 'Let's see where we were. Have you got the minutes, Mr Thomas?'

'"*Where Tawe Flows*,"' said Mr Thomas. '"a Novel of Provincial Life. Chapter One: a cross-section description of the town, Dockland, Slums, Suburbia, etc." We finished that. The title decided upon was: Chapter One, "The Public Town." Chapter Two is to be called "The Private Lives," and Mr Humphries has proposed the following: "Each of the collaborators take one character from each social sphere or stratum of the town and introduce him to the readers with a brief history of his life up to the point at which we commence the story, i.e. the winter of this very year. These introductions of the characters, hereafter to be regarded as the principal protagonists, and their biographical chronicles shall constitute the second chapter." Any questions, gentlemen?'

Mr Humphries agreed with all he had said. His character was a sensitive schoolmaster of advanced opinions, who was misjudged and badly treated.

'No questions,' said Mr Evans. He was in charge of Surburbia. He rustled his notes and waited to begin.

'I haven't written anything yet,' Mr Roberts said, 'it's all in my head.' He had chosen the Slums.

'Personally,' said Mr Thomas, 'I haven't made up my mind whether to have a barmaid or a harlot.'

'What about a barmaid who's a harlot too?' Mr Roberts suggested. 'Or perhaps we could have a couple of characters each?' I'd like to do an alderman. And a gold-digger.'

'Who had a word for them, Mr Humphries?' said Mr Thomas.

'The Greeks.'

Mr Roberts nudged Mr Evans and whispered: 'I just thought of an opening sentence for my bit. Listen Emlyn. "On the rickety table in the corner of the crowded, dilapidated room, a stranger might have seen, by the light of the flickering candle in the gin-bottle, a broken cup, full of sick or custard." '

'Be serious, Ted,' said Mr Evans laughing. 'You wrote that sentence down.'

'No, I swear it came to me just like that!' He flicked his fingers. 'And who's been reading my notes?'

'Have you put anything on paper yourself, Mr Thomas?'

'Not yet, Mr Evans.' He had been writing, that week, the story of a cat who jumped over a woman the moment she died and turned her into a vampire. He had reached the part of the story where the woman was an undead children's governess, but he could not think how to fit it into the novel.

'There's no need, is there,' he asked, 'for us to avoid the fantastic altogether?'

'Wait a bit! wait a bit!' said Mr Humphries, 'let's get our realism straight. Mr Thomas will be making all the characters Blue Birds before we know where we are. One thing at a time. Has anyone got the history of his character ready?' He had his biography in his hand, written in red ink. The writing was scholarly and neat and small.

'I think my character is ready to take the stage,' said Mr Evans. 'But I haven't written it out. I'll have to refer to the notes and make the rest up out of my head. It's a very silly story.'

'Well, you must begin, of course,' said Mr Humphries with disappointment.

'Everybody's biography is silly,' Mr Roberts said. 'My own would make a cat laugh.'

Mr Humphries said: 'I must disagree there. The life of that mythical common denominator, the man in the street, is dull as ditchwater, Mr Roberts. Capitalist society has made him a mere bundle of repressions and useless habits under that symbol of middle-class divinity, the bowler.' He looked quickly away from the notes in the palm of his hand. 'The ceaseless toil for bread and butter, the ogres of unemployment, the pettifogging gods of gentility, the hollow lies of the marriage bed. Marriage,' he said, dropping his ash on the carpet, 'legal monogamous prostitution.'

'Whoa! whoa! there he goes!'

'Mr Humphries is on his hobby-horse again.'

'I'm afraid,' said Mr Evans, 'that I lack our friend's extensive vocabulary. Have pity on a poor amateur. You're shaming my little story before I begin.'

'I still think the life of the ordinary man is most extraordinary,' Mr Roberts said, 'take my own . . .'

'As the secretary,' said Mr Thomas, 'I vote we take Mr

Evans's story. We must try to get *Tawe* finished for the spring list.'

'My *To-morrow and To-morrow* was published in the summer in a heat wave,' Mr Humphries said.

Mr Evans coughed, looked into the fire, and began.

'Her name is Mary,' he said, 'but that's not her name really. I'm calling her that because she is a real woman and we don't want any libel. She lives in a house called "Bellevue," but that's not the proper name, of course. A villa by any other name, Mr Humphries. I chose her for my character because her life is a little tragedy, but it's not without its touches of humour either. It's almost Russian. Mary – Mary Morgan now but she was Mary Phillips before she was married and that comes later, that's the anti-climax – wasn't a suburbanite from birth, she didn't live under the shadow of the bowler, like you and me. Or like me, anyway. I was born in "The Poplars" and now I'm in "Lavengro." From bowler to bowler, though I must say, apropos of Mr Humphries' diatribe, and I'm the first to admire his point of view, that the everyday man's just as interesting a character as the neurotic poets of Bloomsbury.'

'Remind me to shake your hand,' said Mr Roberts.

'You've been reading the Sunday papers,' said Mr Humphries accusingly.

'You two argue the toss later on,' Mr Thomas said.

'"Is the Ordinary Man a Mouse?" Now, what about Mary?'

'Mary Phillips,' continued Mr Evans, ' – and any more interruptions from the intelligentsia and I'll get Mr Roberts to tell you the story of his operation, no pardons granted – lived on a big farm in Carmarthenshire, I'm not going to tell you exactly where, and her father was a widower. He had any amount of what counts and he drank like a fish, but he was always a gentleman with it. Now, now! forget the class war, I could see it smouldering. He came of a very good, solid family, but he raised his elbow, that's all there is to it.'

Mr Roberts said: 'Huntin', fishin' and boozin'.'

'No, he wasn't quite county and he wasn't a *nouveau riche* either. No Philippstein about him, though I'm not anti-Semite. You've only got to think of Einstein and Freud. There are bad Christians, too. He was just what I'm telling you, if you'd only let me, a man of good farming stock who'd made his pile and now he was spending it.'

'Liquidating it.'

'He'd only got one child, and that was Mary, and she was so prim and proper she couldn't bear to see him the worse for drink. Every night he came home, and he was always the worse, she'd shut herself in her bedroom and hear him rolling about the house and calling for her and breaking the china sometimes. But only sometimes, and he wouldn't have hurt a hair of her head. She was about eighteen and a fine-looking girl, not a film star, mind, not Mr Roberts's type at all, and perhaps she had an Oedipus complex, but she hated her father and she was ashamed of him.'

'What's my type, Mr Evans?'

'Don't pretend not to know, Mr Roberts. Mr Evans means the sort you can take home and show her your stamp collection.'

'I will have hush,' said Mr Thomas.

''Ave 'ush, is the phrase,' Mr Roberts said. 'Mr Thomas, you're afraid we'll think you're patronizing the lower classes if you drop your aspirates.'

'No nasturtiums, Mr Roberts,' said Mr Humphries.

'Mary Phillips fell in love with a young man whom I shall call Marcus David,' Mr Evans went on, still staring at the fire, avoiding his friends' eyes, and speaking to the burning pictures, 'and she told her father: "Father, Marcus and I want to be engaged. I'm bringing him home one night for supper, and you must promise me that you'll be sober."'

'He said: "I'm always sober!" but he wasn't sober when he said it, and after a time he promised.'

'"If you break your word, I'll never forgive you," Mary said to him.'

'Marcus was a wealthy farmer's son from another district, a bit of a Valentino in a bucolic way, if you can imagine that. She invited him to supper, and he came, very handsome, with larded hair. The servants were out. Mr Phillips had gone to a mart that morning and hadn't returned. She answered the door herself. It was a winter's evening.

'Picture the scene. A prim, well-bred country girl, full of fixations and phobias, proud as a duchess, and blushing like a dairymaid, opening the door to her beloved and seeing him standing there on the pitch-black threshold, shy and handsome. This is from my notes.

'Her future hung on that evening as on a thread. "Come in,"

she insisted. They didn't kiss, but she wanted him to bow and print his lips on her hand. She took him over the house, which had been specially cleaned and polished, and showed him the case with Swansea china in it. There was a portrait gallery, so she showed him the snaps of her mother and the photograph of her father, tall and young and sober, in the suit he hunted otters in. And all the time she was proudly parading their possessions, attempting to prove to Marcus, whose father was a J.P., that her background was prosperous enough for her to be his bride, she was waiting fearfully the entrance of her father.

'"O God," she was praying, when they sat down to a cold supper, "that my father will arrive presentable." Call her a snob, if you will, but remember that the life of country gentry or near gentry, was bound and dedicated by the antiquated totems and fetishes of possession. Over supper she told him her family tree and hoped the supper was to his taste. It should have been a hot supper, but she didn't want him to see the servants who were old and dirty. Her father wouldn't change them because they'd always been with him, and there you see the Toryism of this particular society rampant. To cut a long story (this is only the gist, Mr Thomas). They were half-way through supper, and their conversation was becoming more intimate, and she had almost forgotten her father, when the front door burst open and Mr Phillips staggered into the passage, drunk as a judge. The dining-room door was ajar and they could see him plainly. I will not try to describe Mary's kaleidoscopic emotions as her father rocked and mumbled in a thick voice in the passage. He was a big man – I forgot to tell you – six foot and eighteen stone.

'"Quick! quick! under the table!" she whispered urgently, and she pulled Marcus by the hand and they crouched under the table. What bewilderment Marcus experienced we shall never know.

'Mr Phillips came in and saw nobody and sat down at the table and finished all the supper. He licked both plates clean, and under the table they heard him swearing and guzzling. Every time Marcus fidgeted, Mary said: "Shh!"

'When there was nothing left to eat, Mr Phillips wandered out of the room. They saw his legs. Then, somehow, he climbed upstairs, saying words that made Mary shudder under the table, words of three syllables.'

'Give us three guesses,' said Mr Roberts.

'And she heard him go into his bedroom. She and Marcus crept out of hiding and sat down in front of their empty plates.

' "I don't know how to apologise, Mr David," she said, and she was nearly crying.'

' "There's nothing the matter," he said, he was an amenable young man by all accounts, "he's only been to the mart at Carmarthen. I don't like t.t.s myself."

' "Drink makes men sodden beasts," she said.

'He said she had nothing to worry about and that he didn't mind, and she offered him fruit.

' "What will you think of us, Mr David? I've never seen him like that before."

'The little adventure brought them closer together, and soon they were smiling at one another and her wounded pride was almost healed again, but suddenly Mr Phillips opened his bedroom door and charged downstairs, eighteen stone of him, shaking the house.

' "Go away!" she cried softly to Marcus, "please go away before he comes in!"

'There wasn't time. Mr Phillips stood in the passage in the nude.

'She dragged Marcus under the table again, and she covered her eyes not to see her father. She could hear him fumbling in the hall-stand for an umbrella, and she knew what he was going to do. He was going outside to obey a call of nature. "O God," she prayed, "let him find an umbrella and go out. Not in the passage! Not in the passage!" They heard him shout for his umbrella. She uncovered her eyes and saw him pulling the front door down. He tore it off its hinges and held it flat above him and tottered out into the dark.

' "Hurry! please hurry!" she said. "Leave me now, Mr David." She drove him out from under the table.

' "Please, please go now," she said, "we'll never meet again. Leave me to my shame." She began to cry, and he ran out of the house. And she stayed under the table all night.'

'Is that all?' said Mr Roberts. 'A very moving incident, Emlyn. How did you come by it?'

'How can it be all?' said Mr Humphries. 'It doesn't explain how Mary Phillips reached "Bellevue." We've left her under a table in Carmarthenshire.'

'I think Marcus is a fellow to be despised,' Mr Thomas said. 'I'd never leave a girl like that, would you, Mr Humphries?'

'Under a table, too. That's the bit I like. That's a position. Perspectives were different,' said Mr Roberts, 'in those days. That narrow puritanism is a spent force. Imagine Mrs Evans under the table. And what happened afterwards? Did the girl die of cramp?'

Mr Evans turned from the fire to reprove him. 'Be as flippant as you will, but the fact remains that an incident like that has a lasting effect on a proud, sensitive girl like Mary. I'm not defending her sensitivity, the whole basis of her pride is outmoded. The social system, Mr Roberts, is not in the box. I'm telling you an incident that occurred. Its social implications are outside our concern.'

'I'm put in my place, Mr Evans.'

'What happened to Mary then?'

'Don't vex him, Mr Thomas, he'll bite your head off.'

Mr Evans went out for more parsnip wine, and returning, said:

'What happened next? Oh! Mary left her father, of course. She said she'd never forgive him, and she didn't, so she went to live with her uncle in Cardiganshire, a Dr Emyr Lloyd. He was a J.P. too, and rolling in it, about seventy-five – now, remember the age – with a big practice and influential friends. One of his oldest friends was John William Hughes – that's not his name – the London draper, who had a country house near his. Remember what the great Caradoc Evans says? The Cardies always go back to Wales to die when they've rooked the cockneys and made a packet.

'And the only son, Henry William Hughes, who was a nicely educated young man, fell in love with Mary as soon as he saw her and she forgot Marcus and her shame under the table and she fell in love with him. Now don't look disappointed before I begin, this isn't a love story. But they decided to get married, and John William Hughes gave his consent because Mary's uncle was one of the most respected men in the country and her father had money and it would come to her when he died and he was doing his best.

'They were to be married quietly in London. Everything was arranged. Mr Phillips wasn't invited. Mary had her trousseau. Dr Lloyd was to give her away. Beatrice and Betti William

Hughes were bridesmaids. Mary went up to London with Beatrice and Betti and stayed with a cousin, and Henry William Hughes stayed in the flat above his father's shop, and the day before the wedding Dr Lloyd arrived from the country, saw Mary for tea, and had dinner with John William Hughes. I wonder who paid for it, too. Then Dr Lloyd retired to his hotel. I'm giving you these trivial details so that you can see how orderly and ordinary everything was. There the actors were, safe and sure.

'Next day. Just before the ceremony was to begin, Mary and her cousin, whose name and character are extraneous, and the two sisters, they were both plain and thirty, waited impatiently for Dr Lloyd to call on them. The minutes passed by, Mary was crying, the sisters were sulking, the cousin was getting in everybody's way, but the doctor didn't come. The cousin telephoned the doctor's hotel, but she was told he hadn't spent the night there. Yes, the clerk in the hotel said, he knew the doctor was going to a wedding. No, his bed hadn't been slept in. The clerk suggested that perhaps he was waiting at the church.

'The taxi was ticking away, and that worried Beatrice and Betti, and at last the sisters and the cousin and Mary drove together to the church. A crowd had gathered outside. The cousin poked her head out of the taxi window and asked a policeman to call a church-warden, and the warden said that Dr Lloyd wasn't there and the groom and the best man were waiting. You can imagine Mary Phillips's feelings when she saw a commotion at the church door and a policeman leading her father out. Mr Phillips had his pockets full of bottles, and how he ever got into the church in the first place no one knew.'

'That's the last straw,' said Mr Roberts.

'Beatrice and Betti said to her: "Don't cry, Mary, the policeman's taking him away. Look! he's fallen in the gutter! There's a splash! Don't take on, it'll be all over soon. You'll be Mrs Henry William Hughes." They were doing their best.

' "You can marry without Dr Lloyd," the cousin told her, and she brightened through her tears – anybody would be crying – and at that moment another policeman – '

'Another!' said Mr Roberts.

' – made his way through the crowd and walked up to the door of the church and sent a message inside. John William

Hughes and Henry William Hughes and the best man came out, and they all talked to the policeman, waving their arms and pointing to the taxi with Mary and the bridesmaids and the cousin in it.

'John William Hughes ran down the path to the taxi and shouted through the window: "Dr Lloyd is dead! We'll have to cancel the wedding."

'Henry William Hughes followed him and opened the taxi door and said: "You must drive home Mary. We've got to go to the police station."

'"And the mortuary," his father said.

'So the taxi drove the bride-to-be home, and the sisters cried worse than she did all the way.'

'That's a sad end,' said Mr Roberts with appreciation. He poured himself another drink.

'It isn't really the end,' Mr Evans said, 'because the wedding wasn't just cancelled. It never came off.'

'But why?' asked Mr Humphries, who had followed the story with a grave expression, even when Mr Phillips fell in the gutter. 'Why should the doctor's death stop everything? She could get someone else to give her away. I'd have done it myself.'

'It wasn't the doctor's death, but where and how he died,' said Mr Evans. 'He died in bed in a bed-sitting-room in the arms of a certain lady. A woman of the town.'

'Kiss me!' Mr Roberts said. 'Seventy-five years old. I'm glad you asked us to remember his age, Mr Evans.'

'But how did Mary Phillips come to live in "Bellevue"? You haven't told us that,' Mr Thomas said.

'The William Hugheses wouldn't have the niece of a man who died in those circumstances —'

'However complimentary to his manhood,' Mr Humphries said, stammering.

' — marry into their family, so she went back to live with her father and he reformed at once — oh! she had a temper those days — and one day she met a traveller in grain and pigs' food and she married him out of spite. They came to live in "Bellevue," and when Mr Phillips died he left his money to the chapel, so Mary got nothing after all.'

'Nor her husband either. What did you say he travelled in?' asked Mr Roberts.

'Grain and pigs' food.'

After that, Mr Humphries read his biography, which was long and sad and detailed and in good prose; and Mr Roberts told a story about the slums, which could not be included in the book.

Then Mr Evans looked at his watch. 'It's midnight. I promised Maud not after midnight. Where's the cat? I've got to put him out; he tears the cushions. Not that I mind. Sambo! Sambo!'

'There he is, Mr Evans, under the table.'

'Like poor Mary,' said Mr Roberts.

Mr Humphries, Mr Roberts, and young Mr Thomas collected their hats and coats from the bannister.

'Do you know what time it is, Emlyn?' Mrs Evans called from upstairs.

Mr Roberts opened the door and hurried out.

'I'm coming now, Maud, I'm just saying good night. Good night,' Mr Evans said in a loud voice. 'Next Friday, nine sharp,' he whispered. 'I'll polish my story up. We'll finish the second chapter and get going on the third. Good night, comrades.'

'Emlyn! Emlyn!' called Mrs Evans.

'Good night, Mary,' said Mr Roberts to the closed door.

The three friends walked down the drive.

WHO DO YOU WISH WAS WITH US?

Birds in the Cresent trees were singing; boys on bicycles were ringing their bells and pedalling down the slight slope to make the whirrers in their wheels startle the women gabbing on the sunny doorsteps; small girls on the pavement, wheeling young brothers and sisters in prams, were dressed in their summer best and with coloured ribbons; on the circular swing in the public playground, children from the snot school spun themselves happy and sick, crying 'Swing us!' and 'Swing us!' and 'Ooh! I'm falling!'; the morning was as varied and bright as though it were an international or a jubilee when Raymond Price and I, flannelled and hatless, with sticks and haversacks, set out together to walk to the Worm's Head. Striding along, in step, through the square of the residential Uplands, we brushed by young men in knife-creased whites and showing-off blazers, and hockey-legged girls with towels round their necks and celluloid sun-glasses, and struck a letterbox with our sticks, and bullied our way through a crowd of day-trippers who waited at the stop of the Gower-bound buses, and stepped over luncheon baskets, not caring if we trod in them.

'Why can't those bus lizards walk?' Ray said.

'They were born too tired,' I said.

We went on up Sketty Road at a great speed, our haversacks jumping on our backs. We rapped on every gate to give a terrific walker's benediction to the people in the choking houses. Like a breath of fresh air we passed a man in office pin-stripes standing, with a dog-lead in his hand, whistling at a corner. Tossing the sounds and smells of the town from us with the swing of our shoulders and loose-limbed strides, half-way up the road we heard women on an outing call 'Mutt and Jeff!' for Ray was tall and thin and I was short. Streamers flew out of the charabanc. Ray, sucking hard at his bulldog pipe, walked too fast to wave and did not even smile. I wondered whom I had missed among the waving women bowling over the rise. My love to come, with a paper cap on, might have sat at the back of the outing, next to the barrel; but, once away from the familiar roads and swinging towards the coast, I forgot her face and voice, that had been made at night, and breathed the country air in.

'There's a different air here. You breathe, It's like the country,' Ray said, 'and a bit of the sea mixed. Draw it down; it'll blow off the nicotine.'

He spat in his hand. 'Still town grey,' he said.

He put back the spit in his mouth and we walked on with our heads high.

By this time we were three miles from the town. The semi-detached houses, with a tin-roofed garage each and a kennel in the back plot and a mowed lawn, with sometimes a hanging coco-nut on a pole, or a bird-bath, or a bush like a peacock, grew fewer when we reached the outskirts of the common.

Ray stopped and sighed and said: 'Wait half a sec, I want to fill the old pipe.' He held a match to it as though we were in a storm.

Hot-faced and wet-browed, we grinned at each other. Already the day had brought us close as truants; we were running away, or walking with pride and mischief, arrogantly from the streets that owned us into the unpredictable country. I thought it was against our fate to stride in the sun without the shop-windows dazzling or the music of mowers rising above the birds. A bird's dropping fell on a fence. It was one in the eye for the town. A sheep cried 'Baa!' out of sight, and that would show the Uplands. I did not know what it would show. 'A couple of wanderers in wild Wales,' Ray said, winking, and a lorry carrying cement drove past us towards the golf links. He slapped my haversack and straightened his shoulders. 'Come on. Let's be going.' We walked uphill faster than before.

A party of cyclists had pulled up on the roadside and were drinking dandelion and burdock from paper cups. I saw the empty bottles in a bush. All the boys wore singlets and shorts, and the girls wore open cricket shirts and boys' long grey trousers, with safety-pins for clips at the bottoms.

'There's room for one behind, sonny boy,' a girl on a tandem said to me.

'It won't be a stylish marriage,' Ray said.

'That was quick,' I told Ray as we walked away from them and the boys began to sing.

'God, I like this !' said Ray. On the first rise of the dusty road through the spreading heathered common, he shaded his eyes and looked all round him, smoking like a chimney and pointing with his Irish stick at the distant clumps of trees and sights of the sea between them. 'Down there is Oxwich, but you can't see it. That's a farm. See the roof ? No, there, follow my finger. This is the life,' he said.

Side by side, thrashing the low banks, we marched down the very middle of the road, and Ray saw a rabbit running. 'You wouldn't think this was near town. It's wild.'

We pointed out the birds whose names we knew, and the rest of the names we made up. I saw gulls and crows, though the crows may have been rooks, and Ray said that thrushes and swallows and skylarks flew above us as we hurried and hummed.

He stopped to pull some blades of grass. 'They should be straws,' he said, and put them in his mouth next to his pipe. 'God, the sky's blue ! Think of me, in the GWR when all this is about. Rabbits and fields and farms. You wouldn't think I'd suffered to look at me now. I could do anything, I could drive cows, I could plough a field.'

His father and sister and brother were dead, and his mother sat all day in a wheel-chair, crippled with arthritis. He was ten years older than I was. He had a lined and bony face and a tight, crooked mouth. His upper lip had vanished.

Alone on the long road, the common in the heat mist wasting for miles on either side, we walked on under the afternoon sun, growing thirsty and drowsy but never slowing our pace. Soon the cycling party rode by, three boys and three girls and the one girl on the tandem, all laughing and ringing.

'How's Shanks's pony ?'

'We'll see you on the way back.'

'You'll be walking still.'

'Like a crutch ?' They shouted.

Then they were gone. The dust settled again. Their bells rang faintly through the wood around the road before us. The wild common, six miles and a bit from the town, lay back without a figure on it, and, under the trees, smoking hard to keep the gnats away, we leant against a trunk and talked like men, on the edge of an untrodden place, who have not seen another man for years.

'Do you remember Curly Parry ?'

I had seen him only two days ago in the snooker-room, but his dimpled face was fading, even as I thought of him, into the colours of our walk, the ash-white of the road, the common heathers, the green and blue of fields and fragmentary sea, and the memory of his silly voice was lost in the sounds of birds and unreasonably moving leaves in the lack of wind.

'I wonder what he's doing now? He should get out more in the open air, he's a proper town boy. Look at us here.' Ray waved his pipe at the trees and leafy sky. 'I wouldn't change this for High Street.'

I looked at us there; a boy and a young man, with faces, under the strange sunburn, pale from the cramped town, out of breath and hot-footed, pausing in the early afternoon on a road through a popular wood, and I could see the unaccustomed happiness in Ray's eyes and the impossible friendliness in mine, and Ray protested against his history each time he wondered or pointed in the country scene and I had more love in me than I could ever want or use.

'Yes, look at us here,' I said, 'dawdling about. Worm's Head is twelve miles off. Don't you want to hear a tramcar, Ray? That's a wood pigeon. See! The boys are out on the streets with the sports special now. Paper! paper! I bet you Curl's potting the red. Come on! come on!'

'Eyes right!' said Ray, 'I's b—d! Remember that story?'

Up the road and out of the wood, and a double-decker roared behind us.

'The Rhossilli bus is coming,' I said.

We both held up our sticks to stop it.

'Why did you stop the bus?' Ray said, when we were sitting upstairs. 'This was a walking holiday.'

'You stopped it as well.'

We sat in front like two more drivers.

'Can't you mind the ruts?' I said.

'You're wobbling,' said Ray.

We opened our haversacks and shared the sandwiches and hard-boiled eggs and meat paste and drank from the thermos in turns.

'When we get home don't say we took a bus,' I said. 'Pretend we walked all day. There goes Oxwich! It doesn't seem far, does it? We'd have had beards by now.'

The bus passed the cyclists crawling up a hill. 'Like a tow

along?' I shouted, but they couldn't hear. The girl on the tandem was a long way behind the others.

We sat with our lunch on our laps, forgetting to steer, letting the driver in his box beneath drive where and how he liked on the switch-back road, and saw grey chapels and weather-worn angels; at the feet of the hills farthest from the sea, pretty, pink cottages – horrible, I thought, to live in, for grass and trees would imprison me more securely than any jungle of packed and swarming streets and chimney-roosting roofs – and petrol pumps and hayricks and a man on a cart-horse standing stock still in a ditch, surrounded by flies.

'This is the way to see the country.'

The bus, on a narrow hill, sent two haversacked walkers bounding to the shelter of the hedge, where they stretched out their arms and drew their bellies in.

'That might have been you and me.'

We looked back happily at the men against the hedge. They climbed on to the road, slow as snails continued walking, and grew smaller.

At the entrance to Rhossilli we pushed the conductor's bell and stopped the bus, and walked, with springing steps, the few hundred yards to the village.

'We've done it in pretty good time,' said Ray.

'I think it's a record,' I said.

Laughing on the cliff above the very long golden beach, we pointed out to each other, as though the other were blind, the great rock of the Worm's Head. The sea was out. We crossed over on slipping stones and stood, at last, triumphantly on the windy top. There was monstrous, thick grass there that made us spring-heeled, and we laughed and bounced on it, scaring the sheep who ran up and down the battered sides like goats. Even on this calmest day a wind blew along the Worm. At the end of the humped and serpentine body, more gulls than I had ever seen before cried over their new dead and the droppings of ages. On the point, the sound of my quiet voice was scooped and magnified into a hollow shout, as though the wind around me had made a shell or cave, with blue, intangible roof and sides, as tall and wide as all the arched sky, and the flapping gulls were made thunderous. Standing there, legs apart, one hand on my hip, shading my eyes like Raleigh in some picture, I thought myself alone in the epileptic moment near bad sleep, when the

legs grow long and sprout into the night and the heart hammers
to wake the neighbours and breath is a hurricane through the
elastic room. Instead of becoming small on the great rock poised
between sky and sea, I felt myself the size of a breathing
building, and only Ray in the world could match my lovely
bellow as I said: 'Why don't we live here always? Always and
always. Build a bloody house and live like bloody kings!' The
word bellowed among the squawking birds, they carried it off
to the headland in the drums of their wings; like a tower, Ray
pranced on the unsteady edge of a separate rock and beat about
with his stick, which could turn into snakes or flames; and we
sank to the ground, the rubbery, gull-limed grass, the sheep-
piled stones, the pieces of bones and feathers, and crouched at
the extreme point of the Peninsula. We were still for so long
that the dirty-grey gulls calmed down, and some settled near us.

Then we finished our food.

'This isn't like any other place,' I said. I was almost my own
size again, five feet five and eight stone, and my voice didn't
sweep any longer up to the amplifying sky. 'It could be in the
middle of the sea. You could think the Worm was moving,
couldn't you? Guide it to Ireland, Ray. We'll see W. B. Yeats
and you can kiss the Blarney. We'll have a fight in Belfast.'

Ray looked out of place on the end of the rock. He would not
make himself easy and loll in the sun and roll on to his side to
stare down a precipice into the sea, but tried to sit upright as
though he were in a hard chair and had nothing to do with his
hands. He fiddled with his tame stick and waited for the day to
be orderly, for the Head to grow paths and for railings to shoot
up on the scarred edges.

'It's too wild for a townee,' I said.

'Townee yourself! Who stopped the bus?'

'Aren't you glad we stopped it? We'd still be walking, like
Felix. You're just pretending you don't like it here. You were
dancing on the edge.'

'Only a couple of hops.'

'I know what it is, you don't like the furniture. There's not
enough sofas and chairs,' I said.

'You think you're a country boy; you don't know a cow from
a horse.'

We began to quarrel, and soon Ray felt at home again
and forgot the monotonous out-of-doors. If snow had fallen

suddenly he would not have noticed. He drew down into himself, and the rock, to him, became dark as a house with the blinds drawn. The sky-high shapes that had danced and bellowed at birds crept down to hide, two small town mutterers in a hollow.

I knew what was going to happen by the way Ray lowered his head and brought his shoulders up so that he looked like a man with no neck, and by the way he sucked his breath in between his teeth. He stared at his dusty white shoes and I knew what shapes his imagination made of them, they were the feet of a man dead in bed, and he was going to talk about his brother. Sometimes, leaning against a fence when we watched football, I caught him staring at his own thin hand; he was thinning it more and more, removing the flesh, seeing Harry's hand in front of him, with the bones appearing through the sensitive skin. If he lost the world around him for a moment, if I left him alone, if he cast his eyes down, if his hand lost its grip on the hard, real fence or the hot bowl of his pipe, he would be back in ghastly bedrooms, carrying cloths and basins and listening for handbells.

'I've never seen such a lot of gulls,' I said. 'Have you ever seen such a lot ? Such a lot of gulls. You try and count them. Two of them are fighting up there; look, pecking each other like hens in the air. What'll you bet the big one wins ? Old dirty beak ! I wouldn't like to have had his dinner, a bit of sheep and dead gull.' I swore at myself for saying the word 'dead'. 'Wasn't it gay enough in town this morning ?' I said.

Ray stared at his hand. Nothing could stop him now. 'Wasn't it gay in town this morning ? Everybody laughing and smiling in their summer outfits. The kids were playing and everybody was happy; they almost had the band out. I used to hold my father down on the bed when he had fits. I had to change the sheets twice a day for my brother, there was blood on everything. I watched him getting thinner and thinner; in the end you could lift him up with one hand. And his wife wouldn't go to see him because he coughed in her face, Mother couldn't move, and I had to cook as well, cook and nurse and change the sheets and hold father down when he got mad. It's embittered my outlook,' he said.

'But you loved the walk, you enjoyed yourself on the common. It's a wonderful day, Ray. I'm sorry about your brother. Let's explore. Let's climb down to the sea. Perhaps there's a cave with prehistoric drawings, and we can write an article and make a fortune. Let's climb down.'

'My brother used to ring a bell for me; he could only whisper. He used to say: "Ray, look at my legs. Are they thinner to-day?"'

'The sun's going down. Let's climb.'

'Father thought I was trying to murder him when I held him on the bed. I was holding him down when he died, and he rattled. Mother was in the kitchen in her chair, but she knew he was dead and she started screaming for my sister. Brenda was in a sanatorium in Craigynos. Harry rang the bell in his bedroom when mother started, but I couldn't go to him, and father was dead in the bed.'

'I'm going to climb to the sea,' I said. 'Are you coming?'

He got up out of the hollow into the open world again and followed me slowly over the point and down the steep side; the gulls rose in a storm. I clung to dry, spiked bushes but the roots came out; a foothold crumbled, a crevice for the fingers broke as I groped in it; I scrambled on to a black, flat-backed rock whose head, like a little Worm's, curved out of the sea a few perilous steps away from me, and, drenched by flying water, I gazed up to see Ray and a shower of stones falling. He landed at my side.

'I thought I was done for,' he said, when he had stopped shaking. 'I could see all my past life in a flash.'

'All of it?'

'Well, nearly. I saw my brother's face clear as yours.'

We watched the sun set.

'Like an orange.'

'Like a tomato.'

'Like a goldfish bowl.'

We went one better than the other, describing the sun. The sea beat on our rock, soaked our trouser-legs, stung our cheeks. I took off my shoes and held Ray's hand and slid down the rock on my belly to trail my feet in the sea. Then Ray slid down, and I held him fast while he kicked up water.

'Come back now,' I said, pulling his hand.

'No, no,' he said, 'this is delicious. Let me keep my feet in a bit more. It's warm as the baths.' He kicked and grunted and slapped the rock in a frenzy with his other hand, pretending to drown. 'Don't save me!' he cried. 'I'm drowning! I'm drowning!'

I pulled him back, and in his struggles he brushed a shoe off the rock. We fished it out. It was full of water.

'Never mind, it was worth it. I haven't paddled since I was six. I can't tell you how much I enjoyed it.'

He had forgotten about his father and brother, but I knew that once his joy in the wild, warm water was over he would return to the painful house and see his brother growing thinner. I had heard Harry die so many times, and the mad father was as familiar to me as Ray himself. I knew every cough and cry, every clawing at the air.

'I'm going to paddle once a day from now on,' Ray said. 'I'm going to go down to the sands every evening and have a good paddle. I'm going to splash about and get wet up to my knees. I don't care who laughs.'

He sat still for a minute, thinking gravely of this. 'When I wake up in the mornings there's nothing to look forward to, except on Saturdays,' he said then, 'or when I come up to your house for Lexicon. I may as well be dead. But now I'll be able to wake up and think : "This evening I'm going to splash about in the sea." I'm going to do it again now.' He rolled up his wet trousers and slid down the rock. 'Don't let go.'

As he kicked his legs in the sea, I said : 'This is a rock at the world's end. We're all alone. It all belongs to us, Ray. We can have anybody we like here and keep everybody else away. Who do you wish was with us ?'

He was too busy to answer, splashing and snorting, blowing as though his head were under, making circular commotions in the water or lazily skimming the surface with his toes.

'Who would you like to be here on the rock with us ?'

He was stretched out like a dead man, his feet motionless in the sea, his mouth on the rim of a rock pool, his hand clutched round my foot.

'I wish George Gray was with us,' I said. 'He's the man from London who's come to live in Norfolk street. You don't know him. He's the most curious man I ever met, queerer than Oscar Thomas, and I thought nobody could ever be queerer than that. George Gray wears glasses, but there's no glass in them, only the frames. You wouldn't know until you came near him. He does all sorts of things. He's a cat's doctor and he goes to somewhere in Sketty every morning to help a woman put her clothes on. She's an old widow, he said, and she can't dress by herself. I don't know how he came to know her. He's only been in town for a month. He's a B.A., too. The things he's got in his pockets! Pincers, and scissors for cats, and lots of diaries. He read me some of the diaries, about the jobs he did in London. He used to go to bed with a policewoman and she used to pay him. She used to go to bed in her uniform. I've never met such a queer man. I wish he was here now. Who do you wish was with us, Ray?'

Ray began to move his feet again, kicking them out straight behind him and bringing them down hard on the water, and then stirring the water about.

'I wish Gwilym was here, too,' I said. 'I've told you about him, He could give a sermon to the sea. This is the very place, there isn't anywhere as lonely as this.' Oh, the beloved sunset! Oh, the terrible sea! Pity the sailors, pity the sinners, pity Raymond Price and me! Oh, the evening is coming like a cloud! Amen. Amen. 'Who do you wish, Ray?'

'I wish my brother was with us,' Ray said. He climbed on to the flat rock and dried his feet. 'I wish Harry was here. I wish he was here now, at this moment, on this rock.'

The sun was nearly right down, halved by the shadowed sea. Cold came up, spraying out of the sea, and I could make a body for it, icy antlers, a dripping tail, a rippling face with fishes passing across it. A wind, cornering the Head, chilled through our summer shirts, and the sea began to cover our rock quickly, our rock already covered with friends, with living and dead, racing against the darkness. We did not speak as we climbed. I thought: 'If we open our mouths we'll both say: "Too late, it's too late."' We ran over the spring-board grass and the scraping rock needles, down the hollow in which Ray had talked about blood, up rustling humps, and along the ragged flat. We stood on the beginning of the Head and looked down, though both of us could have said, without looking: 'The sea is in.'

The sea was in. The slipping stepping-stones were gone. On the mainland, in the dusk, some little figures beckoned to us. Seven clear figures, jumping and calling. I thought they were the cyclists.

OLD GARBO

Mr Farr trod delicately and disgustedly down the dark, narrow stairs like a man on ice. he knew, without looking or slipping, that vicious boys had littered the darkest corners with banana peel; and when he reached the lavatory, the basins would be choked and the chains snapped on purpose. He remembered 'Mr Farr, no father' scrawled in brown, and the day the sink was full of blood that nobody admitted having lost. A girl rushed past him up the stairs, knocked the papers out of his hand, did not apologize, and the loose meg of his cigarette burned his lower lip as he failed to open the lavatory door. I heard from inside his protest and rattlings, the sing-song whine of his voice, the stamping of his small patent-leather shoes, his favourite swear-words – he swore, violently and privately, like a collier used to thinking in the dark – and I let him in.

'Do you always lock the door?' he asked, scurrying to the tiled wall.

'It stuck,' I said.

He shivered, and buttoned.

He was the senior reporter, a great shorthand writer, a chain-smoker, a bitter drinker, very humorous, round-faced and round-bellied, with dart holes in his nose. Once, I thought as I stared at him then in the lavatory of the offices of the *Tawe News* he might have been a mincing-mannered man, with a strut and a cane to balance it, a watch-chain across the waistcoat, a gold tooth, even, perhaps a flower from his own garden in his buttonhole. But now each attempt at a precise gesture was caked and soaked before it began; when he placed the tips of his thumb and forefinger together, you saw only the cracked nails in mourning and the Woodbine stains. He gave me a cigarette and shook his coat to hear matches.

'Here's a light, Mr Farr,' I said.

It was good to keep in with him; he covered all the big stories, the occasional murder, such as when Thomas O'Connor used a bottle on his wife – but that was before my time – the strikes, the best fires. I wore my cigarette as he did, a hanging badge of bad habits.

'Look at that word on the wall,' he said. 'Now that's ugly. There's a time and a place.'

Winking at me, scratching his bald patch as though the thought came from there, he said: 'Mr Solomon wrote that.'

Mr Solomon was the news editor and a Wesleyan.

'Old Solomon,' said Mr Farr, 'he'd cut every baby in half just for pleasure.'

I smiled and said: 'I bet he would!' But I wished that I could have answered in such a way as to show for Mr Solomon the disrespect I did not feel. This was a great male moment, and the most enjoyable since I had begun work three weeks before: leaning against the cracked tiled wall, smoking and smiling, looking down at my shoe scraping circles on the wet floor, sharing a small wickedness with an old, important man. I should have been writing up last night's performance of the *The Crucifixion* or loitering, with my new hat on one side, through the Christmas-Saturday-crowded town in the hopes of an accident.

'You must come along with me one night,' Mr Farr said slowly. 'We'll go down the "Fishguard" on the docks; you can see the sailors knitting there in the public bar. Why not tonight? And there's shilling women in the "Lord Jersey." You stick to Woodbines, like me.'

He washed his hands as a young boy does, wiping the dirt on the roll-towel, stared in the mirror over the basin, twirled the ends of his moustache, and saw them droop again immediately after.

'Get to work,' he said.

I walked into the lobby, leaving him with his face pressed to the glass and one finger exploring his bushy nostrils.

It was nearly eleven o'clock, and time for a cocoa or a Russian tea in the Café Royal, above the tobacconist's in High Street, where junior clerks and shop assistants and young men working in their fathers' offices or articled to stock brokers and solicitors meet every morning for gossip and stories. I made my way through the crowds: the Valley men, up for the football; the country shoppers, the window gazers; the silent, shabby men at the corners of the packed streets, standing in isolation in the rain; the press of mothers and prams; old women in black,

brooched dresses carrying frails, smart girls with shining mackintoshes and splashed stockings; little, dandy lascars, bewildered by the weather; business men with wet spats; through a
mushroom forest of umbrellas; and all the time I thought of the
paragraphs I would never write. I'll put you all in a story by and
by.

Mrs Constable, laden and red with shopping, recognized me
as she charged out of Woolworth's like a bull. 'I haven't seen
your mother for ages! Oh! this Christmas rush! Remember me
to Florrie. I'm going to have a cup of tea at the "Modern."
There,' she said, 'I've lost a pan!'

I saw Percy Lewis, who put chewing gum in my hair at school.

A tall man stared at the doorway of a hat shop, resisting the
crowds, standing hard and still. All the moving irrelevancies of
good news grew and acted around me as I reached the café
entrance and climbed the stairs.

'What's for you, Mr Swaffer?'

'The usual, please.' Cocoa and free biscuit.

Most of the boys were there already. Some wore the outlines
of moustaches, others had sideboards and crimped hair, some
smoked curved pipes and talked with them gripped between
their teeth, there were pin-stripe trousers and hard collars, one
daring bowler.

'Sit by here,' said Leslie Bird. He was in the boots at Dan
Lewis's.

'Been to the flicks this week, Thomas?'

'Yes. The Regal. *White Lies*. Damned good show, too!
Connie Bennett was great! Remember her in the foam-bath,
Leslie?'

'Too much foam for me, old man.'

The broad vowels of the town were narrowed in, the rise and
fall of the family accent was caught and pressed.

At the top window of the International Stores across the street
a group of uniformed girls were standing with tea-cups in their
hands. One of them waved a handkerchief. I wondered if she
waved it to me. 'There's that dark piece again,' I said. 'She's got
her eye on you.'

'They look all right in their working clothes,' he said. 'You
catch them when they're all dolled up, they're awful. I knew a
little nurse once, she looked a peach in her uniform, really
refined; no, really, I mean. I picked her up on the prom one

night. She was in her Sunday best. There's a difference ; she looked like a bit of Marks and Spencer's.' As he talked he was looking through the window with the corners of his eyes.

The girl waved again, and turned away to giggle.

'Pretty cheap !' he said.

I said : 'And little Audrey laughed and laughed.'

He took out a plated cigarette case. 'Present,' he said. 'I bet my uncle with three balls has it in a week. Have a best Turkish.'

His matches were marked Allsopps. 'Got them from the "Carlton"' he said. 'Pretty girl behind the bar : knows her onions. You've never been there, have you ? Why don't you drop in for one to-night ? Gil Morris'll be there, too. We usually sink a couple Saturdays. There's a hop at the "Melba."'

'Sorry,' I said. 'I'm going out with our senior reporter. Some other time, Leslie. So long !'

I paid my threepence.

'Good morning, Cassie.'

'Good morning, Hannen.'

The rain stopped and High Street shone. Walking on the tram-lines, a neat man held his banner high and prominently feared the Lord. I knew him as a Mr Matthews, who had been saved some years ago from British port and who now walked every night, in rubber shoes with a prayer book and a flashlight, through the lanes. There went Mr Evans the Produce through the side-door of the 'Bugle.' Three typists rushed by for lunch, poached egg and milk-shake, leaving a lavender scent. Should I take the long way through the Arcade, and stop to look at the old man with the broken, empty pram who always stood there, by the music store, and who would take off his cap and set his hair alight for a penny ? It was only a trick to amuse boys, and I took the short cut down Chapel Street, on the edge of the slum called the Strand past the enticing Italian chip shop where young men who had noticing parents bought twopennyworth on late nights to hide their breath before the last tram home. Then up the narrow office stairs and into the reporters' room.

Mr Solomon was shouting down the telephone. I heard the last words : 'You're just a dreamer, Williams.' He put the receiver down. 'That boy's a buddy dreamer,' he said to no one. he never swore.

I finished my report of *The Crucifixion* and handed it to Mr Farr.

'Too much platitudinous verbosity.'

Half an hour later, Ted Williams, dressed to golf, sidled in, smiling, thumbed his nose at Mr Solomon's back, and sat quietly in a corner with a nail-file.

I whispered : 'What was he slanging you for ?'

'I went out on a suicide, a tram conductor called Hopkins, and the widow made me stay and have a cup of tea. That's all.' He was very winning in his ways, more like a girl than a man who'd dreamed of Fleet Street and spent his summer fortnight walking up and down past the *Daily Express* and looking for celebrities in the pubs.

Saturday was my free afternoon. It was one o'clock and time to leave, but I stayed on ; Mr Farr said nothing. I pretended to be busy scribbling words and caricaturing with no likeness Mr Solomon's toucan profile and the snub copy-boy who whistled out of tune behind the windows of the telephone box. I wrote my name, 'Reporters' Room, *Tawe News*, Tawe, South Wales, England, Europe, The Earth.' And a list of books I had not written : 'Land of My Fathers, a study of the Welsh Character in all its aspects' ; 'Eighteen, a Provincial Autobiography.' : 'The Merciless Ladies, a Novel.' Still Mr Farr did not look up. I wrote 'Hamlet.' Surely Mr Farr, stubbornly transcribing his council notes had not forgotten. I heard Mr Solomon mutter, leaning over his shoulder : 'To aitch with Alderman Daniels.' Half-past one. Ted was in a dream. I spent a long time putting on my overcoat, tied my Old Grammarian's scarf one way and then another.

'Some people are too lazy to take their half-days off,' said Mr Farr suddenly. 'Six o'clock in the "Lamps" back bar.' He did not turn round or stop writing.

'Going for a nice walk ?' asked my mother.

'Yes, on the common. Don't keep tea waiting.'

I went to the Plaza. 'Press,' I said to the girl with the Tyrolean hat and skirt.

'There's been two reporters this week.'

'Special notice.'

She showed me to a seat. During the educational film, with the rude seeds hugging and sprouting in front of my eyes and plants like arms and legs, I thought of the bob women and the pansy sailors in the dives. There might be a quarrel with razors, and once Ted Williams found a lip outside the Mission to

Seamen. It had a small moustache. The sinuous plants danced on the screen. If only Tawe were a larger sea-town, there would be curtained rooms underground with blue films. The potato's life came to an end. Then I entered an American college and danced with the president's daughter. The hero, called Lincoln, tall and dark with good teeth, I displaced quickly, and the girl spoke my name as she held his shadow, the singing college chorus in sailors' hats and bathing dresses called me big boy and king, Jack Oakie and I sped up the field, and on the shoulders of the crowd the president's daughter and I brought across the shifting-coloured curtain with a kiss that left me giddy and bright-eyed as I walked out of the cinema into the strong lamplight and the new rain.

A whole wet hour to waste in the crowds. I watched the queue outside the Empire and studied the posters of *Nuit de Paris*, and thought of the long legs and startling faces of the chorus girls I had seen walking arm in arm, earlier that week, up and down the streets in the winter sunshine, their mouths, I remembered remarking and treasuring for the first page of 'The Merciless Ladies' that was never begun, like crimson scars, their hair raven-black or silver; their scent and paint reminded me of the hot and chocolate-coloured East, their eyes were pools. Lola de Kenway, Babs Courcey, Ramona Day would be with me all my life. Until I died, of a wasting, painless disease, and spoke my prepared last words, they would always walk with me, recalling me to my dead youth in the vanished High Street nights when the shop windows were blazing, and singing came out of the pubs, and sirens from the Hafod sat in the steaming chip shops with their handbags on their knees and their ear-rings rattling. I stopped to look at the window of Dirty Black's, the Fancy Man, but it was innocent; there were only itching and sneezing powders, stink bombs, rubber pens, and Charlie masks; all the novelties were inside, but I dared not go in for fear a woman should serve me, Mrs Dirty Black with a moustache and knowing eyes, or a thin, dog-faced girl I saw there once, who winked and smelt of seaweed. In the market I bought pink cachous. You never knew.

The back room of 'The Three Lamps' was full of elderly men. Mr Farr had not arrived I leant against the bar, between an alderman and a solicitor, drinking bitter, wishing that my father could see me now and glad, at the same time, that he was visiting Uncle A. in Aberavon. He could not fail to see that I was a boy no longer, not fail to be angry at the angle of my fag and my hat and the threat of the clutched tankard. I liked the taste of beer, its live, white lather, its brass-bright depths, the sudden world through the wet brown walls of the glass, the tilted rush to the lips and the slow swallowing down to the lapping belly, the salt on the tongue, the foam at the corners.

'Same again, miss.' She was middle-aged. 'One for you, miss?'

'Not during hours, ta all the same.'

'You're welcome.'

Was that an invitation to drink with her afterwards, to wait at the back door until she glided out, and then to walk through the night along the promenade and sands, on to a soft dune where couples lay loving under their coats and looking at the Mumbles lighthouse? She was plump and plain, her netted hair was auburn and wisped with grey. She gave me my change like a mother giving her boy pennies for the pictures, and I would not go out with her if she put cream on it.

Mr Farr hurried down High Street, savagely refusing laces and matches, averting his eyes from the shabby crowds. He knew that the poor and the sick and the ugly, unwanted people were so close around him that, with one look of recognition, one gesture of sympathy, he would be lost among them and the evening would be spoiled for ever.

'You're a pint man then,' he said at my elbow.

'Good evening, Mr Farr. Only now and then for a change. What's yours? Dirty night,' I said.

Safe in a prosperous house, out of the way of the rain and the unsettling streets, where the poor and the past could not touch him, he took his glass lazily in the company of business and professional men and raised it to the light. 'It's going to get dirtier,' he said. 'You wait till the "Fishguard." Here's health! You can see the sailors knitting there. And the old fish-girls in the "Jersey." Got to go to the w. for a breath of fresh air.'

Mr Evans the Produce came in quickly through a side door hidden by curtains, whispered his drink, shielded it with his overcoat, swallowed it in secrecy.

'Similar,' said Mr Farr, 'and half for his nibs.'

The bar was too high class to look like Christmas. A notice said 'No Ladies.'

We left Mr Evans gulping in his tent.

Children screamed in Goat Street, and one boy, out of season, pulled my sleeve, crying: 'Penny for the guy!' Big women in men's caps barricaded their doorways, and a posh girl gave us the wink at the corner of the green iron convenience opposite the Carlton Hotel. We entered to music, the bar was hung with ribbons and balloons, a tubercular tenor clung to the piano, behind the counter Leslie Bird's pretty barmaid was twitting a group of young men who leant far over and asked to see her garters and invited her to gins and limes and lonely midnight walks and moist adventures in the cinema. Mr Farr sneered down his glass as I watched the young men enviously and saw how much she liked their ways, how she slapped their hands lightly and wriggled back, in pride of her prettiness and gaiety, to pull the beer-handles.

'Toop little Twms from the Valleys. There'll be some puking to-night,' he said with pleasure.

Other young men, sleek-haired, pale, and stocky, with high cheekbones and deep eyes, bright ties, double-breasted waist-coats and wide trousers, some pocked from the pits, their broad hands scarred and damaged, all exultantly half-drunk, stood singing round the piano, and the tenor with the fallen chest led in a clear voice. Oh! to be able to join in the suggestive play or the rocking choir, to shout *Bread of Heaven*, with my shoulders back and my arms linked with Little Moscow, or to be called 'saucy' and 'a one' as I joked and ogled at the counter, making innocent, dirty love that could come to nothing among the spilt beer and piling glasses.

'Let's get away from the bloody nightingales,' said Mr Farr.

'Too much bloody row,' I said.

'Now we're coming to somewhere.' We crawled down Strand alleys by the side of the mortuary, through a gas-lit lane where hidden babies cried together and reached the 'Fishguard' door as a man, muffled like Mr Evans, slid out in front of us with a bottle or a black-jack in one gloved hand. The bar was empty. An old man whose hands trembled sat behind the counter, staring at his turnip watch.

'Merry Christmas, Pa.'

'Good evening, Mr F.'

'Drop of rum, Pa.'

A red bottle shook over two glasses.

'Very special poison, son.'

'This'll make your eyes bulge,' said Mr Farr.

My iron head stood high and firm, no sailors' rum could rot the rock of my belly. Poor Leslie Bird the port-sipper, and little Gil Morris who marked dissipation under his eyes with a blacklead every Saturday night, I wished they could have seen me now, in the dark, stunted room with photographs of boxers peeling on the wall.

'More poison, Pa,' I said.

'Where's the company tonight? gone to the Riviera?'

'They're in the snuggery, Mr F., there's a party for Mrs Prothero's daughter.'

In the back room, under a damp royal family, a row of black-dressed women on a hard bench sat laughing and crying, short glasses lined by their Guinnesses. On an opposite bench two men in jerseys drank appreciatively, nodding at the emotions of the women. And on the one chair, in the middle of the room, an old woman, with a bonnet tied under her chins, a feather boa, and white gym-shoes, tittered and wept above the rest. We sat on the men's bench. One of the two touched his cap with a sore hand.

'What's the party, Jack?' asked Mr Farr. 'Meet my colleague, Mr Thomas; this is Jack Stiff, the mortuary keeper.'

Jack Stiff spoke from the side of his mouth. 'It's Mrs Prothero there. We call her Old Garbo because she isn't like her, see. She had a message from the hospital about an hour ago, Mrs Harris's Winifred brought it here, to say her second daughter's died in pod.'

'Baby girl dead, too,' said the man at his side.

'So all the old girls came round to sympathize, and they made a big collection for her, and now she's beginning to drink it up and treating round. We've had a couple of pints from her already.'

'Shameful!'

The rum burned and kicked in the hot room, but my head felt tough as a hill and I could write twelve books before morning and roll the 'Carlton' barmaid, like a barrel, the length of Tawe sands.

'Drinks for the troops!'

Before a new audience, the women cried louder, patting Mrs Prothero's knees and hands, adjusting her bonnet, praising her dead daughter.

'What'll you have, Mrs Prothero, dear?'
'No, have it with me, dear, best in the house.'
'Well, a Guinness tickles my fancy.'
'And a little something in it, dear.'
'Just for Margie's sake, then.'
'Think if she was here now, dear, singing *One of the Ruins* or *Cockles and Mussels*; she had a proper madam's voice.'
'Oh, don't, Mrs Harris!'
'There, we're only bucking you up. Grief killed the cat, Mrs Prothero. Let's have a song together, dear.'

'The pale moon was rising above the grey mountain,
The sun was declining beneath the blue sea,
When I strolled with my love to the pure crystal fountain,'

Mrs Prothero sang.
'It was her daughter's favourite song,' said Jack Stiff's friend.
Mr Farr tapped me on the shoulder; his hand fell slowly from a great height and his thin, bird's voice spoke from a whirring circle on the ceiling. 'A drop of out-of-doors for you and me.' The gamps and bonnets, the white gym-shoes, the bottles and the mildew king, the singing mortuary man, the *Rose of Tralee*, swam together in the snuggery; two small men, Mr Farr and his twin brother, led me on an ice-rink to the door, and the night air slapped me down. The evening happened suddenly. A wall slumped over and knocked off my trilby; Mr Farr's brother disappeared under the cobbles. Here came a wall like a buffalo; dodge him, son. Have a drop of angostura, have a drop of brandy, Fernet Branca, Polly, Ooo! the mother's darling! have a hair of the dog.
'Feeling better now?'
I sat in a plush chair I had never seen before, sipping a mothball drink and appreciating an argument between Ted Williams and Mr Farr. Mr Farr was saying sternly: 'You came in here to look for sailors.'
'No, I didn't then,' said Ted. 'I came for local colour.'
The notices on the walls were: ' "The Lord Jersey." Prop.: Titch Thomas.' 'No Betting.' 'No Swearing, B—you.' 'The Lord helps Himself, but you mustn't.' 'No Ladies allowed, except Ladies.'
'This is a funny pub,' I said. 'See the notices?'
'Okay now?'

'I'm feeling upsydaisy.'

'There's a pretty girl for you. Look, she's giving you the glad.'

'But she's got no nose.'

My drink, like winking, had turned itself into beer. A hammer tapped. 'Order! order!' At a sound in a new saloon a collarless chairman with a cigar called on Mr Jenkins to provide *The Lily of Laguna.*

'By request,' Said Mr Jenkins.

'Order! order! for Katie Sebastopol Street. What is it, Katie?' She sang the National Anthem.

'Mr Fred Jones will supply his usual dirty one.'

A broken baritone voice spoiled the chorus: I recognised it as my own, and drowned it.

A girl of the Salvation Army avoided the arms of two firemen and sold them a *War Cry.*

A young man with a dazzling handkerchief round his head, black and white holiday shoes with holes for the toes, and no socks, danced until the bar cried: 'Mabel!'

Ted clapped at my side. 'That's style! "Nijinsky of the Night-world," there's a story! Wonder if I can get an interview?'

'Half a crack,' said Mr Farr.

'Don't make me cross.'

A wind from the docks tore up the street, I heard the rowdy dredger in the bay and a boat blowing to come in, the gas-lamps bowed and bent, then again smoke closed about the stained walls with George and Mary dripping above the women's bench, and Jack Stiff whispered, holding his hand in front of him like the paw of an animal: 'Old Garbo's gone.'

The sad and jolly women huddled together.

'Mrs Harris's little girl got the message wrong. Old Garbo's daughter's right as rain, the baby was born dead. Now the old girls want their money back, but they can't find Garbo anywhere.' He licked his hand. 'I know where she's gone.'

His friend said: 'To a boozer over the bridge.'

In low voices the women reviled Mrs Prothero, liar adulteress, mother of bastards, thief.

'She got you know what.'

'Never cured it.'

'Got Charlie tattooed on her.'

'Three and eight she owes me.'

'Two and ten.'

'Money for my teeth.'

'One and a tanner out of my Old Age.'

Who kept filling my glass ? Beer ran down my cheek and my collar. My mouth was full of saliva. The bench spun. The cabin of the 'Fishguard' tilted. Mr Farr retreated slowly ; the telescope twisted, and his face, with wide and hairy nostrils, breathed against mine.

'Mr Thomas is going to get sick.'

'Mind your brolly, Mrs Arthur.'

'Take his head.'

The last tram clanked home. I did not have the penny for the fare. 'You get off here. Careful !' The revolving hill to my father's house reached to the sky. Nobody was up. I crept to a wild bed, and the wallpaper lakes converged and sucked me down.

Sunday was a quiet day, though St Mary's bells, a mile away, rang on, long after church time, in the holes of my head. Knowing that I would never drink again, I lay in bed until midday dinner and remembered the unsteady shapes and far-off voices of the ten o'clock town. I read the newspapers. All news was bad that morning, but an article called 'Our Lord was a Flower-lover' moved me to tears of bewilderment and contrition. I excused myself from the Sunday joint and three vegetables.

In the park in the afternoon I sat alone near the deserted bandstand. I caught a ball of waste paper that the wind blew down the gravel path towards the rockery, and, straightening it out and holding it on my knee, wrote the first three lines of a poem without hope. A dog nosed me out where I crouched, behind a bare tree in the cold, and rubbed its nose against my hand. 'My only friend,' I said. It stayed with me up to the early dusk, sniffing and scratching.

On Monday morning, with shame and hate, afraid to look at them again, I destroyed the article and the poem, throwing the pieces on to the top of the wardrobe, and I told Leslie Bird in the tram to the office : 'You should have been with us, Saturday, Christ !'

Early on Tuesday night, which was Christmas Eve, I walked, with a borrowed half-crown, into the back room of the 'Fishguard.' Jack Stiff was alone. The women's bench was covered with sheets of newspaper. A bunch of balloons hung from the lamp.

'Here's health !'

'Merry Christmas !'

'Where's Mrs Prothero ?'

His hand was bandaged now. 'Oh ! You haven't heard ? She spent all the collection money. She took it over the bridge to the "Heart's Delight." She didn't let one of the old girls see her. It was over a pound. She'd spent a lot of it before they found her daughter wasn't dead. She couldn't face them then. Have this one with me. So she finished it up by stop-tap Monday. Then a couple of men from the banana boats saw her walking across the bridge, and she stopped half-way. But they weren't in time.'

'Merry Christmas !'

'We got a pair of gym-shoes on our slab.'

None of Old Garbo's friends came in that night.

When I showed this story a long time later to Mr Farr, he said : 'You got it all wrong. You got the people mixed. The boy with the handkerchief danced in the "Jersey". Fred Jones was singing in the "Fishguard." Never mind. Come and have one to-night in the "Nelson." There's a girl down there who'll show you where the sailor bit her. And there's a policeman who knew Jack Johnson.'

'I'll put them all in a story by and by,' I said.

ONE WARM SATURDAY

The young man in a sailor's jersey, sitting near the summer huts to see the brown and white women coming out and the groups of pretty-faced girls with pale vees and scorched backs who picked their way delicately on ugly, red-toed feet over the sharp stones to the sea, drew on the sand a large, indented woman's figure; and a naked child, just out of the sea, ran over it and shook water, marking on the figure two wide wet eyes and a hole in the footprinted middle. He rubbed the woman away and drew a paunched man; the child ran over it, tossing her hair, and shook a row of buttons down its belly and a line of drops, like piddle in a child's drawing, between the long legs stuck with shells.

In a huddle of picnicking women and their children, stretched out limp and damp in the sweltering sun or fussing over paper carriers or building castles that were at once destroyed by the tattered march of other picnickers to different pieces of the beach, among the ice-cream cries, the angrily happy shouts of boys playing ball, and the screams of girls as the sea rose to their waists, the young man sat alone with the shadows of his failure at his side. Some silent husbands, with rolled up trousers and suspenders dangling, padded slowly on the border of the sea, paddling women, in thick, black picnic dresses, laughed at their own legs, dogs chased stones, and one proud boy rode the water on a rubber seal. The young man, in his wilderness, saw the holiday Saturday set down before him, false and pretty, as a flat picture under the vulgar sun; the disporting families with paper bags, buckets and spades, parasols and bottles, the happy, hot, and aching girls with sunburn liniments in their bags, the bronzed young man with chests, and the envious, white young men in waistcoats, the thin, pale, hairy, pathetic legs of the husbands silently walking through the water, the plump and curly, shaven-headed and bowed-backed children up to no sense with unrepeatable delight in the dirty sand, moved him, he thought dramatically in his isolation, to an old shame and pity; outside all holiday, like a young man doomed for ever to the company of his maggots, beyond the high and ordinary, sweating, sun-awakened power and stupidity of the summer flesh on a day and a world out, he caught the ball that a small boy had whacked into the air with a tin tray, and rose to throw it back.

The boy invited him to play. A friendly family stood waiting some way off, the tousled women with their dresses tucked in their knickers, the bare-footed men in shirt-sleeves, a number of children in slips and cut-down underwear. He bowled bitterly to a father standing with a tray before the wicket of hats. 'The lone wolf playing ball,' he said to himself as the tray whirled. Chasing the ball towards the sea, passing undressing women with a rush and a wink, tripping over a castle into a coil of wet girls lying like snakes, soaking his shoes as he grabbed the ball off a wave, he felt his happiness return in a boast of the body, and, 'Look out, Duckworth, here's a fast one coming,' he cried to the mother behind the hats. The ball bounced on a boy's head. In and out of the scattered families, among the sandwiches and clothes, uncles and mothers fielded the bouncing ball. A bald man, with his shirt hanging out, returned it in the wrong direction, and a collie carried it into the sea. Now it was mother's turn with the tray. Tray and ball together flew over her head. An uncle in a panama smacked the ball to the dog, who swam with it out of reach. They offered the young man egg-and-cress sandwiches and warm stout, and he and an uncle and a father sat down on the *Evening Post* until the sea touched their feet.

Alone again, hot and unhappy, for the boasting minute when he ran among the unknown people lying and running loudly at peace was struck away, like a ball, he said, into the sea, he walked to a space on the beach where a hell-fire preacher on a box marked 'Mr Matthews' was talking to a congregation of expressionless women. Boys with pea-shooters sat quietly near him. A ragged man collected nothing in a cap. Mr Matthews shook his cold hands, stormed at the holiday, and cursed the summer from his shivering box. He cried for new warmth. The strong sun shone into his bones, and he buttoned his coat collar. Valley children, with sunken, impudent eyes, quick tongues and singing voices, chests thin as shells, gathered round the Punch and Judy and the Stop Me tricycles, and he denied them all. He

contradicted the girls in the underclothes combing and powder-
ing, and the modest girls cleverly dressing under tents of towels.

As Mr Matthews cast down the scarlet town, drove out the
bare-bellied boys who danced around the ice-cream man, wound
the girls' sunburnt thighs about with his black overcoat —
'Down! down!' he cried, 'the night is upon us' – the young man
in dejection stood, with a shadow at his shoulder, and thought
of Porthcawl's Coney beach, where his friends were rocking
with girls on the Giant Racer or tearing in the Ghost Train
down the skeletons' tunnel. Leslie Bird would have his arms full
of coconuts. Brenda was with Herbert at the rifle-range. Gil
Morris was buying Molly a cocktail with a cherry at the
'Esplanade.' Here he stood, listening to Mr Matthews, the
retired drinker, crying darkness on the evening sands, with
money hot in his pocket and Saturday burning away.

In his loneliness he had refused their invitations. Herbert, in
his low, red sports car, GB at the back, a sea-blown nymph on
the radiator, called at his father's house, but he said: 'I'm not in
the mood, old man. I'm going to spend a quiet day. Enjoy
yourselves. Don't take too much pop.' Only waiting for the sun
to set, he stood in the sad circle with the pleasureless women
who were staring at a point in the sky behind their prophet, and
wished the morning back. Oh, boy! to be wasting his money
now on the rings and ranges of the fair, to be sitting in the
chromium lounge with a short worth one and six and a Turkish
cigarette, telling the latest one to the girls, seeing the sun,
through the palms in the lounge window, sink over the promenade, over the Bath chairs, the cripples and widows, the beach-
trousered, kerchiefed, week-end wives, the smart, kiss-curled
girls with plain and spectacled girl friends, the innocent, swaggering, loud bad boys, and the poms at the ankles, and the
cycling sweet-men. Ronald had sailed to Ilfracombe on the *Lady
Moira*, and, in the thick saloon, with a party from Brynhyfryd,
he'd be knocking back nips without a thought that on the sands
at home his friend was alone and pussyfoot at six o'clock, and
the evening dull as a chapel. All his friends had vanished into
their pleasures.

He thought: Poets live and walk with their poems; a man
with visions needs no other company; Saturday is a crude day;
I must go home and sit in my bedroom by the boiler. But he was
not a poet living and walking, he was a young man in a sea

town on a warm bank holiday, with two pounds to spend; he had no visions, only two pounds and a small body with its feet on the littered sand; serenity was for old men; and he moved away, over the railway points, on to the tramlined road.

He snarled at the flower clock in Victoria Gardens.

'And what shall a prig do now?' he said aloud, causing a young woman on a bench opposite the white-tiled urinal to smile and put her novel down.

She had chestnut hair arranged high on her head in an old-fashioned way, in loose coils and a bun, and a Woolworth's white rose grew out of it and drooped to touch her ear. She wore a white frock with a red paper flower pinned on the breast, and rings and bracelets that came from a fun-fair stall. Her eyes were small and quite green.

He remarked, carefully and coldly in one glance, all the unusual details of her appearance; it was the calm, unstartled certainty of her bearing before his glance from head to foot, the innocent knowledge, in her smile and the set of her head, that she was defended by her gentleness and accessible strangeness against all rude encounters and picking looks, that made his fingers tremble. Though her frock was long and the collar high, she could as well be naked there on the blistered bench. Her smile confessed her body bare and spotless and willing and warm under the cotton, and she waited without guilt.

How beautiful she is, he thought, with his mind on words and his eyes on her hair and red and white skin, how beautifully she waits for me, though she does not know she is waiting and I can never tell her.

He had stopped and was staring. Like a confident girl before a camera, she sat smiling, her hands folded, her head slightly to one side so that the rose brushed her neck. She accepted his admiration. The girl in a million took his long look to herself, and cherished his stupid love.

Midges flew into his mouth. He hurried on shamefully. At the gates of the gardens he turned to see her for the last time on earth. She had lost her calm with his abrupt and awkward going, and stared in confusion after him. One hand was raised as though to beckon him back. If he waited, she would call him. He walked round the corner and heard her voice, a hundred voices, and all hers, calling his name, and a hundred names that were all his, over the bushy walls.

And what shall the terrified prig of a love-mad young man do next ? he asked his reflection silently in the distorting mirror of the empty 'Victoria' saloon. His ape-like hanging face, with 'Bass' across his forehead, gave back a cracked sneer.

If Venus came in on a plate, said the two red, melon-slice lips, I would ask for vinegar to put on her.

She could drive my guilt out; she could smooth away my shame; why didn't I stop to talk to her ? he asked.

You saw a queer tart in a park, his reflection answered, she was a child of nature, oh my ! oh my ! Did you see the dewdrops in her hair ? Stop talking to the mirror like a man in a magazine, I know you too well.

A new head, swollen and lop-jawed, wagged behind his shoulder. He spun round to hear the barman say :

'Has the one and only let you down ? You look like death warmed up. Have this one on the house. Free beer to-day. Free X's.' He pulled the beer handle. 'Only the best served here. Straight from the rust. You do look queer,' he said, 'the only one saved from the wreck and the only wreck saved. Here's looking at you !' He drank the beer he had drawn.

'May I have a glass of beer, please ?'

'What do you think this is, a public house ?'

On the polished table in the middle of the saloon the young man drew, with a finger dipped in strong, the round head of a girl and piled a yellow froth of hair upon it.

'Ah ! dirty, dirty !' said the barman, running round from behind the counter and rubbing the head away with a dry cloth.

Shielding the dirtiness with his hat, the young man wrote his name on the edge of the table and watched the letters dry and fade.

Through the open bay-window, across the useless railway covered with sand, he saw the black dots of bathers, the stunted huts, the jumping dwarfs round the Punch and Judy, and the tiny religious circle. Since he had walked and played down there in the crowded wilderness excusing his despair, searching for company though he refused it, he had found his own true happiness and lost her all in one bewildering and clumsy half a minute by the 'Gentlemen' and the flower clock. Older and wiser and no better, he would have looked in the mirror to see if his discovery and loss had marked themselves upon his face in shadows under the eyes or lines about the mouth, were it not for the answer he knew he would receive from the distorted reflection.

The barman came to sit near him, and said in a false voice; 'Now you tell me all about it, I'm a regular storehouse of secrets.'

'There isn't anything to tell. I saw a girl in Victoria Gardens and I was too shy to speak to her. She was a piece of God help us all right.'

Ashamed of his wish to be companionable, even in the depth of love and distress, with her calm face before his eyes and her smile reproving and forgiving him as he spoke, the young man defiled his girl on the bench, dragged her down into the spit and sawdust and dolled her up to make the barman say :

'I like them big myself. Once round Bessy, once round the gasworks. I missed the chance of a lifetime, too. Fifty lovelies in the nude and I'd left my Bunsen burner at home.'

'Give me the same, please.'

'You mean similar.'

The barman drew a glass of beer, drank it, and drew another.

'I always have one with the customers,' he said, 'it puts us on even terms. Now we're just two heart-broken bachelors together.' He sat down again.

'You can't tell me anything I don't know,' he said. 'I've seen over twenty chorines from the Empire in this bar, drunk as printers. Oh, les girls ! les limbs !'

'Will they be in to-night ?'

'There's only a fellow sawing a woman in half this week.'

'Keep a half for me.'

A drunk man walked in on an invisible white line, and the barman, reeling in sympathy across the room, served him with a pint. 'Free beer to-day,' he said. 'Free X's. You've been out in the sun.'

'I've been out in the sun all day,' said the man.

'I thought you looked sunburnt.'

'That's drink,' said the man. 'I've been drinking.'

'The holiday is drawing to an end,' the young man whispered into his glass. Bye-bye blackbird, the moment is lost, he thought, examining, with an interest he could not forgive, the comic coloured postcards of mountain-buttocked women on the beach and hen-pecked, pin-legged men with telescopes, pasted on the wall beneath the picture of a terrier drinking stout ; and now, with a jolly barman and a drunk in a crushed cap, he was mopping the failing day down. He tipped his hat over his forehead, and a lock of hair that fell below the hat tickled his eyelid. He saw, with a stranger's darting eye that missed no single subtlety of the wry grin or the faintest gesture drawing the shape of his death on the air, an unruly-haired young man who coughed into his hand in the corner of a rotting room and puffed the smoke of his doped Weight.

But as the drunk man weaved towards him on wilful feet, carrying his dignity as a man might carry a full glass around a quaking ship, as the barman behind the counter clattered and whistled and dipped to drink, he shook off the truthless, secret tragedy with a sneer and a blush, straightened his melancholy hat into a hard-brimmed trilby, dismissed the affected stranger. In the safe centre of his own identity, the familiar world about him like another flesh, he sat sad and content in the plain room of the undistinguished hotel at the sea-end of the shabby, spreading town where everything was happening. He had no need of the dark interior world when Tawe pressed in upon him and the eccentric ordinary people came bursting and crawling, with noise and colours, out of their houses, out of the graceless buildings, the factories and avenues, the shining shops and blaspheming chapels, the terminuses and the meeting-halls, the falling alleys and brick lanes, from the arches and shelters and holes behind the hoardings, out of the common, wild intelligence of the town.

At last the drunk man had reached him. 'Put your hand here,' he said, and turned about and tapped himself on the bottom.

The barman whistled and rose from his drink to see the young man touch the drunk on the seat of the trousers.

'What can you feel there?'

'Nothing.'

'That's right. Nothing. Nothing. There's nothing there to feel.'

'How can you sit down then?' asked the barman.

'I just sit down on what the doctor left,' the man said angrily. 'I had as good a bottom as you've got once. I was working underground in Dowlais, and the end of the world came down on me. Do you know what I got for losing my bottom? Four and three! Two and three ha'pence a cheek. That's cheaper than a pig.'

The girl from Victoria gardens came into the bar with two friends; a blonde young girl almost as beautiful as she was, and a middle-aged woman dressed and made up to look young. The three of them sat at the table. The girl he loved ordered three ports and gins.

'Isn't it delicious weather?' said the middle-aged woman.

The barman said : 'Plenty of sky about.' With many bows and smiles he placed their drinks in front of them. 'I thought the princesses had gone to a better pub, he said.

'What's a better pub without you, handsome?' said the blonde girl.

'This is the "Ritz" and the "Savoy," isn't it *garçon* darling?' the girl from the Gardens said, and kissed her hand to him.

The young man in the window seat, still bewildered by the first sudden sight of her entering the darkening room, caught the kiss to himself and blushed. He thought to run out of the room and through the miracle-making Gardens, to rush into his house and hide his head in the bed-clothes and lie all night there, dressed and trembling, her voice in his ears, her green eyes wide awake under his closed eyelids. But only a sick boy with tossed blood would run from his proper love into a dream, lie down in a bedroom that was full of his shames, and sob against the feathery, fat breast and face on the damp pillow. He remembered his age and poems, and would not move.

'Tanks a million, Lou,' said the barman.

Her name was Lou, Louise, Lousia. She must be Spanish or French or a gipsy, but he could tell the street that her voice came from; he knew where her friends lived by the rise and fall of their sharp voices, and the name of the middle-aged woman was Mrs Emerald Franklin. She was to be seen every night in the 'Jew's Harp,' sipping and spying and watching the clock.

'We've been listening to Matthews Hellfire on the sands. Down with this and down with that, and he used to drink a pint of biddy before his breakfast,' Mrs Franklin said. 'Oh there's a nerve !'

'And his eye on the fluff all the time,' said the blonde girl. 'I wouldn't trust him any further than Ramon Navarro behind the counter.'

'Whoops ! I've gone up in the world. Last week I was Charley Chase,' said the barman.

Mrs Franklin raised her empty glass in a gloved hand and shook it like a bell. 'Men are deceivers ever,' she said. 'And a drop of mother's ruin right around.'

'Especially Mr Franklin,' said the barman.

'But there's a lot in what the preacher says, mind,' Mrs Franklin said, 'about the carrying on. If you go for a constitutional after stop-tap along the sands you might as well be in Sodom and Gomorrah.'

The blonde girl laughed. 'Hark to Mrs Grundy ! I see her with a black man last Wednesday, round by the museum.'

'He was an Indian,' said Mrs Franklin, 'from the university college, and I'd thank you to remember it. Every one's brothers under the skin, but there's no tarbrush in my family.'

'Oh, dear ! oh dear !' said Lou. 'Lay off it, there's loves. This is my birthday. It's a holiday. Put a bit of fun in it. Miaow ! miaow ! Marjorie, kiss Emerald and be friends.' She smiled and laughed at them both. She winked at the barman, who was filling their glasses to the top. 'Here's to your blue eyes, *garçon* !' She had not noticed the young man in the corner. 'And one for grand-dad there,' she said, smiling at the swaying, drunk man. 'He's twenty-one to-day. There ! I've made him smile.'

The drunk man made a deep, dangerous bow, lifted his hat, stumbled against the mantelpiece, and his full pint in his free hand was steady as a rock. 'The prettiest girl in Carmarthenshire,' he said.

'This is Glamorganshire, dad,' she said, 'where's your geography ? Look at him waltzing ! mind your glasses ! He's got that Kruschen feeling. Come on, faster ! give us the Charleston.'

The drunk man, with the pint held high, danced until he fell, and all the time he never spilt a drop. He lay at Lou's feet on the dusty floor and grinned up at her in confidence and affection. 'I fell,' he said. 'I could dance like a trooper when I had a beatyem.'

'He lost his bottom at the last trump,' the barman explained.

'When did he lose his bottom ?' said Mrs Franklin.

'When Gabriel blew his whistle down in Dowlais,

'You're pulling my leg.'

'It's a pleasure, Mrs Em. Hoi, you ! get up from the vomitorium.'

The man wagged his end like a tail, and growled at Lou's feet.

'Put your head on my foot. Be comfy. Let him lie there,' she said.

He went to sleep at once.

'I can't have drunks on the premises.'

'You know where to go then.'

'Cru-el Mrs Franklin !'

'Go on, attend to your business. Serve the young man in the corner, his tongue's hanging out.'

'Cru-el lady !'

As Mrs Franklin called attention to the young man, Lou peered shortsightedly across the saloon and saw him sitting with his back to the window.

'I'll have to get glasses,' she said.

'You'll have plenty of glasses before the night's out.'

'No, honest, Marjorie, I didn't know anyone was there. I do beg your pardon, you in the corner,' she said.

The barman switched on the light. 'A bit of *lux in tenebris*.'

'Oh !' said Lou.

The young man dared not move for fear that he might break the long night of her scrutiny, the enchantment shining like a single line of light between them, or startle her into speaking; and he did not conceal the love in his eyes, for she could pierce through to it as easily as she could turn his heart in his chest and make it beat above the noises of the two friends' hurried conversation, the rattle of glasses behind the counter where the barman spat and polished and missed nothing, and the snores of the comfortable sleeper. Nothing can hurt me. Let the barman jeer. Giggle in your glass, our Em. I'm telling the world, I'm walking in clover, I'm staring at Lou like a fool, she's my girl, she's my lily. O love ! O love ! She's no lady, with her sing-song Tontine voice, she drinks like a deep-sea diver ; but Lou, I'm yours, and Lou, you're mine. He refused to meditate on her calmness now and twist her beauty into words. She was nothing under the sun or moon but his. Unashamed and certain, he smiled at her ; and, though he was prepared for all, her answering smile made his fingers tremble again, as they had trembled in the gardens, and reddened his cheeks and drove his heart to a gallop.

'Harold, fill the young man's glass up,' Mrs Franklin said.

The barman stood still, a duster in one hand and a dripping glass in the other.

'Have you got water in your ears ? Fill the young man's glass !'

The barman put the duster to his eyes. He sobbed. He wiped away the mock tears.

'I thought I was attending a *première* and this was the royal box,' he said.

'He's got water on the brain, not in his earhole,' said Marjorie.

'I dreamt it was a beautiful tragi-comedy entitled "Love at First Sight, or, Another Good Man gone wrong." Act one in a boozer by the sea.'

The two women tapped their foreheads.

Lou said, still smiling : 'Where was the second act ?'

Her voice was as gentle as he had imagined it to be before her gay and nervous playing with the over-familiar barman and the inferior women. He saw her as a wise, soft girl whom no hard company could spoil, for her soft self, bare to the heart, broke through every defence of her sensual falsifiers. As he thought this, phrasing her gentleness, faithlessly running to words away from the real room and his love in the middle, he woke with a start and saw her lively body six steps from him, no calm heart dressed in a sentence, but a pretty girl, to be got and kept. He must catch hold of her fast. He got up to cross to her.

'I woke before the second act came on,' said the barman. 'I'd sell my dear old mother to see that. Dim lights. Purple couches. Ecstatic bliss. Là, là chèrie !'

The young man sat down at the table, next to her.

Harold, the barman, leaned over the counter and cupped his hand to his ear.

The man on the floor rolled in his sleep, and his head lay in the spittoon.

'You should have come and sat here a long time ago,' Lou whispered. 'You should have stopped to talk to me in the Gardens. Were you shy ?'

'I was too shy,' the young man whispered.

'Whispering isn't manners. I can't hear a word,' said the barman.

At a sign from the young man, a flick of the fingers that sent the waiters in evening dress bustling with oysters about the immense room, the barman filled the glasses with port, gin, and Nutbrown.

'We never drink with strangers,' Mrs Franklin said, laughing.

'He isn't a stranger,' said Lou, 'are you Jack ?'

He threw a pound note on the table : 'Take the damage.'

The evening that had been over before it began raced along among the laughter of the charming women sharp as knives, and the stories of the barman, who should be on the stage, and Lou's delighted smiles and silences at his side. Now she is safe and sure, he thought, after her walking like my doubtful walking, around the lonely distances of the holiday. In the warm, spinning middle they were close and alike. The town and the sea and the last pleasure-makers drifted into the dark that had nothing to do with them, and left this one room burning.

One by one, some lost men from the dark shuffled into the bar, drank sadly, and went out. Mrs Franklin, flushed and dribbling waved her glass at their departures. Harold winked behind their backs. Marjorie showed them her long, white legs.

'Nobody loves us except ourselves,' said Harold. 'Shall I shut the bar and keep the riff-raff out?'

'Lou is expecting Mr O'Brien, but don't let that stop you,' Marjorie said. 'He's her sugar daddy from old Ireland.'

'Do you love Mr O'Brien?' the young man whispered.

'How could I, Jack?'

He could see Mr O'Brien as a witty, tall fellow of middle age, with waved greying hair and a clipped bit of dirt on his upper lip, a flash ring on his marriage finger, a pouched knowing eye, dummy dressed with a whalebone waist, a broth of a man about Cardiff, Lou's horrible lover tearing towards her now down the airless streets in the firm's car. The young man clenched his hand on the table covered with dead, and sheltered her in the warm strength of his fist. 'My round, my round,' he said, 'up again, plenty! Doubles, trebles, Mrs Franklin is a jibber.'

'My mother never had a jibber.'

'Oh, Lou!' he said, 'I am more than happy with you.'

'Coo! coo! hear the turtle doves.'

'Let them coo,' said Marjorie. 'I could coo, too.'

The barman looked around him in surprise. He raised his hands, palms up, and cocked his head.

'The bar is full of birds,' he said.

'Emerald's laying an egg,' he said, as Mrs Franklin rocked in her chair.

Soon the bar was full of customers. The drunk man woke up and ran out, leaving his cap in a brown pool. Sawdust dropped from his hair. A small, old, round, red-faced, cheery man sat facing the young man and Lou, who held hands under the table and rubbed their legs against each other.

'What a night for love!' said the old man. 'On such a night as this did Jessica steal from the wealthy Jew. Do you know where that comes from ?'

'*The Merchant of Venice*,' Lou said. 'But you're an Irishman, Mr O'Brien.'

'I could have sworn you were a tall man with a little tish,' said the young man gravely.

'What's the weapons, Mr O'Brien ?'

'Brandies at dawn, I should think, Mrs Franklin.'

'I never described Mr O'Brien to you at all. You're dreaming !' Lou whispered. 'I wish this night could go on for ever.'

'But not here. Not in the bar. In a room with a big bed.'

'A bed in a bar,' said the old man, 'if you'll pardon me hearing you, that's what I've always wanted. Think of it, Mrs Franklin.'

The barman bobbed up from behind the counter.

'Time, gentlemen and others !'

The sober strangers departed to Mrs Franklin's laughter.

The lights went out.

'Lou, don't you lose me.'

'I've got your hand.'

'Press it hard, hurt it.'

'Break his bloody neck,' Mrs Franklin said in the dark. 'No offence meant.'

'Marjorie smack hand,' said Marjorie. 'Let's get out of the dark. Harold's a rover in the dark.'

'And the girl guides.'

'Let's take a bottle each and go down to Lou's,' she said.

'I'll buy the bottles,' said Mr O'Brien.

'It's you don't lose me now,' Lou whispered. 'Hold on to me, Jack. The others won't stay long. Oh, Mr Christ, I wish it was just you and me !'

'Will it be just you and me ?'

'You and me and Mr Moon.'

Mr O'Brien opened the saloon door. 'Pile into the Rolls, you ladies. The gentlemen are going to see to the medicine.'

The young man felt Lou's quick kiss on his mouth before she followed Marjorie and Mrs Franklin out.

'What do you say we split the drinks ?' said Mr O'Brien.

'Look what I found in the lavatory,' said the barman, 'he was singing on the seat.' He appeared behind the counter with the drunk leaning on his arm.

They all climbed into the car.

'First stop, Lou's.'

The young man, on Lou's knee, saw the town in a daze spin by them, the funnelled and masted smoke-blue outline of the still, droning docks, the lightning lines of the poor streets growing longer, and the winking shops that were snapped out one by one. The car smelt of scent and powder and flesh. He struck with his elbow, by accident, Mrs Franklin's upholstered breast. Her thighs, like cushions, bore the drunk man's rolling weight. He was bumped and tossed on a lump of woman. Breasts, legs, bellies, hands, touched, warmed, and smothered him. On through the night, towards Lou's bed, towards the unbelievable end of the dying holiday, they tore past black houses and bridges, a station in a smoke cloud, and drove up a steep side street with one weak lamp in a circle of railings at the top, and swerved into a space where a tall tenement house stood surrounded by cranes, standing ladders, poles and girders, barrows, brick-heaps.

They climbed to Lou's room up many flights of dark, perilous stairs. Washing hung on the rails outside closed doors. Mrs Franklin, fumbling alone with the drunk man behind the others, trod in a bucket, and a lucky black cat ran over her foot. Lou led the young man by the hand through a passage marked with names and doors, lit a match, and whispered: 'It won't be very long. Be good and patient with Mr O'Brien. Here it is. Come in first. Welcome to you, Jack!' She kissed him again at the door of her room.

She turned on the lights, and he walked with her proudly into her own room, into the room that he would come to know, and saw a wide bed, a gramophone on a chair, a wash-basin half-hidden in a corner, a gas fire and a cooking ring, a closed cupboard, and her photograph in a cardboard frame on the chest of drawers with no handles. Here she slept and ate. In the double bed she lay all night, pale and curled, sleeping on her left side. When he lived with her always, he would not allow her to dream. No other men must lie and love in her head. He spread his fingers on her pillow.

'Why do you live at the top of the Eiffel Tower!' said the barman, coming in.

'What a climb!' said Mr O'Brien. 'But it's very nice and private when you get here.'

'If you get here!' said Mrs Franklin. 'I'm dead beat. This old nuisance weighs a ton. Lie down, lie down on the floor and go to sleep. The old nuisance!' she said fondly. 'What's your name?'

'Ernie,' the drunk man said, raising his arm to shield his face.

'Nobody's going to bite you, Ernie. Here, give him a nip of whiskey. Careful! Don't pour it on your waistcoat; you'll be squeezing your waistcoat in the morning. Pull the curtains, Lou, I can see the wicked old moon,' she said.

'Does it put ideas in your head?'

'I love the moon,' said Lou.

'There never was a young lover who didn't love the moon,' Mr O'Brien gave the young man a cheery smile, and patted his hand. His own hand was red and hairy. 'I could see at the flash of a glance that Lou and this nice young fellow were made for each other. I could see it in their eyes. Dear me, no! I'm not so old and blind I can't see love in front of my nose. Couldn't you see it, Mrs Franklin? Couldn't you see it, Marjorie?'

In the long silence, Lou collected glasses from the cupboard as though she had not heard Mr O Brien speak. She drew the curtains, shut out the moon, sat on the edge of her bed with her feet tucked under her, looked at her photograph as at a stranger, folded her hands as she folded them, on the first meeting, before the young man's worship in the Gardens.

'A host of angels must be passing by,' said Mr O'Brien. 'What a silence there is! Have I said anything out of place? Drink and be merry, to-morrow we die. What do you think I brought these lovely shining bottles for?'

The bottles were opened. The dead were lined on the mantel-piece. The whiskey went down. Harold the barman and Marjorie, her dress lifted, sat in the one arm-chair together. Mrs Franklin, with Ernie's head on her lap, sang in a sweet, trained contralto voice *The Shepherd's Lass*. Mr O'Brien kept rhythm with his foot.

I want Lou in my arms, the young man said to himself, watching Mr O'Brien tap and smile and the barman draw Marjorie down deep. Mrs Franklin's voice sang sweetly in the small bedroom where he and Lou should be lying in the white bed without any smiling company to see them drown. He and Lou could go down together, one cool body weighted with a boiling stone, onto the falling, blank white, entirely empty sea, and never rise. Sitting on their bridal bed, near enough to hear

his breath, she was farther from him than before they met. Then
he had everything but her body; now she had given him two
kisses, and everything had vanished but that beginning. He must
be good and patient with Mr O'Brien. He could wipe away the
embracing, old smile with the iron back of his hand. Sink lower,
lower, Harold and Marjorie, tumble like whales at Mr O'Brien's
feet.

He wished that the light would fail. In the darkness he and
Lou could creep beneath the clothes and imitate the dead. Who
would look for them there, if they were dead still and soundless?
The others would shout to them down the dizzy stairs or
rummage in the silence about the narrow, obstacled corridors or
stumble out into the night to search for them among the cranes
and ladders in the desolation of the destroyed houses. He could
hear, in the made-up dark, Mr O'Brien's voice cry, 'Lou, where
are you? Answer! answer!' the hollow answer of the echo,
'answer!' and hear her lips in the cool pit of the bed secretly
move around another name and feel them move.

'A fine piece of singing, Emerald, and very naughty words.
That was a shepherd, that was,' Mr. O'Brien said.

Ernie, on the floor, began to sing in a thick, sulking voice, but
Mrs Franklin placed her hand over his mouth and he sucked
and nuzzled it.

'What about this young shepherd?' said Mr O'Brien, pointing
his glass at the young man. 'Can he sing as well as make love?
You ask him kindly, girlie,' he said to Lou, 'and he'll give us a
song like a nightingale.'

'Can you sing, Jack?'

'Like a crow, Lou.'

'Can't he even talk poetry? What a young man to have who
can't spout the poets to his lady!' Mr O'Brien said.

From the cupboard Lou brought out a red-bound book and
gave it to the young man, saying: 'Can you read us a piece out
of here? The second volume's in the hatbox. Read us a dreamy
piece, Jack. It's nearly midnight.'

'Only a love poem, no other kind,' said Mr O'Brien. 'I won't
hear anything but a love poem.'

'Soft and sweet,' Mrs Franklin said. She took her hand away
from Ernie's mouth and looked at the ceiling.

The young man read, but not aloud, lingering on her name,
the inscription on the fly-leaf of the first volume of the collected

poems of Tennyson: 'To Louisa, from her Sunday School teacher, Miss Gwyneth Forbes. God's in His Heaven, all's right with the world.'

'Make it a love poem, don't forget.'

The young man read aloud closing one eye to steady the dancing print, *Come into the garden, Maud.* And when he reached the beginning of the fourth verse his voice grew louder:

> 'I said to the lily, "there is but one
> With whom she has heart to be gay.
> When will the dancers leave her alone?
> She is weary of dance and play."
>
> Now half to the setting moon are gone,
> And half to the rising day;
> Low on the sand and loud on the stone
> The last wheel echoes away.
>
> 'I said to the rose, "The brief night goes
> In babble and revel and wine.
> O young lord-lover, what sighs are those,
> For one that will never be thine?
> But mine, but mine," so I sware to the rose
> "For ever and ever, mine,"'

At the end of the poem, Harold said, suddenly, his head hanging over the arm of the chair, his hair made wild, and his mouth red with lipstick: 'My grandfather remembers seeing Lord Tennyson, he was a little man with a hump.'

'No,' said the young man, 'he was tall and he had long hair and a beard.'

'Did you ever see him?'

'I wasn't born then.'

'My grandfather saw him. He had a hump.'

'Not Alfred Tennyson.'

'Lord Alfred Tennyson was a little man with a hump.'

'It couldn't have been the same Tennyson.'

'You've got the wrong Tennyson, this was the famous poet with a hump.'

Lou, on the wonderful bed, waiting for him alone of all the men, ugly or handsome, old or young, in the wide town and the small world that would be bound to fall, lowered her head and kissed her hand to him and held her hand in the river of light on

the counterpane. The hand, to him, became transparent, and the
light on the counterpane glowed up steadily through it in the
thin shape of her palm and fingers.

'Ask Mr O'Brien what Lord Tennyson was like,' said Mrs
Franklin. 'We appeal to you, Mr O'Brien, did he have a hump
or not?'

Nobody but the young man, for whom she lived and waited
now, noticed Lou's little loving movements. She put her glowing
hand to her left breast. She made a sign of secrecy on her lips.

'It depends,' Mr O'Brien said.

The young man closed one eye again, for the bed was pitching
like a ship; a sickening, hot storm out of a cigarette cloud
unsettled cupboard and chest. The motions of the sea-going
bedroom were calmed with the cunning closing of his eye, but
he longed for night air. On sailor's legs he walked to the door.

'You'll find the House of Commons on the second floor at the
end of the passage,' said Mr O'Brien.

At the door, he turned to Lou and smiled with all his love,
declaring it to the faces of the company and making her, before
Mr O'Brien's envious regard, smile back and say: 'Don't be
long, Jack, Please! You mustn't be long.'

Now every one knew. Love had grown up in an evening.

'One minute, my darling,' he said. 'I'll be here.'

The door closed behind him. He walked into the wall of the
passage. He lit a match. He had three left. Down the stairs,
clinging to the sticky, shaking rails, rocking on see-saw floorboards, bruising his shin on a bucket, past the noises of secret
lives behind doors he slid and stumbled and swore and heard
Lou's voice in a fresh fever drive him on, call him to return,
speak to him with such passion and abandonment that even in
the darkness and the pain of his haste he was dazzled and struck
still. She spoke, there on the rotting stairs in the middle of the
poor house, a frightening rush of love words; from her mouth,
at his ear, endearments were burned out. Hurry! hurry! Every
moment is being killed. Love, adored, dear, run back and whistle
to me, open the door, shout my name, lay me down. Mr O'Brien
has his hands on my side.

He ran into a cavern. A draught blew out his matches. He
lurched into a room where two figures on a black heap on the
floor lay whispering, and ran from there in a panic. He made
water at the dead end of the passage and hurried back towards

Lou's room, finding himself at last on a silent patch of stairway at the top of the house; he put out his hand, but the rail was broken and nothing there prevented a long drop to the ground down a twisted shaft that would echo and double his cry, bring out from their holes in the wall the sleeping or stirring families, the whispering figures, the blind startled turners of night into day. Lost in a tunnel near the roof, he fingered the damp walls for a door; he found a handle and gripped it hard, but it came off in his hand. Lou had led him down a longer passage than this. He remembered the number of doors: there were three on each side. He ran down the broken-railed flight into another passage and dragged his hand along the wall. Three doors, he counted. He opened the third door, walked into darkness, and groped for the switch on the left. He saw, in the sudden light, a bed and a cupboard and a chest of drawers with no handles, a gas fire, a wash-basin in the corner. No bottles. No glasses. No photograph of Lou. The red counterpane on the bed was smooth. He could not remember the colour of Lou's counterpane.

He left the light burning and opened the second door, but a strange woman's voice cried, half-asleep: 'Who is there? Is it you, Tom? Tom, put the light on.' He looked for a line of light at the foot of the next door, and stopped to listen for voices. The woman was still calling in the second room.

'Lou, where are you?' he cried. 'Answer! answer!'

'Lou, what Lou? There's no Lou here,' said a man's voice through the open door of the first dark room at the entrance to the passage.

He scampered down another flight and counted four doors with his scratched hand. One door opened and a woman in a nightdress put out her head. A child's head appeared below her.

'Where does Lou live? Do you know where Lou lives?'

The woman and the child stared without speaking.

'Lou! Lou! her name is Lou!' he heard himself shout. 'She lives here, in this house! Do you know where she lives?'

The woman caught the child by the hair and pulled her into the room. He clung to the edge of her door. The woman thrust her arm round the edge and brought down a bunch of keys sharply on his hands. The door slammed.

A young woman with a baby in a shawl stood at an open

door on the opposite side of the passage, and caught his sleeve as he ran by. 'Lou who? You woke my baby.'

'I don't know her other name. She's with Mrs Franklin and Mr O'Brien.'

'You woke my baby.'

'Come in and find her in the bed,' a voice said from the darkness behind the young woman.

'He's woken my baby.'

He ran down the passage, holding his wet hand to his mouth. He fell against the rails of the last flight of stairs. He heard Lou's voice in his head once more whisper to him to return as the ground floor rose, like a lift full of dead, towards the rails. Hurry! hurry! I can't, I won't wait, the bridal night is being killed.

Up the rotten, bruising, mountainous stairs he climbed, in his sickness, to the passage where he had left the one light burning in an end room. The light was out. He tapped all the doors and whispered her name. He beat on the doors and shouted, and a woman, dressed in a vest and a hat, drove him out of the passage with a walking-stick.

For a long time he waited on the stairs, though there was no love now to wait for and no bed but his own too many miles away to lie in, and only the approaching day to remember his discovery. All round him the disturbed inhabitants of the house were falling back into sleep. Then he walked out of the house on to the waste space and under the leaning cranes and ladders. The light of the one weak lamp in a rusty circle fell across the brick-heaps and the broken wood and the dust that had been houses once, where the small and hardly known and never-to-be-forgotten people of the dirty town had lived and loved and died and, always, lost.

ADVENTURES IN THE
SKIN TRADE*

* The title under which the following three stories were first printed together.

A FINE BEGINNING

1

That early morning, in January 1933, only one person was awake in the street, and he was the quietest. Call him Samuel Bennet. He wore a trilby hat that had been lying by his bedside in case the two house-breakers, a man and a woman, came back for the bag they had left.

In striped pyjamas tight under the arms and torn between the legs, he padded barefoot downstairs and opened the breakfast-room door of his parents' six-room house. The room smelt strong of his father's last pipe before bed. The windows were shut fast and the curtains drawn, the back door was bolted, the house-breaking night could not enter anywhere. At first he peered uneasily into the known, flickering corners of the room, as though he feared that the family might have been sitting there in silence in the dark; then he lit the gaslight from the candle. His eyes were still heavy from a dream of untouchable city women and falling, but he could see that Tinker, the aunt-faced pom, was sleeping before the burned-out fire, and that the mantelpiece clock between hollow, mock-ebony, pawing horses, showed five to two. He stood still and listened to the noises of the house: there was nothing to fear. Upstairs the family breathed and snored securely. He heard his sister sleeping in the box-room under the signed photographs of actors from the repertory theatre and the jealous pictures of the marriages of friends. In the biggest bedroom overlooking the field that was called the back, his father turned over the bills of the month in his one dream; his mother in bed mopped and polished through a wood of kitchens. He closed the door: now there was nobody to disturb him.

But all the noises of the otherwise dead or sleeping, dark early morning, the intimate breathing of three invisible relations, the loud old dog, could wake up the neighbours. And the gaslight, bubbling, could attract to his presence in the breakfast-room at this hour Mrs Probert next door, disguised as a she-goat in a nightgown, butting the air with her kirby-grips; her dapper commercial son, with a watch-chain tattooed across his rising belly; the tubercular lodger, with his neat umbrella up and his basin in his hand. The regular tide of the family breath could beat against the wall of the house on the other side, and bring the Baxters out. He turned the gas low and stood for a minute by the clock, listening to sleep and seeing Mrs Baxter climb naked out of her widow's bed with a mourning band round her thigh.

Soon her picture died, she crawled back grieving to her lovebird's mirror under the blankets, and the proper objects of the room slowly returned as he lost his fear that the strangers upstairs he had known since he could remember would wake and come down with pokers and candles.

First there was the long strip of snapshots of his mother propped against the cut-glass of the window-sill. A professional under a dickybird hood had snapped her as she walked down Chapel Street in December, and developed the photographs while she waited looking at the thermos flasks and the smoking sets in the nearest shop-window, calling 'Good morning' across the street to the shopping bags she knew, and the matron's outside costumes, and the hats like flower-pots and chambers on the crisp, permed heads. There she was, walking down the street along the window-sill, step by step, stout, safe, confident, buried in her errands, clutching her handbag, stepping aside from the common women blind and heavy under a week's provisions, prying into the looking-glasses at the doors of furniture shops.

'Your photograph has been taken.' Immortalized in a moment, she shopped along forever between the cut-glass vase with the permanent flowers and the box of hairpins, buttons, screws, empty shampoo packets, cotton-reels, flypapers, ciga-rette cards. At nearly two in the morning she hurried down Chapel Street against a backcloth of trilbies and Burberries going the other way, umbrellas rising to the first drops of the rain a month ago, the sightless faces of people who would always be strangers hanging half-developed behind her, and the shadows of the shopping centre of the sprawling, submerged town. He could hear her shoes click on the tramrails. He could see, beneath the pastelled silk scarf, the metal badge of Mrs Rosser's Society, and the grandmother's cameo brooch on the vee of the knitted clover jumper.

The clock chimed and struck two. Samuel put out his hand and took up the strip of snaps. Then he tore it into pieces. The whole of her dead, comfortable face remained on one piece, and he tore it across the cheeks, up through the chins, and into the eyes.

The pom growled in a nightmare, and showed his little teeth. 'Lie down, Tinker. Go to sleep, boy.' He put the pieces in his pyjama pocket.

Then there was the framed photograph of his sister by the clock. He destroyed her in one movement, and, with the ripping of her set smile and the crumpling of her bobbed head into a ball, down went the Girls' School and the long-legged, smiling colts with their black knickers and bows; the hockey-legged girls who laughed behind their hands as they came running through the gates when he passed, went torn and ruined into his pyjama pocket; they vanished, broken, into the porch and lay in pieces against his heart. Stanley Road, where the Girls' School stood, would never know him again. Down you go, Peggy, he whispered to his sister, with all the long legs and the Young Liberals' dances, and the boys you brought home for supper on Sunday evenings and Lionel you kissed in the porch. He is a solicitor now. When I was eleven years old and you were seventeen I heard you, from my bedroom, playing the Desert Song. People were downstairs all over the world.

Most of the history sheets on the table were already marked and damned in his father's violet writing. With a lump of coal from the dead fire, Samuel marked them again, rubbing the coal hard over the careful corrections, drawing legs and breasts in the margins, smudging out the names and form numbers. History is lies. Now take Queen Elizabeth. Go ahead, take Alice Phillips, take her into the shrubbery. She was the headmaster's daughter. Take old Bennet and whip him down the corridors, stuff his mouth with dates, dip his starched collar in his marking ink and hammer his teeth back into his prim, bald, boring head with his rap-across-the-knuckle ruler. Spin Mr Nicholson on his tellurion until his tail drops off. Tell Mr Parsons his wife had been seen coming out of the Compass piggyback on a drunk sailor, catching pennies in her garters. It's as true as History.

On the last sheet he signed his name several times under a giant pinman with three legs. He did not scribble on the top sheet. At a first glance there was no sign of interference. Then he threw the coal into the grate. Dust drifted up in a cloud, and settled down again on the pom's back.

If only he could shout at the ceiling now, at the dark circle made by the gas, at the cracks and lines that had always been the same faces and figures, two bearded men chasing an animal over a mountain edge, a kneeling woman with faces on her knees : Come and look at Samuel Bennet destroying his parents' house in Mortimer Street, off Stanley's Grove ; he will never be allowed to come back. Mrs Baxter, have a dekko from under the cold sheets : Mr Baxter, who worked in the Harbour Trust Office, can never come back either. Mrs Probert Chestnuts, your billygoat is gone, leaving a hairy space in the bed ; Mr Bell the lodger coughs all night under his gamp ; your son cannot sleep, he is counting his gentlemen's three and eleven-three half-hose jumping over the tossed blankets. Samuel shouted under his breath, 'Come and see me destroying the evidence, Mrs Rosser ; have a peep from under your hairnet. I have seen your shadow on the blind as you undressed, I was watching by the lamp-post next to the dairy ; you disappeared under a tent and came out slim and humped and black. I am the only gooseberry in Stanley's Grove who knows that you are a black woman with a hump. Mr Rosser married to a camel ; every one is mad and bad in his box when the blinds are pulled ; come and see me break the china without any noise so that I can never come back.'

'Hush,' he said to himself. 'I know you.'

He opened the door of the china pantry. The best plates shone in rows, a willow tree next to an ivied castle, baskets of solid flowers on top of fruits and flower-coiled text. Tureens were piled on one shelf, on another the salad-bowls, the finger-bowls, the toast-racks spelling Porthcawl and Baby, the trifle-dishes, the heirloom moustache-cup. The afternoon tea-service was brittle as biscuits and had gold rims. He cracked two saucers together, and the horn-curved spout of the teapot came off in his hand. In five minutes he had broken the whole set. Let all the daughters of Mortimer Street come in and see me, he whispered in the close pantry : the pale young girls who help at home, calculating down the pavement to the rich-smelling shops, screwing up their straight, dry hair in their rooms at the top of the house; their blood is running through them like salt. And I hope the office girls knock on the door with the stubs of their fingers, tap out Sir or Madam on the glass porch, the hard, bright babies who never go too far. You can hear them in the lane behind the post office as you tiptoe along, they are saying, 'So he said and I said and he said and Oh yeah I said,' and the just male voices are agreeing softly. Shoo them in out of snoring Stanley's Grove, I know they are sleeping under the sheets up to their fringes in wishes. Beryl Gee is marrying the Chamber of Commerce in a pepper-and-salt church. Mrs Mayor's Chain, Madame Cocked Hat, Lady Settee, I am breaking tureens in the cupboard under the stairs.

A tureen-cover dropped from his hand and smashed.

He waited for the sound of his mother waking. No one stirred upstairs. 'Tinker did it,' he said aloud, but the harsh noise of his voice drove him back into silence. His fingers became so cold and numb he knew he could not lift up another plate to break it.

'What are you doing?' he said to himself at last, in a cool, flat voice. 'Leave the Street alone. Let it sleep.'

Then he closed the pantry door.

'What are you doing, ranting away?'

Even the dog had not been wakened.

'Ranting away,' he said.

He would have to be quick now. The accident in the cupboard had made him tremble so much that he could hardly tear up the bills he found in the sideboard drawer and scatter them under the sofa. His sister's crochet-work was too difficult to destroy, the doilies and the patterned tea-cosies were hard as rubber. He pulled them apart the best he could, and wedged them up the chimney.

'These are such small things,' he said. 'I should break the windows and stuff the cushions with the glass.' He saw his round soft face in the mirror under the Mona Lisa. 'But you won't,' he said, turning away; 'you're afraid of the noise.' He turned back to his reflection. 'It isn't that. You're afraid she'll cut her hands.'

He burnt the edge of his mother's sunshade at the gas-mantle, and felt the tears running down his cheeks and dropping on to his pyjama collar.

Even in the first moment of his guilt and shame, he remembered to put out his tongue and taste the track of the tears. Still crying, he said, 'It's salt. It's very salt. Just like in my poems.'

He went upstairs in the dark, with the candle shaking, past the box-room to his own room, and locked the door on the inside. He put out his hands and touched the walls and his bed. Good morning and good-bye, Mrs Baxter. His window, facing her bedroom, was open to the windless, starless early morning, but he could not hear her breathe or sleep. All the houses were quiet. The street was a close grave. The Rossers and the Proberts and the Bennets were still and safe and deep in their separate silences. His head touched the pillow, but he knew that he could not sleep again. His eyes closed.

Come down into my arms, for I shan't sleep, girls asleep on all sides in the attics and spare rooms of the square, red houses with the bay windows looking out on the trees behind the railings. I know your rooms like the backs of my hands, like the backs of your heads in the pictures when you are leaning over on to the next-door shoulders. I shan't sleep again. Tomorrow, today, I am going away by the 7.15 train, with ten pounds and a new suit-case. Lay your curling-pins on my pillow, the alarm at six-thirty will hurry you back to draw the blinds and light the fires before the rest come down. Come down quickly, the Bennets' house is melting. I can hear you breathe, I can hear Mrs Baxter turn in a dream. Oh, the milk-men are waking!

He was asleep with his hat on still, and his hands clenched.

2

The family awoke before six o'clock. He heard them, from a sunken half-asleep, bothering on the landing. They would be in dressing-gowns, stale-eyed and with ragged hair. Peggy might have put two blushes on her cheeks. The family rushed in and out of the bathroom, never stopping to wash, and collided on the narrow top of the stairs as they nagged and bustled to get him ready. He let himself sink deeper until the waves broke round his head again, and the lights of a city spun and shone through the eyes of women walking in his last remembered dream. From the lapping distance he heard his father shout like a man on the opposite shore:

'Have you put the sponge bag in, Hilda?'

'Of course I have,' she answered from the kitchen.

Don't let her look in the china-pantry, Samuel prayed among the women walking like lamp-posts. She never uses the best china for breakfast.

'All right, all right; I just asked.'

'Where's his new hairbrush?'

'That's right, shout my head off. Here it is. How can I give it to you if you're in the kitchen? It's the brush with the initials – S.B.'

'I know his initials.'

'Mother, does he want all these vests? You know he never uses them.'

'It's January, Peggy.'

'She knows it's January, Hilda. You haven't got to tell the neighbours. Can you smell something burning?'

'It's only mother's sunshade,' Samuel said in the locked bedroom.

He dressed and went down. The gas in the breakfast-room was on again. His mother was boiling an egg for him on the gas-stove. 'We'll have our breakfast later,' she said; 'you mustn't miss the train. Did you sleep well?'

'No burglars last night, Sam,' his father said.

His mother brought the egg in. 'You can't expect them every night.'

Peggy and his father sat down in front of the empty grate.

'What do you think you'll do first when you get there, Sam?' said Peggy.

'He'll get himself a nice room, of course, not too central. And don't have an Irish landlady.' His mother brushed his collar as he ate. 'Go and get yourself settled straight away; that's the important thing.'

'I'll get myself settled.'

'Don't forget to look under the wallpaper for bugs.'

'That's enough of that, Peggy. Sam knows a clean place when he sees one.'

He saw himself knocking at a lodging-house in the very centre of the city, and an Irishwoman appearing at the door. 'Good morning, madam. Have you a cheap room?' 'Cheaper than sunlight to you, Danny Boy.' She would not be more than twenty-one. 'Has it got bugs?' 'All over the walls, praise be to God.' 'I'll take it.'

'I'll know what I'm doing,' he said to his mother.

'Jenkins' motor isn't here yet,' Peggy said. 'Perhaps there's a puncture.'

If he doesn't come soon, they'll notice everything. I'll cut my throat on a piece of china.

'Remember to call on Mrs Chapman. Give her all our love from 42.'

'I'll call on her tomorrow, mother.'

The taxi drew up outside. The corners of bedroom blinds would be lifted all over the street.

'Here's your wallet. Don't put it in your handkerchief pocket now. You never know when you'll be wanting to blow your nose.'

'You'll be scattering largesse,' Peggy said. She kissed him on the forehead.

Remind me to wipe it off in the cab.

'You're kissing the editor of the *Times* now,' said his mother.

'Well, not quite that, Sam. Not yet, eh?' His father said, 'Rungs of the ladder,' and then looked away.

'Write tomorrow morning sharp. Send us the news.'

'You send me your news, too. Mr Jenkins is blowing his horn.'

'Better than blowing your trumpet,' Peggy said. 'And there's never any news in Mortimer Street.'

You wait, slyboots. Wait till the flames touch the doilie with the herons on it.

He came down to pat Tinker.

'Come on, don't fuss over the old dog; he's all fleas. It's gone seven.'

Peggy was opening the door of the taxi for him. His father shook him by the hand. His mother kissed him on the mouth.

'Good-bye, Mortimer Street,' he said, and the cab was off. 'Good-bye, Stanley's Grove.'

Through the back window he saw three strangers waving. He pulled down the blind.

3

Sitting with his bag in the lavatory of the moving train, for all the compartments were full, he read through his notebook and tore out the pages in order. He was dressed in a brand-new brown tweed overcoat, a brown town-suit, a white starched shirt with a woolen tie and a tiepin, and black, shining shoes. He had put his hard brown hat in the wash-basin. Here was Mrs Chapman's address next to the telephone number of a Mr Hewson who was going to introduce him to a man who worked on a newspaper; and under these the address of the Literary Institute that had once awarded him a guinea for a poem in a competition: Will Shakespeare at the Tomb of the Unknown Warrior. He tore the page out. Then the name and address, in red ink, of a collected poet who had written him a letter thanking him for a sonnet-sequence. And a page of names that might help.

The lavatory door half opened, and he shut it quickly with his foot.

'I beg your pardon.'

Hear her apologizing down the corridor, full as an egg. She could turn every handle the whole length of the train, and in every closet a fully-clothed man would be sitting with his foot against the door, lost and alone in the long, moving house on wheels, travelling in silence with no windows, at sixty miles an hour racing to another place that did not want him, never at home wherever the train stopped. The handle turned again, and Samuel coughed somebody away.

The last page of the notebook was the only one he kept. Under a drawing of a girl with long hair dancing into an address, he had written: Lucille Harris. A man he met on the Promenade had said as they sat on a bench, looking at the legs passing: 'She's okay. She's a girl I know. She's the best in the world; she'll take care of you. Give her a call when you're up. Tell her you're Austin's friend.' That page he placed in his wallet between two one-pound notes.

The rest of the pages he picked up from the floor, bunched together, and threw down between his legs into the bowl. Then he pulled the chain. Down went the helping names, the influential numbers, the addresses that could mean so much, into the round, roaring sea and on to the rails. Already they were lost a mile behind, blowing over the track now, over the glimpses of hedges into the lightning-passing fields.

Home and help were over. He had eight pounds ten and Lucille Harris' address. Many people have begun worse, he said aloud. I am ignorant, lazy, dishonest, and sentimental; I have the pull over nobody.

The handle turned again.

'I bet you're dancing,' he said to the person the other side of the locked door.

Footsteps pattered away down the train.

First of all, when I reach there, I'll have a Bass and a stale sandwich, he decided. I'll take them to a table in a corner, brush off the cakecrumbs with my hat, and prop my book against the cruet. I must have all the details right at the beginning. The rest must come by accident. I'll be sitting there before noon, cool and calm, my hat on my knees, my glass in my hand, looking not a day under twenty, pretending to read and spying from the corners of my eyes at the waiting, drinking, restless people busily alone at the counter. The other tables will be crowded. There will be women, beckoning without moving, over their cold coffee; old anonymous men with snuff on their cheeks, trembling over tea; quiet men expecting no one from the trains they wait for eagerly every hour; women who have come to run away, to take a train to St Ives or Liverpool or anywhere, but who know they will never take any train and are drinking cups of tea and saying to themselves, 'I could be catching the twelve o'clock but I'll wait for the quarter past'; women from the country with dozens of children coming undone; shop girls, office girls, street girls, people who have nothing worse to do, all the unhappy, happy in chains, bewildered foreign men and women in the station buffet of the city I know from cover to cover.

The door rattled. 'You there,' a voice said outside. 'You've been there for hours.'

He turned on the hot-water tap. It spurted cold water into the basin before he could take his hat out. 'I'm a director of the company,' he said, but his voice sounded weak to him and without assurance.

When the footsteps had faded again, he gathered up his cases and walked out of the lavatory and down the corridor. Standing outside a first-class compartment, he saw a man and a ticket-inspector come to the door and hammer on it. They did not try the handle.

'Ever since Neath,' the man said.

Now the train was losing speed, running out of the lost country into the smoke and a tunnel of factories, puffing past the district platforms and the high houses with broken windows and underclothes dancing in the dirty yards. Children at the windows never waved their hands to the train. It might have been the wind passing.

A crowd of people stood arguing outside the door as the train drew up under a great glass roof.

4

'Nip of Bass, please, and a ham sandwich.' He took them to a table in a corner, brushed off the crumbs with his wet hat, and sat down just before noon. He counted his money : eight pounds nine and a penny, nearly three pounds more than he had ever seen. Some people had this every week. It had to last him until he was dead. At the next table sat a plump, middle-aged man with a chocolate-brown birthmark over his cheek and chin like the half of a beard. He was propping his book against an empty bottle when a young man walked over from the counter.

'Hullo, Sam.'

'Hullo, Ron. Fancy seeing you.'

He was Ronald Bishop who used to live in the Crescent off Stanley's Grove.

'Been up in the smoke for long, Sam ?'

'Just arrived. How's tricks ?'

'Same as me, we must have been on the same train. Oh, so so. Still at the old game, Sam ?'

'Yeah, up on a bit of business. You at the usual ?'

'Yeah.'

They had never had anything to say to each other.

'Where you staying, Ron ?'

'Usual. Strand Palace.'

'Daresay I'll be seeing you, then.'

'Okay, make it tomorrow in the bar, about seven-thirty.'

'Okay.'

'It's a date, don't forget.'

'No fear.'

They both forgot it at once.

'Well, be seeing you.'

'Be good.'

As Ronald Bishop walked off, Samuel said silently into his glass : A fine beginning. If I go out of the station and turn round the corner I'll be back in 42. The little Proberts will be playing doctor outside the Load of Hay. The only stranger anywhere near me is a business-man with a stained face, reading the palms of his hands. No, here comes a woman in a fur coat; she's going to sit next to me. Yes, no, no. I smelt her as she passed; eau-de-Cologne and powder and bed.

The woman sat down two tables away, crossed her legs, powdered her nose.

This is the beginning of an advance. Now she is pretending not to notice that her knees are uncovered. There's a lynx in the room, lady. Button your overcoat. She's rattling her spoon on her saucer to attract my attention, but when I stare at her hand, without smiling, I see she is looking down gently and innocently into her lap as though she had a baby there. He was glad she was not brazen.

Dear mother, he wrote with his finger on the back of an envelope, looking up, between every few invisible words, at the unnoticing woman opposite, this is to tell you that I arrived safely and that I am drinking in the buffet with a tart. I will tell you later if she is Irish. She is about thirty-eight years old and her husband left her five years ago because of her carryings on. Her child is in a home, and she visits him every other Sunday. She always tells him that she is working in a hat shop. You need not worry that she will take all my money as we liked each other on first sight. And you need not worry that I shall break my heart trying to reform her, because I have always been brought up to believe that Mortimer Street is what is right, and I would not wish that on anybody. Besides, I do not want to reform her. Not that I think she is nasty. Her business is very hard on stockings, so I am going to pay the first week's rent for our little room in Pimlico. Now she is going across to the counter to buy another cup of coffee. I hope you will notice that she is buying her own. Everybody in the buffet is unhappy except me.

As she came back to her table, he tore up the envelope and stared at her, unsmiling, for a full minute by the Bovril clock. Once she raised her eyes to his, then looked away. She was tapping her spoon on the side of her cup, then opening and closing the clasp of her handbag, then turning her head round slowly to face him and then looking away again quickly through the window. She must be new, he thought with a sudden compassion, but he did not stop staring. Should I wink? He tilted his hard, wet hat over one eye, and winked: a long,

deliberate wink that screwed up his face and made his burning
cigarette nearly touch the blunt end of his nose. She snapped her
handbag, pushed two pennies under the saucer, and walked
right out of the room, never looking at him as she passed.

She's left her coffee, he thought. And then: My God, she was
blushing.

A fine beginning.

'Did you speak?' asked the man with the birthmark, spying
up. His face was red and purple where it was not brown, faintly
shabby and unshaved, shiftily angry about the eyes as though
his cunning were an irritation impossible to bear.

'I think I said it was a fine day.'

'Stranger in town?'

'Yes, I've just come up.'

'How do you like it?' He did not appear to care at all.

'I haven't been outside the station yet.'

Now the woman in the fur coat would be telling a policeman,
'I have just been winked at by a short boy wearing a wet hat.'
'But it isn't raining, madam.' That would settle her.

He put his hat under the table.

'There's plenty to see,' the man said, 'If that's what you want.
Museums, art galleries.' Without speaking, he went through a
list of names of other attractions, but rejected them all.
'Museums,' he said after a long pause. 'There's one at South
Kensington, and there's the British Museum, and there's one at
Whitehall with guns. I've seen them all,' he said.

Now every table was occupied. Cold, stiff people with time to
kill sat staring at their tea and the clock, inventing replies to
questions that would not be asked, justifying their behaviour in
the past and the future, drowning every present moment as soon
as it began to breathe, lying and wishing, missing all the trains
in the terror of their minds, each one alone at the terminus.
Time was dying all over the room. And then all the tables except
the one next to Samuel's were unoccupied again. The lonely
crowd went out in a funeral procession, leaving ash and tea-
leaves and newspapers.

'You must move out of the station some time, you know,' the
man said, returning to a conversation that held no interest for
him. 'If you want to see around. It's only fair. It's not fair to
come up in a train and sit in the buffet and then go back and
say you've seen London, is it?'

'I'm going out now, quite soon.'

'That's right,' the man said, 'give London a chance.'

He is so tired of talking to me that he is nearly losing his temper, Samuel thought.

He looked around him again, at the mourners fidgeting to the counter, at the quick whisky drinkers in a knot by the tea-urn, at the waitresses listlessly busy with cardboard cakes and small change.

'Otherwise, it's like not getting out of bed, isn't it?' the man said. 'You've got to walk round, you know, you've got to move some time. Everybody does it,' he said in a sudden, dull passion.

Samuel brought another nip of Bass from a girl like Joan Crawford.

'This is the last one, then I'm going,' he said when he had returned to his table.

'Do you think I care how many more you have? You can stay here all day, why should I mind?' The man was looking at the palms of his hands again as his temper mounted. 'Am I my brother's keeper?'

Ronald Bishop still stood at the counter.

Mortimer Street has tracked me down, Samuel thought bitterly, even into this lopsided quarrel with a palmist in a station restaurant. There was no escape. But it was not escape he wanted. The Street was a safe hole in a wall behind the wind in another country. He wanted to arrive and be caught. Ronald stood there like a fury with a rolled umbrella. Come in, Mrs Rosser, in your fawn and beige antimacassar coat, with your tribal hat on your waves, and scream the news of the Street across the table in your whist-drive voice. I could not escape your fury on a birds' rock, your beak gaped open like a shopping bag.

'I hate a nosey parker,' the man said, and got up. On his way to the counter he passed the table where the Irish prostitute had sat and removed the pennies from under the plate.

'Stop, thief!' Samuel said softly. No one could hear. There is a waitress with a consumptive husband who needs those pennies. And two children, Tristram and Eve. He changed the names quickly. Tom and Marge. Then walked over and put a sixpence under the plate just as a waitress came to the table.

'It fell on the floor,' he said.

'Oh yeah?'

As he walked back, he saw that the waitress was talking to three men at the counter and nodding her head in his direction. One man was Ronald Bishop. One was the man with the birthmark.

Oh, fine, fine! If he had not broken the china he would have caught the next train back. The pieces would be swept up by now, but the tears would be running all over the house. 'Mother, mother, he's put my crochet-work up the chimney,' he heard his sister scream in a guard's whistle. Herons, flower baskets, palm trees, windmills, Red Riding Hoods, stuffed up in the flames and soot. 'Get me a rubber to rub out coal, Hilda. I shall of course lose my position. That is only to be expected.' 'Oh my teapot, oh my blue set, oh my poor boy.' He refused to look at the counter where Ronald Bishop inaudibly reviled him. The waitress knew as soon as she saw him that he stole from the begging tins of the blind and led them by the arm into thick traffic. The birthmarked man said that he had shown a certain postcard to a customer in a fur coat. The voices of his parents condemned above the clattering of the cups. He stared hard at his book though the print climbed and staggered as if the tears of the left house had run down after him along the rails and flowed into this hot, suspicious room over the tea-stained air into his eyes. But the image was false and the book was chosen for strangers. He did not like or understand it.

'My bills.' 'My doilies.' 'My willow-plate.'

Ronald Bishop went out on to the platform.

'Be seeing you, Ron.'

Ronald Bishop's face was flushed with the embarrassment of not noticing him.

One pleasure is, Samuel said to himself, that I do not know what I expect to happen to me. He smiled at the waitress behind the counter, and she stared away at once as guiltily as though he had discovered her robbing the till. I am not so innocent as I make out, he thought. I do not expect any old cobwebbed Fagin, reeking of character and stories, to shuffle out of a corner and lead me away into his grand, loud, filthy house; there will not be any Nancy to tickle my fancy in a kitchen full of handkerchiefs and beckoning, unmade beds. I did not think a choir of loose women immediately would sing and dance around the little tables, in plush cloths and advertised brassieres, as I walked into London for the first time, rattling my fortune, fresh as Copperfield. I could count the straws in my hair with one hand.

Hush! I know you, he said, cheater at Patience, keyhole peeper, keeper of nail-clippings and ear-wax, lusting after silhouettes on Laburnum's blind, searching for thighs in the Library of Classical Favourites, Sam Thumb in the manhole prying up on windy days.

I am not like that at all, he said, as the man with the birthmark came over to his table and sat down opposite him.

'I thought you were going,' the man said. 'You told me you were going. You've been here an hour now.'

'I saw you,' Samuel said.

'I know you saw me. You must have seen me, mustn't you, because you were looking at me,' the man said. 'Not that I want the twopence, I've got a house full of furniture. Three rooms full to the ceiling. I've got enough chairs for everyone in Paddington to have a sit down. Twopence is twopence,' he said

'But it was twopence to the waitress, too.'

'She's got sixpence now, hasn't she? She's made fourpence clear. It doesn't do any harm to you just because she thinks you were trying to nip it off her.'

'It was my sixpence.'

The man raised his hands. The palms were covered with calculations in ink. 'And they talk about equality. Does it matter whose sixpence it was? It might have been mine or anybody's. There was talk of calling the manageress,' he said, 'but I put my foot down there.'

They were both silent for several minutes.

'Made up your mind where you're going when you move out of here?' the man said at last. 'Because move you must, some time, you know.'

'I don't know where I'm going. I haven't any idea in the world. That's why I came up to London.'

'Look here,' the man said, controlling his voice, 'there's sense in everything. There's bound to be. Otherwise we wouldn't be able to carry on, would we? Everybody knows where he's going, especially if he's come by train. Otherwise he wouldn't move from where he took the train from. That's elementary.'

'People run away.'

'Have you run away?'

'No.'

'Then don't say it. Don't say it.' His voice trembled; he
looked at the figures on his palms. Then gently and patiently he
began again. 'Let's get the first thing straight. People who have
come must go. People must know where they're going, otherwise
the world could not be conducted on a sane basis. The streets
would be full of people just wandering about, wouldn't they?
Wandering about and having useless arguments with people
who know where they're going. My name is Allingham, I live in
Sewell Street off Praed Street, and I'm a furniture dealer. That's
simple, isn't it? There's no need to complicate things if you keep
your head and know who you are.'

'I'm Samuel Bennet. I don't live anywhere at all. I don't do
any work, either.'

'Where are you going to go, then? I'm not a nosey parker, I
told you my business.'

'I don't know.'

'He doesn't know,' Mr Allingham said. 'Don't think you're
anywhere now, mind. You can't call this place anywhere, can
you? It's breathing space.'

'I've been wondering what was going to happen. That's what
I've been discussing with myself. I came up really to see what
would happen to me. I don't want to make anything happen
myself.'

'He was discussing it with himself. With a boy of twenty.
How old are you?'

'Twenty.'

'That's right. Discussing a question like that with a boy just
out of his teens. What did you expect to happen?'

'I don't know. Perhaps people would come up and talk to me
at the beginning. Women,' Samuel said.

'Why should they talk to you? Why should I talk to you.
You're not going anywhere. You're not doing anything. You
don't exist,' he said.

But all Samuel's strength was in his belly and his eyes. He
should veil his eyes or the marble-topped counter might melt
and all the clothes of the girls behind them peel away and all the
cups chip on the shelves.

'Anyone might come up,' he said. Then he thought of his fine
beginning. 'Anyone,' he said without hope.

A clerk from the Crescent a dozen doors away; a cold,
ordinary woman from Birmingham, driven off by a wink;

anybody, anybody ; a deacon from the Valleys on a mean blind, with his pocket-book sewn in his combs ; an elderly female assistant on holiday from a flannel and calico shop where the change hums on wires. Nobody he had ever wanted.

'Oh, anyone of course. Janet Gaynor,' Mr Allingham said. 'Marion Davies and Kay Francis and . . .'

'You don't understand. I don't expect that kind of person. I don't know what I do expect at all, but it isn't that.'

'Modest.'

'No, I'm not modest either. I don't believe in modesty. It's just that here I am and I don't know where to go. I don't want to know where to go.'

Mr Allingham began to plead, leaning across the table, pulling softly at Samuel's collar, showing the sums on his hands. 'Don't say you don't want to know where to go. Please. There's a good boy. We must take things easy, mustn't we ? We mustn't complicate things. Take one simple question. Now don't rush it. Take your own time.' He gripped a teaspoon with one hand. 'Where will you be tonight ?'

'I don't know. I'll be somewhere else but it won't be anywhere I've chosen because I'm not going to choose anything.'

Mr Allingham put the knotted teaspoon down.

'What do you want, Samuel ?' he whispered.

'I don't know.' Samuel touched his breast pocket where his wallet was. 'I know I want to find Lucille Harris,' he said.

'Who's Lucille Harris ?'

Then Mr Allingham looked at him.

'He doesn't know,' he said. 'Oh, he doesn't know !'

A man and a woman sat down at the next table.

'But you promised you'd destroy him,' the woman said.

'I'll do it, I'll do it,' the man said. 'Don't you worry. You drink your tea. Don't you worry.'

They had lived a long time together, and had grown to resemble one another with their dry, bunched faces and their nibbling mouths. The woman scratched herself as she drank, as she gripped the edge of the cup with her grey lips and shook it.

'Twopence she's got a tail,' Samuel said in a low voice, but Mr Allingham had not noticed them arrive.

'That's right,' he said. 'You have it your own way. And she's covered all over with fur.'

Samuel put his little finger in the neck of the empty bottle.

'I resign myself,' Mr Allingham said.

'But you don't understand, Mr Allingham.'

'I understand enough,' he said loudly. The couple at the next table stopped talking. 'You don't want to make things happen, don't you? I'll make them happen all right. You can't come in here and talk to me like you've been talking. Lucille Harris. Lucy da monk!'

The man and the woman began whispering. 'And it's only half-past one,' the woman said. She shook her cup like a rat.

'Come on. We're going.' Mr Allingham scraped back his chair.

'Where to?'

'Never you mind. It's I'm making things happen, isn't it?'

'I can't get my finger out of the bottle,' Samuel said.

Mr Allingham lifted up the suitcases and stood up. 'What's a little bottle?' he said. 'Bring it with you, son.'

'Father and son, too,' the woman said as Samuel followed him out.

The bottle hung heavily on his finger.

'Where now?' Outside in the roaring station.

'You follow me. And put your hand in your pocket. It looks silly.'

As they walked up the slope to the street, Mr Allingham said, 'I've never been with anybody with a bottle on his finger before. Nobody else has ever had a bottle on his finger. What'd you want to put your finger in the bottle for?'

'I just pushed it in. I'll be able to get it off with soap, there's no need to make a fuss.'

'Nobody else has ever had to get a bottle off with soap, that's all I'm saying. This is Praed Street.'

'It's dull, isn't it?'

'All the horses have gone away,' Mr Allingham said. 'This is my street. This is Sewell Street. It's dull, isn't it?'

'It's like the streets at home.'

A boy passed them and shouted 'Ikey Mo' to Mr Allingham.

'This is 23. See? There's the sign, 23.'

Mr Allingham opened the front door with a key. 'Second floor, first on the right.'

He gave three knocks. 'Mr Allingham,' he said, and they walked in.

The room was full of furniture.

PLENTY OF FURNITURE

1

Every inch of the room was covered with furniture. Chairs stood
on couches that lay on tables ; mirrors nearly the height of the
door were propped, back to back, against the walls, reflecting
and making endless the hills of desks and chairs with their legs
in the air, sideboards, dressing tables, chests-of-drawers, more
mirrors, empty bookcases, washbasins, clothes cupboards.
There was a double bed, carefully made, with the ends of the
sheets turned back, lying on top of a dining table on top of
another table ; there were electric lamps and lampshades, trays
and vases, lavatory bowls and basins, heaped in the armchairs
that stood on cupboards and tables and beds, touching the
ceiling. The one window, looking out on the road, could just be
seen through the curved legs of sideboards on their backs. The
walls behind the standing mirrors were thick with pictures and
picture frames.

Mr Allingham climbed into the room over a stack of mattresses, then disappeared.

'Hop in boy.' His voice came up from behind a high kitchen
dresser hung with carpets ; and, climbing over, Samuel looked
down to see him seated on a chair on a couch, leaning back
comfortably, his elbow on the shoulder of a statue.

'It's a pity we can't cook here,' Mr Allingham said. 'There's
plenty of stoves, too. That's a meat-safe,' he said, pointing to
one corner. 'Just under the bedroom suite.'

'Have you got a piano ?'

'There used to be one,' he said. 'I think it's in the other room.
She put a carpet over it. Can you play ?'

'I can vamp. You can tell what tunes I'm doing, easily. Is the
other room like this ?'

'Two more rooms, but I think the piano's locked. Yes, there's
plenty of furniture,' Mr Allingham said, looking round with

distaste. 'Whenever I say "That's enough now," in she comes with her "Plenty more room, plenty more room." She'll find she can't get in one day, that's what'll happen. Or she can't get out; I don't know which would be the worst. It gets you sometimes you know,' he said, 'all this furniture.'

'Is she your wife, Mr Allingham?'

'She'll find there's a limit to everything. You get to feel kind of trapped.'

'Do you sleep here?'

'Up there. It's nearly twelve foot high. I've measured. I can touch the ceiling when I wake up.'

'I like this room' Samuel said. 'I think it's perhaps the best room I've ever seen.'

'That's why I brought you. I thought you'd like it. Proper little den for a man with a bottle on his finger, isn't it? I told you, you're not like anybody else. Nobody else can bear the sight of it. Got your cases safe?'

'They're there. In the bath.'

'You keep your eye on them, that's all. I've lost a sofa. One more suite and I'll lose my bed. And what happens when a customer comes? I'll tell you. He takes one peek through the door and off he trots. You can only buy what's on the top at the moment, see.'

'Can you get into the other rooms?'

'You can,' Mr Allingham said. 'She takes a dive in, head-first. I've lost all interest in the other rooms, myself. You could live and die in there and nobody'd know. There's some nice Chippendale, too. Up by the skylight.'

He rested his other elbow on a hallstand.

'I got to feel lost,' he said. 'That's why I go down to the buffet; there's only tables and chairs there.'

Samuel sat on his perch, swinging the bottle and drumming his feet against the side of a bath mounted yards above the floor of mattresses. A carpet behind him, laid out flat and wide along the air, having no visible support, bore a great earthenware jar dangerously upon the backs of its patterned birds. High over his head, in the tall room, a rocking-chair balanced on a card-table, and the table's thin legs rested on the top of a cupboard standing up straight among pillows and fenders, with its mirrored door wide open.

'Aren't you frightened of things falling? Look at that rocking-chair. One little prod and over she comes.'

'Don't you dare. Of course I'm frightened,' Mr Allingham said. 'If you open a drawer over there, a wash-stand falls down over here. You've got to be quick as a snake. There's nothing on the top you'd like to buy, is there?'

'I like a lot of things, but I haven't any money.'

'No, no, you wouldn't have money. That's right. Other people have money.'

'I like the big jar. You could hide a man in that. have you got any soap for my finger?'

'Of course there's no soap, there's only washbasins. You can't have a bath, either, and there's five baths. Why do you want a jar big enough to hide a man in? Nobody I've ever met wants to hide a man in a jar. Everybody else says that the jar's too big for anything. Why do you want to find Lucille Harris, Sam?'

'I didn't mean I wanted to hide a man in it. I mean that you could if you wanted to. Oh, a man I know told me about Lucille, Mr Allingham, I don't know why I want to find her, but that's the only London address I kept. I put the others down the lavatory in the train. When the train was moving.'

'Good, good.' Mr Allingham put his hand on the thick, white neck of the naked statue, and tightened his fingers.

The door opened on to the landing. Two people came in, and climbed up the mattresses without a word. The first, a fat, short woman with black hair and a Spanish comb, who had painted her face as though it were a wall, took a sudden dive toward the corner behind Samuel and disappeared between two columns of chairs. She must have landed on cushions or a bed, for she made no sound. The second visitor was a tall, youngish man with a fixed smile; his teeth were large, like a horse's, but very white; his glistening fair hair was done in tight curls, and it smelt across the room. He stood on a spring mattress just inside the door bouncing up and down. 'Come on, Rose, don't be sulky,' he said. 'I know where you've gone.' Then, pretending to see Samuel for the first time, 'Good gracious you look like a bird up there,' he said. 'Is Donald hiding anywhere?'

'I'm not hiding,' Mr Allingham said. 'I'm by the statue. Sam Bennet, George Ring.'

George Ring bowed and bounced, rising a foot from the mattress.

He and Mr Allingham could not see each other. Nobody could see the woman with the Spanish comb.

'I hope you've excused the room to Mr Bennet,' George Ring said. He bounced a few steps in the direction of the hidden statue.

'I don't think it needs any excusing, Mr Ring,' Samuel said. 'I've never seen such a comfortable room.'

'Oh, but it's terrible.' George Ring was moving up and down rapidly now. 'It's very kind of you to say it's comfortable, but look at the confusion. Just think of living here. You've got something on your finger, did you know that? Three guesses. It's a bottle.' He shook his curls and laughed as he bounced.

'You don't know anything yet,' said Mr Allingham's voice. The heavy bouncing had shaken down a carpet on to the hall stand and he was hidden as though in another, lower room. 'You don't know anything about him. You wait. What are you bouncing for, George? People don't go bouncing about like a ball as soon as they come into a room.'

'What don't I know about you?' In one leap George Ring was standing directly below Samuel, craning up his curls.

'He doesn't know where he is going, for one thing. And he's looking for a girl he doesn't know called Lucille.'

'Why are you looking for her?' George Ring's head touched the bath. 'Did you see her picture in the paper?'

'No, I don't know anything about her, but I want to see her because she's the only person I know by name in London.'

'Now you know two more, don't you? Are you sure you don't love her?'

'Of course I'm sure.'

'I thought perhaps she might be a sort of Holy Grail. You know what I mean. A sort of ideal.'

'Go on, you big pussycat,' Mr Allingham said. 'Get me out of here.'

'Is this the first time you've come to London? I felt like that when I came up first, too. Years and years ago. I felt there was something I must find, I can't explain it. Something just round the corner. I searched and searched. I was so innocent. I felt like a sort of knight.'

'Get me out of here,' Mr Allingham said. 'I feel like the whole room's on top of me.'

'I never found it.' George Ring laughed and sighed and

stroked the side of the bath. 'Perhaps you'll be lucky,' he said. 'You'll walk round the corner and there she'll be. Lucille. Lucille. Is she on the telephone?'

'Yes. I've got her number in my book.'

'Oh, that makes it easier, doesn't it. Come on, Rose,' he said. 'I know exactly where you are. She's in a pet.'

Samuel rocked softly on his box in the middle of the furniture. This was the fullest room in England. How many hundreds of houses had been split in here, tables and chairs coming in on a wooden flood, chests and cupboards soaring on ropes through the window and settling down like birds. The other rooms, beyond that jostled door, would be taller and darker even than this, with the mute, black shape of the locked piano mountain-ous under a shroud of carpets and Rose, with her comb like the prow of a ship, driving into their darkness and lying all night motionless and silent where she struck. Now she was dead still on a sunk bed between the column of chairs, buried alive, soft and fat and lost in a grave in a house.

'I'm going to buy a hammock,' George Ring said,. 'I can't bear sleeping under all this furniture.'

Perhaps the room was crowded at night with people who could not see each other, stretched under chairs, under sofas, dizzily asleep on the tops of raised tables, waking up every morning and crying out, 'Earthquake, earthquake!'

'And then I'll go to bed like a sailor.'

'Tell Rose to come and get me out of here,' Mr Allingham said, behind the cloaked hallstand, 'I want to eat.'

'She's sulking Donald. She's mad about a Japanese screen now.'

'Do you hear that, Sam? Isn't there enough privacy in this room? Anybody can do anything, nobody can see you. I want to eat. I want to have a snack at Dacey's. Are you sleeping here tonight?'

'Who?' Samuel asked. 'Me?'

'You can doss down in one of the other rooms, if you think you can get up again. There's enough beds for a harem.'

'Harem,' George Ring said, pronouncing it another way. 'You've got company, Rose darling. Do come out and be introduced.'

'Thank you, Mr Allingham,' Samuel said.

'Didn't you really have any idea at all?' George Ring bounced, and for a moment his scented head was level with Samuel's. One wide, bright, horse-toothed smile, and the head was gone. 'About sleeping and things. I think it's awfully brave. You might have fallen in with all kinds of people. "He fell among thieves." Do you know Sir Henry Newbolt's poem ?'

'He flung his empty revolver down the slope,' Samuel said.

The day was moving carelessly on to a promised end and in a dark room full of furniture where he'd lie down with his bunch of wives in a crow's-nest bed or rock them in a hammock under the ceiling.

'Goodie goodie ! It's so exciting to find someone who knows about poetry. "The voices faded and the hills slept." Isn't that beautiful ? The voices faded . . . ? I can read poetry for hours, can't I, Donald ? I don't care what kind of poetry it is, I love it all. Do you know, "Is there anybody there, said the traveller ?" Where do you put the emphasis, Mr Bennet ? Can I call you Sam ? Do you say, "Is there *anybody* there" or "Is there anybody *there*" ?'

'It isn't natural,' Mr Allingham said, 'for a man not to be able to see anybody when he's sitting right next to them. I'm not grumbling, but I can't see anything, that's all. It's like not being in the room.'

'Oh, do be quiet, Donald. Sam and I are having a perfectly serious discussion. Of course you're in the room, don't be morbid.'

'I think I'd put about the same emphasis on all the words,' Samuel said.

'But don't you find it tends to make the line rather flat ? "*Is* there anybody there, said the traveller,"' George Ring murmured, pacing the mattresses, his head on one side. 'I feel you do want a stress somewhere.'

Will I be alone tonight in the room with the piano ? Samuel wondered. Alone like a man in a warehouse, lying on each bed in turn, opening cupboards and putting my hand in, looking at myself in mirrors in the dark.

'Don't you call me morbid, George Ring,' Mr Allingham said. He tried to move, but the statue fell against his chair. 'I remember once I drank forty-nine Guinnesses straight off and I came home on the top of a bus. There's nothing morbid about a man who can do that. Right on the top of the bus, too, not just in the upper deck.'

Or will the room be full as a cemetery, but with the invisible dead breathing and snoring all around me, making love in the cupboards, drunk as tailors in the dry baths? Suddenly a warm body might dive in through the door and lie in my bed all night without a name or a word.

'I think forty-nine Guinnesses is piggish,' said George Ring.

'It was raining,' Mr Allingham said, 'and I never get truculent. I may sing and I may have a bit of a dance, but I never get nasty. Give me a hand, Sam.'

Samuel took the carpet off the hallstand and pushed the statue away. It had fallen between Mr Allingham's legs. He came up slowly into sight and rubbed his eyes like a man waking.

'I told you,' he said, 'you get trapped. Coming to Dacey's, George?'

'I'll have to stay for hours, you know that,' George Ring said. 'You know I'm the only person who can humour Rosie when she's in one of her states. Oh, come on, Rosie, don't be temperamental. It's ninety per cent temper and ten per cent mental. Just because you're an actress you think you can stay under the furniture all the afternoon. I'll count five . . .'

Samuel followed Mr Allingham to the door.

'Five, six, seven,' George Ring said, as Mr Allingham slammed the door hard, and his voice was lost in the noise of furniture falling. They went down the stairs into the hallway that smelt of cabbage, and out on to the grey street.

'I think it must have been the rocking-chair,' Samuel said.

'Mrs Dacey's is just round the corner,' Mr Allingham said. 'There you are. See the Cadbury sign?'

2

Mrs Dacey's front window was whitewashed from inside, and the words 'High Class' had been scrawled across it. ' "Susan Dacey, licensed to sell tobacco," ' Samuel read aloud. 'Is it a restaurant too?'

'You must tell her that,' Mr Allingham said, opening the door. A bell rang. 'It hasn't been called that before.' He held his foot against the door so that the bell kept ringing. 'She's a woman in a thousand.'

A tall, thin, dignified woman came through the private door at the back of the shop, her hands clasped in front of her. She was dressed in black almost down to the ankles, with a severe white collar, and she held her head primly as though it might spill. God help the other nine hundred and ninety-nine. But she smiled then, and her eyes were sharp and light; the dullness raced from her mouth, leaving it cruel and happy.

'Take your trotter off the door,' she said.

The bell stopped.

'That's better. You made enough noise to wake the dead.' She was a well-spoken woman, clear and precise, like a school-mistress.

'Keeping well, Mrs Dacey? This is a new friend, Sam Bennet. Two pies and two coffees, please. Where's Polly?'

'Up to no good,' said Mrs Dacey, stepping behind the counter. Her grand dress floated around her. 'You're from the country,' she said, over her shoulder, as she turned the coffee tap on the brass urn. 'How did you find Ikey Mo?'

'That's me.' Mr Allingham blushed on one side of his face.

'I'm not from the country really.' Samuel told her where he came from. 'I met Mr Allingham in the station. I'm going to sleep in his flat tonight.'

'I'd sooner sleep in an ashpit,' she said.

The coffee was thick and white and tasteless. They took their cups to a cubicle and Samuel brushed off the crumbs from his chair with his sleeve. His hat was gone. There were small pellets of dirt in the dust at his feet.

'You've got a bottle on your finger,' she said.

'There, you see, everybody notices. Why don't you take it off, Sam? It isn't a decoration, it isn't useful, it's just a bottle.'

'I think my finger must have swollen, Mr Allingham. The bottle's much tighter now.'

'Let me have a look at you again.' Mrs Dacey put on a pair of spectacles with steel rims and a hanging chain. 'He's only a baby.'

'I'm twenty.'

'Ikey Mo, the baby farmer.' She walked carefully to the back of the shop and called, 'Polly, come down here. Polly. Polly.'

A girl's voice called back from high up the house, 'What for, ma?'

'Come and get a gentleman's bottle off.'

'It sounds like a Russian composer, doesn't it, darling?'

George Ring said, at the door. 'What a marvellous dress, you look like a murderess.'

He sat down next to Samuel.

'I couldn't get Rose to move. She's going to lie there all day in a tantrum. Do tell me what's happening, everybody.'

'It's that bottle again,' Mr Allingham said. 'Why didn't he put his finger in a glass or something? I don't know what he was poking his finger about for in the first place. It's an enigma to me.'

'Everything's an enigma to you. You can't understand the slightest touch of originality. I think it must be awful not to have any imagination. It's like a sense of humour.'

'I'm just saying that not to be able to go in and buy a bottle of Bass without having to leave with the bottle on your finger seems to me like a kind of nightmare. That's all I'm saying.'

Samuel heard Mrs Dacey's daughter running downstairs. Then he saw her hand on the edge of the door. In the second she took to push the door open and come in, he made her a hundred faces; he made her talk and walk in all the disguises of his loves at night; he gave her golden hair, black hair, he knew that she would be gypsy-skinned and white as milk. Polly come and put the kettle on with your white, slender, brown, broad hands, and see me waiting like a grenadier or a caliph in the mousey cubicle.

'It's like one of those nightmares when you're playing billiards and the cue's made of elastic,' Mr Allingham said.

In came a girl with a long, pale face and glasses. Her hair was not any of Samuel's colours, but only dark and dull.

'Go and help to pull his bottle off,' said Mrs Dacey.

Polly sat down on the table and took his hand. 'Does it hurt? I've never done it before.' She pulled at his finger.

'I hope you won't ever have to do it again, either,' Mr Allingham said. 'I don't care if I haven't any imagination. I'm glad I'm like I am without anything on my finger.'

Polly bent over Samuel's hand and he saw down her dress. She knew that he was looking, but she did not start back or spread her hand across the neck of her dress; she raised her head and stared at his eyes. I shall always remember this, he said to himself. In 1933 a girl was pulling at a bottle on the little finger of my left hand while I looked down her dress. It will last longer than all my poems and troubles.

'I can't get it off,' she said.

'Take him up to the bathroom then and put some soap on it,' said Mrs Dacey, in her dry, neat voice. 'And mind it's only his bottle.'

George Ring said as they got up to go, 'Scream if you want me, I'll be up in a wink. She's the most terrible person, aren't you, darling? You wouldn't catch little George going up there all alone.'

Polly led the way upstairs.

'I'm not complaining,' Mr Allingham said, 'I'm just making a statement. I'm not saying it isn't all as it should be. He's got a bottle on his finger and I've got a tooth in my pie.'

His voice faded.

3

Someone had drawn the ragged curtains in the bathroom to shut out the damp old day, and the bath was half full of water with a rubber duck floating on it. As Polly closed and locked the door birds began to sing.

'It's only the birds,' she said. She put the key down her dress. 'You needn't be frightened.'

Two cages hung from the ceiling.

But Samuel had looked frightened when she turned the key and put it away where he never wanted to find it, not when the room grew suddenly like a wood in the tangled shadows of the green curtains.

'It's a funny place to have birds,' he said.

'They're mine.' Polly let the hot water run and the birds sang more loudly as though they heard a waterfall. 'Mr Allingham comes here for a bath on Wednesdays and he says they sneer at him and blow little raspberries all the time he's washing. But I don't think he washes very much. Doesn't Mr Allingham make you laugh too?'

He expected her to be smiling when she turned to him, but her face was still and grave, and all at once he saw that she was prettier than any of the girls he had made up in his mind before she opened the door downstairs. He distrusted her prettiness because of the key. He remembered what Mrs Dacey had said when Mr Allingham asked where Polly was. 'Up to no good.' He did not think she was going to put her arms around him.

That would have been different. If she tried to put his head under the water he'd shout for George Ring and up he'd come like a horse, neighing and smelling of scent.

'I only locked the door because I don't want George Ring to come in. He's queer. He puts scent all over his underclothes; did you know that? The Passing Cloud, that's what we call him. The Passing Cloud.'

'You didn't have to put the key where you put it, though,' Samuel said. 'I might push you down and fish for it, I might be that sort.'

'I don't care.'

If only she would have smiled at him when she said that. But she looked as though she really did not care whether he pushed her down or whether he sat on the edge of the bath and touched the duck with his bottle.

The duck floated in circles on the used, greasy water.

'What's your name?'

'Sam.'

'Mine's Mary. But they call me Polly for short.'

'It isn't much shorter, is it?'

'No, it's exactly the same length.'

She sat by his side on the edge of the bath. He could not think of anything to say. Here was the locked door he had often made up in stories and in his head, in bed in Mortimer Street, and the warm, hidden key, and the girl who was willing for anything. The bathroom should be a bedroom and she should not be wearing glasses.

'Will you take off your glasses, Polly?'

'If you like. But I won't be able to see very far.'

'You don't have to see very far, it's only a little room,' he said. 'Can you see me?'

'Of course I can. You're right next to me. Do you like me better now?'

'You're very pretty, I suppose, Polly.'

'Pretty Polly,' she said, without a smile.

Well, he said to himself, here you are, here she is without any glasses on.

'Nothing ever happens in Sewell Street.' She took his hand and let his finger with the bottle on it lie in her lap.

Here you are, he said, with your hand in her lap.

'Nothing ever happens where I come from, either. I think

things must be happening everywhere except where one is. All kinds of things happen to other people. So they say,' he said.

'The man who was lodging next door but one cut his throat like this,' she said, 'before breakfast.'

On his first free days since he was born Samuel sat with a loose girl in a locked bathroom over a tea-shop, the dirty curtains were drawn, and his hand lay on her thighs. He did not feel any emotion at all. O God, he thought, make me feel something, make me feel as I ought to, here is something happening and I'm cool and dull as a man in a bus. Make me remember all the stories. I caught her in my arms, my heart beat against hers, her body was trembling, her mouth opened like a flower. The lotus of Osiris was opening to the sun.

'Listen to the old birds,' she said, and he saw that the hot water was running over the rim of the washbasin.

I must be impotent, he thought.

'Why did he cut his throat like that, Polly? Was it love? I think if I was crossed in love I'd drink brandy and whisky and crème de menthe and that stuff that's made with eggs.'

'It wasn't love with Mr Shaw. I don't know why he did it. Mrs Bentley said there was blood everywhere, everywhere, and all over the clock. He left a little note in the letter-rack and all it said was that he'd been meaning to do it ever since October: Look, the water'll drip right through into the kitchen.'

He turned it off. The birds stopped singing.

'Perhaps it was love, really. Perhaps he loved you, Polly, but he wouldn't say so. From a distance.'

'Go on, he had a limp,' she said. 'Old Dot and Carry. How old are you?'

'Twenty.'

'No, you're not.'

'Well, nearly.'

'No, you're not.'

Then they were silent, sitting on the bath, his hand in her lap. She trailed her pale hand in the water. The birds began again.

'Pale hands I love,' he said.

'Beside the Shalimar. Do you, Sam? Do you love my hands? That's a funny think to say.' She looked dully at the long, floating weed in the water and made a wave. 'It's like the evening here.'

'It's like evening in the country,' he said. 'Birds singing and water. We're sitting on a bank by the river now.'

'Having a picnic.'

'And then we're going to take our clothes off and have a swim. Gee, it'll be cold. You'll be able to feel all the fish swimming about.'

'I can hear the 47 bus, too,' she said. 'People are going home to tea. It's cold without any clothes on, isn't it? Feel my arm, it's like snow, only not so white. Pale hands I love,' she began to sing. 'Do you love me altogether?'

'I don't know. I don't think I feel anything like that at all. I never do feel much until afterwards and then it's too late.'

'Now it isn't too late. It isn't too late, Sam. We're alone. Polly and Sam. I'll come and have a swim with you if you like. In the dirty old river with the duck.'

'Don't you ever smile, Polly? I haven't seen you smile once.'

'You've only known me for twenty minutes. I don't like smiling much, I think I look best when I'm serious, like this.' She saddened her eyes and mouth. 'I'm a tragedienne. I'm crying because my lover's dead.'

Slowly tears came to her eyes.

'His name was Sam and he had green eyes and brown hair. He was ever so short. Darling, darling, darling Sam, he's dead.' The tears ran down her cheeks.

'Stop crying now, Polly. Please. Stop crying. You'll hurt yourself.'

But she was crying pitifully.

'Stop it, Polly, pretty Polly.' He put his arm round her shoulders. He kissed her on the cheek. It was warm and wet. 'Nobody's dead, Polly darling,' he said. She cried and moaned his name in the abandon of her made grief, tore at the loose, low neck of her dress, threw back her hair and raised her damp eyes to the birds in their cages and the cracked heavens of the ceiling.

'You're doing it fine,' he said in despair, shaking her shoulders. 'I've never seen such fine crying. Stop now, please, Polly, please, while you can stop.'

Ninety-eight per cent of the human body is water, he thought. Polly Dacey is all salt water. She sat by his side like a flood in an apron.

'I'll do anything you like if you'll only stop,' he said. 'You'll drown yourself, Polly. I'll promise to do anything in the world.'

She dried her eyes on her bare arm.

'I wasn't really breaking my heart, silly. I was only depicting. What'll you do, then? Anything? I can depict being glad because my lover's not really dead, too. The War Office made a mistake.'

'Anything,' he said. 'I want to see you being glad tomorrow. You mustn't do one after the other.'

'It's nothing to me, I can do them all in a row. I can do childbirth and being tight and – '

'You do being quiet. Do being a quiet lady sitting on a bath, Polly.'

'I will if you'll come and have a swim with me. You promised.' She patted her hair into place.

'Where?'

'In the bath. You get in first, go on. You can't break your promise.'

George Ring, he whispered, gallop upstairs now and bite your way through the door. She wants me to sit with my overcoat on and my bottle on my finger in the cold, greasy bath, in the half-dark bathroom, under the sneering birds.

'I've got a new suit,' he said.

'Take it off, silly. I don't want you to go in the bath with your clothes on. Look, I'll put something over the window so you can undress in the dark. Then I'll undress too. I'll come in the bath with you. Sam, are you frightened?'

'I don't know. Couldn't we take our clothes off and not go in the bath? I mean, if we want to take them off at all. Someone might come in. It's terribly cold, Polly. Terribly cold.'

'You're frightened. You're frightened to lie in the water with me. You won't be cold for long.'

'But there's no sense in it. I don't want to go in the bath. Let's sit here and you do being glad, Polly.'

He could not move his hand, she had caught the bottle between her legs.

'You don't want to be frightened. I'm not any older than you are,' she said, and her whispering mouth was close to his ear. 'As soon as you get in the bath I'll jump on top of you in the dark. You can pretend I'm somebody you love if you don't like me properly. You can call me any name.' She dug her nails into his hand. 'Give me your coat, I'll hang it over the window. Dark as midnight,' she said, as she hung the coat up, and her face in the green light through the curtains was like a girl's under the sea. Then all the green went out, and he heard her fumbling. I do not want to drown. I do not want to drown in Sewell Street off Circe Street, he whispered under his breath.

'Are you undressing? I can't hear you. Quick, quick, Sam.'

He took off his jacket and pulled his shirt over his head. Take a good look in the dark, Mortimer Street, have a peek at me in London.

'I'm cold,' he said.

'I'll make you warm, beautifully warm, Sam.' He could not tell where she was, but she was moving in the dark and clinking a glass. 'I'm going to give you some brandy. There's brandy, darling, in the medicine cupboard. I'll give you a big glass. You must drink it right down.'

Naked, he slipped one leg over the edge of the bath and touched the icy water.

Come and have a look at impotent Samuel Bennet from Mortimer Street off Stanley's Grove trembling to death in a cold bath in the dark near Paddington Station. I am lost in the metropolis with a rubber duck and a girl I cannot see pouring brandy into a tooth-glass. The birds are going mad in the dark. It's been such a short day for them, Polly.

'I'm in the bath now.'

'I'm undressing too. can you hear me?' she said softly. 'That's my dress rustling. Now I'm taking my petticoat off. Now I'm naked.' A cold hand touched him on the face. 'Here's the brandy, Sam. Sam, my dear, drink it up and then I'll climb in with you. I'll love you, Sam, I'll love you up. Drink it all up, then you can touch me.'

He felt the glass in his hand and he lifted it up and drank all that was in it.

'Christ!' he said in a clear, ordinary voice. 'Christ!'

Then the birds flew down and kicked him on the head, carefully between the eyes, brutally on each temple, and he fell back in the bath.

That was all the birds singing under the water, and the sea was full of feathers that swam up his nostrils and into his mouth. A duck as big as a ship sailed up on a drop of water as big as a house and smelt his breath as it spurted out from broken, bleeding lips, like flames and waterspouts. Here came a wave of brandy and birds, and Mr Allingham, naked as a baby, riding on the top with his birthmark like a rainbow, and George Ring swimming breast-stroke through the open door, and three Mrs Daceys gliding in yards above the flowing ground.

The darkness drowned in a bright ball of light, and the birds stopped.

4

Voices began to reach him from a great distance, travelling in lavatories in racing trains along a liquid track, diving from the immeasurably high ceiling into the cold sea in the enormous bath.

'Do you see what I see?' That was the voice of the man called Allingham, who slept under the furniture. 'He's taking a little dip.'

'Don't let me look, Donald, he's bare all over.' I know him, Samuel thought. That's George Ring the horse. 'And he's ill too. Silly Sam.'

'Lucky Sam. He's drunk, George. Well, well, well, and he hasn't even got his bottle off. Where's Polly?'

'You look over there,' Mrs Dacey said. 'Over there on the shelf. He's drunk all the eau de cologne.'

'He must have been thirsty.'

Large, bodiless hands came over the bath and lifted him out.

'He's eccentric,' Mr Allingham said, as they laid him on the floor, 'that's all I'm saying. I'm not preaching, I'm not condemning. I'm just saying that other people get drunk in the proper places.'

The birds were singing again in the electric dawn as Samuel fell quietly to sleep.

FOUR LOST SOULS

_____

1

He sank into the ragged green water for the second time and, rising naked with seaweed and a woman under each arm and a mouthful of broken shells, he saw the whole of his dead life standing trembling before him, indestructible and unsinkable, on the brandy-brown waves. It looked like a hallstand.

He opened his mouth to speak, but a warm wave rushed in.

'Tea,' said Mrs Dacey. 'Tea with plenty of sugar every five minutes. That's what I always gave him, and it didn't do a bit of good.'

'Not too much Worcester, George; don't bury the egg.'

'I won't,' Samuel said.

'Oh, listen to the birds. It's been such a short night for the birds, Polly.'

'Listen to the birds,' he said clearly, and a burning drink drowned his tongue.

'They've laid an egg,' Mr Allingham said.

'Try some Coca-Cola, Donald. It can't do any harm; he's had tea and a prairie oyster and angostura and Oxo and everything.'

'I used to pour the tea down by the pint,' Mrs Dacey said affectionately, 'and up it came, lump sugar and all.'

'He doesn't want a Coca-Cola. Give him a drop of your hair oil. I knew a man who used to squeeze boot-blacking through a veil.'

'You know everybody piggish. He's trying to sit up, the poor darling.'

Samuel wrestled into the dry world and looked around a room in it, at Mrs Dacey, now miraculously divided into one long woman, folding her black silk arms in the doorway, at George Ring arching his smile and hair toward the rusty taps, at Mr Allingham resigned above him.

'Polly's gone,' he said.

It was then that he understood why the three persons in the bathroom were so tall and far. I am on the floor, looking up, he said to himself. But the others were listening.

'You're naked too,' Mr Allingham said, 'under the blanket.'

'Here's a nice wet sponge.' George Ring dabbed and smoothed. 'Keep it on your forehead. There, like that. That better?'

'Eau de cologne is for outside the body,' said Mrs Dacey without disapproval, 'and I'll give our Polly such a clip. I'll clip her on the earhole every time she opens her mouth.'

Mr Allingham nodded. 'Whisky I can understand,' he said. 'But eau de cologne! You put that on handkerchieves. You don't put whisky on handkerchieves.' He looked down at Samuel. 'I don't.'

'No, mustn't suck the sponge, Sam.'

'I suppose he thinks red biddy's like bread and milk,' Mr Allingham said.

They gathered his clothes from the side of the bath and hurriedly dressed him. And not until he was dressed and upright, shivering along the landing to the dark stairs, did he try to speak again. George Ring and Mr Allingham held his arms and guided him toward the top of that winding grave. Mrs Dacey, the one mourner, followed with a rustle of silk.

'It was the brandy from the medicine cupboard,' he said, and down they went into the coarse, earth-like silence of the stairs.

'Give me furniture polish,' Mr Allingham said. 'Crack. Mind your head. Especially when I'm out of sorts in the bath.'

The darkness was settling like more dirt and dust over the silent shop. Someone had hung up a sign, 'Closed', on the inside of the window not facing the street. 'Meths is finicky,' Mr Allingham said.

They sat Samuel down on a chair behind the counter and he heard Mrs Dacey, still on the stairs, calling for Polly up into the dark, dirty other floors and caves of the drunken house. But Polly did not answer.

She would be in her locked bedroom now, crying for Sam gone, at her window staring out on to the colourless, slowly disappearing street and the tall houses down at heel; or depicting, in the kitchen, the agony of a woman in childbirth, writhing and howling round the crowded sink; or being glad at a damp corner of the landing.

'Silly goose,' said George Ring, sitting long-legged on the table and smiling at Samuel with a ferocious coyness. 'You might have been drownded. Drownded,' he said again, looking slyly up from under the spider line of his eyebrows.

'Lucky you left the door open,' Mr Allingham said. He lit a cigarette and looked at the match until it burned his finger. 'I suppose,' he said, his finger in his mouth.

'Our maid at home always said "drownded",' said George Ring.

'But I saw Polly lock the door. She put the key down her dress.' Samuel spoke with difficulty from behind the uncertain counter. The words came out in a rush, then reversed and were lost, tumbling among the sour bushes under his tongue. 'She put it down her dress,' he said, and paused at the end of each word to untie the next. Now the shop was almost entirely dark.

'And Chimbley. You know, for chimney. Well, my dear, the door was open when we went up. No key, no Polly.'

'Just a boy in the bath,' Mr Allingham said. 'Do you often get like that, Sam? The water was up to your chin.'

'And the dirt!'

'It wasn't my dirt. Someone had been in the bath before. It was cold,' Samuel said.

'Yes, yes.' Samuel could see Mr Allingham's head nodding. 'That alters the situation, doesn't it? Dear God,' he said, 'you should have gone in with your clothes on like everybody else.'

'Polly's gone,' said Mrs Dacey. She appeared out of nowhere in the wall and stood behind the counter at Samuel's side. Her rustling dress brushed against his hands, and he drew them sharply back. I touched a funeral, he said to the dazed boy in his chair. Her corpse-cold hand fell against his cheek, chilling him out of a moment's sleep. The coffin has walked upright into my sitting bed.

'Oooh,' he said aloud.

'Still cold, baby?' Mrs Dacey bent down, creaking like a door, and mothered him about the hair and mouth.

There had been little light all day, even at dawn and noon, mostly the close, false light of bedroom and restaurant. All day he had sat in small, dark places, bathroom and travelling lavatory, a jungle of furniture, a stuffed shop where no one called except these voices saying:

'You looked so defenceless, Sam, lying there all cold and white.'

'Where was Moses when the light went out, Mrs Dacey?'

'Like one of these cherubs in the Italian Primitives, only with a bottle on your finger, of course.'

'In the dark. Like this.'

'What did our Polly do to you, the little tart?' Mrs Dacey said in her tidy, lady's voice.

Mr Allingham stood up. 'I'm not listening. Don't you say a word, Sam, even if you could. No explanations. There he was, gassed in the bath, at half-past four in the afternoon. I can stand so much.'

'I want to go out,' Samuel said.

'Out the back?'

'Out.'

Out of the blind, stripping hole in a wall, aviary and menagerie, cold water shop, into the streets, without locks. I don't want to sleep with Polly in a drawer. I don't want to lie in a cellar with a wet woman, drinking polish. London is happening everywhere; let me out, let me go. Mrs Daccy is all cold fingers.

'Out then. It's six o'clock. Can you walk, son?'

'I can walk okay; it's my head.'

Mrs Dacey, unseen, stroked his hair. Nobody can see, he said silently, but Mrs Susan Dacey, licensed to sell tobacco, is stroking my hair with her lizards; and he gave a cry.

'I've got no sympathy,' said Mr Allingham. 'Are you coming, Sue?'

'Depends where you're going.'

'Taking the air down the Edgware Road. He's got to see around, hasn't he? You don't come up from the provinces to drink eau de cologne in the bath.'

They all went out, and Mrs Dacey locked the shop.

It was raining heavily.

2

'Fun!' George Ring said.

They walked out of Sewell Street into Praed Street arm-in arm.

'I'm a fool for the rain.' He shook his clinging curls and danced a few steps on the pavement.

'My new brown overcoat's in the bathroom,' Samuel said, and Mrs Dacey covered him with her umbrella.

'Go on, you're not the sort that puts a coat on in the rain, are you? Stop dancing, George.'

But George Ring danced down the pavement in the flying rain and pulled the others with him; unwillingly they broke into a dancing run under the lamp posts' drizzle of light, Mrs Dacey, black as a deacon, jumping high over the puddles with a rustle and creak, Mr Allingham, on the outside, stamping and dodging along the gutter, Samuel gliding light and dizzy with his feet hardly touching the ground.

'Look out. People,' cried Mr Allingham, and dragged them, still dancing, out on to the slippery street. Caught in a circle of headlights and chased by horns, they stamped and scampered on to the pavement again, clinging fast to each other, their faces glistening, cold and wet.

'Where's the fire, George? Go easy, boy, go easy.' But Mr Allingham, one foot in the gutter, was hopping along like a rabbit and tugging at George Ring's arm to make him dance faster. 'It's all Sam's fault,' he said as he hopped, and his voice was high and loud like a boy's in the rain.

Look at London flying by me, buses and glow-worms, umbrellas and lamp posts, cigarettes and eyes under the water doorways, I am dancing with three strangers down Edgware Road in the rain, cried Samuel to the gliding boy around him. Light and without will as a suit of feathers, he held on to their arms, and the umbrella rode above them like a bird.

Cold and unsmiling, Mrs Dacey skipped by his side, seeing nothing through her misted glasses.

And George Ring sang as he bounced, with his drenched hair rising and falling in level waves, 'Here we go gathering nuts and may, Donald and Mrs Dacey and George and Sam.'

When they stopped, outside the Antelope, Mr Allingham leaned against the wall and coughed until he cried. All the time he coughed he never removed his cigarette.

'I haven't run for forty years,' he said, his shoulders shaking, and his handkerchief like a flag to his mouth. He led them into the Saloon Bar, where three young women sat with their shoes off in front of the electric log fire.

'Three whiskies. What's yours, Sam? Nice drop of Kiwi?'

'He'll have whisky, too,' Mrs Dacey said. 'See, he's got his colour back.'

'Kiwi's boot-polish,' one of the young women whispered, and she bent, giggling, over the grate. Her big toe came out of a hole in her stocking, suddenly, like a cold inquisitive nose, and she giggled again.

This was a bar in London. Dear Peggy, Samuel wrote with his finger on the counter, I am drinking in a bar called the Antelope in Edgware Road with a furniture dealer, the proprietress of a tea-shop, three young women and George Ring. I have put these facts down clearly because the scent I drank in the bath is still troublesome and people will not keep still. I am quite well but I do not know for how long.

'What're you doing, Sam? Looks like you're drawing. I've got a proper graveyard in my chest, haven't I? Cough, cough,' Mr Allingham said, angrily between each cough.

'It wasn't the cough that carried him off,' the young woman said. Her whole plump body was giggling.

Everything is very trivial, Samuel wrote. Mr Allingham is drunk on one whisky. All his face goes pale except his mark.

'Here we are,' Mr Allingham said, 'four lost souls. What a place to put a man in.'

'The Antelope's charming,' said George Ring. 'There's some real hunting prints in the private bar.' He smiled at Sam and moved his long, blunt fingers rapidly along the counter as though he were playing a piano. 'I'm all rhythm. It's like a kind of current in me.'

'I mean the world. This is only a little tiny bit in it. This is all right, it's got regular hours; you can draw the curtains, you know what to expect here. But look at the world. You and your currents,' Mr Allingham said.

'No, really it's rippling out of me.' George Ring tap-danced with one foot and made a rhythmical, kissing noise with his tongue against the roof of his mouth.

'What a place to drop a man in. In the middle of streets and houses and traffic and people.'

The young woman wagged her finger at her toe. 'You be still.' Her friends were giggling now, covering their faces and peeping out at Mr Allingham between their fingers, telling each other to go on, saying 'hotcha' and 'hi de ho' and 'Minnie the Moocher's Wedding Day' as George Ring tapped one narrow, yellow buckskin shoe and strummed on the counter. They rolled their eyes and said, 'Swing it, sister,' then hissed again into a giggle.

'I've been nibbling away for fifty years now,' Mr Allingham said, 'and look at me. Look at me.' He took off his hat.

'There's hair,' whispered the young woman with the hole in her stocking.

His hair was the colour of ferrets and thin on the crown; it stopped growing at the temples but came out again from the ears. His hat made him a deep, white wrinkle on his forehead.

'Here we are nibbling away all day and night, Mrs Dacey. Nibble nibble.' His brown teeth came over his lip. 'No sense, no order, no nothing; we're all mad and nasty. Look at Sam there. There's a nice harmless boy, curly hair and big eyes and all. What's he do? Look at his bloody bottle.'

'No language,' said the woman behind the bar. She looked like a duchess, riding, rising and sinking slowly as she spoke, as though to the movements of a horse.

'Tantivy,' Samuel said, and blushed as Mr Allingham pointed a stained finger.

'That's right. Always the right word in the right place. Tantivy! I told you, people are all mad in the world. They don't know where they're going, they don't know why they're where they are; all they want is love, and beer and sleep.'

'I wouldn't say no to the first,' said Mrs Dacey. 'Don't pay any attention to him,' she said to the woman behind the counter, 'he's a philosopher.'

'Calling everybody nasty,' said the woman, rising. 'There's people live in glass houses.' Over the hurdle she goes, thought Samuel idly, and she sank again on to the hidden saddle. She must do miles in a night, he said to his empty glass.

'People think about all kinds of other things.' George Ring looked at the ceiling for a vision. 'Music,' he said, 'and dancing.' He ran his fingers along the air and danced on his toes.

'Sex,' said Mr Allingham.

'Sex, sex, sex, it's always sex with you, Donald. You must be repressed or something.'

'Sex,' whispered the young woman by the fire.

'Sex is all right,' Mrs Dacey said. 'You leave sex alone.'

'Of course I'm repressed. I've been repressed for fifty years.'

'You leave sex out of it.' The woman behind the counter rose in a gallop. 'And religion,' she said.

Over she goes, clean as a whistle, over the hedge and the water-jump.

Samuel took a pound out of his wallet and pointed to the whisky on the shelf. He could not trust himself yet to speak to the riding woman with the stuffed, enormous bosom and two long milk-white loaves for arms. His throat was still on fire; the heat of the room blazed up his nostrils into his head, and all the words at the tip of his tongue caught like petrol and gorse; he saw three young women flickering by the metal logs, and his three new friends thundered and gestured before him with the terrible exaggeration of people of flesh and blood moving like dramatic prisoners on a screen, doomed forever to enact their pettiness in a magnified exhibition.

He said to himself: Mrs Antelope, pouring the whisky as though it were four insults, believes that sex is a bed. The act of love is an act of the bed itself; the springs cry 'Tumble' and over she goes, horse and all. I can see her lying like a log on a bed, listening with hate and disgust to the masterly voice of the dented sheets.

He felt old and all-knowing and unsteady. His immediate wisdom weighed so heavily that he clutched at the edge of the counter and raised one arm, like a man trapped in the sea, to signal his sinking.

'You may,' Mrs Dacey said, and the room giggled like a girl.

Now I know, thought Samuel beneath his load, as he struggled to the surface, what is meant by a pillar of the church. Long, cold Mrs Dacey could prop Bethesda on the remote top of her carved head and freeze with her eyes the beetle-black sinners where they scraped below her. Her joke boomed in the roof.

'You've dropped a fiver, Sam.' Mr Allingham picked up a piece of paper and held it out on the sun-stained palm of his hand.

'It's Lucille Harris's address,' Samuel said.

'Why don't you give her a ring? The phone's on the stairs, up there.' George Ring pointed. 'Outside the Ladies.'

Samuel parted a curtain and mounted.

'*Outside* the Ladies,' a voice said from the sinking room.

He read the instructions above the telephone, put in two pennies, dialled, and said, 'Miss Harris? I'm a friend of Austin's.

'I am a friend of nobody's. I am detached,' he whispered into the buzzing receiver. 'I am Lopo the outlaw, loping through the

night, companion of owls and murderers. Tu wit to woo,' he
said aloud into the mouthpiece.

She did not answer, and he shuffled down the stairs, swung
open the curtain, and entered the bright bar with a loping stride.

The three young women had gone. He looked at the grate to
see if their shoes were still there, but they had gone too. People
leave nothing.

'She must have been out,' he said.

'We heard,' said Mr Allingham. 'We heard you talking to her
owl.' He raised his glass and stared at it, standing sadly and
savagely in the middle of the room, like a man with oblivion in
his hand. Then he made his choice, and drank.

'We're going places,' he said. 'We're taking a taxi and Sam is
going to pay for it. We're going to the West End to look for
Lucille.'

'I knew she was a kind of Holy Grail,' George Ring said when
they were all in the darkness of the taxi rattling through the
rain.

Samuel felt Mrs Dacey's hand on his knee.

'Four knights at arms, it's terribly exciting. We'll call at the
Gayspot first, then the Cheerioh, then the Neptune.'

'Four lost souls.'

The hand ached on along the thigh, five dry fishes dying on a
cloth.

'Marble Arch,' Mr Allingham said. 'This is where the fairies
come out in the moon.'

And the hurrying crowd in the rain might have had no flesh
or blood.

'Park Lane.'

The crowd slid past the bonnet and the windows, mixed their
faces with no features and their liquid bodies under a sudden
blaze, or vanished into the streaming light of a tall door that led
into the bowels of rich night London where all the women wore
pearls and pricked their arms with needles.

A car backfired.

'Hear the champagne corks?'

Mr Allingham is listening to my head, Samuel thought as he
drew away from the fingers in the corner.

'Piccadilly. Come on Allingham's tour. That's the Ritz. Stop
for a kipper, Sam?'

The Ritz is closed forever. All the waiters would be bellowing behind their hands. Gustave, Gustave, cried a man in an opera hat, he is using the wrong fork. He is wearing a tie with elastic at the back. And a woman in evening dress cut so low he could see her navel with a diamond in it leaned over his table and pulled his bow tie out and let it fly back again to his throat.

'The filthy rich,' he said. My place is among the beggars and the outlaws. With power and violence Samuel Bennet destroys the whole artifice of society in his latest novel, *In the Bowels*.

'Piccadilly Circus. Centre of the world. See the man picking his nose under the lamp post ? That's the Prime Minister.'

3

The Gayspot was like a coal cellar with a bar at one end, and several coalmen were dancing with their sacks. Samuel, at the door, swaying between Mrs Dacey and George Ring, felt his thigh, still frightened. He did not dare look down at it in case even the outside of the trouser-leg bore the inexcusable imprint of his terror in the taxi.

'It's cosmopolitan,' George Ring whispered. 'Look at the nigger.'

Samuel rubbed the night out of his eyes and saw the black men dancing with their women, twirling them among the green cane chairs, between the fruit machine and the Russian billiard table. Some of the women were white, and smoked as they danced. They pussed and spied around the room, unaware of their dancing, feeling the arms around them as though around the bodies of different women : their eyes were for the strangers entering, they went through the hot movements of the dance like women in the act of love, looking over men's shoulders at their own remote and unconniving faces in a looking-glass. The men were all teeth and bottom, flashers and shakers, with little waists and wide shoulders, in double-breasted pin-stripe and sleek, licked shoes, all ageless and unwrinkled, waiting for the flesh-pot, proud and silent and friendly and hungry — jerking round the smoking cellar under the centre of the world to the music of a drum and a piano played by two pale white cross boys whose lips were always moving.

As George Ring weaved Samuel through the dancers to the bar they passed a machine and Samuel put in a penny for a lemon. Out came one and sixpence.

'Who's going to win the Derby, Sam?' said Mr Allingham, behind them.

'Isn't he a lucky poet?' George Ring said.

Mrs Dacey, in half a minute, had found a partner as tall as herself and was dancing through the smoke like a chapel. He had powdered his face to hide a scar from the corner of his eye to his chin.

'Mrs Dacey's dancing with a razor-man,' Samuel said.

This was a breath and a scar of the London he had come to catch. Look at the knickerless women enamouring from the cane tables, waiting in the fumes for the country cousins to stagger in, all savings and haywisps, or the rosy-cheeked old men with buttonholes whose wives at home were as lively as bags of sprouts. And the dancing cannibal-mouthed black razor kings shaking their women's breasts and blood to the stutter of the drums, snakily tailored in the shabby sweat-smelling jungle under the wet pavement. And a crimped boy danced like a girl, and the two girls serving were as harsh as men.

Mr Allingham bought four white wines. 'Go on. He did it on a pin-table. You could bring your Auntie here, couldn't you, Monica?' he said to the girl with the bow tie pouring their drinks.

'Not my Auntie,' Samuel said. Auntie Morgan Pont-Neath-Vaughan in her elastic-sided boots. 'She doesn't drink,' he said.

'Show Monica your bottle. He's got a bottle on his finger.'

Samuel dug his hand deep in his jacket pocket. 'She doesn't want to see an old bottle.' His chest began to tickle as he spoke, and he slipped two fingers of his right hand between the buttons of his shirt on to his bare flesh. 'No vest,' he said in surprise, but the girl had turned away.

'It's a Sunday School,' Mr Allingham said. 'Tasted your wine yet, Sam? This horse's unfit to work. A regular little bun dance. You could bring the vicar's wife in here.'

Mrs Cotmore-Richards, four foot one and a squeak in her stockinged trotters.

'A regular little vestry,' Mr Allingham said. 'See that woman dancing? The one who fell in the flour-bin. She's a bank manager's niece.'

The woman with the dead white face smiled as she passed them in the arms of a padded boy.

'Hullo, Ikey.'

'Hullo, Lola. She's pretendin', see. Thinks she's Starr Faithfull.'

'Is she a prostitute, Mr Allingham?'

'She's a manicurist, Sammy. How's your cuticles? Don't you believe everything you see, especially after it's dark. This is all pretending. Look at Casanova there with the old girls. The last time he touched a woman he had a dummy in his mouth.'

Samuel turned around. George Ring whinnied in a corner with several women. Their voices shrilled and rasped through the cross noise of the drums.

'Lucy got a beating the last time I see her,' said a woman with false teeth and a bald fur. 'He said he was a chemist.'

'Lucille,' George Ring said, impatiently shaking his curls. 'Lucille Harris.'

'With a clothes-brush. He had it in a little bag.'

'There's a chemist,' said a woman, wearing a picture hat.

'He doesn't mean Lucy Wakefield,' another woman said.

'Lucy Wakefield's in the Feathers with a man from Crouch End,' said the bank manager's niece, dancing past. The boy who danced with her was smiling with his eyes closed.

'Perhaps he got a leather belt in his little bag,' said the woman with the fur.

'It's all the same in a hundred years,' said the woman in the picture hat. She went down to her white wine, widening her legs like an old mule at a pool, and came up gasping. 'They put hair oil in it.'

This was all wrong. They spoke like the women who wore men's caps and carried fishfrails full of empties in the Jug and Bottle of the Compasses at home.

'Keeps away the dandruff.'

He did not expect that the nightclub women under the pavement should sing and twang like sirens or lure off his buttons with their dangerous, fringed violet eyes. London is not under the bedclothes where all the company is grand and vile by a flick of the cinema eye, and the warm linen doors are always open. But these women with the shabby faces and the comedians' tongues, squatting and squabbling over their mother's ruin, might have lurched in from Llanelly on a football night, on the arms of short men with leeks. The women at the tables, whom he had seen as enamouring shapes when he first came in dazed from the night, were dull as sisters, red-eyed and thick in the head with colds; they would sneeze when you kissed them or hiccup and say Manners in the dark traps of the hotel bedrooms.

'Good as gold,' he said to Mr Allingham. 'I thought you said this was a low place, like a speakeasy.'

'Speak easy yourself. They don't like being called low down here.' Mr Allingham leant close, speaking from the side of his mouth. 'They're too low for that. It's a regular little hell-hole,' he whispered. 'It's just warming up. They take their clothes off soon and do the hula hula; you'll like that.'

'Nobody knows Lucille,' George Ring said. 'Are you sure she isn't Lucy? There's a lovely Lucy.'

'No, Lucille.'

'"She dwells beside the springs of Dove." I think I like Wordsworth better than Walter de la Mare sometimes. Do you know "Tintern Abbey"?'

Mrs Dacey appeared at Samuel's shoulder. 'Doesn't baby dance?' He shuddered at the cold touch of her hand on his neck. Not here. Not now. That terrible impersonal Bethesda rape of the fingers. He remembered that she had carried her umbrella even while she danced.

'I got a sister in Tintern,' said a man behind them.

'Tintern Abbey.' George Ring pouted and did not turn round.

'Not in the Abbey, she's a waitress.'

'We were talking about a poem.'

'She's not a bloody nun,' the man said.

The music stopped, but the two boys on the little platform still moved their hands and lips, beating out the dance in silence.

Mr Allingham raised his fist. 'Say that again and I'll knock you down.'

'I'll blow you down,' the man said. He puffed up his cheeks, and blew. His breath smelt of cloves.

'Now, now.' Mrs Dacey levelled her umbrella.

'People shouldn't go around insulting nuns then,' Mr Allingham said as the ferrule tapped his waistcoat.

'I'll blow you down,' the man said. 'I never insulted any nun. I've never spoken to a nun.'

'Now, now.' The umbrella drove for his eyes, and he ducked.

'You blow again,' said Mrs Dacey politely, 'I'll push it up your snout and open it.'

'Don't you loathe violence,' George Ring said. 'I've always

been a terrible pacifist. One drop of blood and I feel slimy all over. Shall we dance ?'

He put his arm round Samuel's waist and danced him away from the bar. The band began again though none of the couples had stopped dancing.

'But we're two men,' Samuel said. 'Is this a waltz ?'

'They never play waltzes here, it's just self-expression. Look, there's two other men dancing.'

'I thought they were girls.'

'My friend thought you were a couple of girls,' George Ring said in a loud voice as they danced past them. Samuel looked at the floor, trying to follow the movements of George Ring's feet. One, two, three, turn around, tap.

One of the young men squealed, 'Come up and see my Aga Cooker.'

One, two, three, swirl and tap.

'What sort of a girl is Polly Dacey, really ? Is she mad ?'

I'm like thistledown, thought Samuel. Swirl about and swirl again, on the toes now, shake those hips.

'Not so heavy, Sam. You're like a little Jumbo. When she went to school she used to post mice in the pillar-box and they ate up all the letters. And she used to do things to boys in the scullery. I can't tell you. You could hear them screaming all over the house.'

But Samuel was not listening any more. He circled and stumbled to a rhythm of his own among the flying legs, dipped and retreated, hopped on one leg and spun, his hair falling over his eyes and his bottle swinging. He clung to George Ring's shoulder and zig-zagged away from him, then bounced up close again.

'Don't swing the bottle. Don't swing it. Look out. Sam. Sam.'

Samuel's arm flew back and a small woman went down. She grabbed at his legs and he brought George Ring with him. Another man fell, catching fast to his partner's skirt. A long rip and she tumbled among them, her legs in the air, her head in a heave of bellies and arms.

Samuel lay still. His mouth pressed on the curls at the nape of the neck of the woman who had fallen first. He put out his tongue.

'Get off my head ; you've got keys in your pocket.'

'Oh, my leg !'

'That's right. Easy does it. Upsadaisy.'

'Someone's licking me,' cried the woman at the bottom.

Then the two girls from behind the bar were standing over them, slapping and kicking, pulling them up by the hair.

'It was that one's fault. He crowned her with a bottle. I saw him,' said the bank manager's niece.

'Where'd he get the bottle from, Lola ?'

The girl with the bow tie dragged Samuel up by the collar and pointed to his left hand. He tried to slip it in his pocket but a hand like a black boxing glove closed over the bottle. A large black face bent down and stared into his. He saw only the whites of the eyes and the teeth.

I don't want a cut on my face. Don't cut my lips open. They only use razors in stories. Don't let him have read any stories.

'Now, now,' said Mrs Dacey's voice. The black face jerked back as she thrust out her opened umbrella, and Samuel's hand was free.

'Throw him out, Monica.'

'He was dancing like a monkey, throw him out.'

'If you throw him out you can throw me out too,' Mr Allingham said from the bar. He raised his fists.

Two men walked over to him.

'Mind my glasses.' He did not wear any.

They opened the door and threw him up the steps.

'Bloody nun,' a voice shouted.

'Now you.'

'And the old girl. Look out for her brolly, Dodie.'

Samuel fell on the area step below Mr Allingham and Mrs Dacey came flying after with her umbrella held high.

It was still raining heavily.

4

'Just a passing call,' said Mr Allingham. As though he were sitting indoors at a window, he put out his hand to feel the rain. Shoes slopped past on the pavement above his head. Wet trousers and stockings almost touched the brim of his hat. 'Just in and out,' he said. 'Where's George ?'

I've been bounced, Samuel thought.

'It reminds me of my old man.' Mrs Dacey's face was hidden under the umbrella, as though in a private, accompanying

thunder cloud. 'In and out, in and out. Just one look at him,
and out he went like clockwork.'

Oh, the Gayspot? Can't go there, old man. Samuel winked
seriously in the dark. Oh, carrying a cargo. Swinging a bottle
around. One look at me, out I went.

'He used to carry a little book with all the places he couldn't
go to and he went to them every Saturday.'

Fool, fool, fool, Samuel said to himself.

The steps were suddenly lit up as the door opened for George
Ring. He came out carefully and tidily, to a rush of music and
voices that faded at once with the vanishing of the smoky light,
and stood on Mrs Dacey's step, his mane of curls golden against
the fanlight, a god or a half-horse emerging from the underworld
into the common rain.

'They're awfully cross,' he said. 'Mrs Cavanagh ripped her
skirt and she didn't have anything on underneath. My dear, it's
like Ancient Rome down there and now she's wearing a man's
trousers and he's got legs exactly like a spider's. All black and
hairy. Why are you sitting in the rain?'

'It's safe,' Mr Allingham said. 'It's nice and safe in the rain.
It's nice and rational sitting on the steps in the rain. You can't
knock a woman down with a bottle here. See the stars? That's
Arcturus. That's the Great Bear. That's Sirius, see, the green
one. I won't show you where Venus is. There's some people
can't enjoy themselves unless they're knocking women down
and licking them on the floor. They think the evening's wasted
unless they've done that. I wish I was home. I wish I was lying
in bed by the ceiling. I wish I was lying under the chairs like
Rosie.'

'Who started to fight, anyway? Let's go round the corner to
the Cheerioh.'

'That was ethical.'

They climbed up the street, George Ring first, then Mr
Allingham, then Samuel and Mrs Dacey. She tucked his arm in
hers.

'Don't you worry. You hold on to me. Cold? You're
shivering.'

'It'll be Cheerioh all right.'

The Cheerioh was a bad blaze, an old hole of lights. In the
dark, open a cupboard full of cast-off clothes moving in a wind

from nowhere, the smell of mothballs and damp furs, and find a lamp lit, candles burning, a gramophone playing.

'No dancing for you,' Mr Allingham said. 'You need space. You want the Crystal Palace.'

Mrs Dacey still held Samuel by the arm. 'You're safe with me. I've taken a fancy,' she said. 'Once I take a fancy I never let go.'

'And never trust a woman who can't get up.' Mr Allingham pointed to a woman sitting in a chair by the Speedboat pin-table. 'She's trying to get up all the time.' The woman made a sudden movement of her shoulders. 'No, no, legs first.'

'This used to be the cow-shed,' George Ring said, 'and there was real straw on the floor.'

Mrs Dacey never lets go. Samuel saw the fancy shining behind her glasses, and in her hard mouse-trap mouth. Her cold hand hooked him. If he struggled and ran she would catch him in a corner and open her umbrella inside his nose.

'And real cows,' Mr Allingham said.

The men and women drinking and dancing looked like the older brothers, and sisters of the drinkers and dancers in the club round the corner, but no one was black. There were deep green faces, dipped in a sea dye, with painted cockles for mouths and lichenous hair, sealed on the cheeks; red and purple, slate-grey, tide-marked, rat-brown and stickily whitewashed, with violet-inked eyes or lips the colour of Stilton; pink chopped, pink lidded, pink as the belly of a newborn monkey, nicotine yellow with mustard flecked eyes, rust scraping through the bleach, black hairs axle-greased down among the peroxide; squashed fly stubbles, saltcellared necks thick with pepper powder; carrot-heads, yolk-heads, black-heads, heads bald as sweetbreads.

'All white people here,' Samuel said.

'The salt of the earth,' Mr Allingham said.

'The foul salt of the earth. Drunk as a pig. Ever seen a pig drunk? Ever seen a monkey dancing like a man? Look at that king of the animals. See him? The one who's eaten his lips. That one smiling. That one having his honeymoon on her feet.'

QUITE EARLY ONE MORNING

Quite early one morning in the winter in Wales, by the sea that was lying down still and green as grass after a night of tar-black howling and rolling, I went out of the house, where I had come to stay for a cold unseasonable holiday, to see if it was raining still, if the outhouse had been blown away, potatoes, shears, rat-killer, shrimp-nets, and tins of rusty nails aloft on the wind, and if all the cliffs were left. It had been such a ferocious night that someone in the smoky shipped-pictured bar had said he could feel his tombstone shaking even though he was not dead, or at least was moving; but the morning shone as clear and calm as one always imagines to-morrow will shine.

The sun lit the sea town, not as a whole – from topmost down – reproving zinc-roofed chapel to empty but for rats and whispers grey warehouse on the harbour, but in separate bright pieces. There, the quay shouldering out, nobody on it now but the gulls and the capstans like small men in tubular trousers. Here, the roof of the police-station, black as a helmet, dry as a summons, sober as Sunday. There, the splashed church, with a cloud in the shape of a bell poised above it, ready to drift and ring. Here the chimneys of the pink-washed pub, the pub that was waiting for Saturday night as an over-jolly girl waits for sailors.

The town was not yet awake. The milkman lay still lost in the clangour and music of his Welsh-spoken dreams, the wish-fulfilled tenor voices more powerful than Caruso's, sweeter than Ben Davies's, thrilling past Cloth Hall and Manchester House up to the frosty hills. The town was not yet awake. Babies in upper bedrooms of salt-white houses dangling over water, or of bow-windowed villas squatting prim in neatly treed but unsteady hill streets, worried the light with their half in sleep cries. Miscellaneous retired sea captains emerged for a second from deeper waves than ever tossed their boats, then drowned again, going down down into a perhaps Mediterranean-blue cabin of sleep, rocked to the sea-beat of their ears. Landladies, shawled and bloused and aproned with sleep in the curtained, bombasined black of their once spare rooms, remember their loves, their bills, their visitors – dead, decamped, or buried in English deserts till the trumpet of next expensive August roused them again to the world of holiday rain, dismal cliff and sand seen through the weeping windows of front parlours, tasselled table-cloths, stuffed pheasants, ferns in pots, fading photographs of the bearded and censorious dead, autograph albums with a lock of limp and colourless beribboned hair lolling out between the thick black boards.

The town was not yet awake. Birds sang in eaves, bushes, trees, on telegraph wires, rails, fences, spars, and wet masts, not for love or joy, but to keep other birds away. The landlords in feathers disputed the right of even the flying light to descend and perch.

The town was not yet awake, and I walked through the streets like a stranger come out of the sea, shrugging off weed and wave and darkness with each step, or like an inquisitive shadow, determined to miss nothing – not the preliminary tremor in the throat of the dawn-saying cock or the first whirring nudge of arranged time in the belly of the alarm clock on the trinketed chest of drawers under the knitted text and the done-by-hand water-colours of Porthcawl or Trinidad.

I walked past the small sea-spying windows, behind whose trim curtains lay mild-mannered men and women not yet awake and, for all I could know, terrible and violent in their dreams. In the head of Miss Hughes, 'The Cosy,' clashed the cymbals of an eastern court. Eunuchs struck gongs the size of Bethesda Chapel. Sultans with voices fiercer than visiting preachers demanded a most un-Welsh dance. Everywhere there glowed and rayed the colours of the small, slate-grey woman's dreams, purple, magenta, ruby, sapphire, emerald, vermilion, honey. But I could not believe it. She knitted in her tidy sleep-world a beige woollen shroud with 'thou shalt not' on the bosom.

I could not imagine Cadwallader Davies, the grocer in his near-to-waking dream, riding on horse-back, two-gunned and Cody-bold, through the cactus prairies. He added, he subtracted, he receipted, he filed a prodigious account with a candle dipped in dried egg.

What big seas of dreams ran in the Captain's sleep? Over

what blue-whaled waves did he sail through a rainbow hail of flying-fishes to the music of Circe's swinish island? Do not let him be dreaming of dividends and bottled beer and onions.

Someone was snoring in one house. I counted ten savage and indignant grunts and groans like those of a pig in a model and mudless farm which ended with a window rattler, a wash-basin shaker, a trembler of tooth glasses, a waker of dormice. It thundered with me to the chapel railings, then brassily vanished.

The chapel stood grim and grey, telling the day there was to be no nonsense. The chapel was not asleep, it never cat-napped nor nodded nor closed its long cold eye. I left it telling the morning off and the sea-gull hung rebuked above it.

And climbing down again and up out of the town I heard the cocks crow from hidden farmyards, from old roosts above waves where fabulous sea-birds might sit and cry; 'Neptune!' And a far-away clock struck from another church in another village in another universe, though the wind blew the time away. And I walked in the timeless morning past a row of white cottages almost expecting that an ancient man with a great beard and an hour-glass and a scythe under his night-dressed arm might lean from the window and ask me the time. I would have told him: 'Arise old counter of the heartbeats of alba-trosses, and wake the cavernous sleepers of the town to a dazzling new morning.' I would have told him: 'You unbeliev-able Father of Eva and Dai Adam, come out, old chicken, and stir up the winter morning with your spoon of a scythe.' I would have told him – I would have scampered like a scalded ghost over the cliffs and down to the bilingual sea.

Who lived in these cottages? I was a stranger to the sea town, fresh or stale from the city where I worked for my bread and butter wishing it were laver-bread and country salty butter yolk-yellow. Fishermen certainly; no painters but of boats; no man-dressed women with shooting-sticks and sketch-books and voices like macaws to paint the reluctant heads of critical and sturdy natives who posed by the pint against the chapel-dark sea which would be made more blue than the bay of Naples – though shallower.

I walked on to the cliff path again, the town behind and below waking up now so very slowly; I stopped and turned and looked. Smoke from one chimney – the cobbler's I thought, but from that distance it may have been the chimney of the retired male nurse who had come to live in Wales after many years successful wrestling with the mad rich of southern England. He was not liked. He measured you for a strait-jacket carefully with his eye; he saw you bounce from rubber walls like a sorbo ball. No behaviour surprised him. Many people of the town found it hard to resist leering at him suddenly around the corner, or convulsively dancing, or pointing with laughter and devilish good humour at invisible dog-fights merely to prove to him that they were normal.

Smoke from another chimney now. They were burning their last night's dreams. Up from a chimney came a long-haired wraith like an old politician. Someone had been dreaming of the Liberal Party. But no, the smoky figure wove, attenuated into a refined and precise grey comma. Someone had been dreaming of reading Charles Morgan. Oh! the town was waking now and I heard distinctly insistent over the slow-speaking sea the voices of the town blown up to me. And some of the voices said:

I am Miss May Hughes 'The Cosy,' a lonely lady,
Waiting in her house by the nasty sea,
Waiting for her husband and pretty baby
To come home at last from wherever they may be.

I am Captain Tiny Evans, my ship was the *Kidwelly*,
And Mrs Tiny Evans has been dead for many a year,
'Poor Captain Tiny all alone,' the neighbours whisper,
But I like it all alone and I hated her.

Clara Tawe Jenkins, 'Madam' they call me,
An old contralto with her dressing-gown on,
And I sit at the window and I sing to the sea,
For the sea does not notice that my voice has gone.

Parchedig Thomas Evans making morning tea,
Very weak tea, too, you mustn't waste a leaf.
Every morning making tea in my house by the sea,
I am troubled by one thing only, and that, belief.

Open the curtains, light the fire, what are servants for?
I am Mrs Ogmore Pritchard and I want another snooze.
Dust the china, feed the canary, sweep the drawing-room
   floor;
And before you let the sun in, mind he wipes his shoes.

I am only Mr Griffiths, very short-sighted, B A, Aber.
As soon as I finish my egg I must shuffle off to school.
O patron saint of teachers, teach me to keep order,
And forget those words on the blackboard – 'Griffiths Bat
     is a fool.'

Do you hear that whistling ? – It's me, I am Phoebe,
The maid at the King's Head, and I am whistling like a
     bird.
Someone spilt a tin of pepper in the tea.
There's twenty for breakfast and I'm not going to say a
     word.

Thus some of the voices of a cliff-perched town at the far end
of Wales moved out of sleep and darkness into the new-born,
ancient, and ageless morning, moved and were lost.

A CHILD'S CHRISTMAS IN WALES

One Christmas was so much like another, in those years around the sea-town corner now and out of all sound except the distant speaking of the voices I sometimes hear a moment before sleep, that I can never remember whether it snowed for six days and six nights when I was twelve or whether it snowed for twelve days and twelve nights when I was six.

All the Christmases roll down toward the two-tongued sea, like a cold and headlong moon bundling down the sky that was our street; and they stop at the rim of the ice-edged, fish-freezing waves, and I plunge my hands in the snow and bring out whatever I can find. In goes my hand into that wool-white bell-tongued ball of holidays resting at the rim of the carol-singing sea, and out come Mrs Prothero and the firemen.

It was on the afternoon of the day of Christmas Eve, and I was in Mrs Prothero's garden, waiting for cats, with her son Jim. It was snowing. It was always snowing at Christmas. December, in my memory, is white as Lapland, though there were no reindeers. But there were cats. Patient, cold and callous, our hands wrapped in socks, we waited to snowball the cats. Sleek and long as jaguars and horrible-whiskered, spitting and snarling, they would slink and sidle over the white back-garden walls, and the lynx-eyed hunters, Jim and I, fur-capped and moccasined trappers from Hudson Bay, off Mumbles Road, would hurl our deadly snowballs at the green of their eyes.

The wise cats never appeared. We were so still, Eskimo-footed arctic marksmen in the muffling silence of the eternal snows — eternal, ever since Wednesday — that we never heard Mrs Prothero's first cry from her igloo at the bottom of the garden. Or, if we heard it at all, it was, to us, like the far-off challenge of our enemy and prey, the neighbour's polar cat. But soon the voice grew louder. 'Fire!' cried Mrs Prothero, and she beat the dinner-gong.

And we ran down the garden, with the snowballs in our arms,

toward the house; and smoke, indeed, was pouring out of the dining-room, and the gong was bombilating, and Mrs Prothero was announcing ruin like a town crier in Pompeii. This was better than all the cats in Wales standing on the wall in a row. We bounded into the house, laden with snowballs, and stopped at the open door of the smoke-filled room.

Something was burning all right; perhaps it was Mr Prothero, who always slept there after midday dinner with a newspaper over his face. But he was standing in the middle of the room, saying, 'A fine Christmas!' and smacking at the smoke with a slipper. 'Call the fire brigade,' cried Mrs Prothero as she beat the gong.

'They won't be there,' said Mr Prothero, 'it's Christmas.'

There was no fire to be seen, only clouds of smoke and Mr Prothero standing in the middle of them, waving his slipper as though he were conducting.

'Do something,' he said.

And we threw all our snowballs into the smoke – I think we missed Mr Prothero – and ran out of the house to the telephone box.

'Let's call the police as well,' Jim said.

'And the ambulance.'

'And Ernie Jenkins, he likes fires.'

But we only called the fire brigade, and soon the fire engine came and three tall men in helmets brought a hose into the house and Mr Prothero got out just in time before they turned it on. Nobody could have had a noisier Christmas Eve. And when the firemen turned off the hose and were standing in the wet, smoky room, Jim's aunt, Miss Prothero, came downstairs and peered in at them. Jim and I waited, very quietly, to hear what she would say to them. She said the right thing, always. She looked at the three tall firemen in their shining helmets, standing among the smoke and cinders and dissolving snowballs, and she said: 'Would you like anything to read?'

Years and years and years ago, when I was a boy, when there were wolves in Wales, and birds the colour of red-flannel petticoats whisked past the harp-shaped hills, when we sang and wallowed all night and day in caves that smelt like Sunday afternoons in damp front farmhouse parlours, and we chased, with the jawbones of deacons, the English and the bears, before the motor-car, before the wheel, before the duchess-faced horse, when we rode the daft and happy hills bareback, it snowed and it snowed. But here a small boy says : 'It snowed last year, too. I made a snowman and my brother knocked it down and I knocked my brother down and then we had tea.'

'But that was not the same snow,' I say. 'Our snow was not only shaken from whitewash buckets down the sky, it came shawling out of the ground and swam and drifted out of the arms and hands and bodies of the trees; snow grew overnight on the roofs of the houses like a pure and grandfather moss, minutely white-ivied the walls and settled on the postman, opening the gate, like a dumb, numb thunderstorm of white, torn Christmas cards.'

'Were there postmen then, too ?'

'With sprinkling eyes and wind-cherried noses, on spread, frozen feet they crunched up to the doors and mittened on them manfully. But all that the children could hear was a ringing of bells.'

'You mean that the postman went rat-a-tat-tat and the doors rang ?'

'I mean that the bells that the children could hear were inside them.'

'I only hear thunder sometimes, never bells.'

'There were church bells, too.'

'Inside them ?'

'No, no, no, in the bat-black, snow-white belfries, tugged by bishops and storks. And they rang their tidings over the bandaged town, over the frozen foam of the powder and ice-cream hills, over the crackling sea. It seemed that all the churches boomed for joy under my window; and the weathercocks crew for Christmas, on our fence.'

'Get back to the postmen.'

'They were just ordinary postmen, fond of walking and dogs and Christmas and the snow. They knocked on the doors with blue knuckles . . .'

'Ours has got a black knocker . . .'

'And then they stood on the white Welcome mat in the little, drifted porches and huffed and puffed, making ghosts with their breath, and jogged from foot to foot like small boys wanting to go out.'

'And then the Presents ?'

'And then the Presents, after the Christmas box. And the cold postman, with a rose on his button-nose, tingled down the tea-tray-slithered run of the chilly glinting hill. He went in his ice-bound boots like a man on fishmonger's slabs. He wagged his bag like a frozen camel's hump, dizzily turned the corner on one foot, and, by God, he was gone.'

'Get back to the Presents.'

'There were the Useful Presents: engulfing mufflers of the old coach days, and mittens made for giant sloths; zebra scarfs of a substance like silky gum that could be tug-o'-warred down to the galoshes; blinding tam-o'-shanters like patchwork tea cosies and bunny-suited busbies and balaclavas for victims of head-shrinking tribes; from aunts who always wore wool next to the skin there were moustached and rasping vests that made you wonder why the aunts had any skin left at all; and once I had a little crocheted nose bag from an aunt now, alas, no longer whinnying with us. And pictureless books in which small boys, though warned with quotations not to, *would* skate on Farmer Giles' pond and did and drowned; and books that told me everything about the wasp, except why.'

'Go on to the Useless Presents.'

'Bags of moist and many-coloured jelly babies and a folded flag and a false nose and a tram-conductor's cap and a machine that punched tickets and rang a bell; never a catapult; once, by mistake that no one could explain, a little hatchet; and a celluloid duck that made, when you pressed it, a most unduck-like sound, a mewing moo that an ambitious cat might make who wished to be a cow; and a painting book in which I could make the grass, the trees, the sea and the animals any colour I pleased, and still the dazzling sky-blue sheep are grazing in the red field under the rainbow-billed and pea-green birds.

'Hardboileds, toffee, fudge and allsorts, crunches, cracknels, humbugs, glaciers, marzipan, and butterwelsh for the Welsh. And troops of bright tin soldiers who, if they could not fight, could always run. And Snakes-and-Familes and Happy Ladders. And Easy Hobbi-Games for Little Engineers, complete with instructions.

'Oh, easy for Leonardo! And a whistle to make the dogs bark to wake up the old man next door to make him beat on the wall with his stick to shake our picture off the wall.

'And a packet of cigarettes: you put one in your mouth and you stood at the corner of the street and you waited for hours, in vain, for an old lady to scold you for smoking a cigarette, and then with a smirk you ate it. And then it was breakfast under the balloons.'

'Were there Uncles like in our house ?'

'There are always Uncles at Christmas.

'The same Uncles. And on Christmas mornings, with dog-disturbing whistle and sugar fags, I would scour the swatched town for the news of the little world, and find always a dead bird by the white Post Office or by the deserted swings ; perhaps a robin, all but one of his fires out. Men and women wading or scooping back from chapel, with taproom noses and wind-bussed cheeks, all albinos, huddled their stiff black jarring feathers against the irreligious snow.

'Mistletoe hung from the gas brackets in all the front par-lours ; there was sherry and walnuts and bottled beer and crackers by the dessertspoons ; and cats in their fur-abouts watched the fires ; and the high-heaped fire spat, all ready for the chestnuts and the mulling pokers.

'Some few large men sat in the front parlours, without their collars, Uncles almost certainly, trying their new cigars, holding them out judiciously at arms' length, returning them to their mouths, coughing, then holding them out again as though waiting for the explosion ; and some few small Aunts, not wanted in the kitchen, nor anywhere else for that matter, sat on the very edges of their chairs, poised and brittle, afraid to break, like faded cups and saucers.'

Not many those mornings trod the piling streets : an old man always, fawn-bowlered, yellow-gloved and, at this time of year, with spats of snow, would take his constitutional to the white bowling green and back, as he would take it wet or fine on Christmas Day or Doomsday ; sometimes two hale young men, with big pipes blazing, no overcoats and wind-blown scarfs, would trudge, unspeaking, down to the forlorn sea, to work up an appetite, to blow away the fumes, who knows, to walk into the waves until nothing of them was left but the two curling smoke clouds of their inextinguishable briars. Then I would be slap-dashing home, the gravy smell of the dinners of others, the bird smell, the brandy, the pudding and mince, coiling up to my nostrils, when out of a snow-clogged side lane would come a boy the spit of myself, with a pink-tipped cigarette and the violet past of a black eye, cocky as a bullfinch, leering all to himself.

I hated him on sight and sound, and would be about to put my dog whistle to my lips and blow him off the face of Christmas when suddenly he, with a violent wink, put *his* whistle to *his* lips and blew so stridently, so high, so exquisitely loud, that gobbling faces, their cheeks bulged with goose, would press against their tinselled windows, the whole length of the white echoing street. For dinner we had turkey and blazing pudding, and after dinner the Uncles sat in front of the fire, loosened all buttons, put their large moist hands over their watch chains, groaned a little and slept. Mothers, aunts and sisters scuttled to and fro, bearing tureens. Auntie Bessie, who had already been frightened, twice, by a clock-work mouse, whimpered at the sideboard and had some elderberry wine. The dog was sick. Auntie Dosie had to have three aspirins, but Auntie Hannah, who liked port, stood in the middle of the snowbound back yard, singing like a big-bosomed thrush. I would blow up balloons to see how big they would blow up to ; and, when they burst, which they all did, the Uncles jumped and rumbled. In the rich and heavy afternoon, the Uncles breathing like dolphins and the snow descending, I would sit among festoons and Chinese lanterns and nibble dates and try to make a model man-o'-war, following the Instructions for Little Engineers, and produce what might be mistaken for a sea-going tramcar.

Or I would go out, my bright new boots squeaking, into the white world, on to the seaward hill, to call on Jim and Dan and Jack and to pad through the still streets, leaving huge deep footprints on the hidden pavements.

'I bet people will think there's been hippos.'

'What would you do if you saw a hippo coming down our street ?'

'I'd go like this, bang ! I'd throw him over the railings and roll him down the hill and then I'd tickle him under the ear and he'd wag his tail.'

'What would you do if you saw *two* hippos ?'

Iron-flanked and bellowing he-hippos clanked and battered through the scudding snow toward us as we passed Mr Daniel's house.

'Let's post Mr Daniel a snowball through his letter-box.'

'Let's write, "Mr Daniel looks like a spaniel" all over his lawn.'

Or we walked on the white shore.

'Can the fishes see it's snowing?'

The silent one-clouded heavens drifted on to the sea. Now we were snow-blind travellers lost on the north hills, and vast dewlapped dogs, with flasks round their necks, ambled and shambled up to us, baying 'Excelsior'. We returned home through the poor streets where only a few children fumbled with bare red fingers in the wheel-rutted snow and cat-called after us, their voices fading away, as we trudged uphill, into the cries of the dock birds and the hooting of ships out in the whirling bay. And then, at tea the recovered Uncles would be jolly; and the ice cake loomed in the centre of the table like a marble grave. Auntie Hannah laced her tea with rum, because it was only once a year.

Bring out the tall tales now that we told by the fire as the gaslight bubbled like a diver. Ghosts whooed like owls in the long nights when I dared not look over my shoulder; animals lurked in the cubbyhole under the stairs where the gas meter ticked. And I remember that we went singing carols once, when there wasn't the shaving of a moon to light the flying streets. At the end of a long road was a drive that led to a large house, and we stumbled up the darkness of the drive that night, each one of us afraid, each one holding a stone in his hand in case, and all of us too brave to say a word. The wind through the trees made noises as of old and unpleasant and maybe webfooted men wheezing in caves. We reached the black bulk of the house.

'What shall we give them? "Hark the Herald"?'

'No,' Jack said, "Good King Wenceslas". I'll count three.'

One, two, three, and we began to sing, our voices high and seemingly distant in the snow-felted darkness round the house that was occupied by nobody we knew. We stood close together, near the dark door.

> Good King Wenceslas looked out
> On the Feast of Stephen ...

And then a small, dry voice, like the voice of someone who has not spoken for a long time, joined our singing: a small, dry, eggshell voice from the other side of the door: a small dry voice through the keyhole. And when we stopped running we were outside *our* house; the front room was lovely; balloons floated under the hot-water-bottle-gulping gas; everything was good again and shone over the town.

'Perhaps it was a ghost,' Jim said.

'Perhaps it was trolls,' Dan said, who was always reading.

'Let's go in and see if there's any jelly left,' Jack said. And we did that.

Always on Christmas night there was music. An uncle played the fiddle, a cousin sang 'Cherry Ripe', and another uncle sang 'Drake's Drum'. It was very warm in the little house.

Auntie Hannah, who had got on to the parsnip wine, sang a song about Bleeding Hearts and Death, and then another in which she said her heart was like a Bird's Nest; and then everybody laughed again; and then I went to bed. Looking through my bedroom window, out into the moonlight and the unending smoke-coloured snow, I could see the lights in the windows of all the other houses on our hill and hear the music rising from them up the long, steadily falling night. I turned the gas down, I got into bed. I said some words to the close and holy darkness, and then I slept.

HOLIDAY MEMORY

August Bank Holiday. A tune on an ice-cream cornet. A slap of sea and a tickle of sand. A fanfare of sunshades opening. A wince and whinny of bathers dancing into deceptive water. A tuck of dresses. A rolling of trousers. A compromise of paddlers. A sunburn of girls and a lark of boys. A silent hullabaloo of balloons.

I remember the sea telling lies in a shell held to my ear for a whole harmonious, hollow minute by a small, wet girl in an enormous bathing-suit marked 'Corporation Property.'

I remember sharing the last of my moist buns with a boy and a lion. Tawny and savage, with cruel nails and capacious mouth, the little boy tore and devoured. Wild as seed-cake, ferocious as a hearth-rug, the depressed and verminous lion nibbled like a mouse at his half a bun, and hiccupped in the sad dusk of his cage.

I remember a man like an alderman or a bailiff, bowlered and collarless, with a bag of monkey-nuts in his hand, crying 'Ride 'em, cowboy!' time and again as he whirled in his chairoplane giddily above the upturned laughing faces of the town girls bold as brass and the boys with padded shoulders and shoes sharp as knives; and the monkey-nuts flew through the air like salty hail.

Children all day capered or squealed by the glazed or bashing sea, and the steam-organ wheezed its waltzes in the threadbare playground and the waste lot, where the dodgems dodged, behind the pickle factory.

And mothers loudly warned their proud pink daughters or sons to put that jellyfish down; and fathers spread newspapers over their faces; and sand-fleas hopped on the picnic lettuce; and someone had forgotten the salt.

In those always radiant, rainless, lazily rowdy and sky-blue summers departed, I remember August Monday from the rising of the sun over the stained and royal town to the husky hushing of the roundabout music and the dowsing of the naphtha jets in the seaside fair : from bubble-and-squeak to the last of the sandy sandwiches.

There was no need, that holiday morning, for the sluggardly boys to be shouted down to breakfast; out of their jumbled beds they tumbled, scrambled into their rumpled clothes; quickly at the bath-room basin they catlicked their hands and faces, but never forgot to run the water loud and long as though they washed like colliers; in front of the cracked looking-glass bordered with cigarette-cards, in their treasure-trove bedrooms, they whisked a gap-tooth comb through their surly hair; and with shining cheeks and noses and tide-marked necks, they took the stairs three at a time.

But for all their scramble and scamper, clamour on the landing, catlick and toothbrush flick, hair-whisk and stair-jump, their sisters were always there before them. Up with the lady lark, they had prinked and frizzed and hot-ironed; and smug in their blossoming dresses, ribboned for the sun, in gym-shoes white as the blanco'd snow, neat and silly with doilies and tomatoes they helped in the higgledy kitchen. They were calm; they were virtuous; they had washed their necks; they did not romp, or fidget; and only the smallest sister put out her tongue at the noisy boys.

And the woman who lived next door came into the kitchen and said that her mother, an ancient uncertain body who wore a hat with cherries, was having 'one of her days' and had insisted, that very holiday morning, in carrying all the way to the tram-stop a photograph album and the cut-glass fruit-bowl from the front room.

This was the morning when father, mending one hole in the thermos-flask, made three; when the sun declared war on the butter, and the butter ran; when dogs, with all the sweet-binned backyards to wag and sniff and bicker in, chased their tails in the jostling kitchen, worried sandshoes, snapped at flies, writhed between legs, scratched among towels, sat smiling on hampers.

And if you could have listened at some of the open doors of some of the houses in the street you might have heard :

'Uncle Owen says he can't find the bottle-opener . . .'
'Has he looked under the hallstand ?'
'Willy's cut his finger . . .'
'Got your spade ?'
'If somebody doesn't kill that dog . . .'

'Uncle Owen says why should the bottle-opener be under the hall-stand?'

'Never again, never again . . .'

'I know I put the pepper somewhere . . .'

'Willy's bleeding . . .'

'Look, there's a bootlace in my bucket . . .'

'Oh, come *on*, come on . . .'

'Let's have a look at the bootlace in your bucket . . .'

'If I lay my hands on that dog . . .'

'Uncle Owen's found the bottle-opener . . .'

'Willy's bleeding over the cheese . . .'

And the trams that hissed like ganders took us all to the beautiful beach.

There was cricket on the sand, and sand in the sponge cake, sand-flies in the watercress, and foolish, mulish, religious donkeys on the unwilling trot. Girls undressed in slipping tents of propriety; under invisible umbrellas, stout ladies dressed for the male and immoral sea. Little naked navvies dug canals; children with spades and no ambition built fleeting castles; wispy young men, outside the bathing-huts, whistled at substantial young women and dogs who desired thrown stones more than the bones of elephants. Recalcitrant uncles huddled over luke ale in the tiger-striped marquees. Mothers in black, like wobbling mountains, gasped under the discarded dresses of daughters who shrilly braved the goblin waves. And fathers, in the once-a-year sun, took fifty winks. Oh, think of all the fifty winks along the paper-bagged sand.

Liquorice allsorts, and Welsh hearts, were melting, and the sticks of rock, that we all sucked, were like barbers' poles made of rhubarb.

In the distance, surrounded by disappointed theoreticians and an ironmonger with a drum, a cross man on an orange-box shouted that holidays were wrong.

And the waves rolled in, with rubber ducks and clerks upon them.

I remember the patient, laborious, and enamouring hobby, or profession, of burying relatives in sand.

I remember the princely pastime of pouring sand, from cupped hands or buckets, down collars and tops of dresses; the shriek, the shake, the slap.

I can remember the boy by himself, the beachcombing lone-

wolf, hungrily waiting at the edge of family cricket; the friendless fielder, the boy uninvited to bat or to tea.

I remember the smell of sea and seaweed, wet flesh, wet hair,
wet bathing-dresses, the warm smell as of a rabbity field after
rain, the smell of pop and splashed sunshades and toffee, the
stable-and-straw smell of hot, tossed, tumbled, dug, and trodden
sand, the swill-and-gaslamp smell of Saturday night, though the
sun shone strong, from the bellying beer-tents, the smell of the
vinegar on shelled cockles, winkle-smell, shrimp-smell, the
dripping-oily backstreet winter-smell of chips in newspapers, the
smell of ships from the sun-dazed docks round the corner of the
sand-hills, the smell of the known and paddled-in sea moving,
full of the drowned and herrings, out and away and beyond and
further still towards the antipodes that hung their koala-bears
and Maoris, kangaroos, and boomerangs, upside down over the
backs of the stars.

And the noise of pummelling Punch, and Judy falling, and a
clock tolling or telling no time in the tenantless town; now and
again a bell from a lost tower or a train on the lines behind us
clearing its throat, and always the hopeless, ravenous swearing
and pleading of the gulls, donkey-bray and hawker-cry, harmon-
icas and toy trumpets, shouting and laughing and singing,
hooting of tugs and tramps, the clip of the chair-attendant's
puncher, the motor-boat coughing in the bay, and the same
hymn and washing of the sea that was heard in the Bible.

'If it could only just, if it could only just?' your lips said again
and again as you scooped, in the hob-hot sand, dungeons,
garages, torture-chambers, train tunnels, arsenals, hangars for
zeppelins, witches' kitchens, vampires' parlours, smugglers' cellars, trolls' grog-shops, sewers, under a ponderous and cracking
castle, 'If it could only just be like this for ever and ever amen.'
August Monday all over the earth, from Mumbles where the
aunties grew like ladies on a seaside tree to brown, bear-hugging
Henty-land and the turtled Ballantyne Islands.

'Could donkeys go on the ice?'

'Only if they got snowshoes.'

We snowshoed a meek, complaining donkey and galloped
him off in the wake of the ten-foot-tall and Atlas-muscled
Mounties, rifled and pemmicanned, who always, in the white
Gold Rush wastes, got their black-oathed-and-bearded Man.

'Are there donkeys on desert islands?'

'Only sort-of donkeys.'

'What d'you mean, sort-of donkeys?'

'Native donkeys. They hunt things on them!'

'Sort-of walruses and seals and things?'

'Donkeys can't swim!'

'These donkeys can. They swim like whales, they swim like anything, they swim like – '

'Liar.'

'Liar yourself.'

And two small boys fought fiercely and silently in the sand, rolling together in a ball of legs and bottoms.

Then they went and saw the pierrots, or bought vanilla ices.

Lolling or larrikin that unsoiled, boiling beauty of a common day, great gods with their braces over their vests sang, spat pips, puffed smoke at wasps, gulped and ogled, forgot the rent, embraced, posed for the dickybird, were coarse, had rainbow-coloured armpits, winked, belched, blamed the radishes, looked at Ilfracombe, played hymns on paper-and-comb, peeled bananas, scratched, found seaweed in their panamas, blew up paper-bags and banged them, wished for nothing.

But over all the beautiful beach I remember most the children playing, boys and girls tumbling, moving jewels, who might never be happy again. And 'happy as a sandboy' is true as the heat of the sun.

Dusk came down; or grew up out of the sands and the sea; or curled around us from the calling docks and the bloodily smoking sun. The day was done, the sands brushed and ruffled suddenly with a sea-broom of cold wind.

And we gathered together all the spades and buckets and towels, empty hampers and bottles, umbrellas and fish-frails, bats and balls and knitting, and went – oh, listen, Dad! – to the fair in the dusk on the bald seaside field.

Fairs were no good in the day; then they were shoddy and tired; the voices of hoop-la girls were crimped as elocutionists; no cannon-ball could shake the roosting coco-nuts; the gondolas mechanically repeated their sober lurch; the Wall of Death was safe as a governess cart; the wooden animals were waiting for the night.

But in the night, the hoop-la girls, like operatic crows, croaked at the coming moon; whizz, whirl, and ten for a tanner, the coco-nuts rained from their sawdust like grouse from the

Highland sky; tipsy the griffin-prowed gondolas weaved on dizzy rails and the Wall of Death was a spinning rim of ruin, and the neighing wooden horses took, to a haunting hunting tune, a thousand Becher's Brooks as easily and breezily as hooved swallows.

Approaching, at dusk, the fair-field from the beach, we scorched and gritty boys heard above the belabouring of the batherless sea the siren voices of the raucous, horsy barkers.

'Roll up, roll up!'

In her tent and her rolls of flesh the Fattest Woman in the World sat sewing her winter frock, another tent, and fixed her little eyes, blackcurrants in blancmange, on the skeletons who filed and sniggered by.

'Roll up, roll up, roll up to see the Largest Rat on Earth, the Rover or Bonzo of vermin.'

Here scampered the smallest pony, like a Shetland shrew. And here 'The Most Intelligent Fleas,' trained, reined, bridled, and bitted, minutely cavorted in their glass corral.

Round galleries and shies and stalls, pennies were burning holes in a hundred pockets.

Pale young men with larded hair and Valentino-black side-whiskers, fags stuck to their lower lips, squinted along their swivel-sighted rifles and aimed at ping-pong balls dancing on fountains.

In knife-creased, silver-grey, skirt-like Oxford bags, and a sleeveless, scarlet, zip-fastened shirt with yellow horizontal stripes, a collier at the strength-machine spat on his hands, raised the hammer, and brought it Thor-ing down. The bell rang for Blaina.

Outside his booth stood a bitten-eared and barndoor-chested pug with a nose like a twisted swede and hair that started from his eyebrows and three teeth yellow as a camel's inviting any sportsman to a sudden and sickening basting in the sandy ring or a quid if he lasted a round; and, wiry, cocky, bow-legged, coal-scarred, boozed, sportsmen by the dozen strutted in and reeled out; and still those three teeth remained, chipped and camel-yellow in the bored, teak face.

Draggled and stout-wanting mothers, with haphazard hats, hostile hatpins, buns awry, bursting bags, and children at their skirts like pop-filled and jam-smeared limpets, screamed before distorting mirrors, at their suddenly tapering or tubular bodies and huge ballooning heads, and the children gaily bellowed at their own reflected bogies withering and bulging in the glass.

Old men, smelling of Milford Haven in the rain, shuffled, badgering and cadging, round the edges of the swaggering crowd, their only wares a handful of damp confetti.

A daring dash of schoolboys, safely, shoulder to shoulder, with their father's trilbies cocked at a desperate angle over one eye, winked at and whistled after the procession past the swings of two girls arm-in-arm : always one pert and pretty, and always one with glasses.

Girls in skulled and cross-boned tunnels shrieked, and were comforted.

Young men, heroic after pints, stood up on the flying chairoplanes, tousled, crimson, and against the rules.

Jaunty girls gave sailors sauce.

All the fun of the fair in the hot, bubbling night. The Man in the sand-yellow moon over the hurdy of gurdies. The swingboats swimming to and fro like slices of the moon. Dragons and hippogriffs at the prows of the gondolas breathing fire and Sousa. Midnight roundabout riders tantivying under the fairylights, huntsmen on billygoats and zebras hallooing under a circle of glow-worms.

And as we climbed home, up the gas-lit hill, to the still homes over the mumbling bay, we heard the music die and the voices drift like sand. And we saw the lights of the fair fade. And, at the far end of the seaside field, they lit their lamps, one by one, in the caravans.

THE CRUMBS OF ONE MAN'S YEAR

Slung as though in a hammock, or a lull, between one Christmas
for ever over and a New Year nearing full of relentless surprises,
waywardly and gladly I pry back at those wizening twelve
months and see only a waltzing snippet of the tipsy-turvy times,
flickers of vistas, flashes of queer fishes, patches and chequers of
a bard's-eye view.

Of what is coming in the New Year I know nothing, except
that all that is certain will come like thunderclaps or like comets
in the shape of four-leaved clovers, and that all that is unforeseen
will appear with the certainty of the sun who every morning
shakes a leg in the sky; and of what has gone I know only
shilly-shally snatches and freckled plaids, flecks and dabs, dazzle
and froth; a simple second caught in coursing snow-light, an
instant, gay or sorry, struck motionless in the curve of flight like
a bird or a scythe; the spindrift leaf and stray-paper whirl,
canter, quarrel, and people-chase of everybody's street; suddenly the way the grotesque wind slashes and freezes at a corner
the clothes of a passer-by so that she stays remembered, cold
and still until the world like a night-light in a nursery goes out;
and a waddling couple of the small occurrences, comic as ducks,
that quack their way through our calamitous days; whits and
dots and tittles.

'Look back, back,' the big voices clarion, 'look back at the
black colossal year,' while the rich music fanfares and dead-
marches.

I can give you only a scattering of some of the crumbs of one
man's year; and the penny music whistles.

Any memory, of the long, revolving year, will do, to begin
with.

I was walking, one afternoon in August, along a river-bank,
thinking the same thoughts that I always think when I walk
along a river-bank in August. As I was walking, I was thinking
– now it is August and I am walking along a river-bank. I do

not think I was thinking of anything else. I should have been thinking of what I should have been doing, but I was thinking only of what I was doing then and it was all right: it was good, and ordinary, and slow, and idle, and old, and sure, and what I was doing I could have been doing a thousand years before, had I been alive then and myself or any other man. You could have thought the river was ringing – almost you could hear the green, rapid bells sing in it: it could have been the River Elusina, 'that dances at the noise of Musick, for with Musick it bubbles, dances and growes sandy, and so continues till the musick ceases . . .' or it could have been the river 'in Judea that runs swiftly all the six dayes of the week, and stands still and rests all their Sabbath.' There were trees blowing, standing still, growing, knowing, whose names I never knew. (Once, indeed, with a friend I wrote a poem beginning, 'All trees are oaks, except fir-trees.') There were birds being busy, or sleep-flying, in the sky. (The poem had continued: 'All birds are robins, except crows, or rooks.') Nature was doing what it was doing, and thinking just that. And I was walking and thinking that I was walking, and for August it was not such a cold day. And then I saw, drifting along the water, a piece of paper, and I thought: Something wonderful may be written on this paper. I was alone on the gooseberry earth, or alone for two green miles, and a message drifted towards me on that tabby-coloured water that ran through the middle of the cow-patched, mooing fields. It was a message from multitudinous nowhere to my solitary self. I put out my stick and caught the piece of paper and held it close to the river-bank. It was a page torn from a very old periodical. That I could see. I leant over and read, through water, the message on the rippling page. I made out, with difficulty, only one sentence: it commemorated the fact that, over a hundred years ago, a man in Worcester had, for a bet, eaten, at one sitting, fifty-two pounds of plums.

And any other memory, of the long evolving year, will do, to go on with.

Here now, to my memory, come peaceful blitz and pieces of the Fifth of November, guys in the streets and forks in the sky, when Catherine-wheels and Jacky-jumps and good bombs burst in the blistered areas. The rockets are few but they star between roofs and up to the wall of the warless night. 'A penny for the Guy?' 'No, that's my father.' The great joke brocks and sizzles.

Sirius explodes in the backyard by the shelter. Timorous ladies sit in their back-rooms, with the eighth programme on very loud. Retiring men snarl under their blankets. In the unkempt-gardens of the very rich, the second butler lights a squib. In everybody's street the fearless children shout, under the little, homely raids. But I was standing on a signalling country hill where they fed a hungry bonfire Guy with brushwood, sticks, and cracker-jacks; the bonfire Guy whooped for more; small sulphurous puddings banged in his burning belly, and his thorned hair caught. He lurched, and made common noises. He was a long time dying on the hill over the starlit fields where the tabby river, without a message, ran on, with bells and trout and tins and bangles and literature and cats in it, to the sea never out of sound.

And on one occasion, in this long dissolving year, I remember that I boarded a London bus from a district I have forgotten, and where I certainly could have been up to little good, to an appointment that I did not want to keep.

It was a shooting green spring morning, nimble and crocus, with all the young women treading on naked flower-stalks, the metropolitan sward, swinging their milk-pail handbags, gentle, fickle, inviting, accessible, forgiving each robustly abandoned gesture of salutation before it was made or imagined, assenting, as they revelled demurely towards the manicure *salon* or the typewriting office, to all the ardent unspoken endearments of shaggy strangers and the winks and pipes of clovenfooted sandwichmen. The sun shrilled, the buses gambolled, policemen and daffodils bowed in the breeze that tasted of buttermilk. Delicate carousal plashed and babbled from the public-houses which were not yet open. I felt like a young god. I removed my collar-studs and opened my shirt. I tossed back my hair. There was an aviary in my heart, but without any owls or eagles. My cheeks were cherried warm, I smelt, I thought, of sea pinks. To the sound of madrigals sung by slim sopranos in waterfalled valleys where I was the only tenor, I leapt on to a bus. The bus was full. Carefree, open-collared, my eyes alight, my veins full of the spring as a dancer's shoes should be full of champagne, I stood, in love and at ease and always young, on the packed lower deck. And a man of exactly my own age – or perhaps he was a little older – got up and offered me his seat. He said, in a respectful voice, as though to an old justice of the peace, 'Please, won't you take my seat ?' and then he added – 'Sir.'

How many variegations of inconsiderable defeats and disillusionments I have forgotten ! How many shades and shapes from the polychromatic zebra house ! How many Joseph-coats I have left uncalled-for in the Gentlemen's Cloakrooms of the year !

And one man's year is like the country of a cloud, mapped on the sky, that soon will vanish into the watery, ordered wastes, into the spinning rule, into the dark which is light. Now the cloud is flying, very slowly, out of sight, and I can remember of all that voyaging geography, no palaced morning hills or huge plush valleys in the downing sun, forests simmering with birds, stagged moors, merry legendary meadowland, bullish plains, but only – the street near Waterloo station where a small boy, wearing cut-down khaki and a steel helmet, pushed a pram full of firewood and shouted, in a dispassionate voice, after each passer-by : 'Where's your tail ?'

The estuary pool under the collapsed castle, where the July children rolled together in original mud, shrieking and yawping, and low life, long before newts, twitched on their hands.

The crisp path through the field in this December snow, in the deep dark, where we trod the buried grass like ghosts on dry toast.

The single-line run along the spring-green river-bank where water-voles went Indian file to work, and where the young impatient voles, in their sleek vests, always in a hurry, jumped over the threadbare backs of the old ones.

The razor-scarred back-street café bar where a man with cut cheeks and chewed ears, huskily and furiously complained, over tarry tea, that the new baby panda in the zoo was not floodlit.

The gully sands in March, under the flayed and flailing cliff-top trees, when the wind played old Harry, or old Thomas, with me, and cormorants, far off, sped like motor-boats across the bay, as I weaved towards the toppling town and the black, loud *Lion* where the cat, who purred like a fire, looked out of two cinders at the gently swilling retired sea-captains in the snug-as-a-bug back bar.

And the basement kitchen in nipping February, with napkins on the line slung across from door to chockablock corner, and a bicycle by the larder very much down at wheels, and hats and toy-engines and bottles and spanners on the broken rocking-chair, and billowing papers and half-finished crosswords stacked on the radio always turned full tilt, and the fire smoking, and onions peeling, and chips always spitting on the stove, and small men in their overcoats talking of self-discipline and the ascetic life until the air grew woodbine-blue and the clock choked and the traffic died.

And then the moment of a night in that cavorting spring, rare and unforgettable as a bicycle-clip found in the middle of the desert. The lane was long and soused and dark that led to the house I helped to fill and bedraggle.

'Who's left this in this corner?'

'What, where?'

'Here, this.'

A doll's arm, the chitterlings of a clock, a saucepan full of hatbands.

The lane was rutted as though by bosky watercarts, and so dark you couldn't see your front in spite of you. Rain barrelled down. On one side you couldn't hear the deer that lived there, and on the other side – voices began to whisper, muffled in the midnight sack. A man's voice and a woman's voice. 'Lovers,' I said to myself. For at night the heart comes out, like a cat on the tiles. Discourteously I shone my torch. There, in the thick rain, a young man and a young woman stood, very close together, near the hedge that whirred in the wind. And a yard from them, another young man sat staidly, on the grass verge, holding an open book from which he appeared to read. And in the very rutted and puddly middle of the lane, two dogs were fighting, with brutish concentration and in absolute silence.

RETURN JOURNEY

NARRATOR

It was a cold white day in High Street, and nothing to stop the wind slicing up from the docks, for where the squat and tall shops had shielded the town from the sea lay their blitzed flat graves marbled with snow and headstoned with fences. Dogs, delicate as cats on water, as though they had gloves on their paws, padded over the vanished buildings. Boys romped, calling high and clear, on top of a levelled chemist's and a shoe-shop, and a little girl, wearing a man's cap, threw a snowball in a chill deserted garden that had once been the Jug and Bottle of the Prince of Wales. The wind cut up the street with a soft sea-noise hanging on its arm, like a hooter in a muffler. I could see the swathed hill stepping up out of the town, which you never could see properly before, and the powdered fields of the roofs of Milton Terrace and Watkin Street and Fullers Row. Fish-frailed, netbagged, umbrella'd, pixie-capped, fur-shoed, blue-nosed, puce-lipped, blinkered like drayhorses, scarved, mittened, galoshed, wearing everything but the cat's blanket, crushes of shopping-women crunched in the little Lapland of the once grey drab street, blew and queued and yearned for hot tea, as I began my search through Swansea town cold and early on that wicked February morning. I went into the hotel. 'Good morning.'

The hall-porter did not answer. I was just another snowman to him. He did not know that I was looking for someone after fourteen years, and he did not care. He stood and shuddered, staring through the glass of the hotel door at the snowflakes sailing down the sky, like Siberian confetti. The bar was just opening, but already one customer puffed and shook at the counter with a full pint of half-frozen Tawe water in his wrapped-up hand. I said Good morning, and the barmaid, polishing the counter vigorously as though it were a rare and valuable piece of Swansea china, said to her first customer:

BARMAID

Seen the film at the Elysium Mr Griffiths there's snow isn't it did you come up on your bicycle our pipes burst Monday . . .

NARRATOR

A pint of bitter, please.

BARMAID

Proper little lake in the kitchen got to wear your Wellingtons when you boil a egg one and four please . . .

CUSTOMER

The cold gets me just here . . .

BARMAID

. . . and eightpence change that's your liver Mr Griffiths you been on the cocoa again . . .

NARRATOR

I wonder whether you remember a friend of mine? He always used to come to this bar, some years ago. Every morning, about this time.

CUSTOMER

Just by here it gets me. I don't know what'd happen if I didn't wear a band . . .

BARMAID

What's his name?

NARRATOR

Young Thomas

BARMAID

Lots of Thomases come here it's a kind of home from home for Thomases isn't it Mr Griffiths what's he look like?

NARRATOR

He'd be about seventeen or eighteen . . .   (*Slowly*)

BARMAID

. . . I was seventeen once . . .

NARRATOR

. . .and above medium height. Above medium height for Wales, I mean, he's five foot six and a half. Thick blubber lips; snub nose; curly mousebrown hair; one front tooth broken after playing a game called Cats and Dogs, in the Mermaid, Mumbles; speaks rather fancy; truculent; plausible; a bit of a shower-off; plus-fours and no breakfast, you know; used to have poems printed in the *Herald of Wales*; there was one about an open-air performance of *Electra* in Mrs Bertie Perkins's garden in Sketty; lived up the Uplands; a bombastic adolescent provincial Bohemian with a thick-knotted artist's tie made out of his sister's scarf, she never knew where it had gone, and a cricket-shirt dyed bottle green; a gabbing, ambitious, mock-tough, pretentious young man; and mole-y, too.

BARMAID

There's words what d'you want to find *him* for I wouldn't touch him with a barge-pole . . . would you, Mr Griffiths? Mind, you can never tell. I remember a man came here with a monkey. Called for 'alf for himself and a pint for the monkey. And he wasn't Italian at all. Spoke Welsh like a preacher.

NARRATOR

The bar was filling up. Snowy business bellies pressed their watch-chains against the counter; black business bowlers, damp and white now as Christmas puddings in their cloths, bobbed in front of the misty mirrors. The voice of commerce rang sternly through the lounge.

FIRST VOICE

Cold enough for you?

SECOND VOICE

How's your pipes, Mr Lewis?

THIRD VOICE

Another winter like this'll put paid to me, Mr Evans. I got the 'flu . . .

FIRST VOICE

Make it a double . . .

SECOND VOICE

Similar . . .

BARMAID

Okay, baby . . .

CUSTOMER

I seem to remember a chap like you described. There couldn't be two like him let's hope. He used to work as a reporter. Down the Three Lamps I used to see him. Lifting his ikkle elbow.

(*Confidentially*)

NARRATOR

What's the Three Lamps like now?

CUSTOMER

It isn't like anything. It isn't there. It's nothing mun. You remember Ben Evans's stores? It's right next door to that. Ben Evans isn't there either . . .

(*Fade*)

NARRATOR

I went out of the hotel into the snow and walked down High Street, past the flat white wastes where all the shops had been. Eddershaw Furnishers, Curry's Bicycles, Donegal Clothing Company, Doctor Scholl's, Burton Tailors, W. H. Smith, Boots Cash Chemists, Leslie's Stores, Upson's Shoes, Prince of Wales, Tucker's Fish, Stead & Simpson – all the shops bombed and vanished. Past the hole in space where Hodges & Clothiers had been, down Castle Street, past the remembered, invisible shops, Price's Fifty Shilling, and Crouch the Jeweller, Potter Gilmore Gowns, Evans Jeweller, Master's Outfitters, Style and Mantle, Lennard's Boots, True Form, Kardomah, R. E. Jones, Dean's Tailor, David Evans, Gregory Confectioners, Bovega, Burton's, Lloyd's Bank, and nothing. And into Temple Street. There the Three Lamps had stood, old Mac magisterial in his corner. And there the Young Thomas whom I was searching for used to stand at the counter on Friday paynights with Freddie Farr Half Hook, Bill Latham, Cliff Williams, Gareth Hughes, Eric Hughes, Glyn Lowry, a man among men, his hat at a rakish angle, in that snug, smug, select Edwardian holy of best-bitter holies . . .

(*Bar noises in background*)

OLD REPORTER

Remember when I took you down the mortuary for the first time, Young Thomas? He'd never seen a corpse before, boys, except old Ron on a Saturday night. 'If you want to be a proper newspaperman,' I said, 'you got to be well known in the right circles. You got to be *persona grata* in the mortuary, see.' He went pale green, mun.

FIRST YOUNG REPORTER

Look, he's blushing now . . .

OLD REPORTER

And when we got there what d'you think? The decorators were in at the mortuary, giving the old home a bit of a re-do like. Up on ladders having a slap at the roof. Young Thomas didn't see 'em, he had his pop eyes glued on the slab, and when one of the painters up the ladder said 'Good morning, gents' in a deep voice he upped in the air and out of the place like a ferret. Laugh!

BARMAID

(*Off*) You've had enough, Mr Roberts.
You heard what I said.   (*Noise of a gentle scuffle*)

SECOND YOUNG REPORTER

(*Casually*) There goes Mr Roberts.

OLD REPORTER

Well fair do's they throw you out very genteel in this pub . . .

FIRST YOUNG REPORTER

Ever seen Young Thomas covering a soccer match down the Vetch and working it out in tries?

SECOND YOUNG REPORTER

And up the Mannesman Hall shouting 'Good footwork, sir,' and a couple of punch-drunk colliers galumphing about like jumbos.

FIRST YOUNG REPORTER

What you been reporting to-day, Young Thomas?

SECOND YOUNG REPORTER

Two typewriter Thomas the ace news-dick . . .

OLD REPORTER

Let's have a dekko at your note-book. 'Called at British Legion :
Nothing. Called at Hospital : One broken leg. Auction at the
Metropole. Ring Mr Beynon *re* Gymanfa Ganu. Lunch : Pint
and pasty at the Singleton with Mrs Giles. Bazaar at Bethesda
Chapel. Chimney on fire at Tontine Street. Walters Road Sunday
School Outing. Rehearsal of the *Mikado* at Skewen' – all front
page stuff . . .   (*Fade*)

NARRATOR

The voices of fourteen years ago hung silent in the snow and
ruin, and in the falling winter morning I walked on through the
white havoc'd centre where once a very young man I knew had
mucked about as chirpy as a sparrow after the sips and titbits
and small change of the town. Near the *Evening Post* building
and the fragment of the Castle I stopped a man whose face I
thought I recognized from a long time ago. I said : I wonder if
you can tell me . . .

PASSER-BY

Yes ?

NARRATOR

He peered out of his blanketing scarves and from under his snowballed Balaclava like an Eskimo with a bad conscience. I said : If
you can tell me whether you used to know a chap called Young
Thomas. He worked on the *Post* and used to wear an overcoat
sometimes with the check lining inside out so that you could play
giant draughts on him. He wore a conscious woodbine, too . . .

PASSER-BY

What d'you mean, conscious woodbine ?

NARRATOR

. . .and a perched pork pie with a peacock feather and he tried to slouch like a newshawk even when he was attending a meeting of the Gorseinon Buffalos . . .

PASSER-BY

Oh, *him*! He owes me half a crown. I haven't seen him since the old Kardomah days. He wasn't a reporter then, he'd just left the grammar school. Him and Charlie Fisher — Charlie's got whiskers now — and Tom Warner and Fred Janes, drinking coffee-dashes and arguing the toss.

NARRATOR

What about?

PASSER-BY

Music and poetry and painting and politics. Einstein and Epstein, Stravinsky and Greta Garbo, death and religion, Picasso and girls . . .

NARRATOR

And then?

PASSER-BY

Communism, symbolism, Bradman, Braque, the Watch Committee, free love, free beer, murder, Michelangelo, ping-pong, ambition, Sibelius, and girls . . .

NARRATOR

Is that all?

PASSER-BY

How Dan Jones was going to compose the most prodigious symphony, Fred Janes paint the most miraculously meticulous picture, Charlie Fisher catch the poshest trout, Vernon Watkins and Young Thomas write the most boiling poems, how they would ring the bells of London and paint it like a tart . . .

NARRATOR

And after that ?

PASSER-BY

On the hissing of the butt-ends in the drains of the coffee-dashes and the tinkle and the gibble-gabble of the morning young lounge lizards as they talked about Augustus John, Emil Jannings, Carnera, Dracula, Amy Johnson, trial marriage, pocket-money, the Welsh sea, the London stars, King Kong, anarchy, darts, T. S. Eliot, and girls . . . Duw, it's cold !

NARRATOR

And he hurried on, into the dervish snow, without a good morning or good-bye, swaddled in his winter woollens like a man in the island of his deafness, and I felt that perhaps he had never stopped at all to tell me of one more departed stage in the progress of the boy I was pursuing. The Kardomah Café was razed to the snow, the voices of the coffee-drinkers – poets, painters, and musicians in their beginnings – lost in the willynilly flying of the years and the flakes.

Down College Street I walked then, past the remembered invisible shops, Langley's, Castle Cigar Co, T. B. Brown, Pullar's, Aubrey Jeremiah, Goddard Jones, Richards, Hornes, Marles, Pleasance & Harper, Star Supply, Sidney Heath, Wesley Chapel, and nothing . . . My search was leading me back, through pub and job and café, to the School.

(*Fade*) (*School bell*)

SCHOOLMASTER

Oh yes, yes, I remember him well,
though I do not know if I would recognize him now :
nobody grows any younger, or better,
and boys grow into much the sort of men one would suppose
though sometimes the moustaches bewilder

and one finds it hard to reconcile one's memory of a small
none-too-clean urchin lying his way unsuccessfully out of his
homework
with a fierce and many-medalled sergeant-major with three
children or a divorced chartered accountant;
and it is hard to realize
that some little tousled rebellious youth whose only claim to
fame among his contemporaries was his undisputed right to
the championship of the spitting contest
is now perhaps one's own bank manager.
Oh yes, I remember him well, the boy you are searching for:
he looked like most boys, no better, brighter, or more
respectful;
he cribbed, mitched, spilt ink, rattled his desk and garbled his
lessons with the worst of them;
he could smudge, hedge, smirk, wriggle, wince,
whimper, blarney, badger, blush, deceive, be
devious, stammer, improvise, assume
offended dignity or righteous indignation as though to the
manner born;
sullenly and reluctantly he drilled, for some small
crime, under Sergeant Bird, so wittily nicknamed
Oiseau, on Wednesday half-holidays,
appeared regularly in detention classes,
hid in the cloakroom during algebra,
was, when a newcomer, thrown into the bushes of the
Lower Playground by bigger boys,
and threw newcomers into the bushes of the Lower
Playground when *he* was a bigger boy;
he scuffled at prayers,
he interpolated, smugly, the time-honoured wrong
irreverent words into the morning hymns,
he helped to damage the headmaster's rhubarb,
was thirty-third in trigonometry,
and, as might be expected, edited the School Magazine
                                        (*Fade*)

NARRATOR

The Hall is shattered, the echoing corridors charred where he
scribbled and smudged and yawned in the long green days,

waiting for the bell and the scamper into the Yard: the School on Mount Pleasant Hill has changed its face and its ways. Soon, they say, it may be no longer the School at all he knew and loved when he was a boy up to no good but the beat of his blood: the names are havoc'd from the Hall and the carved initials burned from the broken wood. But the names remain. What names did he know of the dead? Who of the honoured dead did he know such a long time ago? The names of the dead in the living heart and head remain for ever. Of all the dead whom did he know?

(Funeral bell)

VOICE

Evans, K. J.
Haines, G. C.
Roberts, I. L.
Moxham, J.
Thomas, H.
Baines, W.
Bazzard, F. H.
Beer, L. J.
Bucknell, R.
Tywford, G.
Vagg, E. A.
Wright, G.

(Fade)

NARRATOR

Then I tacked down the snowblind hill, a cat-o'-nine-gales whipping from the sea, and, white and eiderdowned in the smothering flurry, people padded past me up and down like prowling featherbeds. And I plodded through the ankle-high one cloud that foamed the town, into flat Gower Street, its buildings melted, and along long Helen's Road. Now my search was leading me back to the seashore.

(Noise of sea, softly)

NARRATOR

Only two living creatures stood on the promenade, near the cenotaph, facing the tossed crystal sea: a man in a chewed muffler and a ratting cap, and an angry dog of a mixed make. The man dithered in the cold, beat his bare blue hands together, waited for some sign from sea or snow; the dog shouted at the weather, and fixed his bloodshot eyes on Mumbles Head. But when the man and I talked together, the dog piped down and fixed his eyes on me, blaming me for the snow. The man spoke towards the sea. Year in, year out, whatever the weather, once in the daytime, once in the dark, he always came to look at the sea. He knew all the dogs and boys and old men who came to see the sea, who ran or gambolled on the sand or stooped at the edge of the waves as though over a wild, wide, rolling ash-can. He knew the lovers who went to lie in the sandhills, the striding masculine women who roared at their terriers like tiger tamers, the loafing men whose work it was in the world to observe the great employment of the sea. He said:

PROMENADE-MAN

Oh yes, yes, I remember him well, but I didn't know what was his name. I don't know the names of none of the sandboys. They don't know mine. About fourteen or fifteen years old, you said, with a little red cap. And he used to play by Vivian's Stream. He used to dawdle in the arches, you said, and lark about on the railway-lines and holler at the old sea. He'd mooch about the dunes and watch the tankers and the tugs and the banana boats come out of the docks. He was going to run away to sea, he said. *I* know. On Saturday afternoon he'd go down to the sea when it was a long way out, and hear the foghorns though he couldn't see the ships. And on Sunday nights, after chapel, he'd be swaggering with his pals along the prom, whistling after the girls.

(*Titter*)

GIRL

Does your mother know you're out? Go away now. Stop following us.

(*Another girl titters*)

GIRL

Don't you say nothing, Hetty, you're only encouraging. No thank *you*, Mr Cheeky, with your cut-glass accent and your father's trilby! I don't want *no* walk on *no* sands. What d'you say? Ooh listen to him, Het, he's swallowed a dictionary. No, I don't want to go with nobody up no lane in the moonlight, see, and I'm not a baby-snatcher neither. I seen you going to school along Terrace Road, Mr Glad-Eye, with your little satchel and wearing your red cap and all. You seen me wearing my . . . no you never. Hetty, mind your glasses! Hetty Harris, you're as bad as them. Oh go away and do you homework, see. Cheek! Hetty Harris, don't you let him! Oooh, there's brazen! Well, just to the end of the prom, if you like. No further, mind . . .

PROMENADE-MAN

Oh yes, I knew him well. I've known him by the thousands . . .

NARRATOR

Even now, on the frozen foreshore, a high, far cry of boys, all like the boy I sought, slid on the glass of the streams and snowballed each other and the sky. Then I went on my way from the sea, up Brynmill Terrace and into Glanbrydan Avenue where Bert Trick had kept a grocer's shop and, in the kitchen, threatened the annihilation of the ruling classes over sandwiches and jelly and blancmange. And I came to the shops and houses of the Uplands. Here and around here it was that the journey had begun of the one I was pursuing through his past.

(*Old piano cinema-music in background*)

FIRST VOICE

Here was once the flea-pit picture-house where he whooped for the scalping Indians with Jack Basset and banged for the rustlers' guns.

NARRATOR

Jackie Basset, killed.

THIRD VOICE

Here once was Mrs Ferguson's, who sold the best gob-stoppers and penny packets full of surprises and a sweet kind of glue.

FIRST VOICE

In the fields behind Cwmdonkin Drive, the Murrays chased him and all the cats.

SECOND VOICE

No fires now where the outlaws' fires burned and the paradisiacal potatoes roasted in the embers.

THIRD VOICE

In the Graig beneath Town Hill he was a lonely killer hunting the wolves (or rabbits) and the red Sioux tribe (or Mitchell brothers).
  (*Fade cinema-music into background of children's voices reciting, in unison, the names of the counties of Wales*)

FIRST VOICE

In Mirador School he learned to read and count. Who made the worst raffia doilies? Who put water in Joyce's galoshes, every morning prompt as prompt? In the afternoons, when the children were good, they read aloud from Struwelpeter. And when they were bad, they sat alone in the empty classroom, hearing, from above them, the distant, terrible, sad music of the late piano lesson.
  (*The children's voices fade. The piano lesson continues in background*)

NARRATOR

And I went up, through the white Grove, into Cwmdonkin Park, the snow still sailing and the childish, lonely, remembered music fingering on in the suddenly gentle wind. Dusk was folding the Park around, like another, darker snow. Soon the bell would ring for the closing of the gates, though the Park was empty. The park-keeper walked by the reservoir, where swans had glided, on his white rounds. I walked by his side and asked him my questions, up the swathed drives past buried beds and loaded utterly still furred and birdless trees towards the last gate. He said:

PARK-KEEPER

Oh yes, yes, I knew him well. He used to climb the reservoir railings and pelt the old swans. Run like a billygoat over the grass you should keep off of. Cut branches off the trees. Carve words on the benches. Pull up moss in the rockery, go snip through the dahlias. Fight in the bandstand. Climb the elms and moon up the top like a owl. Light fires in the bushes. Play on the green bank. Oh yes, I knew him well. I think he was happy all the time. I've known him by the thousands.

NARRATOR

We had reached the last gate. Dusk drew around us and the town. I said: What has become of him now?

PARK-KEEPER

Dead.

NARRATOR

The Park-keeper said:

(*The park bell rings*)

PARK-KEEPER

Dead ... Dead ... Dead ... Dead ... Dead ... Dead.

THE FOLLOWERS

It was six o'clock on a winter's evening. Thin, dingy rain spat
and drizzled past the lighted street lamps. The pavements shone
long and yellow. In squeaking goloshes, with mackintosh collars
up and bowlers and trilbies weeping, youngish men from the
offices bundled home against the thistly wind —
   'Night, Mr Macey.'
   'Going my way, Charlie?'
   'Ooh, there's a pig of a night!'
   'Good night, Mr Swan.' —
and older men, clinging on to the big, black circular birds of
their umbrellas, were wafted back, up the gaslit hills, to safe,
hot, slippered, weatherproof hearths, and wives called Mother,
and old, fond, fleabag dogs, and the wireless babbling.
   Young women from the offices, who smelt of scent and
powder and wet pixie hoods and hair, scuttled, giggling, arm-
in-arm, after the hissing trams, and screeched as they splashed
their stockings in the puddles rainbowed with oil between the
slippery lines.
   In a shop window, two girls undressed the dummies :
   'Where you going to-night?'
   'Depends on Arthur. Up she comes.'
   'Mind her cami-knicks, Edna . . .'
   The blinds came down over another window.
   A newsboy stood in a doorway, calling the news to nobody,
very softly :
   'Earthquake. Earthquake in Japan.'
   Water from a chute dripped on to his sacking. He waited in
his own pool of rain.
   A flat, long girl drifted, snivelling into her hanky, out of a
jeweller's shop, and slowly pulled the steel shutters down with a
hooked pole. She looked, in the grey rain, as though she were
crying from top to toe.
   A silent man and woman, dressed in black, carried the wreaths

away from the front of their flower shop into the scented deadly
darkness behind the window lights. Then the lights went out.

A man with a balloon tied to his cap pushed a shrouded
barrow up a dead end.

A baby with an ancient face sat in its pram outside the wine
vaults, quiet, very wet, peering cautiously all round it.

It was the saddest evening I had ever known.

A young man, with his arm round his girl, passed by me,
laughing; and she laughed back, right into his handsome, nasty
face. That made the evening sadder still.

I met Leslie at the corner of Crimea Street. We were both
about the same age: too young and too old. Leslie carried a
rolled umbrella, which he never used, though sometimes he
pressed doorbells with it. He was trying to grow a moustache. I
wore a check, ratting cap at a Saturday angle. We greeted each
other formally:

'Good evening, old man.'

'Evening, Leslie.'

'Right on the dot, boy.'

'That's right,' I said. 'Right on the dot.'

A plump, blonde girl, smelling of wet rabbits, self-conscious
even in that dirty night, minced past on high-heeled shoes. The
heels clicked, the soles squelched.

Leslie whistled after her, low and admiring.

'Business first,' I said.

'Oh, boy!' Leslie said.

'And she's too fat as well.'

'I like them corpulent,' Leslie said. 'Remember Penelope
Bogan? a Mrs too.'

'Oh, come *on*. That old bird of Paradise Alley! How's the
exchequer, Les?'

'One and a penny. How you fixed?'

'Tanner.'

'What'll it be, then? The Compasses?'

'Free cheese at the Marlborough.'

We walked towards the Marlborough, dodging umbrella
spokes, smacked by our windy macs, stained by steaming
lamplight, seeing the sodden, blown scourings and street-wash
of the town, papers, rags, dregs, rinds, fag-ends, balls of fur,
flap, float, and cringe along the gutters, hearing the sneeze and

rattle of the bony trams and a ship hoot like a fog-ditched owl
in the bay, and Leslie said:

'What'll we do after?'

'We'll follow someone,' I said.

'Remember following that old girl up Kitchener Street? The
one who dropped her handbag?'

'You should have given it back.'

'There wasn't anything in it, only a piece of bread-and-jam.'

'Here we are,' I said.

The Marlborough saloon was cold and empty. There were
notices on the damp walls: No Singing. No Dancing. No
Gambling. No Peddlers.

'You sing,' I said to Leslie, 'and I'll dance, then we'll have a
game of nap and I'll peddle my braces.'

The barmaid, with gold hair and two gold teeth in front, like a
well-off rabbit's, was blowing on her nails and polishing them
on her black marocain. She looked up as we came in, then blew
on her nails again and polished them without hope.

'You can tell it isn't Saturday night,' I said. 'Evening, Miss.
Two pints.'

'And a pound from the till,' Leslie said.

'Give us your one-and-a-penny, Les,' I whispered and then
said aloud: 'Anybody can tell it isn't Saturday night. Nobody
sick.'

'Nobody here to *be* sick,' Leslie said.

The peeling, liver-coloured room might never have been drunk
in at all. Here, commercials told jokes and had Scotches and
sodas with happy, dyed, port-and-lemon women; dejected reg-
ulars grew grand and muzzy in the corners, inventing their pasts,
being rich, important, and loved; reprobate grannies in dustbin
black cackled and nipped; influential nobodies revised the
earth; a party, with earrings, called 'Frilly Willy' played the
crippled piano, which sounded like a hurdy-gurdy playing under
water, until the publican's nosy wife said, 'No.' Strangers came
and went, but mostly went. Men from the valleys dropped in
for nine or ten; sometimes there were fights; and always there
was something doing, some argie-bargie, giggle and bluster,
horror or folly, affection, explosion, nonsense, peace, some wild
goose flying in the boozy air of that comfortless, humdrum
nowhere in the dizzy, ditchwater town at the end of the railway

lines. But that evening it was the saddest room I had ever known.

Leslie said, in a low voice: 'Think she'll let us have one on tick?'

'Wait a bit, boy,' I murmured. 'Wait for her to thaw.'

But the barmaid heard me, and looked up. She looked clean through me, back through my small history to the bed I was born in, then shook her gold head.

'I don't know what it is,' said Leslie as we walked up Crimea Street in the rain, 'but I feel kind of depressed to-night.'

'It's the saddest night in the world,' I said.

We stopped, soaked and alone, to look at the stills outside the cinema we called the Itch-pit. Week after week, for years and years, we had sat on the edges of the springless seats there, in the dank but snug, flickering dark, first with toffees and monkey-nuts that crackled for the dumb guns, and then with cigarettes: a cheap special kind that would make a fire-swallower cough up the cinders of his heart. 'Let's go in and see Lon Chaney,' I said, 'and Richard Talmadge and Milton Sills and . . . and Noah Beery,' I said, 'and Richard Dix . . . and Slim Summerville and Hoot Gibson.'

We both sighed.

'Oh, for our vanished youth,' I said.

We walked on heavily, with wilful feet, splashing the passers-by.

'Why don't you open your brolly?' I said.

'It won't open. You try.'

We both tried, and the umbrella suddenly bellied out, the spokes tore through the soaking cover; the wind danced its tatters; it wrangled above us in the wind like a ruined, mathematical bird. We tried to tug it down: an unseen, new spoke sprang through its ragged ribs. Leslie dragged it behind him, along the pavement, as though he had shot it.

A girl called Dulcie, scurrying to the Itch-pit, sniggered 'Hallo,' and we stopped her.

'A rather terrible thing has happened,' I said to her. She was so silly that, even when she was fifteen, we had told her to eat soap to make her straw hair crinkle, and Les took a piece from the bathroom, and she did.

'I know,' she said, 'you broke your gamp.'

'No, you're wrong there,' Leslie said. 'It isn't *our* umbrella at all. It fell off the roof. *You* feel,' he said. 'You can feel it fell off the roof.' She took the umbrella gingerly by its handle.

'There's someone up there throwing umbrellas down,' I said. 'It may be serious.'

She began to titter, and then grew silent and anxious as Leslie said: 'You never know. It might be walking-sticks next.'

'Or sewing-machines,' I said.

'You wait here, Dulce, and we'll investigate,' Leslie said.

We hurried on down the street, turned a blowing corner and then ran.

Outside Rabiotti's café, Leslie said: 'It isn't fair on Dulcie.' We never mentioned it again.

A wet girl brushed by. Without a word, we followed her. She cantered, long-legged, down Inkerman Street and through Paradise Passage, and we were at her heels.

'I wonder what's the point in following people,' Leslie said, 'it's kind of daft. It never gets you anywhere. All you do is follow them home and then try to look through the window and see what they're doing and mostly there's curtains anyway. I bet nobody else does things like that.'

'You never know,' I said. The girl turned into St Augustus Crescent, which was a wide lamplit mist. 'People are always following people. What shall we call her?'

'Hermione Weatherby,' Leslie said. He was never wrong about names. Hermione was fey and stringy, and walked like a long gym-mistress, full of love, through the stinging rain.

'You never know. You never know what you'll find out. Perhaps she lives in a huge house with all her sisters — '

'How many?'

'Seven. All full of love. And when she gets home they all change into kimonos and lie on divans with music and whisper to each other and all they're doing is waiting for somebody like us to walk in, lost, and then they'll all chatter round us like starlings and put us in kimonos too, and we'll never leave the house until we die. Perhaps it's so beautiful and soft and noisy — like a warm bath full of birds . . .'

'I don't want birds in my bath,' said Leslie. 'Perhaps she'll slit her throat if they don't draw the blinds. I don't care what happens so long as it's interesting.'

She slip-slopped round a corner into an avenue where the neat trees were sighing and the cosy windows shone.

'I don't wand old feathers in the tub,' Leslie said.

Hermione turned in at number thirteen, Beach-view.

'You can see the beach all right,' Leslie said, 'if you got a periscope.'

We waited on the pavement opposite, under a bubbling lamp, as Hermione opened her door, and then we tiptoed across and down the gravel path and were at the back of the house, outside an uncurtained window.

Hermione's mother, a round, friendly, owlish woman in a pinafore, was shaking a chip-pan on the kitchen stove.

'I'm hungry,' I said.

'Ssh !'

We edged to the side of the window as Hermione came into the kitchen. She was old, nearly thirty, with a mouse-brown shingle and big earnest eyes. She wore horn-rimmed spectacles and a sensible, tweed costume, and a white shirt with a trim bow-tie. She looked as though she tried to look like a secretary in domestic films, who had only to remove her spectacles and have her hair cherished, and be dressed like a silk dog's dinner, to turn into a dazzler and make her employer Warner Baxter, gasp, woo, and marry her ; but if Hermione took off her glasses, she wouldn't be able to tell if he was Warner Baxter or the man who read the meters.

We stood so near the window, we could hear the chips spitting.

'Have a nice day in the office, dear ? There's weather,' Hermione's mother said, worrying the chip-pan.

'What's *her* name, Les ?'

'Hetty.'

Everything there in the warm kitchen, from the tea-caddy and the grandmother clock, to the tabby that purred like a kettle, was good, dull, and sufficient.

'Mr Truscott was something awful,' Hermione said as she put on her slippers.

'Where's her kimono ?' Leslie said.

'Here's a nice cup of tea,' said Hetty.

'Everything's nice in that old hole,' said Leslie, grumbling. 'Where's the seven sisters like starlings ?'

It began to rain much more heavily. It bucketed down on the black back yard, and the little comfy kennel of a house, and us, and the hidden, hushed town, where, even now, in the haven of the Marlborough, the submarine piano would be tinning 'Daisy,' and the happy henna'd women squealing into their port.

Hetty and Hermione had their supper. Two drowned boys watched them enviously.

'Put a drop of Worcester on the chips,' Leslie whispered; and by God she did.

'Doesn't anything happen anywhere?' I said, 'in the whole wide world? I think the *News of the World* is all made up. Nobody murders no one. There isn't any sin any more, or love, or death, or pearls and divorces and mink-coats or anything, or putting arsenic in the cocoa . . .'

'Why don't they put on some music for us,' Leslie said, 'and do a dance? It isn't every night they got two fellows watching them in the rain. Not *every* night, anyway!'

All over the dripping town, small lost people with nowhere to go and nothing to spend were gooseberrying in the rain outside wet windows, but nothing happened.

'I'm getting pneumonia,' Leslie said.

The cat and the fire were purring, grandmother time tick-tocked our lives away. The supper was cleared, and Hetty and Hermione, who had not spoken for many minutes, they were so confident and close in their little lighted box, looked at one another and slowly smiled.

They stood still in the decent, purring kitchen, facing one another.

'There's something funny going to happen,' I whispered very softly.

'It's going to begin,' Leslie said.

We did not notice the sour, racing rain any more.

The smiles stayed on the faces of the two still, silent women.

'It's going to begin.'

And we heard Hetty say in a small secret voice: 'Bring out the album, dear.'

Hermione opened a cupboard and brought out a big, stiff-coloured photograph album, and put it in the middle of the table. Then she and Hetty sat down at the table, side by side, and Hermione opened the album.

'That's Uncle Eliot who died in Porthcawl, the one who had the cramp,' said Hetty.

They looked with affection at Uncle Eliot, but we could not see him.

'That's Martha-the-woolshop, you wouldn't remember her, dear, it was wool, wool, wool, with her all the time; she wanted to be buried in her jumper, the mauve one, but her husband put his foot down. He'd been in India. That's your Uncle Morgan,' Hetty said, 'one of the Kidwelly Morgans, remember him in the snow?'

Hermione turned a page. 'And that's Myfanwy, she got queer all of a sudden, remember. It was when she was milking. That's your cousin Jim, the Minister, until they found out. And that's our Beryl,' Hetty said.

But she spoke all the time like somebody repeating a lesson: a well-loved lesson she knew by heart.

We knew that she and Hermione were only waiting.

Then Hermione turned another page. And we knew, by their secret smiles, that this was what they had been waiting for.

'My sister Katinka,' Hetty said.

'Auntie Katinka,' Hermione said. They bent over the photograph.

'Remember that day in Aberystwyth, Katinka?' Hetty said softly. 'The day we went on the choir outing.'

'I wore my new white dress,' a new voice said.

Leslie clutched at my hand.

'And a straw hat with birds,' said the clear, new voice.

Hermione and Hetty were not moving their lips.

'I was always a one for birds on my hat. Just the plumes of course. It was August the third, and I was twenty-three.'

'Twenty-three come October, Katinka,' Hetty said.

'That's right, love,' the voice said. 'Scorpio I was. And we met Douglas Pugh on the Prom and he said: "You look like a queen to-day, Katinka," he said, "You look like a queen, Katinka," he said. Why are those two boys looking in at the window?'

We ran up the gravel drive, and around the corner of the house, and into the avenue and out on to St Augustus Crescent. The rain roared down to drown the town. There we stopped for breath. We did not speak or look at each other. Then we walked on through the rain. At Victoria corner, we stopped again.

'Good night, old man,' Leslie said.

'Good night,' I said.

And we went our different ways.

A STORY

If you can call it a story. There's no real beginning or end and there's very little in the middle. It is all about a day's outing, by charabanc, to Porthcawl, which, of course, the charabanc never reached, and it happened when I was so high and much nicer.

I was staying at the time with my uncle and his wife. Although she was my aunt, I never thought of her as anything but the wife of my uncle, partly because he was so big and trumpeting and red-hairy and used to fill every inch of the hot little house like an old buffalo squeezed into an airing cupboard, and partly because she was so small and silk and quick and made no noise at all as she whisked about on padded paws, dusting the china dogs, feeding the buffalo, setting the mousetraps that never caught her; and once she sneaked out of the room, to squeak in a nook or nibble in the hayloft, you forgot she had ever been there.

But there he was, always, a steaming hulk of an uncle, his braces straining like hawsers, crammed behind the counter of the tiny shop at the front of the house, and breathing like a brass band; or guzzling and blustery in the kitchen over his gutsy supper, too big for everything except the great black boats of his boots. As he ate, the house grew smaller; he billowed out over the furniture, the loud check meadow of his waistcoat littered, as though after a picnic, with cigarette ends, peelings, cabbage stalks, birds' bones, gravy; and the forest fire of his hair crackled among the hooked hams from the ceiling. She was so small she could hit him only if she stood on a chair, and every Saturday night at half past ten he would lift her up, under his arm, on to a chair in the kitchen so that she could hit him on the head with whatever was handy, which was always a china dog. On Sundays, and when pickled, he sang high tenor, and had won many cups.

The first I heard of the annual outing was when I was sitting one evening on a bag of rice behind the counter, under one of my uncle's stomachs, reading an advertisement for sheep-dip, which was all there was to read. The shop was full of my uncle, and when Mr Benjamin Franklyn, Mr Weazley, Noah Bowen, and Will Sentry came in, I thought it would burst. It was like all being together in a drawer that smelt of cheese and turps, and twist tobacco and sweet biscuits and snuff and waistcoat. Mr Benjamin Franklyn said that he had collected enough money for the charabanc and twenty cases of pale ale and a pound apiece over that he would distribute among the members of the outing when they first stopped for refreshment, and he was about sick and tired, he said, of being followed by Will Sentry.

'All day long, wherever I go,' he said, 'he's after me like a collie with one eye. I got a shadow of my own *and* a dog. I don't need no Tom, Dick, or Harry pursuing me with his dirty muffler on.'

Will Sentry blushed, and said: 'It's only oily. I got a bicycle.'

'A man has no privacy at all,' Mr Franklyn went on. 'I tell you he sticks so close I'm afraid to go out the back in case I sit in his lap. It's a wonder to me,' he said, 'he don't follow me into bed at night.'

'Wife won't let,' Will Sentry said.

And that started Mr Franklyn off again, and they tried to soothe him down by saying: 'Don't you mind Will Sentry' ... 'No harm in old Will' ... 'He's only keeping an eye on the money, Benjie.'

'Aren't I honest?' asked Mr Franklyn in surprise. There was no answer for some time, then Noah Bowen said: 'You know what the committee is. Ever since Bob the Fiddle they don't feel safe with a new treasurer.'

'Do you think *I'm* going to drink the outing funds, like Bob the Fiddle did?' said Mr Franklyn.

'You *might*,' said my uncle slowly.

'I resign,' said Mr Franklyn.

'Not with our money you won't,' Will Sentry said.

'Who put dynamite in the salmon pool?' said Mr Weazley, but nobody took any notice of him. And, after a time, they all began to play cards in the thickening dusk of the hot, cheesy shop, and my uncle blew and bugled whenever he won, and Mr Weazley grumbled like a dredger, and I fell to sleep on the gravy-scented mountain meadow of uncle's waistcoat.

On Sunday evening, after Bethesda, Mr Franklyn walked into

the kitchen where my uncle and I were eating sardines with spoons from the tin because it was Sunday and his wife would not let us play draughts. She was somewhere in the kitchen, too. Perhaps she was inside the grandmother clock, hanging from the weights and breathing. Then, a second later, the door opened again and Will Sentry edged into the room, twiddling his hard, round hat. He and Mr Franklyn sat down on the settee, stiff and moth-balled and black in their chapel and funeral suits.

'I brought the list,' said Mr Franklyn. 'Every member fully paid. You ask Will Sentry.'

My uncle put on his spectacles, wiped his whiskery mouth with a handkerchief big as a Union Jack, laid down his spoon of sardines, took Mr Franklyn's list of names, removed the spectacles so that he could read, and then ticked the names off one by one.

'Enoch Davies. Aye. He's good with his fists. You never know. Little Gerwain. Very melodious bass. Mr Cadwalladwr. That's right. He can tell opening time better than my watch. Mr Weazley. Of course. He's been to Paris. Pity he suffers so much in the charabanc. Stopped us nine times last year between the Beehive and the Red Dragon. Noah Bowen, ah, very peaceable. He's got a tongue like a turtle-dove. Never a argument with Noah Bowen. Jenkins Loughor. Keep him off economics. It cost us a plate-glass window. And ten pints for the Sergeant. Mr Jervis. Very tidy.'

'He tried to put a pig in the charra,' Will Sentry said.

'Live and let live,' said my uncle.

Will Sentry blushed.

'Sinbad the Sailor's Arms. Got to keep in with him. Old O. Jones.'

'Why old O. Jones?' said Will Sentry.

'Old O. Jones always goes,' said my uncle.

I looked down at the kitchen table. The tin of sardines was gone. By Gee, I said to myself, Uncle's wife is quick as a flash.

'Cuthbert Johnny Fortnight. Now there's a card,' said my uncle.

'He whistles after women,' Will Sentry said.

'So do you,' said Mr Benjamin Franklyn, 'in your mind.'

My uncle at last approved the whole list, pausing only to say, when he came across one name: 'If we weren't a Christian community, we'd chuck that Bob the Fiddle in the sea.'

'We can do that in Porthcawl,' said Mr Franklyn, and soon

after that he went, Will Sentry no more than an inch behind him, their Sunday-bright boots squeaking on the kitchen cobbles.

And then, suddenly, there was my uncle's wife standing in front of the dresser, with a china dog in one hand. By Gee, I said to myself again, did you ever see such a woman, if that's what she is. The lamps were not lit yet in the kitchen and she stood in a wood of shadows, with the plates on the dresser behind her shining – like pink-and-white eyes.

'If you go on that outing on Saturday, Mr Thomas,' she said to my uncle in her small, silk voice, 'I'm going home to my mother's.'

Holy Mo, I thought, she's got a mother. Now that's one old bald mouse of a hundred and five I won't be wanting to meet in a dark lane.

'It's me or the outing, Mr Thomas.'

I would have made my choice at once, but it was almost half a minute before my uncle said: 'Well, then, Sarah, it's the outing, my love.' He lifted her up, under his arm, on to a chair in the kitchen, and she hit him on the head with the china dog. Then he lifted her down again, and then I said good night.

For the rest of the week my uncle's wife whisked quiet and quick round the house with her darting duster, my uncle blew and bugled and swore, and I kept myself busy all the time being up to no good. And then at breakfast time on Saturday morning, the morning of the outing, I found a note on the kitchen table. It said: 'There's some eggs in the pantry. Take your boots off before you go to bed.' My uncle's wife had gone, as quick as a flash.

When my uncle saw the note, he tugged out the flag of his handkerchief and blew such a hubbub of trumpets that the plates on the dresser shook. 'It's the same every year,' he said. And then he looked at me. 'But this year it's different. *You*'ll have to come on the outing, too, and what the members will say I dare not think.'

The charabanc drew up outside, and when the members of the outing saw my uncle and me squeeze out of the shop together, both of us cat-licked and brushed in our Sunday best, they snarled like a zoo.

'Are you bringing a *boy*?' asked Mr Benjamin Franklyn as we climbed into the charabanc. He looked at me with horror.

'Boys is nasty,' said Mr Weazley.

'He hasn't paid his contributions,' Will Sentry said.

'No room for boys. Boys get sick in charabancs.'

'So do you, Enoch Davies,' said my uncle.

'Might as well bring *women*.'

The way they said it, women were worse than boys.

'Better than bringing grandfathers.'

'Grandfathers is nasty too,' said Mr Weazley.

'What can we do with him when we stop for refreshments?'

'I'm a grandfather,' said Mr Weazley.

'Twenty-six minutes to opening time,' shouted an old man in a panama hat, not looking at a watch. They forgot me at once.

'Good old Mr Cadwalladwr,' they cried, and the charabanc started off down the village street.

A few cold women stood at their doorways, grimly watching us go. A very small boy waved good-bye, and his mother boxed his ears. It was a beautiful August morning.

We were out of the village, and over the bridge, and up the hill towards Steeplehat Wood when Mr Franklyn, with his list of names in his hand, called out loud: 'Where's old O. Jones?'

'Where's old O?'

'We've left old O behind.'

'Can't go without old O.'

And though Mr Weazley hissed all the way, we turned and drove back to the village, where, outside the Prince of Wales, old O. Jones was waiting patiently and alone with a canvas bag.

'I didn't want to come at all,' old O. Jones said as they hoisted him into the charabanc and clapped him on the back and pushed him on a seat and stuck a bottle in his hand, 'but I always go.' And over the bridge and up the hill and under the deep green wood and along the dusty road we wove, slow cows and ducks flying by, until 'Stop the bus!' Mr Weazley cried. 'I left my teeth on the mantelpiece.'

'Never you mind,' they said, 'you're not going to bite nobody,' and they gave him a bottle with a straw.

'I might want to smile,' he said.

'Not you,' they said.

'What's the time, Mr Cadwalladwr?'

'Twelve minutes to go,' shouted back the old man in the panama, and they all began to curse him.

The charabanc pulled up outside the Mountain Sheep, a small, unhappy public-house with a thatched roof like a wig with ringworm. From a flagpole by the Gents fluttered the flag of Siam. I knew it was the flag of Siam because of cigarette cards. The landlord stood at the door to welcome us, simpering like a wolf. He was a long, lean, blackfanged man with a greased love-curl and pouncing eyes. 'What a beautiful August day !' he said, and touched his love-curl with a claw. That was the way he must have welcomed the Mountain Sheep before he ate it, I said to myself. The members rushed out, bleating, and into the bar.

'You keep an eye on the charra,' my uncle said, 'see nobody steals it now.'

'There's nobody to steal it,' I said, 'except some cows,' but my uncle was gustily blowing his bugle in the bar. I looked at the cows opposite, and they looked at me. There was nothing else for us to do. Forty-five minutes passed, like a very slow cloud. The sun shone down on the lonely road, the lost, unwanted boy, and the lake-eyed cows. In the dark bar they were so happy they were breaking glasses. A Shoni-Onion Breton man, with a beret and a necklace of onions, bicycled down the road and stopped at the door.

'Quelle un grand matin, monsieur,' I said.

'There's French, boy bach !' he said.

I followed him down the passage, and peered into the bar. I could hardly recognize the members of the outing. They had all changed colour. Beetroot, rhubarb, and puce, they hollered and rollicked in that dark, damp hole like enormous ancient bad boys, and my uncle surged in the middle, all red whiskers and bellies. On the floor was broken glass and Mr Weazley.

'Drinks all round,' cried Bob the Fiddle, a small, absconding man with bright blue eyes and a plump smile.

'Who's been robbing the orphans ?'

'Who sold his little babby to the gyppoes ?'

'Trust old Bob, he'll let you down.'

'You will have your little joke,' said Bob the Fiddle, smiling like a razor, 'but I forgive you, boys.'

Out of the fug and babel I heard : 'Come out and fight.'

'No, not now, later.'

'No, now when I'm in a temper.'

'Look at Will Sentry, he's proper snobbled.'

'Look at his wilful feet.'

'Look at Mr Weazley lording it on the floor.'

Mr Weazley got up, hissing like a gander. 'That boy pushed me down deliberate,' he said, pointing to me at the door, and I slunk away down the passage and out to the mild, good cows. Time clouded over, the cows wondered, I threw a stone at them and they wandered, wondering, away. Then out blew my uncle, ballooning, and one by one the members lumbered after him in a grizzle. They had drunk the Mountain Sheep dry. Mr Weazley had won a string of onions that the Shoni-Onion man raffled in the bar. 'What's the good of onions if you left your teeth on the mantelpiece?' he said. And when I looked through the back window of the thundering charabanc, I saw the pub grow smaller in the distance. And the flag of Siam, from the flagpole by the Gents, fluttered now at half-mast.

The Blue Bull, the Dragon, the Star of Wales, the Twll in the Wall, the Sour Grapes, the Shepherd's Arms, the Bells of Aberdovey: I had nothing to do in the whole, wild August world but remember the names where the outing stopped and keep an eye on the charabanc. And whenever it passed a public-house, Mr Weazley would cough like a billygoat and cry: 'Stop the bus, I'm dying of breath!' And back we would all have to go.

Closing time meant nothing to the members of that outing. Behind locked doors, they hymned and rumpused all the beautiful afternoon. And, when a policeman entered the Druid's Tap by the back door, and found them all choral with beer, 'Sssh!' said Noah Bowen, 'the pub is shut.'

'Where do you come from?' he said in his buttoned, blue voice.

They told him.

'I got a auntie there,' the policeman said. And very soon he was singing 'Asleep in the Deep.'

Off we drove again at last, the charabanc bouncing with tenors and flagons, and came to a river that rushed along among willows.

'Water!' they shouted.

'Porthcawl!' sang my uncle.

'Where's the donkeys?' said Mr Weazley.

And out they lurched, to paddle and whoop in the cool, white, winding water. Mr Franklyn, trying to polka on the slippery stones, fell in twice. 'Nothing is simple,' he said with dignity as he oozed up the bank.

'It's cold !' they cried.

'It's lovely !'

'It's smooth as a moth's nose !'

'It's *better* than Porthcawl !'

And dusk came down warm and gentle on thirty wild, wet, pickled, splashing men without a care in the world at the end of the world in the west of Wales. And, 'Who goes there ?' called Will Sentry to a wild duck flying.

They stopped at the Hermit's Nest for a rum to keep out the cold. 'I played for Aberavon in 1898,' said a stranger to Enoch Davies.

'Liar,' said Enoch Davies.

'I can show you photos,' said the stranger.

'Forged,' said Enoch Davies.

'And I'll show you my cap at home.'

'Stolen.'

'I got friends to prove it,' the stranger said in a fury.

'Bribed,' said Enoch Davies.

On the way home, through the simmering moon-splashed dark, old O. Jones began to cook his supper on a primus stove in the middle of the charabanc. Mr Weazley coughed himself blue in the smoke. 'Stop the bus,' he cried, 'I'm dying of breath !' We all climbed down into the moonlight. There was not a public-house in sight. So they carried out the remaining cases, and the primus stove, and old O. Jones himself, and took them into a field, and sat down in a circle in the field and drank and sang while old O. Jones cooked sausage and mash and the moon flew above us. And there I drifted to sleep against my uncle's mountainous waistcoat, and, as I slept, 'Who goes there ?' called out Will Sentry to the flying moon.

Appendix
EARLY STORIES

BREMBER

From the stairs, the shadows slid gently down into the hall. He could see the dark outline of the banisters reflected across the mirror, and the arc of the chandelier throwing its light. But that was all. Towards the door, the shadows became larger. Then they were lost in the darkness of the floor and ceiling. He fumbled in his pocket for a match, and lit the taper in his hand. Holding the tiny flame above his head, he turned the handle and stepped into the room. There was a smell of dust and old wood. It was curious how sensitive he was to it, how it quickened his imagination. Old ladies making lace by the light of the moon, their thin, pale fingers stealing along the brocade, their ageless cheeks tinted like a little child's. That was what the room always reminded him of, since the days when he had first tiptoed in, and gazed with terror at the windows opening on to the grey lawn, and the trees beyond. Or when, still a little boy, he had sat at the harpsichord, touching the dusty keys so lightly no one could hear their sound, afraid, and yet entranced as the music rose faintly into the air. It was always sad. He could detect the desolate sadness beneath the lightest fugue; as his hand touched the notes, there were tears in his eyes, a great longing for something he had known and had forgotten, loved but had lost.

That was a number of years ago, and now the same sensation of unreality and of longing came over him as he lit the harpsichord's long candles with his taper, and saw in their spreading light, the walls crowd closer round him, and the heavy chairs hem him in. They keys were as dusty as ever. He brushed them lightly with his sleeve, then let his fingers wander for a moment over them. How frail their sound was. What curious little melodies they made, so sad and yet so perfect. For a moment he thought he heard the sound of childish footsteps outside the door, running down the corridor into the darkness. But then they were gone, and he could but suppose that they had never been. Now there was a hint of laughter sounding in his ears; now it was gone again. As he played, he seemed to hear the soft, rustling noise of a silk skirt dragged along the ground. Then his music grew louder, and, when it was soft again, there was nothing.

Try as he would, he could not analyse his reasons for coming to the house. It terrified him, and yet he could not draw away from it. Out on the road he had suddenly felt the desire to throw apart the veil of the years, to bring back to him all that old house had meant, the dusk, the soft voices in the corridors, the harpsichord, the stairs that wound interminably up into the dark, the thousand details of the rooms, the soft, insinuating fear that looked out of corners, and never went away. He had walked up the drive to the front door. The lion's head on the door-knocker grinned down at him. He lifted it, and struck the wood. No one answered. Again and again he knocked, but the house was quiet. He put his shoulder to the door. It swung open. He had tip-toed along the passages, looked into the rooms, touched the familiar objects. Nothing had changed. And then, when the night had crept out of the leaded windows, he had closed the door of the music-room softly behind him. He was filled with a great relief. The longing always at the back of his mind was realized, the lost thing found, and the forgotten thing remembered. This was the end of the journey.

Momentarily, the candles became brighter. He was able to see further into the room. Rising, he walked across, and picked up a dusty book laid on the table. 'The House of Brember.' He brought it over to the light. Each page was familiar to him, the family, generation by generation, men of thought rather than of action, all visionaries who saw the world from the cloud of their own dreaming. He turned over the pages, until he came to the last: George Henry Brember, last of the line, died . . .

He looked down on his name, and then closed the book.

JARLEY'S

On the day that the travelling waxworks came to town the attendant vanished. Next morning the proprietor called at the employment agency and asked for a smart lad who could talk English. But the smart lads talked Welsh, and the boy from Bristol had a harelip. So the proprietor returned to his lodgings and, passing the canal, saw Eleazar reading on the bank.

'Any luck ?' he enquired.

'I'm not fishing,' replied Eleazar.

He was immediately engaged.

* * *

It was late in the evening, and the last curious visitor had left the tent. The proprietor counted the day's takings and went away leaving Eleazar alone in the dark, wax world. Eleazar removed the last cigarette-end from the ground, and brought out a duster from his pocket. Tremblingly he dusted over the lean, brown body of Hiawatha ; tremblingly he patted the pale cheeks of Charlie Peace ; tremblingly he dusted over the wax neck of Circe.

'You forgot my left calf,' said Hiawatha.

'You forgot my top lip,' said Charlie Peace.

'You forgot my right shoulder,' said the temptress.

Eleazar looked at the wax figures in amazement.

'You heard me,' said Hiawatha.

'You heard me,' said Charlie Peace.

'You heard me,' said the temptress.

Eleazar stared around him. The entrance to the tent was a long way off. There was no escape.

'Calf,' said Hiawatha.

'Lip,' said Charlie Peace.

'Shoulder,' said Circe.

Tremblingly Eleazar dusted over the strong-muscled calf ;

tremblingly he patted the snarling lip; tremblingly he dusted over the wax shoulder.

'That is certainly better,' said Hiawatha. 'You see,' he continued in apology, 'I used to run a lot; and you want your calves dusted then, don't you?'

'I do a lot of snarling,' said Charlie Peace.

'I do a lot of tempting,' said the temptress; 'though, really, I should be losing my fascination by this time; and my shoulder is not all that it was. I had it bitten in Aberdare once.'

'I remember the night well,' said Hiawatha. 'Somebody put an old hat on me.'

'I remember the night,' remarked the murderer, 'when as a child I stuck a needle into my nurse: it was a darning needle.'

'I remember chasing Minnehaha all over the rapids,' said Hiawatha. 'She used to be terribly annoyed when I called her Laughing Water.'

'I remember the sea-green eyes of Jason,' said Circe.

Eleazar could remember nothing. His first fears had vanished to be replaced by a sense of friendly curiosity. He inquired politely if all was well in the state of wax.

'Indeed,' said Hiawatha, 'I have little to complain of. There is a great deal to be said for being wax. One has few troubles. It is difficult to receive injury. The sharpest arrow could do little to me: a momentary impression soon to be filled in with a farthing's worth of wax from the local stores. It is a perpetual source of wonder to me that more people do not realise the advantages of a wax life.'

'How is with you, ma'am?' asked Eleazar.

'There is still the desire to tempt,' replied the temptress, 'that I cannot conquer. And I still remember those confounded sea-green eyes.'

'Murder as a profession,' began Charlie Peace . . .

'Henry Wadsworth,' began Hiawatha . . .

'The history of temptation,' began the temptress . . .

And suddenly the three wax figures were still.

Eleazar shuffled further along the tent.

'Eleazar,' said an ape.

'Sir?' said Eleazar.

'Life,' said the ape, 'is a never-ending mystery. We are born. Why are we born? We die. The reason is obvious. The life of the body is short, and the veins are incapable of holding an eternal supply of blood.'

Eleazar would have continued on his way, but the ape held up its hand. 'Stop,' said the ape. 'Consider the man of flesh and the man of wax. Everything is done for the wax man; he is made painlessly and skilfully; he is found a house in a nice waterproof tent or in the interior of a large and hygienic building; he is clothed, brushed and dusted; he is the cynosure of all eyes. Think of the opportunities he enjoys to study the mentality of his near neighbour-man. Day after day, the faces of men are pressed close to mine; I see into men's eyes; I listen to their conversations. The man of wax is an unchanging, unprejudiced and unemotional observer of the human comedy.'

'Sir,' said Eleazar, 'you talk very well for an ape.'

'Eleazar,' said the ape, 'I have known this frame of wax for two days only. I was the late attendant.'

'Tell me,' said Eleazar, 'do you feel the cold?'

'Neither cold nor warmth.'

'Do you feel hunger?'

'Neither hunger nor thirst. I feel nothing. I want nothing. I am perpetually happy.'

Eleazar removed his jacket and trousers.

'Make room – move up,' said Eleazar.

* * *

Next morning the proprietor called at the employment agency, and asked for a smart lad.

'He must be careful, too,' he explained, 'for my waxworks has just been presented with an expensive new figure.'

'An historical figure?'

'No, no,' said the proprietor; 'the figure of a Welsh Druid in a long white shirt.'

IN THE GARDEN

The boy was more afraid of the dark garden than of anything else in the world. It was frightening enough in the twilight, but when there was blackness above and below and the trees spoke among themselves, the garden was too terrible to think about.

He tried to convince himself that beyhind the red curtains there lay nothing at all, and that there was nothing at all anywhere, only the bright room, his mother, and himself. In the morning, the garden was full of delight; the grass was long and unkempt; there were sunflowers that nobody had planted there. Against the further wall was a summerhouse, the home of beetles, where he kept his collection of strange pebbles and his picture-postcards. There he would sit for as long as the sunlight lasted, with his back against the wood box on the seat, and his feet on an old and mysterious trunk. The trunk was all the more fascinating because there was nothing in it at all. Once he had prised up the rusty padlock with his pocket knife and very fearfully opened the lid, to find only emptiness and the smell of rot. He felt sure that it must have a secret drawer somewhere that held precious stones as bright as the sun, and he planned, when he should discover them, to sell the treasure to a rich merchant, in return for a journey to the parrot-haunted islands.

But as the last rags of the sunset withered away behind the tallest chimney stack, he would hear the warning voices telling him that it was time for him to go, and he knew that somewhere in the approaching shadows were the ugly night-tenants of the garden. Then he would close the door of the summer house very slowly and carefully, and walk up the garden path until he reached the three stone steps that led down to the scullery. These he would take at one leap, and run quickly into the house with all the devils of darkness at his heels.

It was a very hot night. The windows were open, and the spinning jinnies whirled into the house to shake their long legs in the glare of the gas. The boy liked to watch them for as long as they kept to the ceiling, but he hated them when they fell dizzily on to the table cloth or flew blindly into his face, and worst of all he hated the great grey moths that blundered round the room, for he knew they were in league with the things in the garden outside.

'It's hot in here,' his mother said sudenly, 'put out the chairs on the lawn.'

She left him alone in the kitchen. He picked up a chair, then set it down again and went out into the scullery. He opened the garden door, and a great moth flew into his face. Canden he stepped out into the garden and faced the enemies.

Hooded and gloved in black, they lined the paths and stood across the grass. He squared his shoulders and mounted bravely to the top of the steps. He could not see the face of the shadows, but they could see his face, for he was framed in the light from the open door. He thought of the summerhouse in the morning, friendly, dusted with light, and of the trunk where the treasure lay. He went out on to the edge of the grass, and he could not hear the warning of the trees for the drumming of his heart. As he advanced, the shadows curtsied and fell back a little, leaving his path clear to the darkness that was most dreadful of all.

Then he stopped, for he was more afraid than he thought he could ever be. The garden writhed about him, and the walls and the trees shot upward so that he could not see the sky. The pointed roof of the summerhouse shot up the dark like a steeple hat. The boy dared not look behind him, for he knew that he was surrounded by his foes, and that their arms were linked behind his back. Very, very soon, they would close in upon him, as though they were playing an innocent game of Poor Jenny Lies A-Weeping, and one of them would throw a hood over his head. He waited and waited and still nothing happened, only the gradual mounting of the trees, the walls, and the wrongly shaped tower to the sky. He could not see them, for now his hands were over his eyes. The ring closed in upon him. He could hear their feet in the ragged grass and the slipping of their robes over the damp soil.

He threw back his head and stared straight into the eyes of the tallest shadow. For a long while he stared. Then he smiled at his friend the shadow, and held out his arms. The door of the summerhouse swung back in the wind, and he saw that the trunk, lying open on its side, was full of fire. The precious stones poured from it in streams of silver, of gold and of blue. The garden was bright with their colour.

He opened his arms a little wider, and the stones leapt upward to his breast. He smiled at the silent watchers and they dared not meet his eyes. Slowly they melted away, and the trees melted with them. He gathered up the jewels, and, slipping on to his knees, he laid them in the lap of his friend. the door of the summerhouse closed softly with the falling of the latch, the wind dropped, and still the boy smiled and did not move.

His mother called to him. She called to him again, and still he did not answer, so she ran into the garden with his name on her lips. There, in the middle of the grass, she found the boy kneeling, his face in his hands, in the blinding light of the moon.

GASPAR, MELCHIOR, BALTHASAR*

A flying fleet came out of the shadow, [the hangar of shadows,]
and the arsenal of the iron mist, hovered over the island and,
hidden in the smoke of the exhausts, dropped death upon the
cities. The men in the cities raced for shelter, fixing their leather
masks [upon their masks of flesh], their trousers unbuttoned as
they scampered out of the urinals, their hair uncombed as they
climbed out of a purchased sleep, [their typists unfingered as
they] puffed out of tenement offices, cupping their hands for the
exploding manna. Two lovers, struck by the same shell, fell into
bliss. Down thumped a ripper of women, a [lady] *woman* with
rings on her fingers in the [common blood, a starver of babies, a
thief of money, a thief of leisure, and a thief of love in the]
levelling gutter. Bullets broke up the hungry ranks. Crow food
sliced about them [and the flesh of their slave-masters raw in the
streets, they starved in the heart of plenty, starved for the food
of the heart the galvanic wheat that death beat back into the
bone. Death flew over the island cities, and then flew back into
the hangar of the shadow of death.]
The workers in the south and the north of the island, where
death had fallen thinly, were provided with guns and shafts of
steel [and little pinned grenades]. They cocked the guns and
laughed up at the shadow above them[, pointing the barrels at
the high men of the island. They slew the givers of arms. They
looted the shops, and raped the widows, and burgled the hearts
of the dead, finding the keys of hate in the opened pulses. There
was love and hate in the island, out of the spirits of death a new,
reeking life, out of the last hacked coals a new fire]. Street rose
against street, and city against city. In the ruined cities, along
the deserted streets where the dead on the pavements fell apart,

* Square brackets denote deletions and italics indicate superior additions by Dylan
Thomas. This draft of an unpublished story gives an interesting insight into Thomas's
method of revising a draft.

the dying spoke women's names, [and the vermin from the blown sewers gnawed at their chests,] the shadow moved. I saw two ghosts in the avenue by the broken park. They moved among the dead, prying into each shot face, [upon] [on] each [empty] hollow head, and under each folded eye.

The ships were unloaded at the wharves, the engines cold in the stations, the printing presses silent, and the sentries before the island palace stiff[, split like cabbages,] in their boxes. In the parks the birds were singing, a new froth was on the trees, the wind blew the waste paper up the paths. [I remember] I walked all that morning, a ghost [in a springing world, a solid man in a world that was all a ghost]. Wherever I walked, in street or under arch, on the grass of the green parks, through alley and slum down to the edge of the corpsy water, I saw the two ghosts searching. They moved among the dead, questioning each dead eye, invisibly touching the hems of the dresses, the young, triangular breasts, *the* soft heart, [and] *the* hard loins.

The guns grew quieter in the distance. The last of the first revolution died away in the splutter of fire from the east of the great city. [I pattered, silent in my leather like a living man locked and forgotten in a mortuary,] I walked in strange thoroughfares and through the unlit centre of the city, strange itself in its first blindness. As I journeyed through the first stages of the night, coming upon the two ghosts now at a dark corner, now in the shadow of a doorway, and bent forever over the riddled dead, I held my scarf to my face for the smell of the dead flowering Black plague would branch from these blacker plants that shot to heaven through the wounds of the unburied fallen. I made my image as I walked, and the hemlock and the upas sprouted for me from the gutter beds.

It was a minute before midnight that I saw a lantern swinging at the end of a street. It was [a red rose] *bright and sweet* among the flowers that stank at my side, but, as I moved towards it, I felt the wind of the two ghosts as they drifted past me, and I followed them, calling them by name. There were men at the corner, dark-eyed behind their lantern.

'Who goes there?' they [said] cried.

They swung the lantern before my face.

'*Let me pass*', I said.

[Who are you, comrade?] they [said] cried again.

Where are you going?

[Let me pass]

[Who are you, comrade ? they said]

[Of the wise men, I cried, let me pass]

[Where are you going, comrade ?]

[Fools, fools, I cried, and] I waited no longer *but* knocked the lantern from their hands and plunged into the darkness after the windy ghosts. *I ran on and on, with* the noise of the revolvers behind me, [I ran on and on,] through a maze of alleys into a moonlit square.

There stood the two ghosts. At their feet lay a dead woman, naked but for her shawl, with a bayonet wound in her breasts. Slowly I stepped towards her. [Her time had been well upon her when they cut her down.] [But] As I watched, [the] *her* womb [of the dead mother] broke, lifted, through the flesh.

The two ghosts bowed down.

Gold, said [Gaspar] *the first ghost*, [holding] *raising a golden* shadow to the light of the moon.

Frankincense, said [Melchior] *the second ghost* and his shadowy gift smoked from him.

The noise of the guns grew nearer and still nearer.

[Kneeling] *I knelt* where I stood [I] *and* felt the new joy of pain as a bullet drove into my [lung] *breast*. I fell upon the pavement near the two lifted arms, and [, bitter as myrrh,] my [bitter] blood streamed *bitterly* on to the [mother's feet] emerging head.

LIST OF SOURCES

This list has been provided by Walford Davies, who also advised on the text of the stories.

Abbreviations

EPW *Dylan Thomas: Early Prose Writings*, ed. Walford Davies, London & New York, 1971.

ML *The Map of Love* (poems and stories), London, 1939.

Prospect *A Prospect of the Sea and Other Stories and Prose Writings*, ed. Daniel Jones, London, 1955.

QEOM *Quite Early One Morning*, ed. Aneirin Talfan Davies, London, 1954. An enlarged American edition, also with other variations, appeared in the same year.

'After the Fair'. Dated November 1933 in the 'Red Notebook'. This Notebook, now at the Lockwood Memorial Library, the State University of New York at Buffalo, is the initial MS source also for the next eight stories. 'After the Fair' was first published in the *New English Weekly*, 15 March 1934; collected in *Prospect*.

'The Tree'. Dated 28 December 1933 in the 'Red Notebook'. First published in the *Adelphi*, December 1934; collected in *ML* and *Prospect*.

'The True Story'. Entered under the title 'Martha' in the 'Red Notebook', 22 January 1934. First published in *Yellowjacket*, May 1939; collected in *EPW*.

'The Enemies'. Dated 11 February 1934 in the 'Red Notebook'. First published in *New Stories*, June–July 1934; collected in *ML* and *Prospect*.

'The Dress'. Dated March 1934 in the 'Red Notebook'. First

published in *Comment*, 4 January 1936; collected in *ML and Prospect*.

'The Visitor'. Dated April 1934 in the 'Red Notebook'. First published in *The Criterion*, January 1935; collected in *ML and Prospect*.

'The Vest'. Dated 20 July 1934 in the 'Red Notebook'. First published in *Yellowjacket*, May 1939; collected in *EPW*.

'The Burning Baby'. Dated September 1934 in the 'Red Notebook'. First published in *Contemporary Poetry and Prose*, May 1936; collected in *EPW*.

'The Orchards'. Derived from 'Anagram', dated October 1934 in the 'Red Notebook'. First published in *The Criterion*, July 1936; collected in *ML* and *Prospect*.

'The End of the River'. First published in the *New English Weekly*, 22 November 1934; collected in *EPW*.

'The Lemon'. First published in *Life and Letters Today*, Spring 1936; collected in *Prospect*.

'The Horse's Ha'. First published in *Janus*, May 1936; collected in *EPW*.

'The School for Witches'. First published in *Contemporary Poetry and Prose*, August–September 1936; collected in *EPW*.

'The Mouse and the Woman'. First published in *Transition*, Fall 1936; collected in *ML* and *Prospect*.

'A Prospect of the Sea'. First published in *Life and Letters Today*, Spring 1937; collected in *Prospect*.

'The Holy Six'. First published in *Contemporary Poetry and Prose*, Spring 1937; collected in *EPW*.

'Prologue to an Adventure'. First published in *Wales*, Summer 1937; collected in *EPW*.

'The Map of Love'. First published in *Wales*, Autumn 1937; collected in *ML* and *Prospect*.

'In the Direction of the Beginning'. First published in *Wales*, March 1938; collected in *Prospect*.

'An Adventure from a Work in Progress'. First published in *Seven*, Spring 1939; collected in *EPW*.

PORTRAIT OF THE ARTIST AS A YOUNG DOG

Each story was finished close to its individual periodical printing, or as indicated.

'The Peaches'. First published in *Life and Letters Today*, October 1938.

'A Visit to Grandpa's'. First published in the *New English Weekly*, 10 March 1938.

'Patricia, Edith, and Arnold'. First published in *Seven*, Christmas 1939.

'The Fight'. First published in *Life and Letters Today*, December 1939.

'Extraordinary Little Cough'. First published in *Life and Letters Today*, September 1939.

'Just Like Little Dogs'. First published in *Wales*, October 1939.

'Where Tawe Flows'. Completed by early December 1939.

'Who Do You Wish Was With Us?' Completed by early December 1939.

'Old Garbo'. First published in *Life and Letters Today*, July 1939.

'One Warm Saturday'. Completed by July 1938.

First published together in 1940.

ADVENTURES IN THE SKIN TRADE

The work was mainly written May–June 1941. The three parts were separately published as follows.

'A Fine Beginning'. First published in *Folios of New Writing*, Autumn 1941.

'Plenty of Furniture'. First published in *New World Writing*, November 1952.

'Four Lost Souls'. First published in *New World Writing*, May 1953. First published together posthumously in 1953.

'Quite Early One Morning.' Recorded for BBC Wales, 14 December 1944 (broadcast 31 August 1945); published in *Wales*, Autumn 1946; collected in *QEOM*.

'A Child's Christmas in Wales'. Thomas wrote a script called 'Memories of Christmas' for BBC Wales Children's Hour in the autumn of 1945 (broadcast 16 December 1945; published in *The Listener*, 20 December 1945, and *Wales*, Winter 1946; collected in the British edition of *QEOM*). He later wrote a piece on similar material in the form of a 'Conversation about Christmas' for *Picture Post* (27 December 1947). During his first visit to America he amalgamated the 'Memories' and the 'Conversation' for publication in *Harper's Bazaar* (December 1950) as 'A Child's Memories of Christmas in Wales'. This text, the one used here, was also that used for the American edition of *QEOM*.

'Holiday Memory'. BBC Wales Broadcast, 25 October 1946; published in *The Listener*, 7 November 1946; collected in *QEOM*.

'The Crumbs of One Man's Year'. BBC Home Service broadcast, 27 December 1946; published in *The Listener*, 2 January 1947; collected in *QEOM*. 'Return Journey'. Written February 1947; recorded for BBC Home Service, 2 April 1947 (broadcast 9 May 1947); collected in *QEOM*.

'The Followers'. First published in *World Review*, October 1952; collected in *Prospect*.

'A Story'. Written for BBC television, 10 August 1953; published in *The Listener*, 17 September 1953; collected in *QEOM* (American edition) and *Prospect*.

APPENDIX

'Brember'. First published in the *Swansea Grammar School Magazine*, vol. 28, no. 1 (April 1931); collected in *EPW*.

'Jarley's'. Frist published in the *Swansea Grammar School Magazine*, vol. 30, no. 3 (December 1933). Signed 'Old Boy' and attributed to Thomas on the authority of George H. Gwynne, a former master at the school. Thomas had left the school in July 1931. Collected in *EPW*.

'In the Garden'. First published in the *Swansea Grammar Scool Magazine*, vol. 31, no. 2 (July 1934). Signed 'Old Boy'; first attributed to Dylan Thomas, on internal evidence, by Ralph Maud. Collected in *EPW*.

'Gaspar, Melchior, Balthasar'. Dated 8 August 1934 in the 'Red Notebook'. First published in *EPW*.

POETRY
IN EVERYMAN

A SELECTION

Silver Poets of the Sixteenth Century

EDITED BY
DOUGLAS BROOKS-DAVIES
A new edition of this famous
Everyman collection **£6.99**

Complete Poems

JOHN DONNE
The father of metaphysical verse in
this highly-acclaimed edition **£4.99**

Complete English Poems, Of Education, Areopagitica

JOHN MILTON
An excellent introduction to
Milton's poetry and prose **£6.99**

Selected Poems

JOHN DRYDEN
A poet's portrait of Restoration
England **£4.99**

Selected Poems

PERCY BYSSHE SHELLEY
'The essential Shelley' in one
volume **£3.50**

Women Romantic Poets 1780-1830: An Anthology

Hidden talent from the Romantic era,
rediscovered for the first time **£5.99**

Poems in Scots and English

ROBERT BURNS
The best of Scotland's greatest lyric
poet **£4.99**

Selected Poems

D. H. LAWRENCE
A newly-edited selection spanning
the whole of Lawrence's literary
career **£4.99**

The Poems

W. B. YEATS
Ireland's greatest lyric poet
surveyed in this ground-breaking
edition **£6.50**

£5.99

£4.99

£3.50

AVAILABILITY

All books are available from your local bookshop or direct from
**Littlehampton Book Services Cash Sales, 14 Eldon Way, LinesideEstate,
Littlehampton, West Sussex BN17 7HE.** PRICES ARE SUBJECT TO CHANGE.

To order any of the books, please enclose a cheque (in £ sterling) made payable to
Littlehampton Book Services, or phone your order through with credit card details (Access,
Visa or Mastercard) on 0903 721596 (24 hour answering service) stating card number and
expiry date. Please add £1.25 for package and postage to the total value of your order.

SHORT STORY COLLECTIONS
IN EVERYMAN

A SELECTION

The Secret Self
Short Stories by Women

'A superb collection' *Guardian* **£4.99**

Selected Short Stories
and Poems

THOMAS HARDY
The best of Hardy's Wessex in a
unique selection **£4.99**

The Best of
Sherlock Holmes

ARTHUR CONAN DOYLE
All the favourite adventures in one
volume **£4.99**

Great Tales of Detection
Nineteen Stories

Chosen by Dorothy L. Sayers **£3.99**

Short Stories

KATHERINE MANSFIELD
A selection displaying the
remarkable range of Mansfield's
writing **£3.99**

Selected Stories

RUDYARD KIPLING
Includes stories chosen to reveal the
'other' Kipling **£4.50**

The Strange Case of
Dr Jekyll and Mr Hyde
and Other Stories

R. L. STEVENSON
An exciting selection of gripping
tales from a master of suspense **£3.99**

Modern Short Stories 2:
1940-1980

Thirty-one stories from the greatest
modern writers **£3.50**

The Day of Silence and
Other Stories

GEORGE GISSING
Gissing's finest stories, available for
the first time in one volume **£4.99**

Selected Tales

HENRY JAMES
Stories portraying the tensions
between private life and the outside
world **£5.99**

£4.99

£6.99

AVAILABILITY

All books are available from your local bookshop or direct from
**Littlehampton Book Services Cash Sales, 14 Eldon Way, LinesideEstate,
Littlehampton, West Sussex BN17 7HE.** PRICES ARE SUBJECT TO CHANGE.

To order any of the books, please enclose a cheque (in £ sterling) made payable to
Littlehampton Book Services, or phone your order through with credit card details (Access,
Visa or Mastercard) on 0903 721596 (24 hour answering service) stating card number and
expiry date. Please add £1.25 for package and postage to the total value of your order.

CLASSIC NOVELS
IN EVERYMAN

A SELECTION

The Way of All Flesh
SAMUEL BUTLER
A savagely funny odyssey from joyless duty to unbridled liberalism **£4.99**

Born in Exile
GEORGE GISSING
A rationalist's progress towards love and compromise in class-ridden Victorian England **£4.99**

David Copperfield
CHARLES DICKENS
One of Dickens' best-loved novels, brimming with humour **£3.99**

The Last Chronicle of Barset
ANTHONY TROLLOPE
Trollope's magnificent conclusion to his Barsetshire novels **£4.99**

He Knew He Was Right
ANTHONY TROLLOPE
Sexual jealousy, money and women's rights within marriage –
a novel ahead of its time **£6.99**

Tess of the D'Urbervilles
THOMAS HARDY
The powerful, poetic classic of wronged innocence **£3.99**

Wuthering Heights and Poems
EMILY BRONTE
A powerful work of genius – one of the great masterpieces of literature **£3.50**

Tom Jones
HENRY FIELDING
The wayward adventures of one of literatures most likable heroes **£5.99**

The Master of Ballantrae and Weir of Hermiston
R. L. STEVENSON
Together in one volume, two great novels of high adventure and family conflict **£4.99**

£3.99

£2.99

£3.99

AVAILABILITY

All books are available from your local bookshop or direct from
**Littlehampton Book Services Cash Sales, 14 Eldon Way, LinesideEstate,
Littlehampton, West Sussex BN17 7HE.** PRICES ARE SUBJECT TO CHANGE.

To order any of the books, please enclose a cheque (in £ sterling) made payable to
Littlehampton Book Services, or phone your order through with credit card details (Access,
Visa or Mastercard) on 0903 721596 (24 hour answering service) stating card number and
expiry date. Please add £1.25 for package and postage to the total value of your order.

ESSAYS, CRITICISM AND HISTORY IN EVERYMAN

A SELECTION

The Embassy to Constantinople and Other Writings
LIUDPRAND OF CREMONA
An insider's view of political machinations in medieval Europe £5.99

The Rights of Man
THOMAS PAINE
One of the great masterpieces of English radicalism £4.99

Speeches and Letters
ABRAHAM LINCOLN
A key document of the American Civil War £4.99

Essays
FRANCIS BACON
An excellent introduction to Bacon's incisive wit and moral outlook £3.99

Puritanism and Liberty: Being the Army Debates (1647-49) from the Clarke Manuscripts
A fascinating revelation of Puritan minds in action £7.99

History of His Own Time
BISHOP GILBERT BURNET
A highly readable contemporary account of the Glorious Revolution of 1688 £7.99

Biographia Literaria
SAMUEL TAYLOR COLERIDGE
A masterpiece of criticism, marrying the study of literature with philosophy £4.99

Essays on Literature and Art
WALTER PATER
Insights on culture and literature from a major voice of the 1890s £3.99

Chesterton on Dickens: Criticisms and Appreciations
A landmark in Dickens criticism, rarely surpassed £4.99

Essays and Poems
R. L. STEVENSON
Stevenson's hidden treasures in a new selection £4.99

£3.99

£4.99